PRAISE FOR THE NOVELS
OF CAROL BERG

The Spirit Lens

"Superbly realized." —*Publishers Weekly*

"Rich with vivid characters and unforgettable places.... [Berg] spins an infectiously enjoyable series opener that fans of thought-provoking fantasy and intriguing mystery should appreciate." —*Library Journal*

"A super opening to what looks like a great alternate Renaissance fantasy.... Fans will appreciate this strong beginning as science and sorcery collide when three undercover agents investigate the divine and unholy collision of murder, magic, and physics." —Genre Go Round Reviews

"Keeps the reader on edge ... Berg keeps the pages turning." —SFRevu

"Berg is entirely adept at creating a detailed and nuanced fantasy world, made all the more impressive by noting that other books she has written seem to be about other worlds with other rules." —Farenmaddox.wordpress.com

"A genuine page-turner that should please both mystery and fantasy fans." —*Booklist*

Breath and Bone

"The narrative crackles with intensity against a vivid backdrop of real depth and conviction, with characters to match. Altogether superior." —*Kirkus Reviews* (starred review)

"Replete with magic-powered machinations, secret societies, and doomsday divinations, the emotionally intense second volume of Berg's intrigue-laden Lighthouse Duet concludes the story of Valen.... Fans of Marion Zimmer Bradley's Avalon sequence and Sharon Shinn will be rewarded."
—*Publishers Weekly*

"Berg's lush, evocative storytelling and fully developed characters add up to a first-rate purchase for most fantasy collections." —*Library Journal*

continued ...

"Berg combines druid and Christian influences against a backdrop of sorcerers, priestesses, priests, deep evil, and a dying land to create an engrossing tale to get lost in . . . enjoyable."　　　　　　　　　　　　　　　—Monsters and Critics

"An excellent read . . . a satisfying sequel."　　—Fresh Fiction

Flesh and Spirit

"In Carol Berg's engrossing *Flesh and Spirit*, an engaging rogue stumbles upon the dangerous crossroads of religion, politics, war, and destiny. Berg perfectly portrays the people who shape his increasingly more chaotic journey: cheerful monks, cruel siblings, ambitious warlords, and a whole cast of fanatics. But it's the vividly rendered details that give this book such power. Berg brings to life every stone in a peaceful monastery and every nuance in a stratified society, describing the difficult dirty work of ordinary life as beautifully as she conveys the heart-stopping mysticism of holiness just beyond human perception."　　　　—Sharon Shinn, national bestselling author of
The Thirteenth House

"Valen is unquestionably memorable—in what is definitely a dark fantasy as much concerned with Valen's internal struggle as with his conflicts with others."　　　　　　—*Booklist*

"Chilling fantasy."　　　　　　　　　　—*Publishers Weekly*

"Fast-paced. . . . Berg creates a troubled world full of politics, anarchy, and dark magic. . . . The magic is fascinating."
　　　　　　　　　　　　　　　　　　　　—SFRevu

"Carol Berg has done a masterful job of creating characters, places, religions, and political trials that grab and hold your attention. . . . Don't miss one of 2007's best fantasy books!"
　　　　　　　　　　　　　　—Romance Reviews Today

"[Berg] excels at creating worlds. . . . I'm eagerly awaiting the duology's concluding volume, *Breath and Bone* . . . an engrossing and lively tale, with enough action to keep you hungry for more."　　　　　　　　　—*The Davis Enterprise*

The Bridge of D'Arnath Novels

"A very promising start to a new series." —*The Denver Post*

"Berg has mastered the balance between mystery and storytelling [and] pacing; she weaves past and present together, setting a solid foundation . . . It's obvious [she] has put incredible thought into who and what makes her characters tick."
　　　　　　　　　　　　　　　—*The Davis Enterprise*

THE
SPIRIT LENS

A NOVEL OF THE
COLLEGIA MAGICA

CAROL BERG

A ROC BOOK

ROC
Published by New American Library, a division of
Penguin Group (USA) Inc., 375 Hudson Street,
New York, New York 10014, USA
Penguin Group (Canada), 90 Eglinton Avenue East, Suite 700, Toronto,
Ontario M4P 2Y3, Canada (a division of Pearson Penguin Canada Inc.)
Penguin Books Ltd., 80 Strand, London WC2R 0RL, England
Penguin Ireland, 25 St. Stephen's Green, Dublin 2,
Ireland (a division of Penguin Books Ltd.)
Penguin Group (Australia), 250 Camberwell Road, Camberwell, Victoria 3124,
Australia (a division of Pearson Australia Group Pty. Ltd.)
Penguin Books India Pvt. Ltd., 11 Community Centre, Panchsheel Park,
New Delhi - 110 017, India
Penguin Group (NZ), 67 Apollo Drive, Rosedale, North Shore 0632,
New Zealand (a division of Pearson New Zealand Ltd.)
Penguin Books (South Africa) (Pty.) Ltd., 24 Sturdee Avenue,
Rosebank, Johannesburg 2196, South Africa

Penguin Books Ltd., Registered Offices:
80 Strand, London WC2R 0RL, England

Published by Roc, an imprint of New American Library, a division of Penguin
Group (USA) Inc. Previously published in a Roc trade paperback edition.

First Roc Mass Market Printing, January 2011
10 9 8 7 6 5 4 3 2 1

Thanks to all those who helped me bring this story to life. It's impossible to say enough about Linda, my brilliant muse, consultant, and friend—the spirit of Lianelle. And then, of course, Susan, Laurey, Glenn, Brian, Catherine, and Curt, who prod me to be better, and Brenda, who prods me to be. Thanks to Markus, the Fighter Guy, for his valuable consultations. But most especially this is for Pete, the Exceptional Spouse, whose patience and care keep life beautiful and together. I love you all.

PRELUDE

Philosophers claimed the Blood Wars had irredeemably corrupted magic. Historians insisted that Sabria's growing sophistication in physics, astronomy, and alchemistry—the almost daily discoveries that exposed another spell as nonsensical and another magical practitioner as a charlatan—was but a grand human evolution, on the order of our discovery of fire, the wheel, or sail. Whoever had the right of the discussion, a sensible man could not but admit that the practice of magic had lost its glamour—and I was an unendingly sensible man.

Of course it was not good sense, but rather my own incapacity that had caused me to relinquish my aspiration to life as a mage of the Camarilla Magica. Sixteen years' residence at the sole remaining school of magic in Sabria and I could not charm a flea to a dog's back.

With encouragement from my mentor, I had faced disappointment squarely, weathered the storm that followed, and accepted what solace was offered me. Yet somewhere, nurtured by the lost dreams of youth and exposed in the ruthless self-examination required to recover from despair, lay a small, intractable conviction. A seed that would not let me spit it out. A stone that would not be shaken from my shoe. I ought to be more than I was. Even if I lacked the blood-born talents of a mage, somewhere, in some capacity, my service would make a difference in this world. Perhaps that's why the summons intrigued me so, though it made no good sense at all.

The odd missive had arrived in the late afternoon. Spring sunlight streamed through the casements of the collegia library, stretching all the way across the scuffed floor to the book cupboard labeled FORMULARY: POTIONS AND HERBALS. Only incidentally did the beams illuminate the fold of fine paper in my hand.

I peered again at the outside of the page. No insignia had manifested itself in the broken wax seal in the past few moments. The handwriting that spelled out my name remained unrecognizable.

> *Portier de Duplais, Curator of Archives*
> *Collegia Magica de Seravain*

Bold and angular—a man's hand, I judged. Seven years of intensive study in this library and nine more as its keeper, with little companionship but five thousand mouldering manuscripts and a transitory stream of increasingly vapid students, had left me unskilled in the discipline most important to me, but knowledgeable in many arcane branches of learning.

I flipped back to the enigmatic message.

> *Portier de Savin-Duplais:*
>
> *Present yourself at Villa Margeroux on the Ventinna Road no later than 17 Trine on a matter of urgent family business. A mount awaits you at the hostelry in Tigano. We require utmost discretion.*
>
> *Your kinsman*

No personal signature. No politenesses. I had no acquaintance with Villa Margeroux or with any person who lived in the vicinity of Ventinna.

The note could be a prank, perpetrated by some student I had reprimanded for marking in books or dripping lamp oil onto irreplaceable pages. Mage Rutan's much-praised validator, the small pewter charm I had wheedled out of the old sturgeon only with extraordinary groveling, wavered maddeningly between dullness and brilliance, refusing to designate the message as truth or falsehood.

Yet the request was stated with a certain directness uncharacteristic of students. Uncharacteristic, too, was the distance involved; Ventinna lay a good four days' ride westward. And a particular detail tickled my imagination, one that might escape a reader unburdened by the excessive expectations of names and bloodlines—or the private convictions of some greater destiny too embarrassing to mention, even to his longtime mentor. The outer address used my common appellation, *Duplais* being my father's unprepossessing dcmesne. But the inner included *Savin*, the family name I had long discarded, which could not but lead my thoughts to one particular kinsman and couch the imperious tone of the message in an entirely different light. *Present yourself . . . We require . . .*

A prickle of excitement minimized all sober considerations, such as how to request leave from my duties while maintaining *utmost discretion*, and how ridiculous it was to imagine that my fifteenth cousin, the King of Sabria, had summoned me to a clandestine meeting. I had never even met the man.

My finger traced the Savin family device scribed on the back of my left hand at birth, then moved inevitably to the ragged, nine-year-old scar that bisected it, scoring my wrist and vanishing up my sleeve. *If not now, Portier, when?*

In an instant's resolve, I stuffed the missive inside my threadbare doublet, snatched up my compass, journal, and pen case, and locked my desk without so much as returning my books to the shelves. A hastily scribbled note directed students to see Adept Nidallo for access to the archives or the vault. At the modest age of two-and-thirty, I'd spent precisely half my life inside these walls. My bones had near fossilized. Did my royal cousin bid me suckle his children, I'd do it.

"COUSIN PORTIER. WE'VE NOT MET before, I believe." The tall, broad-shouldered man in maroon and silver stood by a grand window that opened onto the sprawling country estate called Margeroux. His clear voice resonated with confidence. His extended hand bore a ruby signet, crested with Sabria's golden tree.

"Indeed, sire, I've not had that privilege." I dropped to one knee and kissed his proffered ring. "How may I serve you?"

I felt immensely relieved and a bit foolish. Four long days in the saddle give a man occasion to recall every synonym for *idiot*. Philippe de Savin-Journia was a sovereign in his prime. His wealth and open-mindedness had artists, explorers, scholars, and academicians of every science flocking to his court. What possible need had he of a librarian, schooled in a fading art? I had decided that, at best, the kinsman awaiting me would turn out to be some moronic relation as bereft of fortune and prospects as I. Worse cases abounded.

But the King of Sabria enveloped my left hand with his own—a broad, hard, warm hand, scribed with the myriad honorable scars of a warrior's life, as well as the same Savin family device that marked mine—and hauled me to my feet. Eyes the deep blue of Sabria's skies took my measure.

"I've a mystery needs solving, cousin. The matter is delicate, and certain aspects require me to seek counsel beyond my usual circles. Where better than with a member of my own family?"

"I'm honored you would think of me, sire." Mystified, to be precise. Curious.

His well-proportioned face relaxed into a welcoming smile. "Good. I've heard decent reports of you over the years and was sure you were the man I needed. I've delayed this unconscionably, hoping— Ah, you'll hear all the sordid complications soon enough. Come along."

He led me on a brisk walk through a series of pleasant, sunny rooms to a deserted kitchen in the back of the house. Pausing only to light a lamp from the banked kitchen fire, which seemed odd in the bright midafternoon, he headed outdoors.

"Tell me, Portier," he said, striding across a shady courtyard. "The methods of sorcerous practice have not changed in these years of my estrangement with the Camarilla, have they? No revelation of opticum or mechanica, no new-writ treatise on anatomy or mathematics or the composition of minerals has altered the teaching of spell-work?"

"Not at all, sire. Indeed some progressive mages believe that instruments such as the opticum will support our understanding of the physical melding of the five divine elements." Not many. Most magical practitioners stubbornly maintained their posture that the *mundane sciences* offered nothing to sorcerers.

"And your brethren yet renounce superstition and daemonology?"

"Mages of the Camarilla work entirely within the bounds of earth. They practice as methodically as do the scientists and natural philosophers you embrace."

Had I ever imagined having the opportunity to seed the king's mind with some good feeling for the art of sorcery, I would have prepared more refined arguments. Philippe was known as a man of lively intellect and devouring curiosity.

"Sire, it seems a sad waste that political disagreements with the Camarilla have so undermined your confidence in an art that has so much to offer your kingdom."

He choked down a laugh. "I will not argue science and magic with you, Portier. My bodyguard reports that you yourself carry a compass rather than some 'directional charm' that might fail inexplicably at the dark of the moon and lead you off a cliff."

We left the path and crossed a dark corner of the yard to a narrow downward stair. Wading through a litter of dead leaves, twigs, and walnut husks, we descended the stone steps to an iron grate that blocked the lower end.

Philippe twisted the latch and tugged a rusty handle, the grate rising more smoothly than its appearance and location would suggest. The low-ceilinged passage beyond, much older than the house, smelled of stagnant water and old leaves. The king adjusted his lamp to shine more brightly. Once the grate slid closed behind us, a fierce sobriety wiped away my cousin's affable demeanor.

"Last year, on the twenty-fifth day of Cinq, an arrow penetrated my mount's saddle, not three millimetres from the great vein in my thigh. By the grace of the Pantokrator's angels, the villain archer's hand wavered, and he lies dead instead of me. Gross evidence implicates my wife."

"Sainted ancestors! I never heard—" Well, perhaps a traveling mage had brought gleeful rumors of a foiled assassination plot, but I'd thought nothing of it. Few mages held excessive love for Philippe, who had set out to dismantle the Camarilla Magica's pervasive influence in Sabrian society, scholarship, and business, and done exceeding well at it. But the queen . . . *the shadow queen*, rumor named her, or *the lady of sorrows*, who had lost one husband already, her parents in a fire, her firstborn to an infant fever, and three others miscarried . . .

We proceeded deliberately through a warren of dank passages. "Few know the complete story, in particular that the nature of the archer, and certain other aspects of the event, evidenced the collaboration of one from your magical fraternity. Somewhere a sorcerer has, for whatever reason, decided that his king ought to be dead. Though her two pet mages have no use for me, I utterly reject the idea that my wife could be involved."

"Sorcery."

"That's why I chose you, cousin. I need a sorcerer to serve as my confidential agent in this matter."

The snaky uneasiness in my belly quickly tangled itself into a familiar knot of disappointment. Though I held no grievance against Philippe, man or king, or his predecessor, King Soren, I forever cursed their presence in my family tree. As early as age ten, I had realized that our royal connection and its excess of expectations had ruined my father, leaving him with no true friends, no money, no useful purpose to his life, and a marital contract sufficient to produce me, but naught else.

At fourteen, I learned that no girl with a wit larger than an acorn would touch a male who wore the interlaced *S* and *V* on the back of his hand. The Camarilla mandated severe penalties for promiscuity, and when one of the parties hailed from the most notable, if not the most vigorous, of Sabria's seventeen remaining magical bloodlines, inquisitorial scrutiny was assured.

In the very year I turned sixteen and began my studies at Seravain, the coolness between the young King Philippe and the Camarilla broke into an open struggle for dominance. Determined to make my way in the society of mages, I had quickly dropped the *Savin* from my name. Seven years later, my ambition had died its humiliating death, my Savin bloodline too weak to carry me farther in a life of sorcery.

"My lord . . ."

At the end of a branched passage, Philippe touched a most ordinary-seeming door of thick oak. The door swung open all of itself. Cool air rushed out, bristling with enchantment. For one moment I allowed the mystical wave to engulf me, a sensory pleasure as deeply human as the smell of damp earth in spring. But nine years of practiced honesty required I speak nature's inescapable verdict.

"My lord, I must confess: I am no sorcerer, nor will I ever be."

He swung around to face me.

"I am failed, sire," I said, lest he had not heard enough. "Incapable of spellwork."

"I see. Yet you excelled in your studies. Reports say you are as intimately familiar with the history and practice of magic as anyone in Sabria—including those who wear the collar of a Camarilla mage. Is that true? Answer squarely, cousin. False modesty has no place here."

The truth was not so simple. Yes, I had read widely. But who would ever separate *knowledge* of sorcery from its practice? "I suppose one could say that, but—"

"Skills can be bought. Knowledge takes much longer to acquire, and the ability to question, analyze, interpret, and deduce longer still. The capacity for loyalty is born in a man, reinforced, I believe, with family connection. I believe you the fit person to pursue a confidential, objective inquiry into a matter of sorcery. The burden of judgment is my duty and my prerogative. But if you take on this task, I shall give you freedom and resources to pursue matters as you think best. If you deem yourself unfit, turn right around and be on your way. My time is exceeding short."

Royal assassination. Magic bent to murder. The queen suspected. Were my eyes wholly dazzled with royal flattery that I would consider treading such dangerous ground? Did unseemly curiosity cloud my judgment? Or was I clinging to the improbable certainty that my life had meaning beyond breathing and dying?

Perhaps reasons didn't matter. My mentor, Kajetan, had instilled in me a determination to honesty, and I allowed that to be my guide. "Beyond the practice of sorcery itself, sire," I said, "I do believe myself fit for such a task."

"Good. Because now I must unnerve you a bit more." Philippe moved through the open door, his boots rapping sharply on the uneven paving of yet another passage. "The last man I set to this investigation, a skilled warrior and experienced diplomat, vanished nine months ago and is not found. For private reasons, I've allowed the public inquiry to lapse. Yet conscience nags that we speak not only of my personal safety, but of the security of Sabria herself."

We halted beside an iron door. Philippe hung his lamp from a bracket and unlocked the door with a plain bronze key, but he did not open it right away. The lamplight ringed his pale eyes with shadow and carved false hollows in his firm-fleshed cheeks.

"I don't believe in magic, Portier. For most of my eight-and-thirty years, I have judged its practice entirely illusion, trickery, or coincidence. Alchemists daemonstrate every day that matter is not limited to sorcery's five divine elements. An opticum lens reveals that *wood* is not homogeneous, but is itself made up of water, air, and fibers.

Water contains unseeable creatures and can be fractured into gaseous matter. *Spark* is but an explosive instance of heat and light and tinder. Similarly with *air* and *base metal*. Natural science brings logic and reason to a chaotic universe. We have discovered more of truth in the past twenty years than in the past twenty centuries, stimulating our minds, benefiting Sabria and her citizens in innumerable ways. However, in this room, it pains me to confess, we find something else again."

He dragged open the door and gestured me in, and though I held ready arguments against his inaccurate understanding of the divine elements, an eager excitement drew me into the small, bare chamber. Swept and brushed, the close room smelled of naught but damp stone and lamp oil. On a stone table at its center lay an arrow, its point, splintered shaft, and ragged fletching stained deep rusty red; a brass spyglass, as a military commander or shipboard officer might use; and an untarnished silver coin. Simple evidence, an observer might say, unless he could sense the enchantment that belched from them in a volcanic spew.

"Sight through the glass, Portier. Then I'll tell you my story of magic and murder."

Magic, as I had told the king, was entirely of the human world and subject to its laws. So it was bad enough that I peered through the enchanted glass and saw a man staggering through a tangle of leafless thorn trees toward a barred iron gate—a view nothing related to the place where I stood. Far worse was my eerie certainty of the land he traveled. To glimpse the Souleater's ice-bound caverns or spy on the surpassing mystery of the Creator's Heaven could be no more fearsome, for every passing soul must first endure the Perilous Demesne of Trial and Journey— Ixtador of the Ten Gates, the desolation that lies just beyond the Veil separating this life from the next. Most unsettling of all was the reason for my certainty. The wailing, exhausted traveler was my father, a man nine years dead.

ONE SHORT HOUR LATER, DREAD, like Discord's Worm, had taken up permanent residence in my bowels. I would have yielded my two legs to return to my dull library.

Less than two hundred years had passed since Sabria had retreated from near dissolution. A century of savagery, fueled by rivalries between the great magical families and between those blood families and the civil authorities, had left our cities in ruins, half of our villages empty or burnt, and more than two-thirds of Sabria's nobles, scholars, and sorcerers dead. Entire magical bloodlines had been wiped out. Even a whisper of those times yet caused cold sweats and shudders in every Sabrian.

Now someone had dredged up the foulest magic of those days to create an assassin and had dispatched him to murder Sabria's golden king. Philippe was convinced that his mysterious enemy, who might or might not be his wife, would make a second attempt on the anniversary of the first, some two months hence. The king's death by unholy sorcery must surely relight the smoldering embers of the Blood Wars, and the mysterious spyglass hinted that this time the conflagration might drive us into realms uncharted. I, Portier de Savin-Duplais, librarian and failed student of magic, was charged to stop it.

"As the secrecy of your investigation must preclude our public relationship, I've engaged you a partner *agente confide*." Philippe led me, still speechless, back into the sunny, peaceful house. I felt out of time, as if I'd just returned from the Souleater's frozen demesne. "Cousin Portier, meet Chevalier Ilario de Sylvae."

A tall, fair, long-nosed young man, garbed in an eye-searing ensemble of red silk sleeves, green satin waistcoat, gold link belt and bracelets, and lace—god's finger, ruffled lace everywhere—swept off a feathered hat and dropped to one knee as we entered the reception room. "Gracious lord. Such a delight to attend you on this glorious spring day—though 'tis a bit warmish for the season—and I am so forever humbled and ennobled to serve you, though my spirit trembles at the requirement for discretion. . . ."

Another hour and I was truly flummoxed. After charging me to halt the revival of the Blood Wars in the span of two short months, the king had paired me with an imbecile.

But I had sworn him my service. Indeed, the implications of the spyglass could not be ignored, and left my first move clear. I needed a sorcerer.

CHAPTER ONE

33 TRINE
64 DAYS UNTIL THE ANNIVERSARY

"Tell me again, good Portier," called my lanky companion over his shoulder, the plumes of his velvet toque bouncing despite the oppressive woodland damp. "Right or left at the chestnut tree? By my sacred mater's nose, headings and inclinations slip through my ears like sand through a sieve. I could lose my way in a bath!"

"Bear right, Lord Ilario," I said, biting back the oh-so-sweet temptation to send the pretty-faced moron the wrong way. "The plowman was most specific. Are you certain you'd not prefer to wait back in Bardeu? There's no need to discomfort—"

"La, brave comrade! How could I, a Knight of Sabria, leave you alone to beard this fearsome mage in his woody den—our first foray into the world as partner *agentes*?" My companion reversed the course of his palfrey with effortless grace, his idiot grin blazing like unwelcome sunrise in a drunkard's eye. "Surely I must collapse in shame, never again able to face our noble king or my fellow knights. Though, naturally, I could not discuss our business with my fellow knights until released from my vow of silence. I don't know that I've taken a vow of silence before. . . ."

With a sigh I checked my compass heading against the map I'd sketched in my journal that morning. All seemed correct. I waved the mewling popinjay onward, hoping to still his prattle with movement if I could neither send him away nor throttle him. Knight of Sabria, indeed. Ilario de Sylvae had been fostered since babyhood with his half sister, Queen Eugenie. If he had ever drawn his fine sword outside Merona's fencing halls, I'd eat my boots.

Philippe had claimed that Ilario's rank could gain me access to information none other could manage and that the young lord's determination to prove his half sister's innocence would provide me a trustworthy ally. Fifteen days together had eliminated my concerns that the fop's motives might be more complicated. Philippe's were yet in question. Even the humiliating need to hire a better sorcerer was easier to bear than the implication that, in my sovereign's eyes, my service ranked on par with an idiot's.

As the spreading canopy of oak and chestnut dimmed the feeble daylight, I spurred my mount past Ilario's. *Turn right from the Carvalho road at the point where it leaves the village,* so the Bardeu plowman had directed me. *Proceed through a beynt of wheat fields and cow pasture (closing the hedge-gate behind you, if you please, sonjeur) and across the weedy bog. Then keep right of the great chestnut and pray the Pantokrator's angels the sorcerer's not bound a confusion spell to lose you in the groves. A well-trod path,* he'd said, his great shoulders shuddering.

Both the obscurity and the local popularity . . . and the shudder . . . had encouraged my decision to seek out this man. Only a skilled mage would be able to explain the spyglass and untangle the workings of complex and illicit sorcery. And every other mage I knew of lived under the inquisitive eye of the Camarilla Magica, scarce an objective position, considering the eighteen years' hostility between the king and Camarilla.

"Halloo! Most fearsome mage, are you to home?" Lord Ilario's cheerful trumpeting caromed off the crowding trees, only to die a quick death in the breathless stillness.

"Chevalier, I must ask again that you adhere to our plan," I said through clenched teeth. "We agreed to be oblique in our approach until we're sure of him. And please, sir, curb your . . . good humor. Rumor names this mage easily offended and unaccustomed to courtly manners."

"Nonsense. Any man of the blood will have had a proper upbringing, whether in the bosom of his family or at Collegia Seravain."

"This mage is unusual, Chevalier. His hand bears no blood family's mark. Nor did he study at Seravain."

That a man not kin to one of the noble families who carried the trait of magical talent, and not formally schooled in the accumulated knowledge of sorcery, much of which was secret, could earn a mage's collar was as likely as a rabbit writing a treatise on the movement of the planets. But so this fellow had done.

Three years previous, he had arrived at Seravain and demanded to sit for examination, naming himself *Exsanguin—Bloodless.* After five rigorous days, he had won through to the rank of master, leaving the collegia faculty in an uproar. Not only had he earned the right to practice sorcery without supervision, and to oversee and instruct other mages, but he was eligible to be named to the Camarilla Prefecture—those who ruled on the accuracy of teachings and charted the course of sorcery in the world. But to the amazement of all, in the same hour his silver collar was sealed about his neck, he had walked away, vanishing into the obscurity from which he'd come.

I had never met Exsanguin, but as Seravain's archivist, I had duly recorded his collaring and the demesne he'd claimed as residence. Twelve days traveling on the back roads of Louvel and much cajoling of reticent villagers had brought Ilario and me to Bardeu. The villagers did not know the sorcerer's true name, either.

"Saints Awaiting!" mumbled Ilario. "Rogue mages are the Souleater's servants. At the least, I've some protection." He pulled a lump of black string, seashells, scarlet beads, and silver bangles from his pocket and dangled it from silk-gloved fingers. "Adept Fedrigo made this for me before I traveled to the sea last summer, as I had expressed my mortal fear of crocodiles. I think it must be a most efficacious charm. For certain, I suffered neither scratch, bite, nor sighting of the wicked creatures. Indeed, I could not even complain about a poor bed upon my travels. Do you think it will suffice in this dismal wood?"

I closed my eyes and inhaled deeply. "Certainly, Chevalier. I'd wager we'll encounter not a single crocodile today."

Hilarity bubbled out of him until he near choked on it. At least he took no offense when my annoyance burst its bounds so injudiciously—damnable idiot.

Our mounts' hooves thudded solidly on the well-beat track through a tunnel of oaks and chestnuts. Stray gleams of sunlight glinted on bits of polished tin hung here and there on the lower branches. No matter the Camarilla's strictures against illicit practice, the ignorant would ever pay hedge witches and marketplace conjurers for such useless trinkets, thinking to ward their travels on perilous paths.

As we rounded a curve, the path opened into a trampled clearing. The unhandsome stone house with sagging thatch might have been a particularly large acorn dropped from one of the thick-boled oaks. I signaled a halt.

"At last!" Ilario flung a long leg over his beast and dropped lightly to the turf. With a flourish, the lanky young lord removed his traveling cloak and tossed it across his saddle, exposing a sky blue satin waistcoat and uselessly thin and tight leather breeches of the fashionable sort deemed suitable for "rustic" excursions. He swept his arm in my direction. "Lead me, good Portier."

I disembarked from my lead-footed mare and smoothed my sober gray tunic. No one would ever call me a "fashionable young twit" or "a preening peacock with a mind less weighty than his feathers." Sighing, I scuffed a clot of dung from my boots. Quite a duet we made—Ilario the Fop, the laughingstock of Merona, and Portier de Duplais, librarian, bound together like a peacock and a tortoise, ready to face the assaults of the unholy.

"Divine grace shine upon thee and thy ancestors, master mage!" I called.

No one answered. Ilario kissed his luck charm, and though his expression maintained a proper sobriety, he winked at me in the intimate manner that I had not yet deciphered, but which felt most unseemly.

I called again, a little louder this time. "Master mage, a word with you, if we might."

No leaf stirred in the thicket of saplings, buckthorn, and laurel that obscured much of the ugly house. No smoke rose from the peak of the roof.

"Bother, if the fellow is away." Ilario pursed his lips, blew a disappointed note, and propped his arms on his saddle, gazing mournfully at me across his beast. Even his plume seemed to droop.

Dried mud, gouged with footprints, bore witness to a great number of visitors—both men and women, many in thick, nailed boots and others on horseback. Some had come in sodden winter; others within the past tennight, as approaching summer tempered the rains. Horses had been tethered here for hours at a time.

"Ill-tempered," the locals had told us. "Wouldn't cross him . . . not for a purse full of kivrae." Yet yeomen, merchants, tradesmen, and even the poorest of husbandmen and laborers sought him out, and he served them willing. "'E fixes them as is cursed in the mind," was the clearest report we'd scavenged. That could mean anything from providing sleeping draughts to excising bits of brain tissue like the storied Mad Healer of Dock Street.

So why the shabby surroundings? Even in these times, when magical practitioners' prestige had ebbed to the level of jongleurs or card cheats, a master mage could live as well as a duc. Privacy could be bought in fairer packages than an ugly hut in a chestnut grove.

I rapped on the door but jerked my hand away. The awareness of living enchantment slithered up my arm like a fiery snake. I'd never felt the like. I grasped a small, smooth stone inside my coin pocket. The courret, a rare wardstone borrowed from Seravain, chilled my fingers, declaring that the lingering enchantment posed no danger. I'd no other way to tell. Disentanglement, discerning the particular nature of the enchantments or magical residues my trained senses perceived, required spellwork, and thus lay beyond my abilities.

Footsteps crunched in the brush.

"Who's there?" The resonant voice was a presence in itself, deep, substantial, brittle, cold as the north wind off the barrens of Delourre.

I whipped my head around.

A lean, wiry man halted at the edge of the trees. His gaunt face was unshaven. The dark hair that dangled wild and loose at front and sides had escaped from a shaggy tail. Despite the imperious greeting, the pick and three iron lever bars dangling from his belt, and the heavy boots, russet tunic, and work-stained canvas slops named him a common countryman. And though he measured scant centimetres taller than my own modest height, I was uncomfortably certain he could snap my scrawny limbs like twigs. He balanced a sizable stone on his shoulder with only one hand. He appeared entirely unlike any mage I had ever met, and yet . . .

"We've come to see the mage on important business, goodman. Is he nearby?" Ilario dabbed his long nose with a kerchief and craned his neck, peering deeper into the trees.

If I could but glimpse the man's neck . . . Mages were forbidden to hide or remove their silver collars, the Camarilla's concession to the fears of the powerless.

"Identify yourselves." The fellow emerged from the gloom and halted in the center of the clearing. Indeed, a seamless band of silver encircled his sinewed neck, wholly incongruous with his rough attire. And the collar's fine gold inlay designated the wearer a master mage. Yet it was the voice that marked him as worthy of note . . . and the eyes set deep under heavy brows. The fiery green of new oak leaves, those eyes could slice paper edge-on. For certain, no common laborer had such.

The fop snapped his hands to his sides and inclined his

head. "Ilario de Sylvae, Chevalier ys Sabria, sir mage. And my good companion, Portier de Duplais."

"Divine grace, Master," I said, bowing with my left hand laid on my right shoulder, the mark of my blood family clearly exposed. "We would appreciate a word with you on a matter of interest."

"I share no interests with aristos."

"I am the archivist at Collegia Seravain," I said. "When examining our records—"

"Go away. I dislike company." The sorcerer hefted his burden a little higher and vanished into the oak and blackthorn scrub crowding the left side of the house.

Ilario bolted after him like a startled doe. "Hold on, sir mage!"

"Please, Master! Chevalier!" My call might have been floating dust for all it slowed them.

I had no choice but to follow. I needed a talented outsider to pursue this investigation. If this mage had skills to match his arrogance, the level of knowledge his collar bespoke, and some quantity of honor that could be claimed or bought, we might have found our man.

Thorny branches snagged my clothes, and my boots sank into the soft earth.

However, the gangly fop darted through the tangle unhindered. "Hear me out, sir mage," he called brightly. "We've brought you an invitation . . . an opportunity, one might say. If we could but sit for a moment, share a glass of wine, perhaps. My mistress will be most distressed if her offer is unheard. Most distressed . . ."

Mistress? Enthroned god! I'd told the fool to let me handle this.

Wrenching my sleeve from the barbed grip of the brush, I stumbled into a small, sunny garden: a few orderly hills and rows of vegetables, and a raised bed of close-planted herbs, swarming with bees. Garlic shoots and thick, low masses of dusty greenery bordered the plot.

Astonishing. From the mage's wild appearance, and the smoldering fury that tainted his words, one might better have expected devilish machinery or smoking pits.

"I've tasks enough to occupy my time. Take your opportunity elsewhere." The earth quivered when he dropped his loaf-shaped stone to the barren ground on the far side of the garden. At least fifty similarly shaped stones lay about the area, some stacked, some scattered randomly, some carefully trimmed and fitted into three walls set square to one another. Chips and flakes of stone littered the dirt.

Ilario blotted his cheeks with his lace kerchief. "Please, good sir mage—"

The mage whirled, his fiery gaze raking Ilario's turnout from purple plume to sleek boots. He flared his nostrils. "If my oven was built, I could bake bread and serve a noble guest and his companion properly. Even a coarse meal would better suit your taste than converse with the likes of me. But my bakefire cannot be lit as yet, so you must leave my home unsatisfied." He removed the pick and the iron bar from his belt and tossed them to the dirt. "*Leave.* Do fine gentlemen like you understand a plain-spoke word?"

Shivers cooled my overheated skin. No welcome here; the villagers had not erred in that.

Squatting with his back to us, the mage shoved the new stone close to the others. His wide, long-fingered left hand palmed the height and width of the block as if to measure it against its fellows. The back of that hand, thick with black hair, was clean of any family mark, as the tale of Exsanguin bespoke. Odd how the right hand stayed so firmly inside his tunic. Was he armed?

Despairing, I ventured into the dismissive silence. "If you would but allow me to explain, Master. My position as archivist led me to your name—"

"We are *sent*, sir mage!" Ilario bellowed at the man's back, while bulging his eyes and waggling his brows at me incomprehensibly. "My mistress believes that current mania for scientific advancement has unfairly turned popular opinion against the mystic arts. She has assembled a consilium of mages, graciously lending her particular prestige to their works." He began to march up and down, bobbing his feathered cap like a cock in a hen roost. "Certainly your next question will be *what works might these be?* Unfortunately, I am incapable of telling you. Though I represent a woman whose intellect scales great heights, my own wit plods along the solid earth. My comrade Portier, here, himself a learned practitioner of your fantastical arts, could explain our aims better, but, of course, he is a modest man of modest rank and shy of intruding in conversation between his betters. Besides, my lady has particularly charged *me* to offer *you* her patronage. . . ."

Blessed saints, the mage would believe we were both flea-wits. The fool Ilario had gotten it wholly muddled. We had agreed that I would assess the mage by luring him into a test of his capability and honor. Only when I was satisfied would we broach the matter of the queen's mages and what we needed him to do. The queen knew—and could know— nothing about this mission.

Yet, indeed, the mage twisted around and stared at Ilario with an intensely curious expression.

"My lady relishes nurturing new talent. I can assure you . . ." Ilario's prattle skidded to a stop under the weight of the mage's scrutiny.

The disconcerting gaze shifted to me. My skin itched. Unease swelled in my belly, reaching full growth, then relaxed again like a flower that buds, blooms, and fades all in the space of ten heartbeats. My soul felt abraded— exposed. Likely it was my conscience. Surely this man recognized the lies.

"What game is this you play?" said the mage softly, returning his attention to Ilario. His dark brows knit a line. "Speak as yourself this time, lord."

Ilario's lips parted, but no sound issued from between them. I, too, felt rendered mute.

"Does truth pain a Sabrian chevalier so much?" The mage extracted a stylus from a jumble of tools in a wooden chest and scored the new block across several of its faces, rolling and marking it entirely with his left hand. "So, one or the other of you can tell me truthfully why you're here. Or I can draw it out of your asses with a billhook. Or you can go away and leave me to my *common labor*."

A sighing breeze shifted the overhanging branches. The sultry gloom deepened. I rubbed my arms through the worn velvet of my doublet.

I was no gullible stable hand who believed charmed cats could cure his pox or pond scum make his wife fertile. Though all agreed that Sabria's greater magic had faded, I had studied the testimony of those who had seen mages soothe whirlwinds and stem the advance of poisoned tides. I myself had felt the balance of the five divine elements and the flow of power through my veins and deepest self—no matter that the result was naught but a sputter in the scheme of the world. But the vibrant and richly textured power swirling about this sunny garden was no more kin to the magic I had experienced than a sunset is cousin to a candle flame. Pressing the back of my hand to my mouth, I fought a compulsion to spew King Philippe's secrets, though the mage had not even raised his uncommon voice.

Ilario's golden skin took on the hue of sour milk. He swallowed, blinked, and dabbed at his quivering lower lip, then straightened his long neck as if for the headsman. "My apologies, sir mage. Allow me to clarify. That my kinswoman defies popular beliefs with support of sorcery is true. What I failed to mention is that she is interested in certain areas of magical pursuit that many people might consider . . . unsavory. And I must confess that my mistress has not yet heard of you. I took this inquiry upon myself after hearing Portier's report—"

"My lord!" Father Creator, he was ready to tell all. "Discretion, sir!"

"We must tell him the truth, Portier! For my lady's sake. Sir mage, some days ago, my friend Portier told me of your unusual collaring at Collegia Seravain. I bade him locate you in hopes you might take an interest in my mistress's needs. In fact, I've been thinking of hiring my own mage. I've no staff at all save my valet, which is highly improper for a person of rank, depending on others to see to my requirements. . . ." Ilario, lost in his prattling deception, flashed me a desperate look. My head threatened to split.

The mage tossed his stylus aside and settled onto the dirt, resting his folded arms on his drawn-up knees, as if prepared to lecture us. "What part of my history leads you or *you*"—he glared ferociously at me—"to believe that I might be willing to be kept in some aristo's menagerie alongside the horses, hounds, and birds? I work as I please and study what I please, and no one demands my time be spent making love philtres or skin glamours or servicing whatever 'unsavory' desires your mistress wishes to indulge. I've countless better things to do."

As I tried not to stare at the mage's now-exposed right hand—a red-scarred, twisted claw living ugly and useless at the end of a well-muscled arm—my mind raced to knit Ilario's unraveled stupidity into a useful story. The fop had skewed the truth just enough to leave me an opening for the very test of skill and character I wished this visit to encompass. If only I knew how to entice the mage into revelations. Obviously, he cared naught for comforts or renown. What induced him to accommodate those who came here seeking his help?

"Because the opportunities we offer are unique," I blurted, insight like a blade between my ears. "Your history and this place"—I waved my hand to encompass his odd home—"and gossip of a forbidding mage who untangles the mysteries of broken minds led me—us—to believe we might find in you a certain . . . nontraditional . . . approach to your work. A talented man interested in puzzles."

"Go on."

Scarce daring to believe I'd guessed right, I laid down another thread. "We could offer virtually unlimited resources to advance whatever studies you wish—books, funds, connections to information and materials from every corner of the known world, the most prominent mages in Sabria as your colleagues. You would have the opportunity to collaborate in magic of a grander scale than you could—"

Mirthless laughter halted me midargument. "So you *are* more fools than villains," said the mage. "Unfortunately for you, it has been many years since I concluded that large-scale magical works are entirely sham and chicanery, and that the 'most prominent mages' in Sabria have not the least concept of true sorcery. In short, your benevolent mistress is misguided at best, some duc's whore perpetuating a fraud at worst, and she could not offer me gold enough to participate in such a mockery."

"Speak no slander, sir!" Ilario's words dropped in the mage's lap like a challenge glove. "We serve the Queen of Sabria."

"Lord Ilario!" I snapped, horrified. The fop had almost got me believing he had a wit.

"The queen?" The mage guffawed. "So the 'prominent' colleagues you offer are the shadow queen's trained Camarilla pups? I'd sooner bed a leper than ally myself with clowns and fools."

No reasoning man could wholly discount the charges laid against sorcerers—that some of us paraded grand illusion in the guise of true sorcery. But this brutish arrogance was insupportable.

"Civilized men do not belittle those they do not know," I snapped, summoning what dignity I could muster ankle deep in a vegetable patch. "You may be gifted, sir, but the mages of the Camarilla have proved their talents over centuries."

He only grew quieter and more contemptuous. "Show me the great work of a Camarilla mage, *student*, and I will show you with what tools a minimally talented hod carrier can duplicate it. Show me one of your own great works. Or perhaps . . . even a small one?"

And so was Ilario's challenge glove returned to my own lap, along with the mage's choice of weapons. I had not thought my failed status so obvious.

Annoyed at my slip of control, I gathered my temper. I had not come here to daemonstrate my own magical worth. If we were to fail at this, all the better this man believe me Ilario's intellectual peer.

"No," I said, crushing doubt and pride alike with the hammer of necessity. "*You* show us. Elsewise, we shall assume you're naught but a trickster with a crude mouth, afraid to speak your own name, and with no better concept of magical truth than those you disdain. I can provide interesting, magically challenging employment for a skilled mage who values truth, scorns danger, and bears no loyalty to the Camarilla or any other magical practitioner."

One corner of his mouth twisted in what might pass for amusement. Far more satisfying was the spark of curiosity that flared in his green eyes. "What employment might that be? You do not sacrifice your pride before a forbidding and unpleasant man for a charm to calm your horse."

Swallowing my discomfiture at his insight, I laid down my challenge. "If you are interested, clean yourself, dress as befits a master mage, and join us at Villa Margeroux, off the Tallemant Road, within three days. A hired mount will await your use in Bardeu. Be prepared to dazzle us with your daemonstration of magical truth. If we are satisfied with your application, Master Exsanguin, we will explain our dangerous proposition."

I bowed to the fop and motioned him back through the underbrush to the horses. Lord Ilario nodded in return and marched away, patting my shoulder as if he had given birth to me.

The green gaze scorched my back as I followed Ilario out of the garden. "Dante," said the uncommon voice behind us. "My name is Dante."

CHAPTER TWO

36 TRINE
61 DAYS UNTIL THE ANNIVERSARY

I had believed the mage intrigued. Something had induced him to yield his name. Dante. *Exsanguin*. Bloodless. By the holy Veil, even the memory of his stare set me glancing over my shoulder. But the third day had almost waned before the Contessa de Margeroux's housekeeper announced a visitor.

"He will not step inside, Conte Olivier." The comfortable gray woman of middling years huffed as if the report scalded her mouth. "He says he's come to see—forgive me, lord, but he's charged me to repeat his words exactly—the student and the dancepole and no . . . inbred aristos. Is it certain he's the person expected? Such a dirty, crude ruffian?"

I doubted the housekeeper's protective loyalty to the elderly Conte de Margeroux and his much younger Lady Susanna was much tested. Though valued friends of the king, the couple lived quietly in this remote demesne. The conte directed an inquiring scowl at Ilario.

"Your report but confirms his identity, good Hanea," said Ilario, shuddering. "And you'd best obey. Cross him and he'll likely change you into an ox. He is entirely yours,

Portier. I've no wish to lay eyes on the creature." He waggled his glittering, ringed fingers, his beloved lace cuffs dangling unchecked into his brandy—a measure of his disturbance. He had determinedly not spoken of Dante since we'd left the chestnut wood.

As I set out to meet our visitor, Conte Olivier retired. I wasn't sure how much the elderly lord and his wife knew of Philippe's personal troubles, but the king clearly trusted their discretion. Not only did they house the assassin's implements, but for fifteen days they had treated Ilario and me as familiar guests, never inquiring of our business.

A bit of wilderness had been allowed to flourish amid the pristine cultivation of Lord Olivier's sprawling demesne. Old joint-pines, creeping laurel, and budding strawberry trees created a fragrant and secluded haven. The footman reported that the visitor had made his way there straightaway.

"Have you an aversion to sunlight, Master Dante?" I said when he spun in his tracks at my approach.

His silver collar shone dully above the same shabby tunic he'd worn three days before, topped by a buff jerkin. Three days' growth had left his chin bristling with black spikelets akin to fen sedge. His dreadful hand was tucked inside his garments. The other hand gripped a white walking stick.

"I've a need to stretch out the knots of beast riding," he said, resuming his brisk pace as soon as I joined him. "Wasn't born to it."

Of all things, I'd never expected to smile in this man's presence. No wonder it had taken him so long to get here.

"I've scorched thighs myself," I said. "Tending a library gives one few opportunities to ride out, even did Seravain have mounts to lend. The chevalier must have a steel ass underneath his silk stockings."

The mage glanced sidewise at me, flaring his nostrils as if an ill odor accompanied us. "How well do you know the pretty peacock?"

I saw no reason to dissemble. "Lord Ilario is harmless and good natured, saints bless his empty-headed ancestors. I did not choose him to partner in this task."

"Perhaps." He slowed to a walk. "So you expected to do the choosing . . . and *you* chose to approach me. Why?"

"As I said, your history speaks of exceptional talents—which you have yet to daemonstrate—and a certain independence of thought—which you most clearly possess. And even after our short meeting, I cannot imagine a danger that would deter you, did you find your work intriguing." Until that moment I had not articulated, even to myself, this certainty that he was the partner we needed. "I cannot and will not say more until I have your assurances—"

"I am no courtier who barters trust like paper words that can be burnt, or ink-drowned, or swept aside by any wind," he snapped. "I speak plain and expect the same respect. You'll get no assurances until I understand the whole of what you want. I don't know why I've wasted my time with you."

I hoped my satisfaction did not show. He did not understand his own hunger. "Clearly a man hiring a mage for a secret and dangerous task cannot reveal everything at once," I said. "So let us proceed step by step. But I'll promise you this: If I decide you are the right person, you will know everything I know before we begin."

He considered that as we strolled deeper into the woodland. "If I agree to the work," he said at last, "I deal with you and not the lordling. I'll not abide deceivers."

"Agreed." My spine relaxed at such easy negotiation. "Now before we proceed, I must inquire about your parentage."

No porcupine could bristle so vividly. "That is *not* your business."

"Bloodlines often hint at areas of expertise. I have been tasked to solve a mystery, and your expertise is your qualification."

"Bloodlines are irrelevant. I've queried witnesses who vouch this body burst from my common mother's womb thanks to my common father's seed. The two of them bequeathed me naught but this." He yanked out his ruined hand. "Speak not to me of blessed ancestors or blood-born magic. I've neither worth the telling."

"But your talents . . ."

"Everything I possess of spellmaking is learnt or discovered." He thrust his maimed hand back into hiding, planted the walking stick, and moved on, visibly quenching his flared temper. "Does that intrigue you, Portier de Duplais, failed student?"

He sped his steps, and I could not read his back. What kind of *agente confide* could I be if a new acquaintance could deduce my own history so easily?

"Show me, Master," I said, more forcefully than I intended. "You boast and scoff, and I hear naught but a marketplace shill, luring me into a diviner's tent where I'll be told the name of my true love for a mere two kivrae. Teach me your *discovered* truth of magic. I may be only a student who has discerned his natural limits, but I am a very *good* student."

He halted, waiting for me, his folded arms resting on his chest, the staff tight in the crook of his arm. His mouth twisted oddly, narrowed eyes gleaming fierce in the failing light. Assessing me. I did my best not to squirm.

"All right, then. I presume you have memorized the formulas for many spells. You've learnt to balance the five divine elements—water, wood, air, spark, and base metal—by choosing appropriate particles to embody each formula and adjusting those particles according to the spell's particular requirements: selecting a smaller shard of limestone to make a gate ward less rigid, or choosing three spoons of dust to increase the proportion of air and wood, allowing a sleeping fog to be easily dispersed, or adding a lock of hair from the person to be healed or warded or glamoured so that your enchantment will be tight bound to its focus. But tell me, are the particles themselves—or any other natural object—ever altered by your spellworking?"

"Certainly not." Certainly not in my case—but not in anyone else's case, either. "A particle can be glamoured—disguised with light to fool the eye—but the other senses would reveal its unchanged state. Or the particle, as any other object, can be used as a receptacle, linked to the spell so the enchantment can be transported. But magic itself is ephemera. Dust is naught but dust. Stone is stone. A thistle is a thistle. The Pantokrator has rendered nature immutable."

We rounded a corner and came to an open glade. At one end of the clearing, stones had been stacked and fitted and a flow of water channeled to imitate a rocky waterfall. A stone bench sat to one side of the burbling font.

"Yet we melt silver and shape it," said Dante, motioning me not to the bench, but to the ground in front of the font. "We alloy zinc and copper to make brass. We steep leaves in water to make tea."

Irritated at his condescending tone, I cleared away a litter of thorny branches and last year's leaves and sat crosslegged on the cool ground like a child in village school. A rabbit scuttered through the underbrush to find a new hiding place. "I am not an idiot, mage. Such are blendings or reshaping, not fundamental alterations. Brass is but a variant formulation of the divine elements. The metalsmith has added spark, and the new metal's properties—weight, mass, hardness, malleability—remain appropriate to the combined elements. It is not magic."

"Just what I'd expect a squawking parrot to report. Sit knees together, close your eyes, and quiet your thoughts."

Curiosity—and a determination to see through whatever conjury he planned—goaded me to obey. From beyond my eyelids came a shifting and scraping and a grunt of effort. Whatever I expected, it had naught to do with an anvil being set in my lap. *No, not an anvil, but one of the stones from the font.* The cool solidity weighed heavy on my knees.

"Your masters at Collegia Seravain would have you believe they can recreate a memorized formula and bind a potion to smooth the skin of an old woman or generate a finger of holy fire to ensure a royal counselor's honesty. They preen when they succeed and provide a litany of excuses when the crone dies wrinkled and the counselor is caught embezzling from the treasury. They fail to inform their patrons that a common laborer could hold the lenses they've used to focus beams of light or that any decent herbalist can provide a salve of apricots and olive oil to improve the skin as long as the woman is not *too* old and eats well and stays out of the sun."

The mage's warm fingers arranged my hands side by side on the cool flattish stone in my lap. His hardened palm remained atop my hands. "True sorcery begins with small things," he said, his ever-present scorn yielding to something more kin to reverence. "Every natural object in this world—tree, stone, person, honeybee—carries with it a pattern of sound and light that our eyes and ears cannot perceive. Some call it the object's *cast*. . . ."

I released my held breath. What a hypocrite! *Cast* was naught but oldwife twaddle—the trickster's love philtres, ghekets, and fairy rings this man purported to disdain. Yet before I could protest, the space behind my eyes—the center of my thinking self—began to heat like a glowing ember.

". . . but it is more accurately called *keirna*, for this patterning lies beyond our natural senses. A properly disciplined mind can perceive these patterns, just as refined lenses can perceive stars invisible to our eyes. Consider this particular object you hold. . . ."

Against the dark background inside my eyelids appeared lines of shimmering gray light, some lighter, some darker, stacked one atop the other like some arcane glyph, the line at the bottom thicker than the one at the top. I'd never experienced the like.

"The pattern reflects the solidity and strength that is the stone's nature. . . ."

As the mage spoke, another line appeared at the top of the stack curving gracefully around to connect at the bottom, touching every other line in the array.

". . . as are its continuity, enclosure, boundedness. Now consider the specifics of *this* rock, the minerals it contains, the shape and weight and source and history that make it like no other."

And woven in and out of the gray lines appeared slender threads of bright red, dull gold, and other colors I could not name. Permeating all was a low thrum, a sound so precise it was almost visible, a pulse that gave the pattern life.

"Were I to strike the rock with a chisel, I would alter this pattern—its keirna—but only in small ways. Because I study the language of keirna, the pattern would yet speak to me of stone, cut from yonder crags, formed in fire in the recesses of history and shaped apurpose to build this font."

Ridiculous. Stone was stone—an amalgam of the divine elements of wood, water, and base metal. Stone was softer or harder—more or less of the wood that made it firm and the base metal that made it impermeable. It was black or red or white, grainy or smooth. Such properties helped us judge the concentration of the elements in a particle and create the proper balance to bind spells. No magical *essence* hung about it.

"Human thoughts have patterns, as well." The mage's rich and resonant voice seemed strained, as if he balanced fifty such stones high above his head, daemonstrating their shapes and sizes to the world. "Those of true talent—and though there are more of them in this world than you might suspect, few wear mage's collars or reside in palaces—are capable of extending their patterns of thought and will to touch keirna, to link and bind and manipulate the keirna of various objects . . . creating . . . magic."

Into my vision intruded a finger of light, a pinpoint of dark blue brilliance with a tail of silver and crimson. The finger shredded the thick lower line and picked out some of the thinner weavings. In that same moment, as the surety of enchantment settled over me like a garment, I would have wagered my life that someone lifted the stone from my knees, though my hands told me it had not moved and had not changed in length or breadth or thickness. And when I opened my eyes, unable to contain myself longer, indeed *nothing* had changed but the weight of the massive stone. A burden little heavier than a pebble rested on my lap.

No, no, you cannot alter the fundamental properties of a particle—an object of the Pantokrator's creation. I lifted my hands, shoving his away, and shifted my knees, expecting to disrupt his illusion. Nothing changed. I inserted my fingers between the stone and my thighs and hefted it.

Turned it over. Shook it. Held it in one hand and raised it higher than my head, before resting it in my lap again and staring at it. A child could have tossed the thing into the air or skipped it on a pond. Illusions deposited a faint magical residue the texture of dry meal. Dante's left the air crackling like summer lightning.

The green eyes bored into mine, watching, waiting, judging me. I stared into their fiery depths and felt the foundations of my world crack.

The mage did not smile, but nodded as if a conversation had been concluded. "That, student, is the truth of sorcery."

His clawed hand gripped his walking stick, and he rested his head on it. A sighed word and the stone's full weight pressed down on my knees again.

I could not ask him how he'd learned it. To do so would have been to admit that I had failed not only in my aspiration, but in my striving. That I had wasted sixteen years. That my chosen masters, the priests of my mind's temple, the most honored mages of history— By the Ten Gates to Heaven, I had *read* their teachings hunting answers to my failure, and none gave a moment's credence to *cast*—the idea that magic lived not solely in the blood and will of a practitioner, but in all of nature, waiting to be drawn out. How could they all be wrong about the fundamental truths of the world?

I wanted to scream at Dante that he was the Souleater's servant, a trickster daemon. Yet I knew better. Illusions deceived the external senses, but this strange patterning of light and sound had appeared inside my mind where only I could render judgment. Unless I was myself a madman, he had shown me truth.

Perhaps he understood the lump the size of his rock that had lodged itself in my throat, for he spoke quietly and without rancor or hubris. "The mages at Seravain proclaim that only those they choose, only those born of proven bloodlines, only those who memorize their lists and follow their formulas, can work magic. Sorcery acknowledges no such limits. Most of the truly gifted work their small magics by rote, imitating what their grannies told them, or by instinct, because they have not separated themselves from nature by dividing all things into five divine boxes. Some of these people actually sense keirna and are able to manipulate a pattern as I did."

"Why don't we hear of this?" I said, grasping at arguments that evaporated with my touch. Fools and tricksters everywhere swore by their charms, philtres, wards, by their mother's healing power or their uncle's virility potion. What few claims ever proved true had been traced to a blood family's bastard or some true practitioner's deception.

"All those I've met work blind," said Dante, scritching the end of his staff in the dirt. "None claim to see the actual structure of keirna or attempt to display it for another as I did with you. Yet even if they did, who would believe? The Camarilla would name them cheats and deceivers and fine them into starvation, or torture them until they recant and brand them on the forehead, all to prove that collared mages alone hold the mighty reins of power. Cursed be their blackguard souls—"

He bit off a snarl, and his good hand tugged at his silver collar, as if it chafed; as if the masters at Seravain, jealous of his talent and despising his rude manner, had left a burr inside its enchanted circle or unbalanced its elements so that it would not accommodate the play of his muscles. No wonder they had been happy to forget him. His results and the lack of a blood mark on his hand must have confounded them. And he was correct; if the Camarilla had any idea of the magical heresies he propounded, they would bury him so far below Sabria's deepest dungeon, he would never see light again.

The mage had leaned his back against the fountain and closed his eyes as if to sleep. Not a peaceful sleep, but that of a wary traveler on an unknown road. "So, do I pass your test?"

I could not accept an entire reversal of my beliefs. Somewhere between his truth and mine must lie a connection I was too simple to recognize. But I could not deny him. Sainted ancestors, if all this were true, my mind could not encompass the possibilities of his talent.

I raised my head and sucked in the heaviness that weighed upon my spirit far more than the stone I had rolled off my knees. "If you agree to the terms of our partnership, I'll show you what we face and what I propose for you to do about it."

OF COURSE, DANTE ACCEPTED MY terms: absolute secrecy, loyalty to Sabria's interests, and acknowledgment of my direction. These were not difficult oaths for him, I thought, a man who had secrets of his own. He clearly cared naught for the gold or political gain that could come from betrayal. More significant to my mind, this unpleasant and forbidding man had opened a small window into himself and shown me the one thing in the world he cared about—magic. What greater offering of trust exists than that? I liked him.

As night fell on Lady Susanna's wild garden, I led Master Dante down the courtyard stair to the Conte Olivier's iron-bound cell. "Fifteen days ago, I was brought down here, sworn to the same oath I asked of you, and told a strange story. One afternoon nigh on a year ago, the King of Sabria rode out to exercise with his household guard—the Guard Royale—as he does every tennight. He jousted, sparred with his favored partners, shot close targets with a pistol, and practiced with his longbow. His captain of the guard, a man who had stood at his back since he was crowned, challenged him to a wrestling match—a sport he much enjoyed in his youth. Though the king was soundly thumped, both he and the captain were laughing at the end of it."

I unlocked the door with the key my royal cousin had entrusted to me. The arrow, the spyglass, and the coin lay on the stone table, exactly as the king and I had left them.

"As His Majesty rode from the field, this arrow struck his saddle, scarce missing the great vein in his thigh, to the peril of his life"—I locked the door behind us and hung the lamp from a wire loop above the table—"for, naturally, he had not donned his armor after the wrestling. The horse fell, but the king managed to leap free, unharmed.

"His guardsmen scoured the field, in a fury that so bold an attempt was made in their very midst. Two of them noted a man wearing their own livery drop his bow behind a tree. They attempted to question him, but discovered the man incapable of speech. Before they could alert their comrades, he hamstrung one of his captors and strangled the other. As he ran away, he dropped this spyglass. When he retrieved it, the hamstrung guardsman threw his ax, and fortunately or unfortunately as you may see it, felled the assailant before he himself died. The villain would have gone free if he'd kept running."

Dante's brow creased. He leaned his walking stick in the corner and squatted low to get a closer look. He did not touch the artifacts. "Go on."

"The guard captain stripped the corpus in search of his identity, and instantly forbade any other to come near. The man's arms and legs were scored and scabbed, bruising, scars, and cupping marks every centimetre. . . ."

"Transference," said Dante softly, his two fingers tracing the line of the half-split arrow shaft without actually touching it. "The archer was a source—a mule. And the sorcerer who leeched the archer's blood to grow his own power persuaded . . . induced . . . forced him to wield the nasty bit of weaponry. Did the arrow deliver poison?"

"The king assumes so, as the horse convulsed and died. Philippe immediately commanded his most loyal friend, Michel de Vernase, Conte Ruggiere, to investigate the assault. The conte ordered the horse and saddle burned in place as a precaution against a contaminating poison or a lingering spell-trap. With a mage implicated, Vernase-Ruggiere chose not to call in a practitioner to examine the arrow."

"But you've looked at it."

"I detect no extant enchantment, only a strong magical residue. But I've no skill to analyze it."

He took no note of my admission. "I'd guess the aristo lackwit had the assassin-mule's corpse burnt, as well."

"They could not allow word to get out." A hint that an unknown mage was practicing blood transference would send blood families running to their fortresses, unraveling two centuries of concord between factions. "The conte immediately arrested the guard captain, for on any other exercise day, the king would not have shed his armor before leaving the practice field. And there the problem becomes infinitely more complex."

The mage glanced up at me, sharp-eyed. "Could it be the *queen* set the captain to propose the grapple?"

No longer amazed at his quickness, I nodded. "There is a history of strain between our liege and his wife—their marriage when she was widowed so young, her failure to birth a living heir since their first boy died, disagreements over the role of sorcery in their aligned households, and more, I think, that he did not tell me. His own counselors have long pressured him to set her aside. Yet he holds determined faith in her innocence and would not . . . and will not . . . have her questioned."

"So what is the coin?"

"Likely nothing," I said, "though you'll see it is a double strike. Some people consider a two-faced coin lucky. The conte found it in the mule's jerkin, the sole item he carried. I sensed no enchantment on it, yet—" I could not explain the sensation that had come over me when I'd first held the coin. It was as if I'd been thrown into a plummeting waterfall and emerged to the nauseating certainty that my body had been turned wrong side out or hung up by my feet, and all the blood rushed to my head. "There is a strangeness about it."

"The noble investigator has no theories?"

And so to the next element of the mystery. "A month after the attempt, Michel de Vernase wrote a letter to the king stating he'd found new evidence and hoped to have a solid case before too many more days passed. He said he planned 'a second visit to Collegia Seravain.' No one has seen or heard from him since."

"Mayhap he found the villain he was hunting." Dante's attention shifted to the spyglass. "And this?"

I swallowed hard and glared at the instrument, its tarnished surface gleaming dully in the light. It seemed wrong that such a fine invention, a marvel not so many years ago, could so strike my heart with dread.

"Naught is known of its origin or purpose. But when you sight through it, you'll understand why our dilemma is so much more than marital disaffection, more even than the revival of such evil practice as blood transference. And you'll see why we need a talented mage to help unravel this mystery." The memory of my own looking made me wish to creep into a cave and hide.

Dante drew his fingers along the artifact's tarnished case and around each of its knurled grips. He brushed dust and damp from the lenses, and while bracing it awkwardly with his scarred right fingers, he examined its construction, expanding and collapsing its length and twisting the grips.

"This was not expertly made," he said. "Its mechanisms are unbalanced, its material impure." He glanced up. "This takes no magic to learn, if you're wondering, but only the teaching of a skilled instrument maker. But the making shapes its keirna, and it's nae possible to comprehend keirna without understanding function and composition."

Stepping back from the light, he balanced the brass instrument in the claw of his ruined hand and peered through the eyepiece. The color drained from his cheeks as it surely had from mine. He set the instrument gingerly upon the stone table and snatched his hands away, breath rapid, lips compressed, his eyes squeezed tight as if a dagger had pierced his skull.

Dante did not tell me what he'd seen. But as we locked the cell door, I guessed that he, too, had glimpsed a scene beyond this life—a scene not even the most sophisticated enchantments should be able to show us.

"The Veil teachings have never made sense to me," he said. "Why would a god who bothers to create living persons suddenly decide to ship them off someplace worse than this life when they're dead, all in hopes of some heaven that no one can describe? If I have to depend on my kin or some benevolent stranger to get me through ten gates to a paradise that might or might not be better than this, I might as well give up right now. Dead is dead, or so I've claimed. . . ."

I disliked such bluntness. In my youth I had accepted what I'd been taught at the temple: that the Blood Wars had brought humankind to such a state of depravity that the Pantokrator had altered his creation, setting the bleak and treacherous Ixtador between the Veil and Heaven. Those souls who journeyed the trackless desolation and passed Ixtador's Ten Gates would be well purified, worthy of the Pantokrator's glory. Those who failed would be left for the Souleater to devour on the last day of the world.

Unfortunately the dead could do little to further their own cause. The honor and virtuous deeds of the family left behind must provide the strength and endurance for a soul's journey. As I came to see that my weak family connections were unlikely to provide much support for Ixtador's trials, and that my prospects for improving the situation were exceedingly poor, I had shoved such concerns to the back of my mind, unwilling to relinquish either hope or belief. The spyglass insisted I confront the issue.

The mage rubbed the back of his neck tiredly and tugged at his silver collar again. "But then we must ask what is this devilish glass? Gods, if you think I can answer that for you, you've less wit than that rock in the garden. It would take a deal of study. Experimentation. So that's the job, is it? To find out the use of these things. Or, I suppose, it's truly to tell your employer, who is the *king*, I'm guessing, and not his treacherous wife"—he paused and waited; I nodded and shoved open the outer cell block door— "what sorcerer in this blighted kingdom could create such enchantments and why an assassin—a voiceless mule— would carry them." He ground the heel of his staff into the stone. "Did anyone see the mule *use* the glass?"

"Not that we know."

"His Dimwit Majesty ought to question his queen. I could do *that* for him."

I had no doubt he could. His rumbling undertone shook me like the earth tremors I'd felt when I was a boy, on the day a godshaking had razed the city of Catram eight hundred kilometres away.

"Yes, the king wants to know who's responsible for

transference and attempted murder," I said. "He wants his queen exonerated. He wants to know how this instrument can show him a sixteen-year-old battlefield disgorging its dead men, many of whom he knows, into a wilderness that perfectly fits every description of Ixtador Beyond the Veil. And he very much desires to know what's become of Michel de Vernase. Though he's received no demand for ransom or favor in exchange for Michel's life, he refuses to accept that his friend is dead."

We started up the dungeon stair.

"Beyond all that lies his duty to Sabria. The king believes magic is dying, and he bids it good riddance. He sees it as a chain that binds us to superstition and causes us to descend into myth-fed savagery such as the Blood Wars. This event tells him that someone is attempting exactly that, seeking power of such magnitude as to touch the demesne of the dead. But for what purpose? As Sabria's protector, he must understand what's being done and by whom and why. He doesn't trust the Camarilla . . . the prefects . . . any mage . . . knowing how they resent him."

"But for some reason he trusts you, who lives and works among them. You're his spy."

"I prefer the title *agente confide*." It bore a certain gentility; less resonances of ugly execution. "As it happens, I am His Majesty's distant kinsman—fortunately for you, *very* distant, so I'll not take exception to your loose-tongued name calling. Though we'd never met until a half month ago, my cousin subscribes to the old virtues in the matter of family, thus has charged me to protect his life and search out the answers he needs. He believed I was—"

Again came the uncomfortable confession. Nine years previous, Master Kajetan had first forced me to admit failure aloud. As my mentor, he had insisted I speak the verdict to my parents, else I would be tempted to live forever with a delusion. My father, who had ever lived in his own delusions, had taken umbrage. I still wore the scars—within and without. The ugly episode had left me shy of discussing my paucity of talent.

Dante waited. I inhaled deeply. "As you judge correctly, Master, I cannot even begin to unravel such magic. Though

I have informed the king of my lacks, he insists he trusts me to solve his mystery. As for the spying—well, for that we must include the chevalier in our conversation. Are you willing to go on, Master Dante? It is time for yea or nay, in or out."

The lamplight scarce touched the bottomless well of the descending stair, and the sinewy, black-haired mage with the unsettling gaze might have been Dimios himself, returning to the world of light for his annual visit, the blighted hand the manifest evidence of his corruption. He halted just below me.

"I doubted you could present me a mystery that I would take on—a librarian with self-loathing so exposed as to make him bold. But I don't like events that contradict my view of the world. So, go on, tell me the rest."

I took that as a *yea*.

CHAPTER THREE

36 Trine
61 DAYS UNTIL THE ANNIVERSARY

Ilario's lanky frame sprawled like a creeping vine over an armchair at Lady Susanna's card table. He was spinning his crocodile charm above his head like a pinwheel, occasionally rattling a crystal-globed lamp or clinking his wineglass. The lady herself, a serene, intelligent beauty with the most luxuriant black hair I had ever seen, laid down her fan of cards when I tapped on the open door. She was a gracious hostess indeed to tolerate Ilario for more than a tennight without the least ripple of aggravation.

"Pardon, my lady," I said, bowing. "I'm sorry to steal your company. Chevalier, you wished to speak to our visitor. . . ."

"No matter," said Susanna, shifting a richly colored shawl to her shoulders as she rose. Her smile illumined her large eyes and the deep cinnamon glow of her complexion. "I am a hopeless night bird. My husband is long to bed, and I have teased poor Ilario into one game too many in search of evening's amusement. Though he carries the most perfect tenor, he will sing only when we play at cards. Alas, he seems to have run out of cheerful ditties."

Indolence abandoned, Ilario contracted his spread

limbs and slithered to the edge of his chair, peering curiously through the empty doorway behind me. "Your exceptional loveliness demands excellence, dear lady, a responsibility that weighs heavy on my bardic soul. My supply of drivel is endless; my supply of poetry not so, especially when awaiting a visit from a fiend. My companion Portier, as you see, is of a depressive cast of mind, but this fellow who's come to visit us makes Portier appear but a frippery. Where is the devilish visitor, good curator?"

"He awaits us in the wild garden," I said.

"You must persuade him to come inside," said the lady. "The night closes very dark. If he prefers more privacy, Hanea will open the guesthouse."

Ilario got out an answer more quickly than I. "Lovely Susanna, I fear indelible bruises on your innocent soul must result were his company forced upon you."

Lady Susanna laughed, a throaty ripple that issued from a deep center, and then kissed the fop on his flaxen head. "Sweet Ilario, innocent? Me? You must quit all indulgence in wine. I'll leave you to your fiendish visitor, but rest assured, naught can bruise my soul. I am well hardened."

She had scarce vanished, when she poked her head back around the doorjamb, her eyes glimmering with pleasure. "One matter of interest, Sonjeur de Duplais. Our son, Edmond, returns home tomorrow on leave from his posting in the south. You needn't fear; he is reliable and discreet. Yet I would not have him . . . compromised . . . by awkward situations. You understand."

She didn't wait for confirmation, but glided out of sight in a whisper of silk. Ilario gazed after her, as if admiring the afterglow such a luminary must leave behind. "Is any woman so much a vision of Heaven's angels? How fortune leads us. . . ." Then he lifted his head abruptly. "I could have had her, you know. She wasn't highborn. Even an offside pedigree such as mine would have raised her up. Yes, she's a few years older, but egad . . . this fossil she's got instead! Eugenie says Conte Olivier was His Majesty's first commander. Taught him everything about leading troops and bedding down in muck and staying on his feet in a battle. He was Soren's first commander, too, but I doubt he taught the shitheel much. Soren believed he knew everything already."

Eugenie de Sylvae—Ilario's half sister—had been but a child when wed to King Soren, Philippe's predecessor and an even more distant cousin of mine. When Soren fell in a miscalculated raid on the witchlords of Kadr, he had not yet bedded the girl, much less begat an heir. Through a happenstance of Sabrian custom, my fifteenth cousin, a wild young duc entirely unprepared for the throne, had inherited the demesne of Sabria. To preclude any dispute of his position, Philippe had immediately wed Soren's child widow, inheriting her virginity, the support of her powerful relatives, and her bastard half brother, Ilario. My overly sentimental mother had insisted that political necessity had grown into a true love match between Philippe and Eugenie—despite the burden of the ridiculous half brother. But who could say what love meant, especially in such rarified circles? I doubted my mother knew.

"Thanks be, young Edmond got his mother's wit as well as her looks," mused Ilario. "Old Olivier has the cleverness of a turnip in anything but war making and wife picking."

Feeling the press of time, I dropped my voice. "I've judged that Mage Dante's talents will . . . suffice. And he agrees that the level of magic the glass signifies is extraordinary."

Ilario bobbed his fair head and clapped his hands. "Excellent, Portier. I knew he would work out." As if he'd thought of it. "Go to it."

"If we are to be partner *agentes*, the three of us must agree on our next steps."

He flared his straight nose and stretched his long saffron-colored legs in front of him. "Heaven's messengers, I near piss myself when he glares at me, and these are my favorite hose."

My royal cousin had insisted that Ilario was trustworthy and that his close bond with his half sister could help us discover the truth. I could accept that, but playing nursemaid to the fop would test a saint's patience. "You must attend, Chevalier. It is your duty as a Knight of Sabria, your sister's champion, one might say."

"Oh. Quite right." He jumped to his feet and inhaled until his bony ribs threatened to pop the buttons on his gold waistcoat. "You understand, Portier, Eugenie could not have done this thing—conspired. It is not in her nature."

I had never seen him so somber when he wasn't frighted out of his wits or reeling drunk. Thus I found myself believing him—which was entirely foolish so early on. I had vowed to withhold judgment in *all* these matters until evidence led me to the truth.

"I understand, Chevalier. We do this for her safety as well as His Majesty's . . . and Sabria's." I didn't think a reminder of our larger purposes would go amiss. Uncounted thousands of Sabria's people had died in the Blood Wars, the flower of her nobility, the most powerful of her magical families. A second orgy of death and ruin would destroy us all.

THE EVENING HAD COOLED. SCENTS of thyme, lavender, and waking earth rose in the spring damp, and the soft rasping twitter of tree crickets engulfed the trees. Ilario steeled his courage by clutching his spalls—the shards of onyx and jade he carried to remind him of the ancestors he held sacred: surely including the father he shared with Queen Eugenie, and her mother, who had so generously taken her husband's bastard infant into her home and raised him as her own.

We found the stone bench empty when we reached the glade. I whirled in a full circle, relieved when the lamplight caught a band of silver near the font. "Master! I feared you'd left us."

The dark figure hunched on the ground raised his eyes. Ilario promptly dropped his pouch, scattering his spalls across the rocks.

Dante's lip curled. "I was relishing the *quiet*."

His collection retrieved, the lord sank to the end of the stone bench farthest from the mage. I took the other end of the bench, which set me between them, a position I feared might become familiar. As I set down the lamp and pulled out my journal, I searched for the right words to launch our odd collaboration.

"So we are to be spies," I said. "No matter how distasteful the word, I suppose we must accustom ourselves to it. Michel de Vernase made a public show of his investigation. The king refuses to believe his disappearance coincidence, which is why *we* must work in secret."

"In secret?" said Dante, scornfully. "With one of us the guilty queen's pet?"

"A fair question," I said, laying a hand on Ilario's arm to prevent him drawing his sword. "We are investigating treason, with all its heavy consequences. But His Majesty believes entirely in Lord Ilario's sincere determination to keep our secrets unshared. I choose to accept the king's word."

Though the pooled lamplight showed Dante's face impassive, his restless energies roiled the deepening night. I hastened onward, opening my journal to the notes I had made thus far, my eyes automatically deciphering my encoded script.

"So to our case and our plan. As far as the king knows, Michel learned very little. The assault on King Philippe occurred at Castelle Escalon. The assailant, who was never identified, wore royal livery. The evidence of his scars and bruises named him a mule used to feed a mage's power. Thus, we know he was of the blood. He wore no mage collar, and unfortunately, de Vernase reported his handmark obscured by scars. So we are hunting a mage with talent and knowledge enough to work transference and the . . . complex . . . spyglass spells."

Dante stirred from his contemplative posture. "Hired by the shadow queen?"

"The queen's suggestion to the guard captain that he persuade the king to wrestle and thus divest himself of armor might only be a wife's concern for her husband's amusement. We shall not be privy to the personal disagreements between their majesties that feed the king's disturbance. However, the queen does support two household mages, and it only makes sense to investigate them first." I deferred to Ilario, tapping his knee when he failed to take my cue. "Chevalier?"

"Orviene is pleasant enough," he said, avoiding the mage's heated gaze, "though a bit oily to my taste, always smarming after ladies above his station. But Gaetana is frightful. Women so large are surely an aberration of Father Creator, and she glares at me quite as much as you do."

"Orviene has an indifferent reputation at Seravain," I said, trying to add more pertinent information, "competent, reasonable, pleasant enough. He has never achieved a master's rank. Gaetana has. She is reputed to be quite brilliant, but left teaching years ago, as she is more interested in research than students. Neither ever instructed me. They've resided in the queen's household since the mortal illness of the infant Prince Desmond seven years ago. Gaetana returns frequently to Seravain for study and research. She is polite but never familiar, and, alas, it has never been my habit to pry into what mages study in my library."

"These two have apprentices, I presume," said Dante.

"Several, who seem to change quite often . . ."

"Only Adept Fedrigo and Adept Jacard have been at court more than a year," said Ilario. "Fedrigo is quite gentleman-like and ever helpful. I don't know Jacard, as he is presently loaned out to some friend of my foster mother's. The rest scurry about like ants, fetching and sweeping, or they disappear into the mages' laboratorium for days at a time, only to reappear unkempt and entirely too exhausted to do a man a favor."

I dipped my head in acknowledgement and continued. "Neither the king nor Lord Ilario knows of any other mage with access to the queen's household, and both have expressed a feeling that Orviene and Gaetana have . . . insinuated . . . themselves between the queen and her family. Unfortunately, the lady made it known to her husband, and thus to Michel de Vernase, that no one in her household would be available for questioning. Without more specific evidence linking her to the assault, the king is unwilling to contradict her in the matter."

Dante shrugged and drew his walking stick across his lap. "Dancing about tender feelings will never get you answers. Did these mages inquire about the spyglass? Hunt for it?"

"Not that we know—which means very little. Evidently, Michel de Vernase never made any secret of his disdain for sorcery or his belief that a sorcerer planned the attack on the king. He tried to interrogate the Camarilla prefects without prior negotiation—a violation of the Concord de Praesta—and when refused, took his inquiries to Seravain. With such—"

"The conte quite insulted poor Fedrigo," blurted Ilario. "Called him a 'trickster taking advantage of his station' just because he makes these excellent charms for Eugenie's friends."

"With such a bullheaded approach," I concluded, "I doubt the conte could have learned the door warden's name at Seravain. No one directed him to my library, I can tell you."

"But if no one saw the mule use the spyglass, why was it there at all?" said Dante.

A good question that pricked not a hint of an answer in *my* mind. "The larger problem," I said, "is that even if the queen allows her mages to be questioned, they're not going to tell me—or any interrogator—the kind of information we seek. They'll deny knowing the assassin. They'll deny building instruments that show us the demesnes of the dead. They will most certainly deny any knowledge of transference or other prohibited practices. Thus we need someone to join their little consilium and learn what they're about. Only a person of their own rank might have a chance to observe their practices and judge if they are capable of the sorcery we've seen."

I paused, awaiting the explosion. It came quietly, but with intensity that near knocked me off the stone bench.

"You want *me* to pose as a court mage?" said Dante, blowing a derisive breath. "I thought you had a semblance of mind, Portier. My reputation is fairly earned. I've no manners. I know naught of bowing or titles or mouthing pleasantries to fools. You see my finest garments." He spread his arms, his grotesque hand purple in the lamp-light. "Hardly what's expected of a queen's puppet."

"A certain distance might work to your advantage, Master." I dropped my eyes that he might not think me staring at his ropelike scars. "And with your permission, of course, we can teach you whatever you need to know of court life, can we not, Chevalier?"

Ilario hunched his shoulders without even a sidewise glance at Dante. "I'll loan my tailor and my barber, but . . . some tasks are impossible."

Dante hoisted himself up with his stick and strode back toward the path and the house. Before I could decide whether to chase him down, he halted, spun in place, and jabbed a finger toward Ilario. "Dress me like this strutting cock, and I still could not get near them. Do I walk up to the gate and apply for the position of queen's assassin?"

"I made you an offer three days ago," said Ilario, dabbing at his nose with a lace kerchief. "You scoffed."

"And in which layer of lies was this offer couched?"

"Please, Master. Please, Chevalier!" How was I to harness these two most irritating men, both of whom out-ranked me? "We are charged with our kingdom's safety. Philippe has reason to believe another attempt at murder will be made on the twenty-fifth day of Cinq—the anniversary of last year's attempt, which happens also to be the seventh anniversary of his infant son's death—which happens to be one-and-sixty days from this. Each of you has a unique gift to bring to the task."

"Give me the daemonish glass, and I'll divine its use," said Dante, "perhaps even something of its maker. Give me the coin and the arrow. Such mysteries intrigue me. But do not expect me to pretend I care for an aristo's domestic troubles. I'm as like to spit on him and be done with the matter. And it's sure I'll end up prisoned myself anyway, when the Camarilla gets wind of my heretical opinions. Find another plan."

I reached for patience. "Lord Ilario . . . graces . . . society throughout Castelle Escalon and the royal city. As he mentioned at our first meeting, his half sister has set herself the charge to support magical scholarship in rivalry to the king's support of the new sciences. It would be only natural for the chevalier to bring her a new talent he has encountered. He can secure you a position—"

"Pursuing magics that 'many people might consider unsavory'? Those were your words, were they not, Chevalier?" snapped the mage. "So tell me, what are these unsavory wishes your mistress might ask me to indulge? Transference, perhaps? Enough to set me up as scapegoat for this crime?"

"Certainly not," I said. "Lord, you must explain."

No matter his pique, no matter his care for the queen's reputation, Ilario could not hide this last piece of our puzzle. Neither could he pass it off with his usual foolery. "My lady has suffered an overburden of griefs in her life: our beloved parents lost to fire not a year after her too-early marriage; an adored husband, the late king, fallen in battle; her own child dead before his first birthday, a daughter stillborn, and two more miscarried. She seeks . . . solace."

"Surely these two jackleg mages can concoct a sleeping draught. Or is it illusions she wants?"

Dante's brutal frankness drove Ilario to his feet and into the night beyond the pool of lamplight. "Portier, this is most unseemly. I'll not discuss a gracious lady with a damnable rogue."

"Mage Dante is our partner in this endeavor, lord chevalier, and has sworn to keep private all he hears. If you don't tell him all, then I must, else we'll never lift this cloud of suspicion from your royal sister. Better this come from one who can tell us her true mind . . . gently."

Evidently, Michel de Vernase had disdained Ilario, never bothering to interview him. And until Philippe himself had spoken to the chevalier, he did not comprehend the nature and intensity of his wife's unhealthy yearnings.

"They've tried illusions with varying success," said Ilario, his breath shaking. "But more than anything in the world, my sister desires her mother's comforting hands and our father's shoulder on which to weep. She yearns to hear that her dead children are not frightened as they assay the trials of Ixtador."

The mage stiffened. "Necromancy?" he said in hushed

fury. "She's mad. You're all mad. Even if it's possible—
and naught's certain of that—lest you've forgotten, muck-
ing with the dead is frowned upon. If the Temple were to
get wind of this ... gods ... the tetrarchs might slap a
queen's wrists, but they'll hang the sorry practitioner in
the temple square by his thumbs as fodder for rats and
ravens."

"We're aware of that," I said, intestines clenching at
thoughts of both the crime and the punishment.

The Camarilla discouraged deadraising; many said because they no longer knew how to do it. But the Temple
claimed that to breach the Veil between life and death was
to violate creation itself. Ixtador was our penalty for the
depredations of the Blood Wars, including transference
and necromancy. Did we transgress again, the tetrarchs
and prophets implied we would be barred from Heaven
everlastingly. No matter how pallid one's private convictions, the sway of public sentiment kept deadraising a dangerous activity.

"I'd not want you to mistake the possible complications, Master. But we're not asking you to practice necromancy, only to hint that you could. That you might. To
daemonstrate skills that suggest you are capable. The
queen's mages claim they are unable to satisfy her wishes
for these very reasons you name. But we must wonder if a
spyglass that seems to focus in Ixtador, and a mule whose
very existence speaks of unholy practice, indicate that
they are, in fact, attempting such wickedness. This is the
way for you to get close to the queen and her mages and
find out what we need to know."

Eyes closed, Dante crossed his arms over his bent head
as if to smother the curiosity that—I hoped—would drive
him to find answers. Ilario kept mercifully quiet. An owl
flapped away from a nearby oak, the rushing spread of
wings near stopping my heart.

At last the mage clasped his walking stick and tapped
its heel on the packed dirt. "So, peacock," he said, "have
you ever seen your little sister playing with this naughty
glass?"

"This is insupportable." Ilario waved his arms weakly, his protest lackluster beside Dante's resonant conviction. I kept silent, giving him no permission to back away.

The chevalier heaved a suffering sigh. "Her Majesty does not include me in her mages' rituals. It is a *great kindness*, for she knows they frighten me. I've never seen her or anyone else using that foul implement. I suppose I could ask her. . . ."

My chest constricted. "No, no, best avoid any appearance of interest in such activities. Forget about the spyglass altogether when in her presence. Your caution is the best help you can give . . . along with your gift of a new mage, who will help dismiss these foul suspicions. Agreed?"

I waited until Ilario flicked his hand to acknowledge my warning before turning to our new partner. "Master, unless you suggest something better, I propose that Lord Ilario present you to the queen seven days hence. You will say what is necessary to secure employment in her household. Once you are assigned chambers in the palace, I will arrange for the spyglass, the arrow, and the coin to be delivered to you there." I tapped a forefinger on my journal. "Time is critical. Tomorrow is the first day of Qat. We've sixty-one days."

"What of you, student?" said Dante. "If a brutish sorcerer is to be made into a courtier, and a peacock into an informant, where is *your* place in Castelle Escalon? No one will say anything useful in the hearing of a king's kinsman."

I smoothed the pages of my journal and closed it, happy no one had ever deciphered its encoding. My future likely held a potful of frustrations to express outside the public eye. "Once Lord Ilario has secured your position at court, I shall follow you to Castelle Escalon, where I intend to have a flaming public row with my royal cousin and take on a dismal, unhappy palace job of my own just to flout him. Everyone will pity me and believe I am dreadfully abused, and, I hope, divulge all manner of useful things."

"What job?" For the first, and likely last, time, Ilario and Dante spoke in unison.

"Lord Ilario's private secretary. It was the worst thing I could think of."

For the first, and likely last, time, the three of us together burst out laughing.

ON THE NEXT MORNING, I stood in the cool, sheltered carriageway with Lady Susanna and her son, Edmond, who had arrived sometime in the night. The tall, sleepy-headed young officer indeed reflected his handsome and intelligent mother.

After worrying at the problem for a fruitless hour, I had solicited my hostess's assistance in preparing Dante for his introduction at court. "He and Ilario get along like a wildcat and a magpie," I said. "The chevalier insists *I* see to it, but I've business that can't wait."

"I'll gladly do what I can," said the lady.

"Let me take it on," said Edmond. "I've been tasked with the very same duty for young officers promoted in the field. And, begging your pardon, my most refined and gracious mother"—he beamed at Lady Susanna—"some men don't appreciate a lady's introducing them to forks and serviettes and chamberpots. As it happens I've supply dispatches need delivering in Merona. The mage and I could stay on in our town house. I'll not embarrass the fellow . . . nor you nor Papa, either."

Shadows dimmed Lady Susanna's smile, and her dark eyes darted from her son to me. "I don't think . . . Perhaps this is too private a matter. You've duties here, Edmond."

But to me it sounded ideal. Edmond de Roble exuded his mother's serenity in a stalwart, soldierly package. "If you're willing, Greville, it could save several lives at once. I'll introduce—"

A bellow exploded from the inner courtyard. The three of us raced through the vine-covered gate to find Ilario flattened to the brick wall like a lizard caught between the blooming bougainvillea and honeysuckle. The tip of Dante's white staff was pressed to the chevalier's throat, in vivid illustration of our dilemma.

"Touch this again, peacock," said Dante in the quiet

manner that shivered my toes, "and it will burn a hole straight through this dainty flesh." The mage tightened his grip on the carved stick, eliciting a squirm from Ilario. "Do you comprehend?"

Ilario emitted some unintelligible squeak. As the glowering mage jerked his stick away and stepped back, the bedraggled chevalier stumbled across mounds of alyssum and wallflowers, not stopping until he stood at my shoulder, glaring back at his attacker. "Madman," he croaked between coughing spasms. "I . . . was just . . . interesting carving . . . just looking . . ." He sucked greedily at an opaline flask he'd pulled from his cloak.

"You agreed I'd deal with you alone, Portier," snapped the mage. "Not with a sniveling, creeping aristo who thinks he has rights to anything he chooses."

"Divine grace, sonjeur." Edmond inhaled sharply as sun glints sparked from the silver band circling Dante's neck, but the young man did not hesitate to incline his back. "Excuse me . . . Mage. I am Edmond de Roble, Greville in the Guard Royale. I understand you're to be presented at Castelle Escalon. May I offer my services as escort to Merona and your host as you get your bearings in the city?"

In moments, all was calm and ordered at Villa Margeroux. If only Philippe had assigned this young man to our partnership instead of the dithering Ilario, I might have better hopes of success.

CHAPTER FOUR

10 QAT
51 DAYS UNTIL THE ANNIVERSARY

The shutters of the palace waiting room had not yet been opened to the mild spring air, and scented candle smoke, the cloying aroma of blooming orchids, and the stifling heat had my stomach in full rebellion. Or perhaps it was only anxiety. My court debut awaited me in the Royal Presence Chamber.

"Dame Renche, present yourself." An aide in red and gold livery awaited my companion in misery—a wilting dowager come to petition the king for her son's reassignment to a regiment quartered in Tallemant. The young man was currently billeted on the *Destinne*, the vessel chosen to sail beyond the Mouth of Hedron in search of the legendary Isles of Koshavir. The woman claimed she needed her son to manage her vineyard, but her effortless domination of her serving man and the succession of footmen, secretaries, and aides a petitioner encountered en route to this room led me to conclude she did not want for managerial skills. As she repeatedly referred to voyages of exploration as "frivolous and ungodly," and the *Destinne*, in particular, as an ill-omened ship, I assumed she just didn't want to risk her boy.

The lady swept from the room. I waited and churned.

From my persistent difficulties in obtaining this audience, I assumed Ilario had outlined my scheme to His Majesty. And from the lack of any alternative information since their arrival in Merona, I presumed that young Edmond de Roble-Margeroux had survived his sevenday with Dante, and that Ilario had successfully introduced Dante to his royal sister. Barring disaster, I had forbidden them from communicating with me.

Another rivulet of sweat dampened my threadbare velvet doublet.

"Sonjeur de Duplais, present yourself."

I adjusted my attire and trailed after the stiff-backed aide through a series of more elaborate waiting rooms and across a puddled courtyard, steamy with the previous night's rain. Halfway down a majestic promenade, footmen swung open a pair of bronze doors to reveal an expansive chamber and an eye-filling swarm of ruffed collars, plumed hats, curled beards, jeweled necks, and billowing skirts. My escort motioned me inside.

Truly this meeting place of king and subject had been designed to impress. My royal cousin sat beneath a gold-mosaic dome, where chips of lapis, tourmaline, and malachite depicted a Sabrian monarch accepting the gifts of earth, sea, and sky from the enthroned Pantokrator. On the barreled ceiling vaults hovered painted angels so lifelike, one could believe the damp, flower-scented breeze that wafted through the chamber's open arches a product of their wings. Or perhaps the shifting air emanated from the exquisite planetary suspended in the vault behind the king—the gleaming brass model of Heaven's fiery orb, circled unendingly by its five children planets in the mathematical precision calculated by Philippe's astronomers.

A half circle of ten to fifteen courtiers stood in favored attendance on Philippe. Across the dais to his right, a separate group of eight or ten clustered about a velvet-cushioned chair—empty on this day.

"I had hoped to present my petition to both king and queen," I whispered to the stiff-backed aide at my side.

"The queen no longer attends His Majesty's public audiences," he said, his eyes fixed forward. "Be ready."

So rumor was correct in that respect, at least.

Ilario's height and flaxen hair left him easy to spot at the back of the queen's party. But it was two wearing silver collars who drew my interest. The statuesque master mage, Gaetana, held the position of favor at the immediate right of the queen's chair. The First Counselor's iron gray hair was twisted tight at the back of her head. Her pale gaze reflected chilly disinterest. The tidy, elegantly gray-haired mage standing in her formidable shadow would be Orviene. Dante was not present.

" . . . thus it is our best judgment that Augustin de Renche receive no exception to his sworn obedience." Whether by virtue of wizardry or architecture, my cousin's natural voice rang clear even at this remotest end of the chamber. "Indeed, sonjeura"—Philippe leaned down from his gilt chair and spoke with perfectly audible intimacy—"I surmise that your son's share of the *Destinne*'s discoveries shall enable you to hire three bailiffs and an entire crew of vineyard overseers next season. *Judis ainsi.*"

Philippe's formal assertion of conclusion brought a liveried aide to whisk the dowager Renche away.

"Portier de Savin-Duplais, present yourself." Was it only imagination that the herald's announcement of my name quieted the bustle of skirts and gossip? Certainly a fervid mumbling swelled as the aide escorted me up the long central aisle and pointed to a tiled circle at the foot of the dais. Head bowed, I sank to one knee and waited.

Curse the arrogant devil, where was Dante? It would be nice to know the mage was safely in play before enduring this unpleasantness.

"*Savin*-Duplais? Do we know you?"

A twitch of the aide's gloved hand brought me to my feet. Philippe's expression—clear eyes, the light brows that matched his neatly trimmed mustache and beard— held steady, cool, and disinterested.

All right then. The game was on. Time to destroy, at

least for the present, what hopes I held of sober reputation in the wider circles of the world.

"Heaven's grace be with you, Majesty. My late father, Onfroi de Savin-Duplais, scholar and gentleman, was fourteenth-degree Savin out of Renferre de Savin-Gorsiet. But alas, you and I have never met, gracious sire, a seeping wound which is the matter of my petition this day. The intermediaries who rightly defend your presence from the common hordes have taken it upon themselves to refuse your kinsman private audience."

The fair brows lifted. I plunged onward, trying to ignore the titters that broke here and there.

"Insulted and demeaned by these servants, your devoted cousin has been forced to resort to this public airing of his necessities . . ." I allowed the pause to extend just past comfort. "Unless your most gracious majesty would overrule them and consent to retire behind yon doors that I might speak in private."

"Our householders reflect our mind and our instructions, *cousin*. What could you have to say that would require abandoning these other honored petitioners?" The king's wave encompassed the crowd of gaping, sniggering courtiers. I doubted many were public petitioners. "Speak, kinsman. What necessity has brought you?"

"My desire to serve you, lord. For fifteen years, my family has petitioned a place in your household appropriate for one who bears the Savin name." I tossed a bundle of letters onto the mosaic dragon whose scarlet tail encircled my feet. "Refused. Every one. Nine years ago, my honored father passed beyond the Veil. I have strived to aid his journey through the Ten Gates by prayer, virtuous living, and honorable study and employment at Collegia Seravain. But temple readers assess his tessila"—to the inhaled breath of the onlookers and a modicum of guilt on my own part, I produced the palm-sized carving of red jasper sanctified by my father's spirit—"and tell me he does not progress. He waits for his only son to supply deeds of proper quality to advance him toward his heavenly life. It is my conviction that those deeds must fall under the aegis of family. And so, gracious sire, I have dedicated myself to seek worthy service at your side."

Philippe collapsed laughing into the depths of his great chair. "Collegia Seravain!" he bellowed in great humor. "By the Ten Gates, have we a kinsman mage?"

"Nay, Majesty." I rubbed my bare neck as if to show him. "An acolyte only, but I—"

"So you have mastered reading and writing arcana, but daemonstrate no skills of the blood—even by the assessment of those who *believe* in skills of the blood?"

The presence of the queen's mages only heightened the humiliation of the wretched confession. "True, sire, but—"

"Fortunately for you, Portier de Savin-Duplais, we take but small offense at this odor of failure attached to our family name. Clearly you have been cloistered with your supernatural fraternity too long and are sorely misinformed. We employ no mages in our household. No adepts. And indeed, not even acolytes. The Camarilla Magica exists by our royal sufferance, but without credence in our counsels. Thus you must seek employment elsewhere. We would advise you look to mathematics, physics, and astronomy"—he opened his hand in the direction of the gleaming planetary—"to find the true magic the Pantokrator has granted humankind. *Judis ainsi.*"

Cheeks ablaze, I sank to my knee and winced at the risks of violating protocol by opening my mouth again. But, truly, a night in the public stocks could heap no worse disgrace upon my name than what I had just done, and a little stalwart whining should entrench my character in the public perception. Thus, when the aide tapped my shoulder to vacate my position, I rose to a posture of offended dignity. "I *shall* find a way to serve in your house, Majesty. For my honored father's soul, I shall."

"Impertinent cousin!" Philippe roared, flicking a finger at the aide. "Ill manners reap one night's service at least—in our household jail. Alas for you, Lady Justice requires a balanced hand, even for those who bear the Savin name. *Judis ainsi!*"

The aide scooped up my hastily manufactured letters and stuffed them into my arms. The soldiers of the Guard

Royale gripped my shirt collar, propelled me down the long aisle, and shoved me through the door.

PHILIPPE'S PRIVATE JAIL HOUSED A prisoner in comfort when compared to a public dungeon or the Spindle, the bleak tower perched on a barren rock in the deepest channel of the river Ley. Plastered walls surrounded a real bed with sheets and blanket, approximately clean. A tin washing bowl and covered night jar sat in one corner. A small window at eye level, albeit barred, opened to a moldy brick courtyard cluttered with dustbins. Yet the sturdy lock on the thick door and the lack of any illumination source to supplant the failing sunlight could not but reinforce a vague nausea at my first experience of prisoning.

Sitting on the bed, propped against the outer wall, I consoled myself that it was one night only, and necessary to make my humiliation real. I flicked a finger at two spiders that crept down the peeling wall and kicked a large beetle out of the sheets.

Truly, the "row" had gone well. If I was to be the king's pawn, it was reassuring that he was an intelligent manipulator. Yet, even though I knew his opinions, Philippe's bald declaration of scorn for sorcery had shocked me. He had, in essence, called his wife's mages cheats as the two of them stood not fifteen metres from him. I wished I had dared look up to gauge their expressions. Surely *marital discord* must be too sweet a term to describe the friction between the two royal households. What an ugly mess.

A fractured laugh escaped my throat at my naive hopes that Philippe's summons would somehow lead to my imagined "destiny." I'd not even two months to unravel a mystery whose chief suspects I was forbidden to question. And what if we were wrong about Orviene and Gaetana and had to look in some entirely different direction?

The lock scraped and rattled, reminding my stomach that hunger might be causing my gut's upheaval. A full day had passed since I'd supped.

But the short, robust young woman who entered my cell bore a lamp, not dinner. The ring of keys dangling from her leather belt evidenced responsibilities, yet her jeweled earrings, smoothly coiled hair, and full-sleeved gown of indigo silk hardly bespoke a jailer.

"I'll knock when I'm ready to leave," she announced to the hesitant guard. "I doubt Sonjeur de Duplais poses any risk to health or virtue."

Of a sudden acutely aware of my unseemly posture, I kicked off the sheets and jumped to my feet. My spall pouch dropped to the floor. I bent to retrieve it, noting the regrettably threadbare state of my stockings. My cheeks flamed. Alas, the guards had taken my shoes and belt, and I had to settle for buttoning my gaping doublet with the spall pouch inside and running fingers through my straggling hair. *Dithering fool.* But then, far more time had passed since a woman had graced my bedchamber than since I had dined.

"Divine grace, damoselle," I said, bowing, left hand properly exposed on my shoulder.

"Maura ney Billard," she said, baring her own left hand.

Though many might judge the lady plain, the earthen hues of her hair, eyes, and round cheeks glowed warmly in the lamplight. Her voice, on the other hand, was decidedly cool and precise.

After a brisk survey of my chamber, eyeing the rumpled bed where the beetle and several of its friends had taken up residence again, she seated herself on the three-legged stool in the corner. Its proximity to the bare floor did no more to diminish her self-assurance than did her diminutive height or her brief nose. "I serve as administrator of the queen's household, including the *Consilium Reginae*—Her Majesty's advisors in matters of sorcery. Please sit down."

I perched on the edge of the bed, near swallowing my tongue. Were we found out? Ilario . . . Dante . . . Ixtador's Gates, what had they done?

The lady cocked her head and leaned forward, examining me as if she were a kennelmaster considering a new pup. "I witnessed your petition to the king, sonjeur. This afternoon, as someone recounted the tale to Her Majesty, Mage Gaetana mentioned that you had served as archivist and librarian at Collegia Seravain. Is that true?"

"Yes, my lady."

"Her Majesty has just taken on a new advisor," said the lady, setting her lamp on the floor, "a master mage unfamiliar with court life. The mage deems an assistant necessary, in particular an acolyte or adept who might acquire and maintain the books he needs for his duties. Never having retained his own assistant, he has no name in mind and has left the hiring to me. I am here to offer you the position."

Caught between relief and confusion, my mind snarled like a sprung clockwork. *Ilario*, not Dante, was supposed to put about that he was in desperate need of a personal secretary.

"But I—" What to say? This was all wrong. If I refused her offer . . . insulted this lady or somehow made myself undesirable . . . how could I then apply to work for Ilario?

"Your determination to serve the royal family would be well satisfied by this position, sonjeur. And your qualification of good family and sincere piety, as well as your experience, seems a fortuitous match. Naturally, we would require references, but I've no doubts they'll be satisfactory and see no reason to delay."

"References . . ." Blood pounded my temples. This was absurd. I couldn't work for Dante. I needed to go places he'd have no reason to go; inquire about things he had no reason to know. Dante had agreed with my plan.

Think, Portier. I breathed deeply twice, a remedy I'd often used to force time and thought to slow. Dante was not stupid. He must have some compelling reason to contravene our plan. And this whole matter . . . the woman's haste . . . seemed odd.

Billard. A major blood family. She would have numerous contacts at Seravain and elsewhere—adepts and acolytes who would relish court service. And her use of *ney* Billard, instead of *de* Billard, indicated that her mother's family outranked her father's, which often meant even *more* relatives eager for advancement. Why would she choose an unknown? She embodied a quiet authority, yet her plump fingers had twined themselves into a knot in her lap.

"I would need to write letters," I said, slowly—testing. "Explain my need for references. It could take a tennight or two, perhaps a month. But I could certainly consider your kind offer."

Disappointment melted her cool mask, and rue tweaked a friendly smile. "I abhor dissembling, Sonjeur de Duplais, and thus I must inform you that this offer promises no comfortable employment. I pounced upon your qualifications both because of your desire to be at court and also because the longer this new mage resides at Castelle Escalon, the more difficult it will be to fill the position. Master Dante is a most . . . *intense* . . . man."

"How so, lady? You intrigue me." I buried my mouth in my hands, lest the smile grown on my own face give me away. She had caught Dante perfectly.

She frowned and stared at the ceiling for a moment, as if determining how to couch her description. To her credit, when she spoke, she looked me square on. "His words, his opinions, and his scrutiny carry weight beyond the usual. I can't describe it better than that. His manners daemonstrate little grace. His frankness is more akin to flaying than speech, and he has no patience with frivolity or hesitation. Yet he comes highly qualified, recommended by persons Her Majesty trusts. Her Majesty was entirely satisfied after their private interview."

All right. Perhaps she didn't want to subject any personal friends to the strange mage's whims. That made sense. She was here because Dante had demanded an assistant in such terms that I was the glaringly obvious choice. He knew my plan and the reasoning behind it. I had to trust him.

I rose to my stockinged feet and bowed. "Damoselle ney Billard, your honesty becomes you and honors your mistress. I hear naught to make a determined spirit quake. Indeed, this prospect, while daunting, saves me the difficulties of exploring other opportunities in the royal household that would likely result in situations far less suited to my experience. In short, I am humbly grateful and accept the position."

She popped up from the stool, as if the weight of the sky

had lifted from her shoulders. "Consider me in your debt, Sonjeur de Duplais. If the situation becomes too burdensome, I insist you come to me and I shall seek remedy from Her Majesty. The mage has been brought in to do my lady service, and I've no doubt that any who aid him will also reap her deepest gratitude."

My skin crept at recalling the *service* Eugenie de Sylvae desired of Dante. Royal gratitude could certainly be useful, but the mage had better have a damned good reason for this.

DAMOSELLE MAURA WAS NOTHING IF not efficient. Morning brought a plate of cold lamb and olives with her compliments. Still groggy from a night of empty dreams, I'd scarce dug in when the lady herself arrived.

"Did you sleep well in this unfortunate place, sonjeur?" she asked, wrinkling her nose. The door remained open behind her, and the draft from the courtyard outside the barred window strengthened the miasma of mold and urine.

"As well as could be expected, damoselle," I said, scrambling off the bed while dabbing at my greasy mouth with the back of my hand. Few activities are less graceful than eating, especially when one lacks knife, spoon, or serviette. "I feel thoroughly chastised. My court protocol shall certainly *not* slip again."

She did not quite laugh, as if the bounds of her business kept such daemonstrations inside her. Yet the heightened glow of her richly colored skin and the evidence of a slight dimple in one cheek made the prospects of the day immensely brighter.

"The guard holds your release papers and personal belongings. As Master Dante insists you attend him right away, I've come to show you the way to his chambers myself."

"My deepest gratitude, damoselle. I cannot tell you—" But she was already out the door, leaving my tongue hanging out like a thirsty pup's.

I blotted my mouth again, wiped my hands quickly on

the bed sheets, and followed, reciting to myself the unfortunate realities of family connection that had kept my life celibate. The lady, daughter of a blood family, would know the rules. The door guard returned boots, belt, journal, compass, and the silver phial my mentor had given me with his best potion for my recurrent headaches. The courret remained tucked away in my spall pouch.

Once out of the cell, I felt as if I'd shed an excessively tight suit of clothes. But I could not forget I had a role to play, even if Dante had changed the playscript out from under me.

"Damoselle, if you please," I said, catching up to her. "Why would the mage need me so soon? I mean, I'm happy to go, but after a night confined, I feel unkempt. If this mage is very exacting . . . Are you certain he will accept me?"

"Her Majesty is providing the assistant her servant has requested. He'll not dare refuse." A pleasant animation softened the blunt assertion. A bold young woman indeed.

The open galleries and gardens of Castelle Escalon were built in the sprawling Fassid style. As Damoselle Maura briskly navigated the confusing route from my cell, housed in the cellar of an old barracks, I did my best to memorize landmarks. A long gray underground passage. A round crossing-room banded by lozenge-shaped window openings. A fragrance garden. An arcade where a Fassid love poem had been scribed in the tiled floor and its erotic images painted on panels in the vaulted ceiling.

"You're very kind to show me the way," I said. "It would be easy to get lost here."

"Her Majesty's household comprises the entire east wing," she said, pointing beyond three wide steps of whorled rose marble flanked by sculpted oak trees. "Her ladies, her brother Lord Ilario, and her counselors, including her mages, all live here."

At the top of the steps a broad gallery swept a long curve, its open arches overlooking the slate rooftops of Merona and the wide band of the river Ley, shimmering in the morning light. Just before the gallery ended in a wide, upward stair, a passage branched off to the right.

"These are Mage Gaetana's apartments," said the lady, pointing to the first doors along the soft-lit passage. "These Mage Orviene's, and these"—we arrived at the single door closest to the far end of the passage—"Mage Dante's."

The administrator's brisk knock elicited a curt, "Enter."

The lady gasped as we stepped through the door. Gray smoke wafted from the hearth, stinging our eyes and offending our nostrils with a sulfurous stench. Despite the discomfort, I had to smother amusement, even while breathing a prayer the mage would not get himself booted out of the palace too quickly. Luxurious draperies of heavy, blood-colored satin had been tied up in ugly knots, spilling sunlight from the broad windows across a scene of destruction. Armchairs, cushions, ebony tables, and delicate statuary had been piled haphazardly on damask couches shoved against the walls. At least three crumpled rugs had been thrown atop the pile.

A deep, narrow groove had been gouged into the rare mahogany floor, forming a circle some four metres in diameter. Clad in his old russet tunic, rather than one of the embroidered jackets Edmond de Roble had provided him before leaving Villa Margeroux, the mage knelt inside the circle, tracing the deep channel with the still smoking end of a charred stick.

"Master Dante, what have you—?" The woman visibly choked back a reprimand. "I've brought your new assistant, Portier de Savin-Duplais."

"Good. He can finish this while I get on with the underlayment." He glanced up and caught Damoselle Maura's displeasure. "What? Do these other mages not *work* at Her Majesty's business? Perhaps that's why they achieve no results. To prepare a new circumoccule for every trial is inefficient and error-prone. Accuracy. Precision. Repeatability. Without them, you've naught but accidents and happenstance."

He popped to his feet, thrust the smoldering stick into my hand, and crouched beside the hearth. The offending stench and smoke rose from a crucible set upon a tripod over an unnaturally intense fire. "I need worktables," he said as he dropped yellow clots from a paper packet into the crucible, causing rills of blue flame to flare across his stinking mixture. "Three of them, each exactly three metres long. One with a polished stone surface, the others planed oak. And cupboards with lockable doors. Two at the least. Four would be better."

"You didn't inform the steward of these needs, when we spoke to him yesterday?"

"How was I to expect that folk hiring a mage had no idea what a mage needs to do his work?" He poked at the belching contents of the crucible with a stirring rod, then glared at me over his shoulder. "Well, get on then, apprentice. The sooner you've done, the sooner we clear this damnable stink."

"Sonjeur de Duplais is King Philippe's cousin, Master Dante," stated the lady firmly, "engaged to acquire and catalog books. If you need manual labor, we can fetch a workman."

"He might be the Pantokrator's maiden aunt for all I care. He does what I tell him in the manner I prescribe or he's no good to me and might as well dive headfirst out the window right now. Is that understood?"

Arrogant. Unyielding. Ungraceful. Even the cool Damoselle ney Billard fumed.

"I serve at the queen's pleasure, Master," I said quickly. "To that end, I shall be honored to take on whatever tasks you assign and to learn whatever you might teach." Especially why a man who disdained common sorcerous practice needed a circumoccule, a ring used to enclose particles arranged for traditional spellworking. And to learn why he had dragged me into a position that would make our investigation impossible. And to learn why this chamber thrummed as if a hundred musicians played at once, all of them different tunes.

Raising my brows and venturing a grin to soothe the lady's concerns, I shrugged out of my wrinkled doublet and bent to the work, first reheating the smoldering end of the stick—once a chair rung, I guessed—then shoving it through the gouge. Soot and char brought a minimal useful balance of spark, air, and wood to spells that focused heavily on the elements of base metal and water. A standard practitioner would embed other preferred particles into a permanent ring—fragments of colored glass, perhaps, or a few well-chosen herbs, and always nuggets or links of silver—the most perfect substance, encompassing all five of the divine elements. But who knew what Dante's plan was? The sulfur bespoke unsavory complexities.

"Get it hotter and move faster," snapped Dante. "The wood must be well seared as I lay down the lead."

"Very well then," said the administrator, equanimity recovered, though the toe of her elegantly small foot tapped rapidly on the ruined floor. "Have Sonjeur de Duplais bring a list of your additional requirements to my office this afternoon. Shall I have these excess furnishings removed?"

"Aye," said Dante, carefully ladling the first dipper of molten lead into a charred segment of the groove. "And the window rags as well. They're useless and ugly. I'll keep yon bed and the eating table and such." He jerked his head toward an open doorway in the end wall. "And you can leash your simpering maidservants and prancing footmen. None sets foot in my chambers unless I give them leave. The assistant will clean what needs cleaning. Now out with you, and let us to our work."

"Certainly, Master. Divine grace, and to you also, Sonjeur de Duplais. As I mentioned earlier, I am at your service." The lady gazed at me intently, communicating a sincere concern and intent to help, which pleased me considerably. I acknowledged her kindness as well as I could from my ungraceful posture on the floor.

My task completed, I sat back on my heels. I expected Dante would stop once Maura had gone, but in fact his focus narrowed, his capable left hand dribbling an almost perfect thread of molten lead in the grooved circle. It was easy to overlook his doing almost everything one-handed. His ruined appendage had remained out of sight the entire time the lady was in the room. A touch of vanity, perhaps.

When he had closed the circle of lead, he returned his ladle to the empty crucible and used his staff to disperse the pile of white-hot coals across the floor of the hearth. If I hadn't been watching so carefully, I might have missed the moment when he pressed his narrow lips together as if muting a word they were intending to shape. The coals dulled instantly and fell to ash. For that one moment, I would have sworn I'd gone naked and feathers stroked my skin.

Dante rose, hurried to the windows, and threw open the casements, clinging to the iron frames as he heaved great breaths of the morning air. "Discord's realm . . . This place is going to drive me mad." Then he spun in place, his gaunt face hungry, his green eyes snapping and sparking like the fires of midsummer. "But it will be a fine madness, student. We've so much nastiness afoot in Castelle Escalon, it will take us a year to sort it out. They've found another corpse—another mule."

CHAPTER FIVE

It was an unfortunate fact that the actual blood of someone like me could so dramatically enhance another sorcerer's spellmaking, when it could not provide me enough power to work magic of my own. Transference, the direct infusion of magical blood into a sorcerer's veins, had been practiced since the awakening of magic. A few practitioners bled themselves, distilled the product, and reinfused their own strengthened ichor. But as this led determinedly to self-destruction, most incidents of transference involved an unwilling victim, leeched to provide magical sustenance for the unscrupulous. Some blood family's bastard, feeble-minded brother, or demented aunt might "wander off" or "take a sudden fever," perhaps to reappear bruised, pale, and scarred, perhaps never to be seen again.

Until the practice had exploded into a plague of abduction, torture, and murder in service of the grand power rivalries that came to be called the Blood Wars, no one had acknowledged its use among otherwise respectable members of the Camarilla Magica. And only then did ordinary Sabrians learn of mules—victims repeatedly bled until their veins collapsed and their minds disintegrated. The Temple tetrarchs declared that the mules' souls bled away as well, an irretrievable corruption.

The Concord de Praesta, the accord that ended the Blood Wars, required every mage to wear the permanent silver collar that supposedly kept his or her workings well scrutinized. And all children born to the blood were permanently marked on the back of the left hand and required to display that mark at every encounter, warning others that we might be purveyors of illicit magic. Abductions were punishable by death, and promiscuity among blood families by public penance and heavy fines, lest unrecorded bastards provide temptation for evildoers—or provide more evildoers. Despite all such precautions, it appeared that someone was bleeding poor sods into mindless idiots right under the nose of the Camarilla, the Temple, the king, and the educated citizenry of Merona. Two mules discovered within a tenmonth would strike fear in any heart. It could not be coincidence.

"A mule, are you sure?"

"Yestermorn the queen's chief panderer summoned me to his chambers." Dante perched on the broad window seat, the sunlight at his back. His white staff lay across his lap. "This Orviene, as sweet a talker as any marketplace barker, was wheedling at me to tell where I'd trained, and dancing about talk of necromancy. He even offered to lend books and materials, though revealing naught of his own skills or current work, to be sure. Yon crucible and such came from his stock, so I decided to make good use of them while I waited for you to arrive. Never thought to hear you'd got yourself thrown in jail. You were to be the *hidden* partner."

"Exactly so," I said. "So Orviene told you of the mule?"

"No. The woman Gaetana's chambers are right across the passage from Orviene's. While I was with Orviene, one of her adepts brought her a message that 'the verger would not release the dead mule.'"

"Are you sure you heard the report accurately from such a distance?" Across a passage?

"I've a spell . . . my staff . . . it's not important."

"Not *important*?" Sorcery could trick the senses; it could not alter their quality, any more than it could enable a man to eat poison without consequence.

"Gaetana was furious. Agitated. She felt"—he closed his eyes and waved his hands about his head as if grasping for the right word—"betrayed. This . . . this mule's death . . . this risk of their exposure . . . isn't supposed to be happening, which means we must take advantage before they seal whatever wall of secrets has been breached."

"Without thinking hard, I can devise fifty possibilities that would bring an agitating message to Gaetana. The last thing we need is to fly off on imaginings."

"I *must* see that corpse," he said. "You are the planner, the leader, so make it happen before they burn the creature."

Impossible that he could have surmised so much from a message muffled by two walls and a passageway. Yet his belief was as undeniable as a hurricane.

"All right. I'll do what I can. Find the deadhouse. Get you in there today." And then find a way to renege on my agreement with Damoselle Maura without jeopardizing my chances for Ilario's position. "Surely you could have come up with a simpler scheme to see the body than to engage me as your assistant. Something to do with Orviene's questions, the deadraising . . ."

"But they've no idea I know about the mule. Don't you see? If they suspect I can hear beyond walls, they'll never trust me near them."

Unreasonably reasonable. "All right. But I cannot work with you beyond this. I *must* have the freedom of opportunity Lord Ilario's employ can give me."

"Do what you must, but get me in to see this new corpse. What use is a plan if it hides the very truth we need to examine?"

That was inarguable.

I hadn't even poked my arms into my discarded doublet when the mage dragged a crate of jumbled metal strips, spools, and packets into the center of his circumoccule. "Hold on. We've work to do while you consider your course. Lay the strips of tin to either side of the lead. The bronze links should lie at the sixteen compass points. You *are* capable of determining true compass headings, are you not?"

My bewildered fumbling for my compass must have impressed him as a *no*, for he snatched up his staff, rubbed his thumb on some particular bit of carving, and used the soot stick to place sixteen marks on the scarred mahogany rim of his circle.

"Braid the linen, cotton, and silk thread together and lay it around the outer edge. Then fill in all the gaps and holes with wood shavings; there's a rasp in the box, and I don't care which wood you use. Spread a thin layer of sand over all. When you've done, I'll seal the ring with fire."

Exasperated, I shook my head. "Master, I'm not going to—"

"I might as well have use of you while you're in my service. Meanwhile I'll write the list of materials I need from that housekeeper or whatever she is. She pities you, so you should be able to get whatever I want. I doubt she'll be so generous when I'm on my own again." He vanished into the other room.

Mumbling unseemly responses at his vanished back, I snatched up the spall pouch I had laid aside with my doublet. I had no intention of continuing his humiliating little game of master and servant now Maura had gone. But as my thumb traced the outline of the red jasper tessila inside the heavy little bag, the glimmering of a plan took shape. A Damoselle Maura who pitied me could surely tell me where to find the palace deadhouse, and Dante's list would give me a perfect excuse to seek her out right away. Grumbling, I threw my doublet aside, knelt inside the circumoccule, and bent to the mage's work.

As I crawled about the sooty floor placing the metal and braided threads and converting the rest of a broken chair into splinters and shavings enough to fill the trough, I considered what else we needed to know about the dead mule. But the odd construction of Dante's circumoccule soon distracted me. Sand created a dispersed weight of base metal and wood. Braided threads effected proximity of silk's component water and linen's wood. But why cotton? The juxtaposition of particles fit no formula I knew. I argued with myself that Dante's chosen materials were not based on the balance of the five elements, but rather on this keirna he believed in, and then wondered for the fiftieth time if his magic relied upon particles at all. By the time I'd poured a thin layer of sand from the hearth box atop the filled ring, I was wholly filthy and wholly confused.

"I've finished, Master," I said, poking my head through the doorway in the end wall, "and I—"

Dante sat at a small writing desk next to an open window. The desktop was littered with paper, pens, and an ink bottle, and he'd wedged a small knife blade into the wood at one side, which puzzled me until the scattered shavings explained that this was how a man with one useful hand sharpened his quills. But the mage was not writing and did not acknowledge my presence. His elbow rested on the desk, and his forehead rested on his curled left fist as if he were in the deepest contemplation. His staff, wedged in the claw of his damaged hand, quivered almost imperceptibly.

"Master, are you ill?" I whispered, not truly believing it so. His posture was too deliberate, the vibrant energies of the small room as vivid as midsummer sunlight along Aubine's seacoast.

Indeed he did not move or answer, and I lowered myself to the tidy bed lined up against the adjoining wall. This was a much smaller chamber than the other, intended as a wardrobe or manservant's quarters, scarce room to walk between the bed, the desk, the night cupboard, and a small table. At the foot of the bed, atop an unopened traveling case, sat a worn leather satchel, stuffed to bursting with books and papers. Nowhere did I spy altar stone, tessila, spall pouch, or the smallest ikon of the Pantokrator. Not only was he heathen, but he didn't care who knew it, a more honest display than some of us dared.

The open satchel tempted me to discover what books he valued, but a distant bell striking the quarter hour stayed my hand. Just as well, for only moments later, Dante stirred and propped his staff against the wall. Grimacing, he massaged his temple, then ran his fingers down the scribbled papers on the desk as if to remind himself of what he'd written. "Are you finished yet, student?" he bellowed, without lifting his attention from the page. "Time passes."

"A while ago, Master," I said, childishly pleased that he near knocked over his chair as he jerked around to find me so near. "You're not ill." A statement, not a question.

"No." Curt and stone-faced, he gathered a stack of sheets and passed them over. "Here's what I need to begin work—both on the mystery and the deadraising—and enough things I *don't* need to confuse anyone who reads the list. The last page tallies books. Most I've only heard about; don't know if they really exist. Perhaps you'll know better ones."

Resigned that he would reveal nothing until he was ready, I glanced through the lists. "A boar's tooth, three pearls, camphor oil, black alder bark, an Arothian dagger, myrrh . . . all right. But nightshade? Smut rye? Shepherd's purse? You think they're going to supply a stranger with poisons, especially these last two that cause women to *miscarry*?"

He shrugged and grabbed his staff. "If it gives them pause, so be it. I did warn the queen that if I am to tease Death itself, I must work with things that Death enjoys. She agreed. When can I get the spyglass and the other things?"

"I'll send for them today. Three or four days and we should have them. These books"—I glanced over the odd amalgam of standard texts, guessed titles, and terse descriptions—"can you read any of the ancient languages?"

"I've a skill with languages. I'm likely better with Aljyssian than Orcasi."

Orcasi. Only people native to remote Coverge named our common tongue *Orcasi* instead of *Sabrian*. The ill-educated population of Sabria's northernmost demesne scarce admitted six hundred years of Sabrian hegemony and spoke an ugly, guttural dialect of their own. That a man grown up in harsh, mountainous Coverge could read was astonishment enough, no matter that he could work the sorcery of a master mage. It explained a great deal about Dante's rough manners.

"If you ever need to leave anything for me, stuff it in that satchel," he said. "It will always be out, but won't necessarily be in the same place. No one can take aught from it. . . ."

Naturally, my fingers were drawn to test his declaration.

"Ouch!" Invisible steel teeth near ripped my fingernails out by their roots. I fell back on the bed, clutching my hand and groaning.

"Not even you. The sensation gets worse, the longer one keeps contact with it. Eventually it would—well, you'll know to be quick and not stuff my satchel with rubbish."

Wriggling my stinging fingers and cursing the day I lured Dante from his forest hovel, I followed him into the great chamber, where he was circling the ring, inspecting my work.

"I've never seen a circumoccule quite like it," I said.

"Good. I intend it to keep them guessing." He leaned heavily on his staff.

"Them? The other mages?"

"Whoever it was sneaked in here in the late watches. I weened it might take a bit longer for them to grow so bold, but then I've no experience of palace custom in the matter of sneaking. I suppose the Camarilla's been dithered about me these three years past, yes?" Grimacing, he tugged at the band about his neck. "Every day of my life I suspect they put some devilish poison in this collar to drive me mad and bring me back to Seravain."

Understanding seeped through my thick skull. Naturally the two mages would be mad to know what Dante was up to. One of them—or some trusted adept or acolyte—would certainly try to examine his work. If they probed his circumoccule, they'd be flummoxed by its odd composition. "Yes. They're most certainly curious. They'll judge this worthless"

"And then, someday perhaps, I'll raise a dead man in the center of it." Eyes fixed on the center of the circle, he could not have seen me stop breathing.

"Your purpose is not to *practice* necromancy, Master."

He shrugged, refusing to meet my gaze. "Likely any true sorcery would confuse them."

"If all goes well, I'll fetch you to the deadhouse tonight after sunset. Then we'll decide how to dissolve this unfortunate connection so I can begin asking some questions."

He nodded and folded his arms. Silently, dark brow drawn up in a knot, he watched me dab at the sorry grime of my shirt collar and gather his lists.

"Divine grace, Master," I said when I felt ready.

He did not return the farewell, but as I laid a hand on the door latch, words spilled out of him as boiling water breaks over the rim of a pot. "Tell your king to be wary. Some violence is brewing, but I can't say what as yet."

"How—?" But he had already retreated into the little bedchamber and slammed the door behind him.

DAMOSELLE MAURA HELD COURT IN a writing room three corridors and two courtyards away from the mage's apartments. A footman waved me to a velvet-cushioned bench beside the passage wall, where I waited alongside several other supplicants and stewed over Dante's mysterious warning.

"Present, Adept Fedrigo de Leuve."

I glanced up at a dark-bearded, bull-necked giant wearing an adept's gray gown and a red sash. His nose looked to have been broken a number of times. So this was the perpetrator of Ilario's crocodile charm and other "excellent magics" for Queen Eugenie's household. Evidently his business was not as simple as the other supplicants'. Even the thick door could not mask the sound of agitated voices. He emerged, red-faced, after a lengthy consultation and stormed away.

"Present, Sonjeur de Duplais," said the footman, pointing at the door.

The administrator welcomed me warmly. "So soon? Is all well with you?"

"Perhaps better than with you," I said, inclining my head toward the door.

"We must all deal with thorns in our shoes," she said,

wrinkling her nose. "Some are more difficult to be rid of than others. Ah, you've brought your thorn's lists."

An hour we spent puzzling out Dante's requirements. The lady accepted the more sinister materials with better grace than I had, and did not balk at oddities such as a *barrel of battleground soil* or a *used rat trap*.

"Everyone in my family practices the art, sonjeur. I myself attended Collegia Seravain. But I found the constant study and repetition tedious, and when I heard that Her Majesty was searching for ladies of rank who were comfortable with magic, I leapt at the chance to move on." A rosy flush deepened the rich brown of her complexion.

Likely she had found little more success at Seravain than I. Though she had surely attended during my tenure as archivist, I'd neither met nor heard reports of her. Not so unusual. Seravain's tutorial schedules were tight and demanding, and some students found little use for the library.

"Unfortunate for the collegia, you didn't find your proper calling there," I said. "They need administrators so accommodating and efficient . . . and kind." I'd met few people so easy to talk to. Women over age seventeen generally left me in mumbling incoherence.

She radiated pleasure. "Here I serve only three mages, nine adepts, and seventy householders, not Seravain's three hundred fifty. And I much prefer a royal budget to an academic one. Which reminds me, we must see to your accommodations. . . ." She jumped up.

Ignoring two waiting supplicants, the lady herself escorted me first to the palace steward to obtain the keys to an apartment in the male householders' wing, and then to his accommodating third secretary to arrange for someone to fetch my belongings and for delivery of letters and parcels. With entrancing wit, the lady dispensed bits of history to accompany each landmark along our route. By the time we returned to her writing room, I was wholly and entirely smitten.

"From the traffic in this room, you must surely administer more than the queen's consilium," I said, struggling to revert to my more sinister business.

She settled back in the chair behind the writing desk. "I accommodate Her Majesty's family and a few other courtiers, as well—juggling apartments or personal servants, ordering books, hiring musicians for special occasions, making use of the contacts I've developed in my regular work. I know everyone in the palace and most tradesmen in Merona." She tilted her head and peered at me closely. "Tell me, sonjeur, is something troubling you?"

I steepled my fingers and pressed them to my mouth, attempting a show of contemplation before forging ahead. Perhaps not entirely a show. The subjects of death, faith, and Veil passages always left me discomforted. "No. No. I don't think . . . You've done more than I can thank you for already."

"There, you see, something preys on your mind. Come, tell me. Mage Dante is despicably rude, setting you to such low tasks. I could speak a word to Her Majesty . . . release you. . . ."

"Please no, damoselle. I am determined to stay on in the royal household. A few insults are bearable." First things first. "I'm wondering—perhaps you could make a recommendation. After my presentation to His Majesty yesterday, I'm sore in need of a temple reader. Surely my father's spirit flags after my injudicious references to his journey. And I must have his tessila resanctified after profaning it so selfishly. This fire in me has been so strong, I fear I failed in judgment."

She leaned across her writing table in great concern and laid a kind hand on mine. "Your devotion must surely speed your father on to Heaven. We have a temple minor here and so, three readers. But, of course, the only reader who can also sanctify tessilae is a deadhouse verger. . . ."

And being precise and efficient as she was, Damoselle Maura drew me a small map to find the deadhouse, set between the temple minor and the swan garden. And she dispatched a note to Verger Rinaldo de Soinfe, saying that Portier de Duplais would be visiting him in the late evening for a reading and sanctification.

I took Damoselle Maura's small, warm hand and bowed over it. "You have been most kind, lady."

"There are more than just you who seek meaningful service in the world, sonjeur. If I can aid your search, I'm glad of it."

Lies I had expected in the role of *agente confide*; crass manipulation of sincere good feeling, I had not. I left the administrator's office feeling soiled in more than my garments.

I NEEDED TO DO SOMETHING about my crumpled, sooty attire before visiting the verger, so I sped off to locate my new apartment. No sooner had I opened the door than a trim young fellow carrying a pillow and towel darted in, skidded to a stop, and gave a jerky bow.

"Divine grace, sonjeur." He dashed a lock of yellow hair from his eyes. "I'm Heurot, manservant for your honored self and four other gentlemen as lives on this passage. I'll empty slops, lug your wash water, and such. Leave your boots outside the door each night and I'll see to 'em before morning. And what clothes need cleaning, lay out atop yon chest in the morning. Ye'll take meals in the gentlemen's refectory at the end of the passage. Have ye nowt I should put away, sonjeur?" He peered around the bare little room as if clothing and boots might pop out of the woodwork.

"A small case should be arriving soon. More in a few days. But I don't need much looking after. I value my privacy."

No more than sixteen, he displayed a ready grin. "I'm pleased to leave ye to yerself. Four gentlemen's already a race to handle."

It was impossible not to return his breathless cheer. "Two small requests before you go. Are paper and ink available? And a clothes brush, if you would."

"Paper in the desk cupboard, sir; brush in the chest." He yanked at a sticky door latch on the cupboard mounted above the writing table. Behind the door were two shelves and a shallow drawer, containing a sheaf and an ink bottle. "If it's not enough, I can fetch more."

"These will do nicely."

He wielded the clothes brush with a deft hand and youthful vigor, ridding my doublet and breeches of prison dirt and Dante's soot and sawdust. "Thank you, Heurot. Divine grace go with you. Oh—"

My abortive call halted him in the doorway. "Sonjeur?"

"You wouldn't know . . . I've an appointment at the deadhouse this night, and I've heard a man was found dead within the palace precincts some few days ago. Are there funeral rites tonight? I'd not like to intrude."

"I've heard nowt of any such. There's only Contessa Bianci dead as I know of, Lady Antonia's waiting lady what popped off in her sleep this morning, and high time, too, the old pecking crow—angels forgive me for speaking ill of the dead. I doubt her rites'd be so soon. But a friend of mine, Grinnel, is a guardsman and's posted evening watch at the temple gate this tennight. He'll know."

"Fine. Good. Well done. I'll seek him out."

The youth vanished in a breath of soap and boot polish.

I made grateful use of the lukewarm water and towel that waited atop the washing table. Then I unstoppered the ink and set to work.

As the palace bells rang sixth hour of the evening watch, I threaded my way through the palace maze. Letters to my mother, her steward, and the family's man of business, giving notice of my changed residence, went into the steward's post bag, along with a brief commission to a tailor in the village of Margeroux. In only a few days I should receive a package containing a new skirted doublet suitable for court wear, along with a silver coin, a bloody arrow, and a most unusual spyglass. Satisfied, I headed off to question a temple guardsman, fetch the mage, and visit the dead.

CHAPTER SIX

11 QAT
50 DAYS UNTIL THE ANNIVERSARY

The deadhouse gates swung open at my touch. The garden beyond lay quiet in the night, its thick plantings like a second wall, a moat of scent and thorn completely enclosing the blocklike stone building. Lantana and prickly juniper clogged the air with sickly, pungent aromas, and ghastly white blooms masked the sharp spines of blackthorn trees. Sabrians did not encourage the dead to linger. We wanted them to find their way through Ixtador to Heaven, lest the Souleater devour them on the last day of the world.

The echo of the gate bell faded. But from the vast palace precincts behind me rose a mournful cry that chilled my soul, sounding far more like a despairing human than dog or feral cat. The business that awaited could not but make a man skittish and heartsick. The dead mule we'd come to see was a girl, so Heurot's guardsman friend had told me.

A balding, moon-faced man awaited me in the flickering yellow torchlight of the entry. "Sonjeur de Duplais?"

he said, exposing his left hand on his shoulder. "I am Verger Rinaldo."

"Divine grace," I said, swiping thumb to forehead in respect before exposing my own hand. "I appreciate your seeing me so late of an evening."

"I'm happy to serve your need, sonjeur." He held the door open.

I resisted the temptation to glance over my shoulder. Dante should be hidden in the shadowed peripheries of this garden. As I crossed the threshold, I dragged my hand across the mechanism of the lock, scraping it with the brass ring he had given me. No sooner had I whispered the key *inclavio*, than I snatched my hand away and stuffed it under the opposite elbow. My fingers stung as if I'd dipped them in a wasp nest. The mage had warned me his spell was crudely made and lacked shielding for the user.

Much of a student's first year at Seravain was spent training the senses to detect the existence of bound enchantments, the active energies of their release, and the residue that remained after some or all of those energies were used. Unlike the subtle sensations I had learned to associate with spellwork, Dante's magic nipped at my senses like a wolverine's bite—sharp, vital, as ferocious as everything else he did. I bled envy.

The mage's precaution to ensure his passage served well, as the verger shot the bolt once we were inside. Easy to see why. A thousand lamps hung from the age-mottled ceiling—lamps small and large, wrought of silver and gold, ancient lamps of the simplest design, others intricately wrought, etched, filigreed, or set with gems and jewel-hued glass. The Revelation of the Veil taught us that families could speed an ancestor's progress through Ixtador's Ten Gates only by honor and righteous living, not with material offerings. That was a difficult teaching for those who believed gold and jewels could buy anything.

Only a few of the lamps were lit, just enough to illumine our way across the foyer and through the circles of stone benches that surrounded a display of sand, miniature gates, and glazed water bowls. From the Chamber of Contemplation wide marble steps descended into a maze of polished walls etched with the names of the dead who had passed through this house.

Rather than continuing down a second stair to visit the Chamber of the Dead, where those brought to the deadhouse were washed and wrapped to lie in peace until their funeral rites, or to the tessilactory, where craftsmen shaped the stone artifacts to be sanctified at those rites, the verger led me down a side passage to a reading room. Built to exact dimensions, two and a half metres in height, width, and length, the close little chamber reeked of incense and scented soap from the verger's purification.

Already my head throbbed unmercifully. Incense forever induced the headaches that had plagued me since the explosive ending of my magical studies—the day I confronted my father with the truth of my failure and reaped the whirlwind.

Rinaldo scribed my father's full name on his slate and lit three-and-fifty candles, one for each year of my father's life. We sat cross-legged on either side of the loaf-sized altar stone, and I laid out the smoothed shape of red jasper and its matching spall—the little wedge chipped from the tessila on my father's funeral day.

"Now why do you believe you have profaned your father's memory?" asked the verger kindly.

"In passion and duty resulting from a recent temple reading . . ." I recounted my braid of lies yet again, feeling vaguely guilty and vaguely heretical—and decidedly foolish for such emotions. My beliefs about Ixtador and its perilous gates had been uncertain for many years. Yes, I kept my altar and carried a spall pouch and judged my every deed as to its efficacy for my honored dead. But extensive reading had brought me to view the Revelation as merely a historically necessary call to reformation after the Blood Wars. Now the spyglass vision had wholly confused my beliefs.

A gentle man, Rinaldo did not condemn me for my "dutiful zeal," but counseled me to leave the tessila in its proper place on my home altar next time I needed to grovel before the king and to carry only the unsanctified spall as a reminder of my family duty. "Let us step through the resanctification first. Then I'll attempt to assess your father's progress."

"Many thanks, Verger."

He raised his hands in supplication. "Holy angels, messengers of Heaven, bear my petition for hearing and grace to sanctify this memorial of Onfroi Guillame de Savin-Duplais. . . ."

As the verger recited the lengthy prayers and blessings required to purge the tessila of profanation, he poured and drank a thimble-cup of thick red liquid and lit the dish of herbs that sat on the altar beside the tessila and spall. I tried not to fidget as I imagined Dante slipping through the enspelled door lock and seeking out the mule's corpse. I tried not to breathe as the vapors roiled my stomach, and sharp-edged visions of curved swords and smoking battlefields etched themselves into my pounding head.

Just after the palace bells clanged the quarter hour, Rinaldo lapsed into the trancelike state of a reader probing the mysteries of Ixtador. I shook off my own drowsy half dreams, retrieved a pinch of sleeping herbs from my spall pouch, and dropped it into the smoldering dish. Rinaldo's trance state would be a bit deeper than usual and last for at least half an hour. I rose quietly and sped down the passage and the lower stair into the Chamber of the Dead.

Ranks of blocklike catafalques stood like some morbid army, silhouetted against the deeper blackness of the frigid chamber. Few were occupied. The soft white gleam from Dante's staff directed me to our quarry, a plain bier in a corner roped off for the unsanctified—suicides, felons, blasphemers, and mules.

As my mind encompassed the obscenity laid out on the stone slab, sin and grief took on new meanings for which my sheltered existence could not have prepared me. The bruised, lacerated body that lay amid the tousled grave wraps belonged to a once-fair girl of no more than sixteen summers. Scars defiled every portion of her pale skin, their number and varied age witnessing to years, not months, of torment. Even did the sorcerer extract but a thimbleful at each bleeding, a body could not replenish so much in any shorter span. Worse yet, life and mystery knotted so tightly that each wound screamed from my own flesh. For I knew her. *Ophelie* . . .

"The leech is expert," said Dante, his finger tapping the ranks of pale scars along the girl's arm and those on her neck, exposed when someone had hacked her dulled hair to a knucklebone's length. "Clean. Precise. Methodical. But I believe the mule began by bleeding herself. These oldest cuts on her thighs are ragged and tentative. And this"—he exposed the ugly red ruin of her left hand, where her family mark would be—"the mutilation of her identity was done quite recently." He dropped the flaccid limb onto the stone slab. "The body's keirna reveals—"

"She is not just a body, not just a mule," I blurted harshly, throttling a rising anger.

I could not but glimpse the flash of golden hair in the lamplight of the Seravain library, hear her spritely laughter in the company of her friends. I disliked children and resented when the younger students invaded my library. But the age of fourteen saw some become tolerable, especially the brightest minds as they began to comprehend the true dimensions of the world, the wonders that lay in life, in books, in magic. . . .

"Her name was Ophelie de Marangel," I said, "a diligent student, intelligent and insightful. Three or four years ago, she stood on the verge of dismissal, incapable of spellwork. Then, as happens from time to time, she all at once broke through that . . . barrier." The barrier that separates those who reach for power and find magic in their grasp from those who reach, but find their palms empty.

I could still hear Ophelie's desperation when she had come to me in confidence, begging me for some volume that might open the gates of magical understanding. I'd had to tell her no such work had ever been written. I had rejoiced to learn of her awakening. But evidently her palms had gripped a lancet and no true power at all. Self transference—reinfusing her own blood to fuel her magic. Only a child's perverse reasoning would judge slow death a sensible exchange for magic. And then, what? What villain, what filth, what maggot-souled fiend had discovered Ophelie's secret sin and taken up the task?

Dante glanced up from his examination of a small wound beneath her breastbone. "You discovered so much from a guardsman?"

I shook my head, unable to remove my eyes from the translucent skin stretched over her fine bones like gossamer sails on a master-wrought ship. She could have no flesh beneath that skin. With purpose and without mercy, a sorcerer had bled her dry.

A fury woke in me, hardening into certainty of purpose. "I knew her at Seravain. Last year, not long after passing her second adept's testing, we heard she fell ill and was sent back to her family in Challyat. She never returned to school." I inhaled the blended reeks of lamp oil, incense, and dead flesh, scribing the sight and stink upon my memory with the indelible medium of outrage. "The temple guardsman knew only that a knight found a dead girl at the base of the orchard wall with a dagger in her gut. The Guard Royale assumed she had climbed the outer wall in an attempt to breach the palace precincts and attack the king, but lost her grip and fell on her own weapon."

"Unlikely." Dante uncurled her hand, and I quickly averted my eyes. The girl's fingers were little more than ragged, blood-crusted stubs. "She'd never have topped any wall with hands like these. More likely she was trying to get *out* of the palace precincts."

"Why would anyone do that to her?" I said, swallowing hard. "Was stealing her blood not cruel enough?" What could be more dreadful than watching your own blood stolen drop by drop, knowing that your soul must eventually drain away with it?

"Identification," said the mage, crouching beside the bier, touching each torn stub in turn, using a small blade to scrape dried blood into a glass vial. I could not bear to watch. "We leave a trace of ourselves on every spell we work."

"And the Benocke test on her fingers might reveal it," I murmured. The old formula purported to link a sorcerer and a worked spell, though I had never seen it work successfully.

"There are surer ways, but yes. Not only did our knaves

leech her blood to empower magic, but I'd also guess they induced her to work some spell they wanted, just as they forced the assassin to shoot the arrow at the king. But they didn't want her work identified, which tells me that they expected someone to be analyzing her spells." He glanced up, his eyes dark pits in the gloom. "Remember the coming violence I spoke of? Odds on, she was to be a part of it."

"We should take these despicable mages down," I snapped. "Have them arrested right now."

"Without knowing what spells she's worked? Without knowing if a trap is already in place?" Dante slipped around the end of the catafalque, cut off a snippet of the girl's hair, and moved on to examine her right hand. "The actual removal of her fingers occurred a tennight or more past, which suggests her work was complete. This fresh damage comes from her attempt to climb the wall. If we cannot establish a connection between the queen's mages and either one of the mules, the Camarilla could as easily blame this on me."

Certainly the miscreants must be terrified at the girl's exposure. The discovery of a second mule would warn the king of a coming attempt. And if someone recognized the girl, the lie about her "illness" could be traced to an accomplice at Seravain. I'd have wagered my life that Ophelie's family believed her still at the collegia, too busy with her studies to write.

"I'll find the connection," I said, skin and soul ablaze. Fifty days yet remained until the anniversary of Prince Desmond's death. "Now, will you stop touching her? It's unseemly."

Ignoring my protest, the frowning mage again palpated the knife wound beneath her breast. Though she had not been washed, little blood and only a small bruise marked the hole.

"This guardsman's story makes no sense," he said, looking up at me. "How could she have a knife? She'd no strength to disable a jailer. She'd have been desperate to escape and would never have taken time to hunt a weapon she could not wield. As she could not climb, she could not have fallen on it by accident. Even the placement of the wound is odd. So precise. How likely is it to 'fall on a knife' in the exact spot and at the exact angle to instantly stop the heart?"

"But her captors didn't kill her. You said Gaetana was upset at her exposure. They'd never have abandoned her corpse where she could be found."

Dante tapped the deadly puncture. "Find me the weapon that did this. Its keirna will tell us—"

From beyond the silent stairs and chambers behind us a clanging bell broke the silence, and a resounding thud signaled the opening of the great bronze door. "Verger Rinaldo?" bellowed a man's voice. "Would a bit of light be too much to ask in a house of the dead? Bring that torch, Jacard. The rest of you, wait here." Heavy footsteps echoed through the upper chambers.

"Sainted bones," I whispered. "I've got to get back."

Abandoning Dante to tuck the coarse grave cloth about Ophelie, I pelted through the aisles and crept up the lower stair. The last of the hanging lamps were sputtering, as I threaded the maze of the Chamber of Remembrance and dodged down the side passage into the reading room.

The verger had not moved. I dropped to the kneeling cushion opposite him just as heavy boots crossed the vestibule.

"We require Verger Rinaldo," snapped the elderly gentleman who filled the reading room doorway. The egg-sized emerald that fastened his black velvet cloak, the high starched ruff, and a heavy pectoral chain, carrying an amulet of woven silver and amber, testified to his exalted station.

"Pardon, lord," I whispered. "We are engaged in a reading."

"I don't care about your reading!" he bellowed. "My wife lies profaned!"

Wife!

Rinaldo's shoulders jerked. The verger pressed his fingers to his eyes before staring across at me and then up to the newcomer. Dazed, he wobbled to his feet. "Conte Bianci . . ."

The name quickly erased my shock. My valet had spoken of a newly deceased waiting woman.

"Verger, is it true that a corrupt corpus lies in your deadhouse alongside my wife?"

"Indeed not," said the verger, his back stiff and his eyes clearing. "That is, a corrupted body lies in the house, but we provide separate accommodation for the unsanctified. No harm shall come to your lamented lady."

"I'll not have it. Corrupt dead are to the Souleater's minions as honey to flies. Rid this house of the unsanctified, or I shall carry my wife to the Temple Major in my arms. The tetrarchs will strip you of your office. You'll be washing bodies and scrubbing floors."

"Come, come, good lord . . ."

Dante had been right to press for a quick viewing. Saints grant, this uproar might cover his departure. There was no outside exit from the Chamber of the Dead.

Those hopes died quickly. The verger swept his arms toward the doorway. "Let us set your mind at rest. You'll see that every care has been taken. Grief must not spur haste."

As the conte stepped out, mumbling sentiments to the effect that proximity less than the moon's distance would be too close, Rinaldo laid a hand on my shoulder. "Pardon this unfortunate interruption, Sonjeur de Duplais," he whispered. "Were it anyone but a man who's lost his wife of nine-and-forty years, I'd send him packing. In any case, your father's reading seemed dreadfully confused. Come back another time, and we'll try again."

A slender, sharp-featured young man in adept's robes lit the passage with a jeweled lamp. My blessing words trailed after the verger, as he, the conte, and the adept swept out. I scooped up my tessila and spall and hurried after, willing Dante to be up the stairs and out of the deadhouse before the conte reached the lower chamber. We must not have our interest—or our confederacy—exposed.

"Adept Jacard, would you please tend the stairway lamps?" asked Verger Rinaldo, gesturing the conte to wait before descending into the dark. As I held quiet at the end of the passage, the nimble young man used the verger's long-handled brass taper to light a good third of the hanging lamps over the downward stair. *Blast!* No one would pass beneath them unseen.

Cursing Dante for leaving the entry door unlatched, I climbed the upward stair. I was nearing the main level when a clamor broke out both from above and below me. Conte Bianci shouted unintelligibly from below, while from the direction of the foyer, a ferocious baritone intoned, "Portier de Duplais, show yourself, you talentless maggot!"

I raced upward, unable to mistake Dante's resonant tones. A handful of gentlemen cowered in front of the entry doors.

The mage stood in the center of the foyer, his staff belching flames and a thundering noise that rattled the hanging lamps and set them swaying, chains and pendants jangling as in a whirlwind. "Where is my *servant*?" he bellowed.

As my mouth opened and closed soundlessly, the mumbling conte boiled up the stair behind me. "Burn that cursed mule tonight, Verger!"

As if propelled forward by the nobleman's wrath, I stumbled into the foyer, straight into Dante's glare. "There you are, insect!"

The conte's party halted at my back. "What in the infernal depths—?"

"Did I give you permission to pursue your own activities, apprentice?" Dante's visage pulsed the purpled black of a stormy sunset. "Floors unswept. Materials scattered. Accounts incomplete. Never . . . *never* . . . do you take it upon yourself to decide when to come or go. Return to my chambers and finish your work or I'll encase your feet in lead before the next sunrise."

He reversed direction and waved his flaming staff at the oaken entry doors. One of them flew open, crashing against the wall as if a battering ram had struck it. At least ten nearby lamps smashed into the tiled floor, sending the cringing gentlemen attendants scurrying to Conte Bianci's side. The sharp features of Bianci's adept glazed with awe. Mine likely did, as well.

As the mage swept into the thorny garden, one scheme, then another, careened through my head. For better or worse, I was left with the span of a moment to set my course. I had best trust my original plan.

I folded my arms around myself and set my shoulders shivering. "Witness, great lord, holy verger, good gentlemen," I said with appropriately trembling voice, "that I resign my commission as Master Dante's apprentice as of this hour. Should I fail to survive the night, I beg you invoke the Camarilla to avenge this affront."

As the white flames vanished beyond the hedges, I tucked my chin into my chest and fled, leaving the gentlemen attendants jabbering like magpies and young Adept Jacard laughing.

CHAPTER SEVEN

O n the next morning, Lord Ilario perched atop a waist-high wall in a private courtyard, feet dangling in the yellow wallflowers. His mouth gaped with a horror grown throughout my recounting of the deadhouse venture.

"Honestly, lord chevalier, the venture itself could not have worked out better," I said, attempting to ease his concern before he toppled backward into the fishpond. "Damoselle Maura placated Dante by assuring him that she would have me fetch his books from Seravain until she could assign him a new assistant. Then she offered me the position as your secretary, as we've planned all along."

My appreciation for the lady had increased yet again after I had burst in upon her the previous night, begging her to release me from Dante's service. I had not needed to feign awe at his magics, and my outrage at Ophelie's fate had sufficed for trembling.

"But, Portier, encased in lead!" He stretched his long legs straight out and gawked at his elegant boots. "You would be crippled forever! Well, I suppose you might drag your feet one by one, unless"—a sharp inhale signaled a new imagining—"he might encase them both in one block. You would have to be hauled about in a barrow!"

"He never would have done it, lord," I said, halfway between exasperation and amusement. "Dante wanted to make Conte Bianci's men forget that he had not entered through the outer door. The story of his outburst has spread throughout the palace and everyone is terrified and in awe of his magic. Just as we wish."

Certainly my spirit yet stung with the memory of Dante's enchantment. The thrill of power had raged through the deadhouse foyer like untamed lightning, filling the emptiness that gaped inside me as the ocean fills a sea cave.

"Truly, he did well. I've been freed to serve you, yet I've a perfect excuse to come and go in his chambers."

"Bless the Saints Awaiting, I did not see the poor girl." Ilario shuddered dramatically. "I would surely dream of it over and again."

After a sleepless night hearkening to Ophelie's pleas for vengeance, I could not argue. "Dante needs the weapon that killed her. But I've no idea what might have been done with it and no excuse to inquire. You do understand the questions surrounding the girl's death, Chevalier?"

"Certainly I understand," he said, springing from the wall as gracefully as a dancer. "I have a mind, after all, Portier."

"I didn't mean to imply—"

"Indeed you did. I'm not wholly unaware of what's said. No one credits that a gentleman who understands fashion and proper manners and refuses to dwell on upsetting matters in the presence of ladies can also be quite serious and scholarly." He dabbed at his hands and dusted the grit from his white hose with a lace kerchief, before tucking it into his sleeve. "The orchard, you say? I suggest that if we wish to know about the weapon, we speak to Audric de Neville. Would the present moment suit, or must you hurry off to attend to my trivial concerns or your own more sober ones?"

He strutted across the flower-filled yard toward an open gate without waiting for my answer, waving one hand as if he were an orator in the public forum. "I believe I shall enjoy having a private secretary. I have decided to host an exposition. How I love that word! *Exposition.* It sounds delightfully modern and studious. I daresay such a display shall reverse this canard that has been spread about my sobriety. You shall make all the arrangements. . . ."

"But we've more pressing—?" As he vanished into the larger garden beyond the gate, my thoughts gummed like feathers in pine sap. I hurried after him.

Only after we had traversed the flower garden, innumerable courtyards and corridors, three kitchens and a vast kitchen garden, and descended a short slope toward a forested bend of the great palace wall did Ilario's long legs slow enough to allow me to ask who was Audric de Neville. Yet by then the pungent scents of lemon and almond blossoms rising from ordered ranks of trees left the question unnecessary. A house knight had found Ophelie dead in an orchard.

The red-liveried chevalier was sleeping, back against the sun-drenched wall, jaw dropped in the way of the very old. His perfectly shined black boots stuck out in front of him as if he'd folded in the middle and sat straight down from standing guard. A pink almond blossom petal had settled on his white hair.

"He's the only knight in Castelle Escalon posted in an orchard," Ilario confided. "A noble spirit and proper chevalier. Philippe assigned him to guard this corner of the wall for as long as he chooses to serve. Lamentably, his attention doesn't last so long as it once did."

Ilario waved me forward and propped his knee on an empty crate left among the unbloomed pomegranate trees.

"Divine grace, Chevalier Audric," I said as I crossed the grassy strip paralleling the wall.

The old knight jerked and snorted and struggled to his feet, watery yellow eyes blinking rapidly. "Who comes?"

I exposed my hand and bowed. "Portier de Duplais. I've come about the dead girl found here. The mule."

"Daemon hand! Souleater's servant!" His rapier was in hand with a speed entirely unlikely for a man his age, and his face wore the wrath of the Pantokrator casting out Di-

mios at the founding of the world. "I'll see you dead—
I'll—Ah!"

Breathing hard as if he'd run the length and breadth of
his orchard post, the old man choked back the sentiments
that sudden waking had startled out of him.

"I am the girl's friend," I said, "her mourner, rather. My
employer, a kindly man horrified by this tale, has ordered
me to identify the girl and contact her family."

"Don't know aught. How could I? Found her dead." His
hands trembled so violently, his blade hummed. As the
emotion trying to escape him so belied this mumbled answer, I did not believe him in the least.

"We must tell her family how she died, what weapon
finished her, so they might speed her way through Ixtador's gates." My bare hand stilled his blade. " 'Twill be a
mercy to all. Tell us, Chevalier."

As quickly as he'd drawn his weapon, the old man
sagged to his knees. Sword dropped to the emerald grass,
he crossed his arms and gripped his shoulders as if to keep
his heart from flying out of his breast. "She begged me.
Soon as she found the wall too steep to climb. Wild, she
was. Could scarce speak and most of it babbling nonsense.
But she shed no tears. Not a one. I'm damned forever to
have done it, though she promised to carry word to the
saints to defend me."

"Damned? But *you* didn't—" I shook off a grotesque
image of the old man leeching her. It wasn't leeching he
spoke of. "You found her *alive*. What did she tell you?"

"Claimed a devil woman bled her. Claimed the two
forced her to terrible sin. To treason and murder. To the
betrayal of a good man. Yet she'd no strength to save herself. She pawed at me. Tore at me. Begged on her knees
and pressed the tip to her breast. Mad, as if the Souleater
himself had gnawed her reason. I couldna refuse her. Do
ye see that? I had to save her."

Dread truth stared me in the face yet again, as Audric
uncrossed his arms and lifted his rapier on open palms.

Suicide. The old chevalier's rapier might have pierced
her breast, but the Pantokrator, the all-seeing Judge,
would know she had driven him to it. What sin could

frighten her more than traversing the Veil corrupt—a mule who had sought her own death? Ixtador's gates would be barred to her.

I swallowed bile and accusation. "A name, Chevalier. In all this, did she speak a name?"

"Only near the end. She held my hand and spake it over and over in the midst of her weeping, so's I didn't know what to make of it. *Michel . . . captured . . . betrayed . . . Altevierre . . . save me . . .* Over and over. *Michel . . . captured . . . betrayed . . . Altevierre . . . save me . . . Michel . . .*"

Michel de Vernase . . . Our first word of Philippe's lost investigator. My blood raced.

Half-crazed with shame and guilt too long suppressed, the old knight poured out his story. It illumined little. He could provide no clue to assassination plots; no hint as to Michel de Vernase's fate; no identification of Ophelie's captors beyond the *devil woman* and the vague *two*; no idea what the word *Altevierre* referred to, and yes, it might have been something other, but his hearing was so cursed feeble. . . .

The Guard Royale had not questioned the bloodied poniard Audric had left with the girl as if she'd fallen on it. Audric had told no one that he'd found Ophelie living. The deception had likely saved his life.

We plied the old knight with valerian tea from the opaline flask Ilario carried for his digestion. Now that the boil of his shame had been lanced, Audric vowed to perpetuate his silence. To soothe his conscience, I suggested he sanctify a tessila for the mysterious girl. "If she sought to avoid forced sin, then perhaps her soul was not entirely expended in unholy magic. Though you're not blood kin, your deed, for good or ill, has surely bound you to her fate."

Audric, eased by that consideration or the valerian or both, insisted on remaining at his post.

I was near dancing with urgency. We were closing on information of importance. Michel de Vernase had vanished nigh a year ago and nothing had been heard of him, so Philippe had told me. No sightings. No demands. Everything had pointed to his death. And Ophelie had come to Audric from *inside* the castle walls, as Dante had surmised.

"Where could these mages hold secret prisoners?" I demanded, once a swath of trees separated Ilario and me from the knight. "If Ophelie and Michel were held prisoner together, it must be somewhere close." *Perhaps he is still there*, I dared not say aloud. *Perhaps he is in the same state as Ophelie.*

Ilario blotted his forehead, then wagged the knotted kerchief northward. An ancient blocklike keep squatted atop a low mound near the northern wall like a wart upon Castelle Escolon's warm yellow face. "Eugenie and I used to play in the old dungeons. Yet watchmen wander in from time to time, so you couldn't keep a secret prisoner." He swiveled westward toward the river. "Then there's the Spindle. . . ."

"Spindle Prison is outside the walls, and Ophelie didn't row a boat to get away. She was held here at the palace. A place the mages could come and go unremarked, with thick walls or well out of the common way. They'd not want anyone to hear what was going on." Cries for help. Pleading, as a child's blood was drained away. *Father Creator, forgive.*

Ilario pivoted full circle, mumbling the merits and demerits of various possibilities as his gaze traversed kitchen buildings, courtyard walls, guard towers; nurseries, toolsheds, and stables; deadhouse, swan garden, and the marble-columned temple minor. His brow lifted and smoothed. "There," he declared with the certainty of a man choosing white bread over brown.

I summoned patience. "The temple? But there's no—"

"The royal crypt lies underneath," he said, setting off at a brisk pace. "The King's Gate is kept locked until a sovereign dies, is crowned, or takes a notion to alter the name of his heir. But Eugenie found another way down." He shuddered dramatically. "She wanted to explore the secret chambers. She forced me to go. Called me a ninny, but I kept imagining those fifty kings, sitting in their niches in the dark, rotting."

As we crossed the sweltering gardens, his pace slowed

and he lowered his voice. "Michel could not be used as a mule, you know. He's as common as a barnyard—most certainly not of the blood. And he despises sorcery. Cursed preachy about it, too. Stubborn as the pox."

"A perfect hostage, however," I said, matching his quiet voice. "The king's closest friend."

"True enough." Ilario shrugged and aimed his unfocused eyes in the direction of the sun-washed temple roof. "They served together for years. Drank one another's wine and covered one another's sins. Long before anyone knew Philippe was Soren's heir, Michel took a sword strike for Philippe that near cost his arm. Philippe stood goodfather to Michel's children, and Michel did the same for Prince Desmond, angels guide the poor dead mite."

A white stone chip appeared in Ilario's hand. He touched the spall to his heart, forehead, and lips, before returning it to the silk pouch at his waist, scarce interrupting his commentary.

"Philippe's first act when crowned was to name Michel his First Counselor, displacing old Baldwin whose family had held the office since the Founding. Then he granted Michel the Ruggiere demesne that's never been held by less than royal kin, and without so much as consulting its overlord. Neither move was at all fitting. Geni's always felt the two of them were closer—" Ilario swallowed the sentiment, jerked the string closure on his spall pouch, and angled across the temple lawn.

It struck me as no surprise that a friendship founded on youth and war might bloom more intimate than a marriage founded on political necessity. But the tenor of Ilario's words gave me pause, serious as they were, and threaded with such profound dislike. I observed him closely.

Eyeing me sidewise, he wrinkled his mouth like a dried currant. "Well, all right. You've caught me out. Michel de Vernase and I get along like cats and fish. He is a brute and a bully and has not the least sense of fashion or manners or respect. He usurps places that are not his. But I'd not wish that"—he jerked his head in the direction whence we'd just come—"on anyone."

Nor would I. Nonetheless, I had been proceeding on the assumption that Michel de Vernase's disappearance had resulted solely from his position as investigator, that the king's regard for his friend had somehow made Michel's own character unimportant. *A lesson, Portier: Judge each player objectively, individually, and entirely.*

"Who is the overlord of the Ruggiere demesne?"

Ilario snapped his head around. "Dumont, of course. The Duc de Aubine." He narrowed his eyes. "No, no, Portier, quiet your nefarious imaginings. Dumont is not at all your man. He cares for naught but his birds. Now, back when Philippe granted Ruggiere to Michel, the demesne was held by Dumont's grandfather, who was as friendly as a rabid dog. He called the grant *theft*. If not for my foster mother, the old devil would have hauled Michel out of Ruggiere naked and bound in thorn ropes."

Comprehension required some wrestling with bloodlines and inheritance. King Soren had married Eugenie de Sylvae when she was but a child, and his mother, Lady Antonia, had fostered Eugenie and her half brother, Ilario, after their parents died in a fire. "So Lady Antonia persuaded her father, the *old* duc of Aubine, not to fight Philippe's grant to Michel?"

"Antonia is very persuasive. And she believes a king can grant what he wills. It helped that the slavering old hound doted on her until the day he died choking on an olive." Ilario waved his hand dismissively. "As for the present duc—Dumont—I promise you he doesn't care who holds his demesnes unless they've beaks and feathers. Michel de Vernase earned plenty of enemies elsewhere."

A serving man was sweeping the wide, shallow steps of the temple portico as we approached. A few ladies stood in the breezy shade of the pediment, as triumphant angels, painted scarlet, emerald, and gold, bent down from the facade as if to eavesdrop on their gossip.

Ilario bowed gracefully to the women as he tripped lightly up the steps and crossed the portico. As I entered the dim vestibule, he was disappearing, not into the light-filled vastness of the temple nave, but through a lesser doorway on the left. "It's far too long since I venerated my father's tomb," he was declaiming loudly. "I've been thinking it requires a new offering urn. You must arrange for it, secretary."

Two veiled women trudged past us. We hurried down the broad passage between a wall of carved memorial stones and a rank of increasingly elaborate sarcophagi. Midway down the aisle, Ilario's closed fingers touched his lips, then brushed a vault of rosy marble capped with the sculpted figure of a Knight of Sabria.

We halted in a memorial bay at the farthest end of the aisle. With a glance back down the aisle—now deserted—Ilario ducked under the bay's gilded rail and dodged behind a massive carving of some saintly king. I followed.

The dark alcove stank of musty wine and ancient incense. "Make us a light," Ilario said, from somewhere ahead of me. "Twiddle your fingers or whatever you sorcerers do."

"Twiddle . . ." My cheeks heated. Any more and they'd provide flames enough to see by.

I retreated past the effigy and the rail, returning moments later with a votive lamp from some marquesa's tomb hidden under my cloak. "This will have to do."

In the first moment I uncovered the lamp, I caught Ilario frowning at me. "Well, I assumed you could do *something* magical."

He dropped to his knees and probed the latch with a dainty knife more suited to picking teeth than breaking locks. Twice he fumbled and dropped the implement with a clatter. "Blast!" he said. "This used to be easier."

"Let me try," I said, trading him the lamp for the knife.

"This is the Tetrarch's Gate," Ilario whispered over my shoulder. "On coronation day, the new sovereign has to go down to the crypt to scribe the name of his heir. He uses the King's Gate—behind the font in the temple nave. A tetrarch is supposed to greet the new king down below in the name of all the dead kings, but it appears rude if he bullies past to descend first. So, instead, he slips aside and goes down this way."

In a moment's whimsy, I attempted a simple spell I'd used with some success when a child—a marvel that had sparked my magical ambitions. I broke off a thread dangling from the hem of my doublet. Twisting the thread about the knife blade and touching the latch with the knife, I blew upon their intersection—adding air to the balance of wood and metal—and infused the simple spell with my will. Not the least trickle of power cooled my veins. *Idiot.*

I twisted the handle and yanked on the door in frustration. To my astonishment, it flew open.

"Well done!" said Ilario, beaming.

"It was already unlocked," I snapped, angered at my inability to let go of what was ended.

"Impossible. No one ever goes down here. And this gate is always latched from the inside."

Impossible. Always. Dangerous words for an investigator. "Perhaps Ophelie escaped this way," I said.

Ilario blanched, blew a shaky breath, and motioned me through the opening. We closed the door softly and tiptoed down a spiraled stair. At the end of a downsloping passage lay a cavernous vault, hewn from the great rock underlying Castelle Escalon.

Massive columns incised with Fassid symbols, centuries older than the temple they supported, crowded the vast chamber. Censers of tarnished silver and brass dangled from the damp-stained ceiling like old moss, glittering and fading in our lamplight as we threaded a path between them. Every breath reeked of old incense, old stone, and old earth.

Not a step, not a breath, disturbed the stillness. What prisoner might have been held down here was no longer.

A single red lamp beamed brightly through the forest of columns, marking a great black stone bowl set atop a stepped pyramid some eight or ten metres across. Disproportionately elongated figures of men and women, hacked roughly from the gray stone, supported the bowl.

"The Coronation Font," said Ilario quietly. "Step up and take a look. It's a marvel."

The rounded lip felt cold to my hands as I peered into the font. Five half-height pillars protruded a few centimetres above the dark, still surface of the water, providing stepping stones to the center, where the watch lamp's ruby glow illumined a marble pedestal. A stone tablet lay on the pedestal. "Is that the Heir's Tablet?"

"The thing itself."

It behooved a sovereign to be specific when he scribed the name of the one who would succeed him, should he die without issue. Soren had written the *Duc de Journia*, who at the time was Armand de Savin, the white-haired Chancellor of Sabria. By the time Soren died, the Duc de Journia was the late chancellor's twenty-one-year-old son, Philippe, whom Soren detested.

"I thought it would be locked away," I said, astonished, "so no one could tamper with it."

"No need," said Ilario, from below me. "Stretch your hand out over the water."

When I did so, the water began to churn. Swirling, burbling, the dark flood quickly swelled upward toward the lip of the font, swamping the half columns.

I snatched my hand away, and the heaving water calmed. The residue of massive enchantment settled on my skin like spiderwebs, smelling of musty leaves and mildew.

"Happens it requires a few drops of an anointed king's blood to prevent all that folderol," said my companion. "And if a person gets swept off the stepping stones into the water, a hellacious clamor breaks out in the temple, and people come running and pull you out half drowned, and you think some pompous temple aide is going to slap you into one of these cells for the rest of your life, though you just wanted to get a look. . . ."

Ilario's rueful expression—and the image of a lanky young boy's dripping humiliation—elicited an unexpected laugh. But I was quickly sobered by a serious question that should have been the first out of my mouth when my royal cousin handed me this mess.

"Lord Ilario, whose name is scribed on that tablet? Since the boy died . . ."

Prince Desmond had died seven long years previous, and three more babes had failed since. Even as the distraught queen grew more reclusive, the suspicion grew that the sad lady was cursed and Philippe should be rid of her. No matter how devotedly my cousin believed his wife would yet produce a living heir, I could not imagine Philippe abandoning his beloved Sabria to the closest male of the Savin line, the near-illiterate Conte Parnasse.

"No one can pry it out of him," said Ilario. "After Catalin was stillborn, he came down here and scribed a new name, but he told no one *whose* name. Not even Eugenie. He said only that she didn't need to fret; that if the worst befell, his heir would be a person of strong and noble heart, who would care for her as his own sister . . ."

He tapped one elegant toe. Then he huffed, sighed deeply, and climbed the black stone steps to stand at my side. I waited, grasping that his thought was not quite ended.

"And then, a month later, on the anniversary of Desmond's death—that would be not quite two years ago now—Philippe's horse went mad and threw him. Broke his leg and three ribs. Damned bad luck. I offered to fetch him a charm from Fedrigo, but, as always, he scoffed."

I gaped at Ilario, who in turn stared at the tablet, its secret barricaded with enchantments I doubted any mage of our day could duplicate. And I wondered about luck and coincidence and if, perhaps, my royal cousin's certainty that his son's deathday would bring him mortal danger was based on more than a single incident. "Have there been other unfortunate occurrences on Prince Desmond's deathday?"

"The year prior to the mad horse, their daughter, Catalin Jolie, was stillborn."

Holy saints! When Philippe named a new heir, had the queen been relieved that the burden of Sabria's future did not rest in her womb, or had she been angry that her husband's throne would pass to someone she did not know, as if he had lost faith in her? Or perhaps . . . Rumor said Queen Eugenie had first brought mages to Castelle Escalon when the little prince lay dying.

"Lord Ilario, does your sister blame the *king* for Prince Desmond's death?"

"Certainly not. The boy was sickly from birth." Ilario

spun in place and tripped down the stepped dais. "We'd best move on. We came looking for evidence of Michel."

The royal tombs of Sabria's kings nestled in cold, dark bays between the heavy piers. Thick iron doors broke the occasional spaces of flat wall.

"Preparation rooms, chapels, storehouses, who knows what they were?" said Ilario, as we peered into the airless chamber behind one such door. Anyone of adult stature would have to duck to enter. Despite the cramped doorway, the ceiling stood at a reasonable height. "The verger says the lintels were built low so dead souls could not escape." He shuddered.

We opened and closed every door. Some revealed bare cells. Some revealed heaps of what might be rotted carpeting, or worse. We found splintered shelves, broken chisels, and a rusty vise.

The crypt must have held fifty royal tombs—some sarcophagi little more than stone boxes, carved with symbols, some marked with elaborately adorned altars and graven memorial stones, some adorned with carvings of horses, wine casks, and other symbols of wealth and prosperity. More than once I jumped when our lamp revealed a pale face with solid black eyes—a nouré, a statue erected to honor the dead, its naked form swathed in real garments and jewelry, lacking only lifelike eyes so as not to be mistaken for the departed one.

Time had ravaged most of the tombs. Once-bright paint had faded on walls and furnishings. The fine garments that draped the nouri hung threadbare, ravaged by insects, vermin, and damp. Gemstones sat in tarnished settings or had been dug out and replaced with less precious stones.

The weight of so many tombs and altars, pillars, and cells oppressed my soul. The black, accusing stare of the nouri from their dark recesses dredged up my own long-buried darkness. And when I caught a whiff of cedar, the old wounds hidden underneath my doublet flared with pain, igniting searing memory. . . .

The hammering fire so unexpected . . . and then another piercing blow comes fast. The world explodes in pain and blood. Shoulder. Back. Searing agony, accompanied by a flailing blade and madman's cries: "Failure! Fool! Incapable."

"Father . . . don't!"

Lancing fire splits my left arm elbow to wrist. Life escapes in warm floods. Knees buckle. Side skewered with flame . . .

"Master, help me! Dufreyne . . . Garol . . . Mother!"

"Get up, get up. On your feet or die this moment. Sweet angels defend! He's strong as a rabid dog. Grab his wrist. Ignore the pummeling; that *hand holds no blade."*

The earth wavers . . . light shimmers . . . fades into gray . . . Let go of his knife hand and you die. Hold on and you'll collapse . . . and die. So, let go, then. Aim for his throat. One chance . . .

"Soren's tomb is the farthest in. I hope he's kept his clothes on at the least. Viewing your sovereign in the raw is different when you actually *knew* the fellow."

Ilario's prattle dispersed my vision as the wind scatters feathers. But the pain lingered, and I could still smell the reek of blood and mortal panic. The scent of dry cedar never failed to rouse these persistent fragments of horror— memories of the day my father had tried to kill me, and I killed him instead.

"Portier, are you quite well?"

"Yes, yes, I'm fine," I said, near breathless from a burgeoning headache. Half-sick, hands trembling and hot as if yet drenched in nine-year-old blood, I fought to lock away the cursed past like a stray book in its proper cupboard.

When I opened my eyes, Ilario wore an expression of drawn worry so at odds with his raked cap and dangling feathers, I had to smile. "All right, I am not fine," I said. "As with you, Chevalier, crypts and deadhouses give me the frights. Now, what were you saying about Soren?"

Soren's tomb was the newest memorial, erected only eighteen years past, so it was only to be expected that it would show less deterioration than the others. Rosemary and lavender had been sprinkled liberally about the alcove to deter insects, and the rich colors of its frescos had been laid on deeply. But not only did the nouré's robes of silk and ermine appear to have been taken from the royal wardrobe that very morning, but at least three hundred candles burned in wrought-iron sconces. Fresh-cut iris and purple flax bloomed in pewter urns.

"The crypt must not be so unvisited as you thought," I said.

Ilario stared at the tomb bathed in candlelight, one arm folded across his sleek doublet, elbow resting in his hand, allowing him to chew a thumb thoughtfully. "Whatever are you doing, *caeri*?"

My skittish nerves prompted a rude answer. But I bit it off. The softly voiced question was not for me, but rather for the dear *one* he believed had supplied these adornments.

After a few moments, he snapped his head around. "It's surely Antonia who maintains all this. Soren was her only true son, nigh a god to her. Though, certainly, she has been all kindness to Geni and me. She had no need to adopt us . . . me, especially."

He returned his gaze to the altar, and the half-again-larger-than-truth nouré of his foster brother looming. I didn't think he believed his assertion. Queen Eugenie, wed to another man—another king—had been lavishing her dead husband's tomb with love. How much more evidence against her would Philippe need?

"Onward," said Ilario, with far less enthusiasm than he'd shown up to now.

When Ilario pulled open the iron door tenth from Soren's tomb, the chamber sighed a tainted breath: sweat, ordure, and the acrid stink of pain, torment, and despair that seeped from walls and ceiling. Our lamplight pooled on a stained stone floor, and a litter of long, pale shards of freshly splintered wood.

A single sturdy chair stood bolted to the floor in the center of the room. An accusation. A monument to evil. Even as my soul recoiled, the *agente confide* inside me noted that I would need to bring Dante to examine its stained arms. Perhaps some residual enchantment might identify the devils who had tormented a young girl in this pit. The metallic flavor of blood drowned my tongue, as if the stolen ichor hung in the air like mist.

"*Sancte angeli*," whispered Ilario, touching the chain dangling from the ancient wall—steel links not rusted, but new and sleek and merciless. The manacle at its end gaped open, warped and twisted, a jagged break splitting the thick metal. "However did the girl manage this?"

He held out the torn metal. The cursed thing pricked my fingers like stinging nettle.

"Magic," I croaked, cramming my fingers under my arm and fighting not to drop the lamp. "Someone's magic broke it. Perhaps her own . . . but a mule so near the end . . . unlikely."

Swallowing bile, I held the lamp high and circled the chamber, examining every centimetre of the damp walls. Ophelie had learned Michel's name. But the conte had no power for magic. There should be one more chain, at the least, two if the sorcerer who had freed Ophelie had been a prisoner as well.

On the wall opposite the dangling chain, another bolt had been fixed to the wall. Close examination revealed more. "Chevalier, come. . . ."

I shone the lamp on markings scratched in the wall near the floor, scarce distinguishable from the dirt and mold that crusted the stone. A series of minute tick marks— eleven in a ragged row, with the first nine crossed over in the manner of one counting off a tenday. More interesting were what appeared to be an *R*, encircled by a twisted rope or vine, and a word scratched in tiny letters—*Altevierre*.

Ilario, crouched beside me, touched the first mark. "The Ruggiere device," he said, confirming my guess. "Michel was here." But wherever the conte had gone, his chains and manacles had gone with him. If the tick marks indicated the length of Michel's imprisonment in this cell, then he had been held here only a short time.

Neither of us knew what *Altevierre* might signify, only that Ophelie had repeated it in her dying mania. As I sketched the wall markings in my journal, Ilario hunted more, but without success.

"We need to take the manacle," I said. "Dante might be able to identify the spellworker."

Without speaking the need aloud, we moved with accelerating urgency. Those who had used this room knew verger's schedules and little-used stairways better than we did. Even Ilario would have difficulty explaining our presence.

With a rusty gripping tool left in the crypt by some ancient bronzeworker, I worried a small piece of the torn manacle free and dropped it in my spall pouch. The shard had to be enough. Our lamp was fading. Then, as if our anxieties had made themselves manifest, a distant grind of metal heralded light footsteps on the grand stair and women's voices murmuring.

I pressed the chevalier's arm. Shielding the lamp with our cloaks, we glided through the maze of columns, past the glistening black font. Thready enchantments brushed spirit and flesh like a storm of spiderwebs.

Halfway from the font to the Tetrarch's Stair, our lamp died. *Saints and angels!* Blinded, I stretched out my arms.

"You feel it, lady? Someone's here." The woman's voice came from the direction of the King's Gate. "Who's there? Step out!" Yellow beams danced through the forest of pillars.

Edging one foot forward, I cursed my stubborn pride for refusing to commission charms. A guidespell would have been useful. But as I slid around the next pillar, a fan of pale blue light stretched out in front of me, just bright enough to enable me to avoid inconveniences like dangling lamps waiting to collide with my head. Astonishingly, the light emanated from Ilario's hand.

"Stop right where you are!"

We dodged through the remaining pillars, ducked into the passage, and raced up the Tetrarch's Stair. Guided by better light than Ilario's blue fan, the footsteps pounded the lower stair at the same time I poked my head through the door.

"All clear," I whispered. The side aisle was deserted, but we had no hope of getting away before our pursuers emerged behind us. Venturing into the temple nave would be even more foolish, as the domed vastness offered no better cover than a few benches and potted flowers.

"Duck behind Albriard," said Ilario, as we shut the

door quietly and huddled in the memorial alcove. "He'll not mind. Stay put until they've gone."

It took me a moment to realize *Albriard* was the kingly statue looming over my head. As I weighed the wisdom of remaining three steps from the doorway, Ilario darted down the aisle. He dropped to his knees before the tomb he'd venerated on our arrival and touched forehead to stone.

The door burst open, sending me deep into the shadow of King Albriard's effigy. A tall, gray-haired woman paused a handsbreadth from me and glared down the aisle. I did not breathe. Of formidable stature, sturdy limb, and smooth, well-defined features, she might have stepped off a temple fresco—the very image of the warrior angel who cast the Souleater into the abyss. Once one had met Mage Gaetana, one would not forget her.

Another woman passed the Tetrarch's Door. Clothed in emerald silk, she, too, stood above an average woman's height, though unlike that of her robust companion, this woman's presence scarce moved the air. Slender-boned, frail, her luminous skin pale as moonlight framed in heavy loops of ebon hair, she seemed almost transparent. "Who is it?" she said, in breathless quiet.

"Your bastard brother is the only visitor I see," said the sorceress, her muted contralto as chilly as the stones and tinged with hostility. "What would he be doing down below?"

A laugh rippled like starlight on water. Gentle humor, in no wise mocking. "Ilario? Ah, dear Gaetana, my brother would not visit the crypt were his tailor to set up shop there. Dark places frighten him terribly—my fault, I fear. It's only some temple aide or a wayward child has visited the kings today. Go back. I'll rejoin you soon."

The Queen of Sabria glided down the memorial aisle, laid a hand on Ilario's shoulder, and knelt beside him, making the same ritual gesture—a kiss of her fingers to lay on the stone. After a few moments, sister and brother stood and embraced.

"I was missing him today, Geni," said Ilario, as they strolled down the aisle arm in arm, the dark head and the fair almost touching. "You'll not tell anyone, will you? Of all things in the world, I'll *not* be seen as a Moping Mariah who lurks about tombs. My reputation!"

Gaetana stepped back through the Tetrarch's Door and closed it softly behind her. Expelling my long-held breath, I sagged against King Albriard's monument.

Eugenie laid her head on Ilario's shoulder. "Ah, sweet brother, I miss him, too. So very much. Someday . . ." They moved out of hearing before she completed her thought.

Was it possible Philippe and Ilario were so wrong about this lovely woman? Could one who appeared so fragile wreak the Souleater's own torments on a girl of sixteen? Heaven bless that I was but the investigator of this mystery and not the judge.

Only as the two walked away did I notice the implement dangling from Ilario's left hand. Absurdity filled the dark voids left by our delving and my own brief odyssey into past despair, and I slid to the floor with a disbelieving chuckle. Our guiding light had come from Ilario's crocodile charm.

CHAPTER EIGHT

"I'll say this investigating is not half so entertaining as I thought it would be. Murders. Mules. Crawling around in dreadful places." Goblet of wine in hand, Ilario leaned on his wrought-iron balcony rail that overlooked the swan garden.

Though sunlight, clear skies, and potent refreshment made the royal crypt seem a world distant, only a day had passed since our venture into the wretched dark. A day of frustration. Twice I had tried to take Dante the shard of Ophelie's broken manacle. Twice I'd found his apartments locked and strongly warded. What was he up to?

"I've written to Ophelie's family," I said, setting aside my own cup. "I hope to find out if anyone from Collegia Seravain contacted them about her 'illness.' *Someone* spread the lies about her leaving school. I need to go to the collegia soon, as well. Perhaps I can discover what Michel was looking for or what he might have uncovered that led to his disappearance. Why would someone risk taking such a prominent hostage, then not tell anyone what they want for him?"

Ilario wagged a long finger at my nose, his gold ring

and its ruby-eyed phoenix flashing sunbeams in my eyes. "We must also begin arrangements for my exposition. I require it to be spectacular, splendors of science and magic displayed side by side for the entire court to witness."

I leaned my elbows on the iron rail, pressing fingers to temples to stave off another headache before the world went gray. I had been ready to dismiss Ilario's folly of an "exposition." Yet preparations for such an event could give me reason to speak to a variety of people, and Dante needed to observe and analyze some large-scale work of the queen's mages. If they did not accept him into their circle, such a ruse might be the only way.

Ilario rattled on. "Perhaps I could design a cloud and lightning display. Mage Orviene would certainly work the caelomancy for me, especially if Eugenie encouraged him. She has him tend the weather over her family's vineyards—not to any beneficial effect that I've ever seen. But he's a good sort of fellow. Congenial. Well mannered."

"Lord Ilario, consider—" I clamped my lips before I lashed out at his thoughtlessness. Had he forgotten so soon that Mage Orviene might have bled a child to self-murder to fuel his weather-working?

Despite the day's warmth, I shivered and rubbed the back of my left hand. Consideration of the Blood Wars chilled anyone of the blood. The very mark that identified us as potential sorcerers also identified us as potential mules.

"Very well," I said. "But as I take care of these other matters, you must do all you can to watch for clues. Anything to do with the queen's mages or their assistants. Anything sudden or surprising, because Ophelie's escape must surely alter the villains' plans. Even the smallest matters—those they speak to, those they dine with, what small magics they work, how they prepare for your exposition—might be important. That is the role you agreed to."

I could not but hope that the sister Ilario so clearly adored was not stained with the foulness we had glimpsed. But neither could I forget her words: *I miss him, too. So very much. Someday . . .* She longed to speak to her dead parents. She had hired Dante to bring them back. The spy-glass seemed to reach beyond death, linking assassination, unholy magic, and the queen's unhealthy desires.

"I'll do what's needed," said Ilario, who had drained his wine cup and moved indoors to flop on a couch. "Though I don't like deception. If I'd not spoken out and asked Eugenie why she'd come to the temple, I'd never have remembered it was Soren's deathday."

The queen's answer might explain the flowers and extra candles, but had addressed neither Gaetana's presence nor the nouré's wealth of jewels and silks, nor the wax built up so thickly on candlesticks and altar stone that one must conclude the attentive vigil had lasted years, not days. Did Philippe know?

Gratefully, I followed Ilario out of the sultry heat. "One more thing, Chevalier. We must pass this new information to His Majesty. Dante's warning of violence, Ophelie and the possibility that Michel is alive and captive. Can you manage that without anyone's remarking it?" I could not afford an audience with Philippe. I was too visible as yet, so soon after my introduction at court and Dante's well-reported tirade.

"Oh, there's a way." Ilario's face soured like that of a boy commanded to kiss an ill-favored aunt. "The king enjoys trouncing me at stratagems. Does anyone but mention the tedious game, he insists on a match, no matter that he knows how I detest it. Who dares refuse a king's whim? But I oft insist on a private venue to deprive him of an audience for his triumph. None will remark it."

"Excellent," I said, unable to imagine flighty Ilario shifting knights, warriors, tetrarchs, and queens through the complex landscape of a stratagems board. "We'll not take advantage too often."

As if pricked by a hay fork, Ilario leapt from his couch, snatched up a feathered hat, and tucked his pale locks behind one ear to reveal a dangling earring of rainbow-colored stones. "Come along, Portier," he said, charging across the carpet toward the door. "Enough of maudlin business. If it is Third-day, as I suspect, and midafternoon, as I notice, then it is time for my foster mother's salon. I

dare not shirk my duty, as I am charged to amuse the ladies especially. Today, I shall display my sober side. All
shall marvel that I have myself a private secretary."

He halted abruptly, pressing his back to the outer door,
and examined me head to toe. "Do you have that journal
you're forever messing about with?"

"Always."

"Get it out. It makes you look properly serious and sec-
retarial. We'll say your luggage has been lost and you've
had to borrow clothes from your valet. La, we must get you
to my tailor and my barber soon, else the entire court will
guess you're a spy. None will believe I've hired a shaggy-
headed slip of a fellow who wears velvet in spring."

I sighed and followed him. I would much rather have
sought out Philippe's disgraced guard captain or re-
searched the meaning of *Altevierre*—the word scratched
on the crypt wall and flown from Ophelie's lips as she
begged for death. But Antonia de Foucal had stood at the
center of Castelle Escalon as queen, queen mother, and
now as Eugenie and Ilario's adoptive mother. She must
know everyone and everything. What better resource for
an investigator?

ILARIO SWEPT INTO LADY ANTONIA'S grand drawing room
like a benevolent west wind, touching, ruffling, and tweaking every sleeve, cheek, and temper within view. A head
taller than everyone else, and adorned in blazing scarlet,
he could not vanish into any crowd. He wept over a deceased cat with a thready dowager and commiserated with
a fellow dandy over the poor quality of Hematian bro-
cades. He promptly threatened a duel with a local tetrarch
when a weak-chinned marquesa reported that the clergy-
man had complained of Ilario juggling eggs on the temple
lawn. Without noting scornful smirks or guests rolling
their eyes, he declared his longing that one of the sainted
Reborn could choose ridding the world of crocodiles as his
heroic task.

I heeled like a well-trained hound. From time to time,
Ilario would pause his conversation, spin around, and

point at me, declaring, "Make a note that I must speak to Teb about the exposition," or, "Pen a letter to my old swordmaster, Portier. I shall require practice before this duel."

I would acknowledge with a half bow and scratch notes in my journal, all the while learning names, listening, observing.

Ilario's sole temperate moment occurred when he encountered a man wearing the phoenix badge of the Cult of the Reborn. Cultists believed the saints to be souls who had willingly relinquished their hope of Heaven in order to serve the needs of humankind in this life, reborn time and again at the Pantokrator's whim. I thought it nonsense.

"You must be the new secretary. Duplais, is it? *Savin-Duplais?*" Based on her unimposing height, unexceptional figure, and unguessable age, the mature woman who stood at my shoulder could have been any court lady. Yet she had shunned the heavy, smooth-woven coils of current fashion and organized her gray-streaked black hair into masses of small, stiff curls about her face—a style one saw only on thousand-year-old Fassid carvings. And just like those ancient figures, she had completely plucked out her eyebrows, giving herself a permanent look of ingenuous surprise. Such flagrant defiance of fashion demanded concentrated attention. No common courtier would be so bold.

"Indeed, my lady," I said, making all proper deference. "I am Portier de Savin-Duplais, though it might serve me ill to emphasize the *Savin* at present."

Her laugh rippled, pleasant and knowing. "Royal relations tread a more strenuous road than any outside our odd circle might suspect. You must join me for tea some afternoon. We shall exchange strategies for maintaining our equilibrium."

"I would forever prize such an event." I appreciated the absence of scorn in her good humor. Swallowing my usual inhibitions, I did not stop with politeness. "May I speak to your secretary to set a day?"

Her painted eyes widened. "What a bold young snippet! Not so craven as I was told."

She patted me on the cheek with three jeweled fingers and swept onward without answering, instantly the center of each group she encountered. She could be none but the Lady Antonia.

When Ilario spied her, he spun in a whirl of silken cloak and dangling jewelry and dropped to one knee, spreading his arms as if awaiting a message from Heaven. "Divine grace, lady mother."

Lady Antonia acknowledged this overeager obeisance with a touch to his shoulder and a pained expression. She moved on before he could rise or open his mouth again.

Sighing hugely, Ilario scrambled to his feet and took up the tale of his recent sojourn on the Aubine seacoast for two young ladies whose pasted smiles begged for escape. Perhaps they, as well as Lady Antonia, had heard the tales of crocodile charms and therapeutic mud bathing too often already.

My spirits rose when I spied Damoselle Maura poised in the doorway. Yet before I captured her notice, she set course for two wind-scoured gentlemen. Sober blue jackets, trimmed in gold, and broad-brimmed hats pinned up on one side suggested naval connections. Maura smoothed their path around the refreshment and card tables to an elaborately draped corner where Lady Antonia now bantered with a cluster of admiring ladies and gentlemen.

Though Maura lacked the dainty perfection of Ilario's bejeweled ladies or the languid elegance of the ingenue who enthralled five gallants in the garden doorway, I found the softer curves of her body and the spare authority of her movements quite pleasing. When she glanced up and caught me watching her, I'd have sworn a smile crinkled the corners of her eyes, though she continued to participate fully in her conversation with Sabria's dowager queen.

Not wishing to be rude, I shifted my attention to the refreshment table, browsing the quails' eggs and pickled leeks, the sweetmeats and lemon tarts, while observing the comings and goings. My interest focused sharply when a tidy, wide-browed mage entered from a side chamber. His gray-threaded locks were sleekly dressed, his doublet as elegantly skirted as Ilario's. His mage's collar gleamed amid his starched shirt ruffles. On the occasion of my ignominious debut in court society, he had stood behind Gaetana. Orviene, certainly.

Was it possible that this newcomer who floated from one group to the next, extending a quiet greeting or a smile, touching a young woman's hand, laughing, and offering referrals to magical practitioners who could help with every condition from limp hair to lingering curses, had hacked off Ophelie's fingers and prisoned her in a crypt next to fifty dead men? It struck me as a fearful thing that such depravity might be couched in so ordinary a figure. Surely a monster should wear a horned cap and blood soaked black, reeking of brimstone, and not peacock blue brocade and hair pomade.

"The daemonish mage has not wreaked vengeance on you, has he?"

My head snapped around, and I near bit my tongue. Maura had somehow got across the room without my noticing it. Her round cheeks glowed with her smile, as terror constricted my throat. Had I somehow voiced my thoughts?

"I've promised to find him a new assistant." Dante. She referred to Dante.

"No vengeance," I said. "But then I've not yet encountered the devil again. Will he be here?"

The administrator clasped her hands modestly at her waist and knotted her brow in mock sobriety. "I doubt anyone has thought to invite him. I'm not sure even Mage Orviene's generosity would extend so far."

Generosity? Only a considered breath kept me from choking. "I'm not sure I'm ready to meet Mage Orviene, either," I said. "I would like to establish some solid reputation at court before greeting its most formidable figures."

Maura's eyes livened with amusement. Some might call her stiff, but she seemed to me a well-contained person, her feelings clear to anyone who took the time to observe her closely. Even before her descent into permanent genteel hysteria, my mother had lived in a constant state of fractured emotions, liberally shared with anyone within reach, and the female students at Seravain seemed forever thrashing about between the overexcited activity of squirrels and the argumentative despondency of hibernating bears.

"Mage Orviene is anything but formidable," she said. "He ever has a kind word for those who seek his help. You should speak to him. That's the purpose of a lady's salon."

"My mother hosted such events when I was a boy. Awful, awkward afternoons. I am wholly out of practice. Lord Ilario insisted I accompany him today, else I'd have spent a happy hour on his latest whim. He intends to sponsor a scientific exhibition in the coming months."

"Indeed." She ducked her head, and her finger pressed a smile from her lips. "I've heard rumor of this . . . uh . . . fancy. If you need advice . . ."

I bowed. "An accomplished administrator who knows everyone at court and most of the tradesmen in Merona could save my life. Again."

Her laughter bubbled just beneath the surface, a pleasing animation of mouth and eyes that was at once unembarrassed and quite private. Warmth flooded through my limbs and . . . everywhere. Gracious angels, it had been so long.

Of a sudden Maura's brows lifted and she tilted her head as if to see better beyond my shoulder. Then she leaned forward slightly and spoke directly into my chest, "On your guard, good sir. Thy nemesis doth approach."

I shifted around slowly, as if adrift in the sea of conversation. Framed in the doorway to the outer passage stood Dante. Clean shaven, dressed in black knee breeches and hose with an elegant short cloak swept over his right arm, he cut a fine, if sober, figure. A plain, silver earring adorned one ear. I offered fervid thanks to young Edmond de Roble and his tailor, and, foolishly, felt quite proud. Relieved, too; Dante did not carry his staff.

Across the room, Mage Orviene laughed with another admirer. Lady Antonia embraced two bejeweled ladies at once. Ilario's prattling floated atop the general buzz of voices like a gemsflute against a room full of hurdy-gurdies.

Dante's gaze swept the room like a sea storm, rousing a first tremor of uncertainty. Voices faded. Heads turned.

His attention seemed to settle on a destination, and as he moved forward, the guests parted to let him through. His broad left hand cupped a glittering heap of glass or jewelry. He halted in front of Ilario.

Ilario aborted his monologue in midsentence.

"A serving man graced me these'n yestertide, along with your requirements for 'an enchanted musical gaud, suitable for a gift to an aged baroness.'" None in the large chamber could fail to hear the measured menace in Dante's quiet statement, issued in the rough patois of Coverge. "I spoil for to clarify a few mots as to your request." With a twist of his hand, he tossed the heap into the air.

Ilario's young ladies gasped, and the chevalier himself leapt backward. Yet the glittering pieces did not strike any guest, nor did they plummet. Rather they hovered a handsbreadth from Ilario's long nose—a jumble of colored glass shards, small mirrors, strings of pearls, lapis, jade, and slips of metal.

The guests withdrew into a gaping circle. As every eye widened in wonder—mine not least—the shimmering mass rose toward the coffered ceiling, organizing and collecting itself into a revolving fountain of light and music. Rings of glass prisms focused light into crossed beams; rings of mirrors reflected the light in a hundred dazzling directions. The colored beads twisted and draped like a canopy of ribbons; dangling bits of bronze and silver rang clear and joyous as the structure spun.

The guests pointed and gasped, shocked murmurs growing into laughter and expressions of awe and admiration. Yet how many of them could truly comprehend the magnificence of what they saw? This was no illusion, no scant veil of sensory deception draped over a decorated wire frame. Naught supported these glittering elements or interlaced their light beams but purest magic.

"Is this what you had to mind, great lord?"

Ilario moved underneath the sparkling font of light, bobbing his head, whirling on his heeled boots. "Oh, yes! Magnificent! Marvelous!"

Only those who heeded the mage's tight voice, only those who tore their eyes from the creation to the creator, would have seen Dante brush his silver earring, then point a steady finger at the spinning enchantment.

The glancing light soured to a thunderous purple; the melodic jingle rose to a mind-jarring cacophony.

"Lord, beware!" I darted forward and yanked Ilario from underneath the quivering folly just as it shattered, raining splintered glass and fractured beads.

Ladies screamed. Gentlemen shouted and pressed the circle of onlookers backward. Ilario tripped on my feet and stumbled to his knees.

Dante stood over Ilario, pinning him to the floor with his scorn. "I do *not* make gauds. I do *not* take orders from trivial men. Sorcery is *not* an amusement."

Before a speechless Ilario could rise, Dante had gone.

Whispers rushed through the shocked crowd like a swarm of insects. *Illusion . . . Madman . . . Who is he? Insufferable . . . dangerous . . . Who?*

Lady Antonia pushed through the frantic crowd and gazed down at the mess, Orviene at her side. The mage dropped to a knee. Closing his eyes, he swept widespread fingers over the debris in a dramatic, but entirely unnecessary, gesture. An experienced examiner sensed magical residue on his skin, on his tongue, in his bones.

As he bounced to his feet, Orviene palmed a few slips of silver and colored beads from the floor and slid them into his doublet. *Yes, test them. Feel them. I'll wager you've never felt the like.* The residue of Dante's enchantment sparkled and shimmered through my skin and spirit as no fragments of glass or metal could ever do. *Well done,* I thought. *Very well done.* Orviene could not but be impressed with his new colleague's talents.

The dapper mage waved dismissively. "No enchantment remains. You are all quite safe."

A twitch of Lady Antonia's fingers brought liveried servants with brushes and dustpans to collect the not-at-all illusory debris. The crowd sighed as one and the anxious murmurs grew into a strident babbling.

I gave Ilario a hand up and a raised brow of inquiry. He shook his head ever so slightly. He had not prompted the event. No sooner was he on his feet than he was besieged by ladies and gentlemen alike. "Dante," he said, "his name is Dante. A master mage. I brought him here to amuse Eugenie, but I never imagined . . . I am wholly flummoxed."

Dante and his display were the primary topics of conversation for the next hour. Ilario repeated his story of finding Dante by way of his search for a new crocodile-slaying spell at least a hundred times, elaborating as he went along. I retired to the wine steward.

I'd scarce downed a sip when Maura joined me, dragging Mage Orviene alongside her. "Portier, meet Her Majesty's Second Counselor, Orviene de Cie. Orviene, this is Portier de Savin-Duplais, Lord Ilario's new secretary."

"Divine grace, Mage," I said, trying not to stare.

"And with you, sonjeur, an acolyte yourself, I hear." The mage's pale eyes moved from my exposed hand to my face in polite interest. "Fresh from Seravain."

"My studies ended many years ago, sir. I've served as the collegia librarian for almost a decade." The courret tucked into my waist pocket remained chilly. Surely it should react in the presence of evil, as it would for poisons or unsheathed weapons.

With another not quite a smile that near melted my bones, Maura excused herself.

Orviene smiled broadly. "A scholarly gentleman with an appreciation of the mystical arts will always be welcome in the household. *Common* breeding will ever display itself, eh?" Though he leaned close, as if to share a confidence, any guest within ten metres could have heard. "If your duties allow, you must stop by my chambers and I'll introduce you to my assistants. Though I'd gladly show you our current work, I doubt you'd quite grasp the intricacies."

The mage did not so much as take a breath, much less register my embarrassment. "I'd be interested to hear news of Seravain. . . ."

For half an hour, he plied me with questions about the collegia, allowing no more than a bell's strike for me to answer. Each query would launch a humorous anecdote or a reminiscence of his own student days. Eventually he ceased bothering to ask anything, but provided avuncular advice as to court dress—modesty served best for those of us in service, even when family connection supported more opulent attire—court ladies—Sabria's most luminous treasures—perfumes—best kept muted so as not to compete with the ladies—and wine—I should seek out Giorgio, the third wine steward, for the best recommendations if I planned to entertain.

By the time the mage apologized that he really must move on and attend to a few more acquaintances, my head swam with trivia. Either Orviene was the most skilled deceiver in Sabria or he was a genial, self-important, silvertongued gadfly, who truly believed that his most critical decisions each day were which coat and scent to wear as he monitored the queen's wards and charms. I was entirely confused.

"Many thanks for the introduction, damoselle," I said when, to my delight, I encountered Maura at the refreshment table. "Not so fearsome after all."

She smiled sagely. "I told you—"

"Excuse me, damoselle." Ilario, appearing from nowhere, snatched my arm, and dragged me away. "Come, come, Portier. No time for self-indulgence. Important business awaits."

Quivering like a captive bird, he urged me insistently toward the doorway, snatching the cup from my hand and shoving it at the first person we passed, a startled Mage Orviene. "Ah, sir mage! I do hope you and your colleagues will grace us with your participation in my Grand Exposition. My private secretary here will be handling the arrangements. But excuse us; we've urgent business waiting."

"Tell me, Chevalier, have you seen Adept Fedrigo today?" Orviene called after us. "Three days he's missed an important tutorial. I know you often preempt his time for small projects. . . ."

"Not for aeons," said Ilario, whisking me into the passage and around the corner before Orviene's question had faded.

"It's the *Destinne*," he burst out the moment his ornately carved door slammed behind us. His earrings and jeweled bracelets jangled as he hurried across the thick carpet to shut the paned garden doors. "She is scheduled to sail on the morning tide, day after tomorrow. Her captain just informed Antonia. His first officer, the other fellow who was there, is some grandnephew's cousin's eldest boy or something like."

"The exploration voyage?" I struggled to switch my thinking away from spinning gauds and unexpected mages.

"Don't you see? You told me to listen for sudden changes. The sailing date's been moved up by more than a month." Ilario threw his hands in the air as if expecting me to congratulate him.

"I'm sure there's good reason for the change. The tides . . ."

"But, Portier, it *had* been scheduled for the twenty-fifth day of Cinq."

My heart stuttered. "Prince Desmond's deathday. The anniversary." Our deadline.

Ilario lapped the room with his long strides, his brow drawn up in a knot. "Philippe chose that date apurpose, as he's dedicated the voyage to Desmond, you see, to honor the child and see him through Ixtador. Now something's changed and the *Destinne* sails early."

"The king will insist on being at the docks to send her off," I said. "Out in the open where there will be a thousand places to lurk and a thousand times a thousand places for spell-traps to be hidden. A perfect place for a public murder."

"So I was right that this was important?"

"Saints and angels, yes. You must play that game of stratagems with Philippe tonight. Put him on his guard. And whatever you need do to arrange it, Dante and I must be near the king that day."

Scarce more than a day. Too little time to send sorcerers to detect spell-traps. Too few courrets remaining in the world for them to use. This was too soon. We didn't know enough.

CHAPTER NINE

On my way to apprise Dante of the new threat, I devised an excuse to stop in at the palace steward's office. The steward's third secretary, Henri de Sain, had been a friendly sort and had invited me to return if I needed anything. I needed information.

I found the harassed secretary jotting notes in his ledger book about a large, ill-smelling crate at his feet. "It's the dung," he said, when I slapped a kerchief to my nose. "Rare mushrooms growing in a crate full of dung. As if we didn't have enough trouble with this business of the *Destinne*..."

In fact, the steward's office was in an uproar, taxed with hasty arrangements for honor guards, musicians, a viewing stand, a celebratory feast with an invocation from the High Tetrarch, a smooth-tongued diplomat to coax the prefects of the Camarilla to attend in a show of unity, and little more than a day to do it all. But nothing in the reports of the changed sailing enlightened me.

"By the way," said Henri, as I rose to leave, "you may not need my tailor's service after all. Not an hour ago, we received a box from a tailor in Margeroux and sent it on to your apartment."

From Margeroux . . . The arrow and spyglass! I hadn't thought I could feel *more* urgency. Without so much as a thank-you, I bolted.

"How can a captain change the sailing day on his own?" With his skilled left hand, Dante unraveled the last knot binding the canvas-wrapped box from Margeroux. He'd set himself and the bundle on the floor at the center of his circumoccule immediately on my arrival.

"The captain holds full authority on his ship," I said. "Not even the king can gainsay him. The steward's secretary says the crew was near mutiny at sailing on a prince's deathday."

My cousin had sapped his own authority in the first year of his reign, issuing a declaration that disenfranchised the Camarilla in maritime matters. Until Philippe's pronouncement, the Camarilla had required every vessel to carry a mage, who could overrule a captain's decision at a whim. To mollify the prefects, enraged at their loss of influence, Philippe had decreed that neither temple nor civil officials could overrule a ship captain, either.

I helped myself to wine from the pitcher on a low bench. Dante's apartments had been transformed in the past two days. The heavy draperies and excess furnishings had been removed. Two chairs, one long couch, and one small table remained in front of the tall east windows, while his required cupboards and worktables had been installed about the rest of the room. A variety of implements had been tossed on the worktables alongside a clutter of boxes and bins.

"Your king's a fool if he goes to the docks," said the mage. "Let the ship sail and make his prayers at home if he must."

Dante had heeded my news of the *Destinne*'s new launch with only half his attention, clearly more interested in the artifacts of the first assassination attempt than in anything we might do to prevent a second. He had responded to my congratulations on his "salon debut" with a shrug. "I assumed you'd control Lord Fool's reaction."

Even my report of Ophelie's death and her prisoning in the crypt had elicited few questions. My eager offering of her broken manacle had prompted a promise to "look into it" when he'd more time. Indeed, I had not pushed. Our first priority must be to protect Philippe.

"Kings are not so easily dissuaded," I said. "Especially warrior kings turned natural philosophers, who have staked their kingdom's prosperity on voyages such as this. Surely, if we can locate the threat, you can do something to protect him."

He didn't bother to answer, but yanked the thin rope loose from the dusty canvas. I needed to engage him. "I've a courret."

That caused him to look up even as the wrapping fell away to expose a flat leather case near as long as my arm. "Indeed? And how would a librarian come by such a rarity? Not a mage living knows how to make a wardstone."

I squirmed under his stare, green as jade and hot as a smith's furnace. "It's borrowed."

"Daemonfire, you've stolen it!" Pure astonishment erased the wariness and suspicion he wore like a temple dancer's mask. "*You*—that I thought might be the first honest man I've ever met."

"I did *not* steal it," I said, exasperated that we'd wandered so easily from the needs of the hour, confounded again that I could be so easily read. "I found it in a crate of texts we brought from a ruin in Xarles two years ago. The courret was likely the only decent thing to come out of that house. The Mondragoni were—"

No. Better not to speak of them, though they had been on my mind since the inception of this enterprise.

But Dante's hand had fallen still. "*What* were they?"

Ixtador's Gates, the man's ears must be keener than a hawk's to hear what lingered unspoken on a man's tongue. "Necromancers," I said. "Leeches. Daemonists. Torturers. A blood family that was everything foul and unholy. Some say their overreaching fired the Blood Wars. The few of them not wiped out in the wars were beheaded after, and none have ever disputed the rightness of it."

"Ah." He twisted the brass key I'd given him to unlock

the leather case. The latch clicked. "I'd give a deal to see those texts—if I'm to make a show of deadraising. Orviene and Gaetana may not have the talent they think, but they'll not be easily deceived."

I pulled out my journal, my hand itching for my pen. I'd only plummet to hand, but I could ink the reminder later: *Bring Dante the Mondragon texts*.

Puzzled, I stared at the open page and the words already taking shape. I had no intention of fetching the Mondragon books.

I glanced up. Dante's eyes had fixed on the case, but his hand had stilled.

"Stop this immediately, Master." I slammed my journal onto the worktable before fury—or fear—crumpled it.

Dante hungered for knowledge as the poor hunger for evidence of the god. And because providing access to the filthiest underside of our art was the last thing I would do for anyone, friend or foe, I knew for certain this time that the compulsion I felt was entirely unnatural. No one should be able to influence a man so . . . directly.

"I don't know what spell you've worked on me, Master Dante, but you will stop it now. Tell me what you want. Tell me why. And when I make my own choice, yes or no, argue with me if you will, but with honest words, not sorcery. If you persist in this, our partnership is ended."

"I've told you what I want and why. So will you bring me these Mondragon texts or will we argue it?" Stubborn. Prideful. Contemptuous. The manners of a badger, as Ilario had said.

Streaming sunlight transformed the circumoccule's glassy surface into a ring of amber encircling the mage. With a pair of locking forceps, he lifted the bloodstained arrow from its nest of Lady Susanna's worn silks and laid it on the floor beside his staff. The spyglass remained snugged in its wrappings. He closed the case and set it outside the circle.

I gripped my convictions tightly. "Fortunately, in this matter, I've no choice. The Mondragon scripts are locked in the Seravain vault. And do not *will* me to break the locks. The texts are encrypted and entirely unreadable. I kept them . . ." I could not say why I'd kept them, save that destroying works of such antiquity did not come easy to me. Kajetan, my mentor, the chancellor of the collegia, and a prefect of the Camarilla, had supported my judgment.

I wasn't sure Dante heard me. Hunched over where he could see it closely, he nudged the arrow with the forceps once, then again and again, examining its length with each rotation.

The hour ticked away in silence. I waited as long as I could bear before curiosity trumped anger. "Dante, tell me what you're—"

"Deeping fires!" Dante slammed his implement to the floor. "When did you transform into a babbling idiot like the peacock? Have you no discipline? No patience? No wonder you're incapable of spellwork."

I did not rise to the insult. "What do you see, Master?"

"What does your *borrowed* courret tell you?"

I'd not even thought of it. Which meant . . . The silver pebble I pulled from my waist pocket was as cold as the first day of Estar on Journia's highest peak. A poisoned arrow less than two metres distant should have it scorching. "It's telling me nothing."

"Step inside the circumoccule." He pulled a flask from his pocket and dribbled its contents in a small oval close around the arrow. "And bring a willow wand with you, one with a forked end. There's a basket of them over there." He gestured vaguely in the direction of the worktables.

By the time I found the basket and rummaged through the fifty or so slender branches to find what he wanted, the painted oval had dried to brown.

"Well come along. If you want to *know*."

I stepped across the amber ring of the circumoccule and promptly dropped the courret. The wardstone clattered to the floor and rolled toward Dante. It had near burnt a hole in my palm. "Gates of Heaven!"

"One needs a secure enclosure to work on dangerous matters," he said, nudging the silver pebble in my direction. "This circumoccule suffices. The painted boundary merely isolates the object of our study from other objects, enchanted or otherwise. As we've no idea of its dangers, you'd best use the branch to touch the arrow. Willow, simple and known, will disturb its keirna far less than a finger attached to a human person, especially one who disciplines his spirit no better than a bumpkin child."

Leaving the courret where it lay, I knelt facing Dante, the arrow and its enclosing strip of paint between us, the forked end of the willow wand wedged snugly about the arrow shaft. The mage touched the joined arrow and wand with his staff and closed his eyes, visibly retreating into that state of profound stillness I had witnessed in his bed-chamber two days before. I didn't need him to tell me to close my eyes as well.

"Quiet your spirit," he said after a moment. "Naught can reflect on a turbulent sea. Calm it."

I tried. Fear—or excitement—at the revelations to come hollowed my belly. The day's urgencies could not be dismissed by merely willing it so. I shifted position. Stretched my neck and shoulders. Breathed deep. Yet I saw naught but blackness.

Determined not to miss what he would teach me, I accepted Dante's command as literal instruction. I imagined my internal landscape as the roiling ocean beyond the shores of Tallemant, and my will as the finger of the Creator at the dawn of the world. I calmed each wave, smoothed each ripple, stilled its unsettled surface until my mind's slate gleamed black as obsidian.

Against the shining blackness, a font of deep, healthy green surged upward . . . quickly overlaid with wedges of brilliant yellow and blue, angled sharp as the arrow point itself, and a series of brown marks like the crosshatching motifs on old pottery, save for an unpleasing irregularity. From the base of the rune, as I thought of the display, pooled an inky black splotch that stretched into a long, straight line twined with bruised purple. A faint waved line appeared below it.

"The keirna—this pattern you see writ in shapes and colors—tells us that this is an implement of death, precisely made from living wood, steel, and poison." Dante spoke softly, as if sharper words might jar our tenuous connection. "Splintered now—see the irregularity of the hatching—but made to fly . . . straight . . . to penetrate . . ."

A very long while passed and I thought perhaps to see no more. But then, outside my head, the mage expelled a great sigh of effort, while inside, a sparkling net of white scored the darkness and enclosed the colored marks, binding, containing, masking its entirety.

". . . everything."

After a moment of quiet, I felt the shift of limbs clothed in fabric and leather and a release as Dante dissolved the bond between us. The pattern vanished. Wood scraped softly on wood.

When I opened my eyes, Dante sat cross-legged on the floor, the carved staff across his lap. He was staring puzzled at the arrow, which had changed neither its position nor its rusty tale of a dead horse and a lucky king and the twisting yank of whoever had withdrawn it from its victim.

I waited, confident the mage would tell me what bothered him so, for I had a sudden inspiration that sharing this marvel had not been his original intent, but an apology for his brutish attempt to manipulate me, offered in the only coin he knew. He would always prefer to investigate magic's mysteries alone.

"They were overeager, our assassins," he said at last. "That's all I can calculate. So determined to cast blame on Her Gullible Majesty that they concocted this foolery of guard captains and wrestling matches. Or perhaps that whole complication was naught but coincidence, and your guard captain the unluckiest of men."

Penetrate everything. "You're saying the arrow would have penetrated the king's armor no matter what, so there was no point in getting him out of it."

In one startling motion, he picked up the arrow and slammed it to the mahogany plank beside him. The impact left the stained head buried in the wood and a magical residue stinging my eyes like blown sand.

"This arrow would penetrate a marble slab," he said. "An iron cliff."

Stunned, I could not budge my gaze from the quivering shaft protruding from the floor. Yet my mind raced. I did not believe in coincidence. "Perhaps casting blame on the queen was never the end, but a means—a confusion to embroil an investigator in domestic argument, masking the true perpetrators."

"Or perhaps the murderous wife did not trust her mages to do what they promised," said Dante, dry as the deserts of Aroth. "The wrestling ploy marked the game as amateur."

"No amateur worked transference or enspelled an arrow to penetrate iron." What was this protective instinct already so plain in Philippe and Ilario where Eugenie de Sylvae was concerned? I'd need to do better. Philippe was relying on me to be thorough and objective.

The mage, distracted, acknowledged my point with head and hand. He closed his eyes and knotted his brow, not quiet this time, but tapping his fingers on his staff. After only a few moments, he launched the staff across the room, growling in frustration.

"There's something more here," he said, as staff and a stack of boxes clattered on the floor. "Keirna tells a story, and the story of this arrow seems clear. Only the human conspiracy surrounding it tangles our minds. Yet I've this notion . . . Some piece of the pattern is missing. If I'd studied a hundred poisoned arrows launched at kings, I might know better what to look for."

"I'll find out what more I can about that day," I said, retrieving my courret and stepping quickly outside the circumoccule before the silver pebble set my pocket afire. "But the day after tomorrow looms much larger just now. You *will* come to the docks."

"If I must." Dante dragged his horrid right hand out of his tunic and crossed his arms atop his knees, glaring at the arrow as if it had thwarted him apurpose. "I'll need those texts, you know. With some work, I can likely break the ciphers. If I'm to tease death and wickedness . . ."

He must work with them. My mind completed his assertion, as he knew it would. I pretended not to hear. I chose to go in search of Calvino de Santo, former captain of His

Majesty's personal guard, condemned to serve his former underlings for his failure in judgment. Perhaps *he* would answer my questions.

MY FIRST STOP IN MY search for the disgraced soldier was a cluttered temple guardpost. Its sole occupant, a craggy-faced veteran with red hair and huge feet, was quite willing to recommend where a newcomer to Merona could get the best view of the king and the launch of the *Destinne*. Bored and alone in his watch, the soldier was easily coaxed into a lengthy discussion of the difficulties of protecting a monarch who insisted on mingling with his subjects.

"Of course, I've heard the closest to death the king's come in years occurred last year among his own guards," I said, as if I didn't know what Guardsman Veryl's red livery signified. I perched on a stool, watching him light the lamps in the sooty corners of the guardroom. The place smelled of cleaning oil, musty boots, and the spreading lawn of the temple minor beyond the open door. "Heard a guardsman near killed him."

The soldier's back stiffened, and his overlarge lower lip pooched out even farther from his red beard. "'Tweren't no fault of the guards. Nor even the cap'n's, though he's paid the price and will do till he passes the Veil."

"He's still alive? After betraying the king? I'd have wagered a year's pay the hangman had dropped him into the Souleater's maw long since." I was becoming well practiced at disingenuous surprise.

Veryl pulled a cloth-wrapped bundle from a leather pocket and extracted a slab of coarse bread spread thickly with nettle cheese and olive paste. "Nawp, you'll see the cap'n round all the posts here, wiping floors or hauling coal." He nodded to the filled scuttle beside the brazier. "He's forbid to speak to us, though we oft hear him crying out in the night. Pity. He was a decent officer got led down the path by—" He bit off a large chunk of the pasty bread and stuffed the rest back into its wrapping. "I'd best be off now. I've rounds to make."

"Sorry to delay you." I jumped up, wishing I dared push

harder. But I couldn't afford to be remarked. "It's just . . . I thought I'd feel safer inside Castelle Escalon's walls than out in the countryside. But rumors of scarred assassins with no blood left in them get a man's mind working, especially when his blood skills fall short."

Veryl's gaze darted to my marked hand. As he hitched the leather pocket over his shoulder, he jutted his thick jaw toward the open door, as if it represented all of the wide world. "I was on the practice field that day, but never saw aught for myself. Just hunted the bowman and heard the rumors like everyone else. The fellow what took that shot was carried off and burnt so fast, naught but a few ever saw his body, and they wouldn't talk about it. But if I wore such a mark on my hand as you do, I'd keep close to my lord, no matter he's a fool, and not wander the palace nor city nor dockside at night. Just my thought on it."

That's the way life had been during the Blood Wars. Hired rogues lurking in the dark places, ready to snatch those fool enough to walk out alone. Anyone remotely kin to a blood family stalked and whisked away at the first misstep, never to be seen again. And now we were marked.

I laid fist to breast and inclined my back in respect. "Divine grace, guardsman, and angels companion all who protect Sabria and my lords and such poor accounts as me."

Veryl shouldered a halberd and grunted his own farewell blessing. As he marched into the night, I pulled out my journal and reviewed my sketches of Castelle Escalon's geography. I would visit the guardposts one by one until I found Calvino de Santo.

Left skitterish by the guardsman's warning, I hurried through the darkening alleyways with an extra urgency in my steps.

THE SEVENTH POST I VISITED, a brightly lit room off the wall walk near the postern, resounded with boisterous invocation of those saints and daemons who chart the fall of dice. The middle-night watch bells had just rung. Uncertain at confronting more guardsmen with the same false story, wishing I'd brought my own lantern, and feeling an increasing burden of futility, I held back in the dark courtyard below, uncomfortable in a night that seemed to twine itself about my limbs like a sneaking cat.

"Sante Calvino!" shouted a thick-tongued figure who appeared in the lit doorway. "This butt's gone dry! Do we shrivel of thirst, our wives'll take rakes to your traitorous hide."

I near cracked my head on the brick wall, startled when a dark figure darted from behind a pile of emptied crates and casks piled in a corner of the yard and vanished into the base of the tower. The man soon reappeared rolling an ale cask. As the heavy butt rumbled up the ramp to the wall walk and the tower room, all I could note was that he was a big, bearded man of dark complexion.

The arrival of a full cask was greeted with cheers, whoops, and no few references to its handler's "holiness" and "exemplary leadership." The man soon reappeared, rolling an empty cask down the ramp. Each time the butt insisted upon wedging itself in the crooks of the wall, he jarred it loose with a violent kick. Though spared the traitor's doom of headsman or hangman, a proud soldier and once-trusted captain could find such base servitude naught but torment. What kept such a man from slamming his head into a wall?

He shoved the emptied cask into the corner, threatening to topple the entire stack, then retreated into the shadows whence he'd come. As I crossed the yard, I made sure he could see me in what light fell from the tower room. "Calvino de Santo?"

"I'm bound by law to warn thee: Royal judgment forbids me speak to any man of arms, any squire, any woman, child, or servant, or any who's weak-minded or foolish." Bitterness as thick as old honey flowed from the shadows.

"I am none of those. Nor am I here to shame you, nor to condemn or defend your past actions. Rather, I am a servant of Sabria tasked to find answers to certain questions about the very incident that resulted in this heavy judgment. To fulfill my charge, I call upon what core of honor caused you to devote your life's service to the Guard Royale, and what desire you might harbor to expose the deeper truth of that terrible event."

A harsh laugh accompanied the big man to the edge of the shadow. What tale his filthy slops, unwashed skin, ragged hair, and bleak eyes began, his half-cropped ears must complete. The hideous scars named him a convicted dupe to an unconvicted treacher, condemned to unending humiliation in the only employment that would ever be open to him.

"What gives you to think honor or truth mean aught to me, servant of Sabria?"

To avoid a glib answer required careful consideration. "You are alive. That fact speaks of inner strength. It speaks of a history and character that convinced your king your failings were in judgment, not loyalty, at a time when no other witness would speak for you."

His glare weighed on my shoulders like an iron yoke. When he retreated into shadow again, I followed, but assumed I'd lost my gamble that honesty might outweigh contrivance. I was wrong.

"I told Vernase-Ruggiere everything I knew," he said, in earnest pain. "Fifty times, I told him. I answered everything he asked me, and never did I waver from my story, not when he showed me the headsman's ax and told me it was too good for me, not when he let me hear him order gallows built. Not during that ruination of a trial, nor after, when he brought in the butcher . . . Shite!"

"But you were terrified and angry, disbelieving and confused—as any man would be. Now, months have passed, and you've had time to think. You've gone over it all a thousand times. Surely something has revealed itself to you—a word . . . a look . . . a detail."

When he did not deny it right away, I knew I'd lanced the proper vein.

My eyes could pick out his shape now. He had slumped to the ground, his back to the wall. I crouched low and dropped my voice. "The events set in motion that day have not yet been graven in history, despite what hard experience tells you. I cannot—*will* not—drive you with unsubstantial hopes, but surely truth cannot hurt you more than this."

"You know naught of hard experience. Why do you roust a dogsbody when those as might tell all remain unquestioned? I'm forbid to speak, forbid to say who it was suggested I wrestle the king that day. But I hear enough to know who sits on silk cushions and eats fresh figs and who hides protected behind her skirts. Not my wife, who's disowned me and gone back to her parents. Not my children, who will ne'er again in this world hear my name nor speak it. Not the poor stupid wretch whose blood got stolen by devils, nor any of those *he* cared for."

His fury might be justifiable indignation or the sour dregs of failed conspiracy, but his meaning lay clear. "You *knew* him! The mule who lofted that cursed arrow. By the Ten Gates, man, who was he? I'll swear—" What could I offer for such a prize? My cousin had granted me no power of pardon and no purse full enough to salve the wounds of this man's disgrace. But perhaps I could ease his fears.

"I am partnered with a very powerful man, Captain. He bears no loyalty to those you blame and is joined with me to see this truth uncovered. We can do naught for the dead man, save name him with pity in our prayers. But I promise you, the two of us shall stand between those you would protect and those whose wrath you fear."

I left it there and waited while he sounded my words as I had sounded his.

"You trust this other?"

If I hoped to gain de Santo's trust, I must not delay an answer. Thus I spilled the first words that flitted into mind. "He has trusted me with what he values most, and he knows my own shame, yet treats me as an honest man. Our safety and our pride are bound up with each other's secrets."

"Naught of evil will come down on the mule's family or mine?"

"No sorcerer of the Camarilla, no adept, no acolyte, no blood-marked man or woman will learn that you spoke this name unless you give me leave. With every resource I can muster, I will see to his family's sustenance and your family's as well. I give you my hand on it."

"His name was Gruchin." Though he ignored my proffered hand, he sounded relieved to share what he knew. "At first I didn't recognize him; he was so changed. When I saw the assassin was a mule, I kept everyone away, so none could be harmed by whatever spells or corruption might linger on him. Thus no one else saw him to recognize." De Santo leaned forward, knees drawn up, hands covering his mutilated ears. "I've quarters in the barracks, but I've no peace when I'm with other men. I'd rather stay out here. But the nights get long, and I don't sleep well . . . and I see him every night."

"In your dreams."

He near choked on a barbed laugh. "Dreaming, I see him. Waking, I see him. I see him in alleys, in courtyards, on the walls, in the trees, inside my eyelids. That bloodless, battered wreck of a face was the last I saw that wasn't calling me traitor, and now he'll not leave me be. Gruchin was an expert bowman, but a sniveling sort of fellow. Always complaining. Always insisting I promote him. It was well after I took him on that I discovered he was of the blood—some laggard of a family mostly died out. One night he was in his cups and starts whining about his ill luck and how he had tried to be a mage, but got booted out of Seravain. Claimed he'd played adept to the queen's mage, but only—"

"To Orviene?"

"Nay, the woman mage. But she'd dismissed him. Accused him of leeching. *Him*." Another despairing laugh. "Not a day after Gruchin told me this, he started with the shakes. Soon he couldn't hit a cliff from ten paces. Within a month I had dismissed him, too, and never gave him another thought. It's only fit we spend our nights together now."

"And his family?"

"He'd a wife in Riverside and a girl child same age as mine. I think of her . . . the little one . . . and wonder . . . Great Kingfather of us all, what if the devil took her, too?"

His voice broke, and I rose to go, thankful for the night

and shadows that gave him a measure of privacy, if not comfort. Yet I needed an answer to one more question. "You told Michel de Vernase that the mule—Gruchin— ran away, then came back to retrieve a dropped spyglass, and one of your men killed him as he ran off again. Did Gruchin do anything else with the glass? Work magic . . . ?"

"He never ran. Hrogar said Gruchin *walked* away to pick up the glass, then came back and stood there. Hrogar flung his ax and hit the vein in his thigh. As if— Souleater's fire, he wasn't two metres away and just stood there. Hrogar, poor sod, mostly dead himself, couldn't have hit anyone running."

Such a difference to hear the exact story, knowing of Ophelie. Had Gruchin, too, preferred death to infamy? But then . . . he'd already lofted the spelled arrow. What further infamy awaited? Was it more bleeding he feared? Or the glass? "Where did you find the spyglass?"

"Had to pry it from Gruchin's hand."

So Gruchin hadn't intended to hide it or dispose of it or even to use it. That made no sense. "Tell me, did you look through it?"

"Aye," he said harshly. "A man does, doesn't he? As if it might tell him something."

"But you didn't see anything . . . unusual?"

"Naught but Gruchin laying there dead, and he's naught but bones and skin, looking back at me with eyes sunk into his skull. In the two years since I'd sacked him, I'd never asked what became of him. My own soldier. I'd never asked if his family was eating. The king sent Michel de Vernase to clean up the mess, and I gave him the glass along with everything else and told him all I learned from them as saw anything. Then the whoreson *arrested* me."

"And no one's ever come asking you about it since then?"

"None. By every saint and daemon, I'd see them all strung up and bled like pigs." He buried his head in his arms, muffling a roar of anguish.

"Divine grace, Calvino," I said softly, leaving him to his misery. "I'll do what I can for you."

Mind reeling with thoughts of desperate mules and unfathomable motives, I retraced my route, too far from any familiar venue to risk a shortcut. My boots rang on the cobbled paths and bounced off the courtyard walls, far too loud. The deserted storehouses and bakehouses looked different from this direction. Bigger. Darker. And the air in the cramped alleys felt dank and chill as if Desen's month yet lingered there from wintertide.

I did not believe in ghost hauntings. No spirit, no incorporeal being swathed in mist, wandered the demesne of the living after the heart ceased its beating. I believed the Veil a barrier of iron, not silk. Whatever happened after a person's final breath was beyond our knowing, unless the spyglass could penetrate that barrier to show us truth. . . .

From the night-filled alleys and courtyards behind me rose a wild, despairing, terrified howl that echoed from the storehouses, barracks, and corner towers. I broke into a run and squeezed my eyes to a slit. I didn't want to see what made Calvino de Santo wail.

CHAPTER TEN

The moment I arrived at his apartments the next morning, Ilario whisked me off on a round of calls: the chambers of the chancellor, the king's appointment secretary, the current captain of the Guard Royale, and ten other untitled dignitaries. "I've a plan for tomorrow," he said. "You'll see. You told me we should do something unexpected."

After an hour, my nerves felt shredded. While my lord nattered about racehorses, shared tea, inquired about relatives, slandered an errant bootmaker, and wheedled some concession about "placement" and "accompaniment" and "appropriate honors," I sat on cushioned benches and fidgeted. I needed to tell Dante of my encounter with de Santo. Some crumb or tidbit in my talk with the ruined guard captain taunted me with overlooked importance, and I could not grasp it. Dante's acid reason might.

As we returned from our morning's excursions, I slipped over to the mages' passage. Dante was not in his chambers, so I tore a transcript of Calvino de Santo's testimony from my journal and stuffed it in his warded satchel. I hoped he could pick up the thread that escaped me.

"Philippe agreed to be on his guard tomorrow," Ilario said when I rejoined him in his apartments. He fluffed the lace of his third change of attire since breakfast. "But he offered no assistance with our placement for the launch. Honestly, the man has no patience with me even at a game table where he is sure to win. You'd think we stood at Carabangor itself, he takes the cursed play so seriously."

"And the girl . . . the news of Michel . . . of the crypt? What did he say when you told him?"

"First he wiped out my entire line of warriors, both tetrarchs, and my queen. I do hate it when he takes both tetrarchs, as I think they are the most exquisite pieces. . . ."

"Lord, what did he *say*?"

"He said those responsible would pay dearly, and that we—the three of us—should continue. Truly, Portier, I thought he would snatch me up and toss me into the box with the game pieces!"

Ilario's reference to Carabangor described no trivial testiness on Philippe's part. The costly victory at the desert city, ending eighteen years of barbaric incursions from Kadr, stood as Philippe's first great achievement as sovereign. It was friends and good soldiers fallen at Carabangor that the spyglass had shown him wandering in an arid wasteland—lost, terrified, and despairing.

"But after our game"—Ilario leaned close, as if spies might have embedded themselves among the brocade doublets, satin cloaks, and silk shirts stuffing his wardrobe room—"he wanted to view the cell in the crypt. Portier, it was clean! No chains. No filth. No chair."

"You're sure it was the same?" Of course, he would be sure. Yet another twist tightened my knotted gut. "And Soren's tomb?"

Had the light in the wardrobe room been better, I might have been surer of the flush that colored Ilario's cheeks. "The display was . . . reduced. He did not note it. Come, Portier, don't look so grim. You'll ruin your complexion. Even Philippe said it was only to be expected that they'd clear out that wretched hole."

Yes, but the timing was so close. The queen and her sorceress knew someone had been poking about in the crypt. The king had commanded me to withhold judgment, but that was becoming more and more difficult.

"Now, dust yourself off. I've more calls to make."

I could glean no more specific report of their talk, nor could I break away to consult Dante, for Ilario fussed and threatened tantrums until I accompanied him. "If you insist on my accomplishing these tedious tasks, Portier, then the least you can do is provide me this smidge of assistance. My dislike of all serious business is well-known. I simply refuse to suffer frown lines and hair falling out all over. Besides, my gifts lie so completely in the area of gentle amusements and refined sport, it would be seen as simply greedy were I to strive for the same accomplishment in business or arms. But I'm finding that if I travel with a private secretary, I am instantly accorded a certain respect that allows serious conversation. So you see, it is your own fault. . . ."

Ilario's life flowed like a river flooded out of its banks—senseless, directionless, yet hugely impossible to divert. The afternoon visits took us to a hunchbacked dowager, whose town house smelled like soured apple parings, but boasted a sweeping view of the Ley and the bristling masts clustered at its wharves; then on to a black-bearded marqués, and the pink marble halls of the collegia botanica. As the sun slipped into the western sea, Ilario exchanged whispers and drank tiny cups of spiced tea with a Fassid silk merchant whose silk-draped display pavilion could have held my entire family estate.

I could not recall a single word of sense spoken in those hours. Yet at the end of the day, the fop set off to play another game of stratagems and inform the king of his arrangements. A party of important personages, representing all elements of the city's society, would accompany the king and queen to the launch of the *Destinne*. Rather than mounting a viewing platform on shore or anywhere Philippe and Eugenie might be expected, they would observe the launch from the private, well-secured pleasure barge of the Fassid silk merchant. It was a good scheme—perhaps enough to confound an assassin. Perhaps.

SCARLET AND GOLD PENNANTS WAFTED lazily against the sheeted silver of the dawn sky. The merry strains of shawm and sackbut danced across the water. As the broad river Ley rippled and slurped against piers and barges and muddy banks, cockboats ferried the last supplies to the caravel *Destinne,* lying so grand at her anchorage in the center of the channel.

As I clung to the rail of the *Swan*, Massimo Haile's elegantly outfitted pleasure barge, the sight of the *Destinne* struck hard upon my imagining. In less than an hour, it would set sail for the lands of diamond-crusted streets, trees taller than temples, cities ruled by naked women, or whatever truly lay across the seas beyond the Mouth of Hedron. Or perhaps her brave crew would sail the *Destinne* off the edge of the world and plummet into the Souleater's abyss, as some few yet believed. To embark on such a voyage on such a morning must surely drive mind and spirit to the highest reaches. Gracious saints, what I would give for such purpose and adventure. The king's evermore-sordid mystery had stripped the warmth and color from my already-sober world, leaving it danker and grayer yet.

Despite the early hour and the damp from overnight rain, the dockside lanes and merchants' wharves teemed with people. Bread and tea sellers cried their morning wares. Dockhands and carters, beset by swooping, screeching gulls, bawled at women and romping boys to clear a path. Viewing stands had been hastily constructed on the mud flats and draped in soggy buntings. A platform near the shore had been reserved for a crowd of scholars, displaying their distinctive regalia—brick red gowns and berets for the collegiae astronomica, sky blue for the collegiae mathematica, green gowns and black velvet tams for the collegiae botanica.

A circle of the Guard Royale kept the crowd well away from our mooring, and the slowly brightening morning revealed liveried archers atop the warehouses and pikemen posted at every door and alleyway. Massimo Haile's sturdy hirelings controlled access to the pleasure barge. They claimed to have manned their posts all through the night.

Even so, I had clutched my courret and traversed every centimetre of the gilded barge: the promenade along the elaborately carved, newly painted bulwarks; the open-air viewing galleries fore and aft; the lounging pavilion tucked behind billowing draperies in the center of the barge, and each of its cushioned couches, inlaid tables, and hanging lamps. I had even visited the cramped wine and food store beneath the exotic arch of the *Swan*'s tail, and the forward rowing banks where sixteen bare-chested Fassid of impressive physique stared insolently while stretching backs and arms or downing mugs of ale. My talisman had indicated no untoward risks anywhere aboard, yet I felt no easier. The attempt would come today, not six-and-forty days from now.

Cheers rolled through the crowd as trumpet blasts and the royal ensign heralded the king's arrival. As Philippe traversed the wharfside, he tossed memorials—buttons, coins, or somewhat—into the crowd, leaving a wake of scrabbling backsides. He dismounted at the cordoned-off foot of Haile's gangway, exchanging greetings with two dignitaries in starched ruffs and wide-brimmed hats. Haile's dockhands unloaded a number of tight-rolled bundles, wider than my armspan, from a waiting dray, then carried the linen rolls and the king's furled ensign up the ramp. Our rail-thin host and two fellow merchant princes wrapped in fur-lined mantles waited under a silken canopy on deck.

The cheering faded into scattered shouts and rolling murmurs, as a blue painted coach passed the guarded perimeter. First out, aided by a footman in the queen's livery, was Damoselle Maura. Rising from her curtsy, she spoke an earnest message to Philippe. Unease nibbled at my gut. Though too far away to hear her, I had no difficulty in reading the king's displeasure at her news. My cousin strode angrily up the gangway. Maura trailed after him alone, as the coach rolled away. Queen Eugenie had not come.

What I would not give for Dante's spell to hear across distances! What could possibly keep the queen from the launch of an expedition honoring her son's memory? What wicked magic had the villains planned for Ophelie to work this day, and who would work it in her stead? What role was planned for a captive Michel de Vernase?

Sainted ancestors! I massaged my aching jaw. My teeth had near ground themselves flat these past two days. No matter which way I turned, my back felt vulnerable. I returned to the small, forward gallery, tucked between the lounging pavilion and open hull where the rowers sat. The venue allowed me to observe ship, shore, and a sky now hazed with scudding clouds.

Two rows of elaborately carved posts, more than twice a man's height and topped with gold-and-red painted birds, formed a great rectangle at the center of the barge. From slender crossbeams hung garlands of flowers, the silken draperies that shielded Massimo Haile's lounging pavilion from the public eye, and the stretched canopies that protected his guests on the aft gallery from excess sun. The silk merchant's dockside crew stretched new spans of line even higher on the posts between the carved birds. To each taut span the dockhands lashed one of the linen rolls—celebration banners, I guessed.

A steward hoisted the king's black and silver stag above the *Swan*'s high curved tail. The ensign snapped sharply, near ripped from its mooring by a stray gust.

Ilario arrived with the guests of the queen's party—the black-bearded marqués, the hunchbacked dowager, and, to my astonishment, all three mages. Mage Orviene paused for a laughing conversation with a Fassid aide before mounting the gangway. Gaetana swept aboard with the other guests. Dante, his long hair plaited, his black brows and gaunt cheeks made more severe by a black tunic and deep blue gown, ascended the ramp alone. Both guests and crew kept their distance, which likely suited him very well.

Though immeasurably relieved to see Dante, I was not sure whether to be fearful or reassured at the presence of our two principal suspects. Yet I doubted their own hands would be soiled with this day's work. Once more I scanned every person on the barge, the ring of guards, the people lining the wharves, the dinghies and shallops that dotted the broad reaches of the river. Where would the attack commence? It *would* come; I was sure of it.

Deckhands hauled in the gangway. I forced myself to breathe.

The bargemaster barked orders from a small railed platform facing the oarsmen. *"Seiche mar!"* Rowers settled into position and grasped the oars. *"Disema!"* Deck boys dressed in red tunics and gold arm rings cast off the mooring lines. *"Kise fa!"* Sixteen oars raised as one. *"Kise diche!"* As one the sweeps dipped into the murky water. Smooth as its namesake, the *Swan* glided away from its berth above Merona's port and eased into the channel up-river, between the *Destinne* and the grim stone finger of Spindle Prison.

The rising wind shifted the furled banners and billowed the barge's filmy draperies and silken canopies. The king's ensign set up a steady whapping. I grabbed my narrow-brimmed hat to prevent it from making its own journey beyond the Mouth of Hedron.

"Slack water!" We'd not yet dropped anchor when the cry echoed through every bobbing boat, shallop, and skiff on the river. Another wave of raucous cheers and merry music swelled on shore. On board the caravel, copper-skinned seamen scrambled into the rigging, and more gathered at the *Destinne*'s bow and stern.

Philippe, Haile, Ilario, the marqués and marquesa gathered at the *Swan*'s stern rail, to watch a *Destinne* sea-man hoist Sabria's scarlet and gold. Guests crowded behind them on the grand gallery. A few, including two Fassid merchants and Maura, strung out along the star-board rail. I abandoned the chanting rowers and strolled toward Maura, thinking to find out why her mistress was not here.

"Sonjeur de Duplais." I swiveled. Gaetana had come up behind me, serenely sober, as if bleeding young girls for power had never occurred to her. Dante, sour faced, stood a few steps behind.

"Divine grace, Master Gaetana, Master Dante," I said, inclining my head. "Indeed a bright day." Yet the hazy sky was shading anything but fine at present. We'd see storms by afternoon.

"Dante, have you met Lord Ilario's secretary, Portier de Savin-Duplais?" asked the woman mage, extending a hand toward each of us. "Portier was our quite-competent librarian at the collegia. Knowledgeable as far as a layman can be." The barbed compliment reflected the sentiments of most at Seravain.

Dante's stare could have frosted flame. "I've doubts as to competence. But until yon female overseer finds me a proper servant, this knock-kneed craven's to fetch my books—assuming he can manage a task for a body with a *mind* attached." Ilario's current boisterous recitation of "The Lay of Hedron's Mouth" in the stern gallery would do naught to dispel Dante's scorn.

"Chevalier de Sylvae is a loyal supporter of our art," said Gaetana. "Her Majesty favors him."

A trumpet fanfare from Philippe's heralds made further conversation impossible. The stern anchor raised, the *Destinne*'s crew now hauled on their bow cable as if to draw the great ship all the way upstream to the Spindle by strength of their arms. But a shouted command loosed the spritsail, and the caravel began to come about. When the bow anchor lurched free, another scrap of sail high in the rigging was unfurled, and to the roar of Merona's delighted citizenry, the *Destinne* harnessed the quartering wind and rounded slowly into the Ley's current and the outgoing tide.

Gaetana beckoned Dante to resume their movement aft, toward the king's party. But as Dante passed between me and the furled banners, he swiveled suddenly and grabbed my neck. His iron hand shut off my breath. Green eyes blazing, he pressed me to the rail and snarled. "Do you think me deaf? I'll have no murmured resentments as I pass. Keep out of my sight until you are summoned, librarian. The stink of failure offends me."

A brutal twist and a powerful shove and I crashed to the deck, sliding headfirst toward the chanting rowers.

Chest burning, cheek scraping the polished planks, I was only vaguely aware of blaring trumpets.

From a corner of my watering eye, I glimpsed Haile's man haul on the lines. A cascade of painted linen unfurled from the bird-topped posts, first the king's own black and silver standard, then the gold-on-scarlet tree of Sabria, and lastly a new ensign—a sky blue field with a white ship, a golden sun, and the words HONOR and REMEMBER and a third word that might have been DESTINNE, only the banners' unfolding tails crackled and spat, and the world an arm's length above my head erupted into a blinding spray of white flame.

Chaos erupted in every quarter. Gluttonous flames swallowed the *Destinne*'s banners as if they had never been and raced along greased ropes and varnished crossbeams, quickly engulfing the next banner and the next, and licking at the billowing canopies.

Rolling, scrambling away from the fire, I tumbled over the edge of the gallery decking into the open hull, very nearly into a shocked oarsman's lap. My right hand sirened pain, as if sparks of molten iron had penetrated flesh and bone.

Bellowing oarsmen shot up from their benches, brushing frantically at skin and hair. A writhing, screaming few jumped into the river, while still others tried to slosh water over the bulwarks to douse the burgeoning fires. The bargemaster, whose platform had placed him directly in front of the forward-facing banner, lay draped over his handrail, unmoving, pitted skin smoking like a field of geysers. Heavenly angels . . . Philippe!

Eyes streaming, I strained to see the rear of the barge where I'd last seen my cousin, but billowing smoke and flame obscured the way. The whoresons who'd done this could not have found better tinder than the inked linen banners, the silken furnishings, and the *Swan*'s newly painted wood.

The oarsman nearest me twisted and danced in macabre torment, screaming and clawing at his face. I lurched upward and reached out to steady him, but the current and the changing tide caught the barge and swung it around drunkenly. We both staggered. His partner in the lead bank, a brawny fellow with a gold strap across his chest, shoved us aside and yelled, *"Seicha mar! Seicha mar!"*

A few men grabbed flapping oars and sat, though flames had burst out here and there like daemonic seeds scattered from a plowman's hand. I needed to move. But the back of my right hand had become a paralyzing agony, the raw wounds smoking . . . great Heaven . . . as if I burned from the inside out.

As the lead oarsman yelled and the few at the sweeps took up a ragged rhythm, I ripped the cloth band from my hat, dipped it in the water, and wrapped it tightly about my hand. I wasn't going to be able to do anything if I started screaming, too. I needed to get aft . . . to the king . . . to Maura . . . Ilario . . . Dante.

Cradling my hand, I scrambled onto the gallery deck. Blistering heat, dense white smoke, and licking flame barred the promenades on either side of the lounging pavilion. The only way to make it aft was to forge straight through the pavilion itself. Greedy flames licked at the sagging roof canopy and gnawed at the support poles. I took a deep breath and charged in.

Impossible. The smoke was blinding; the walls ablaze. I tripped over a couch and crashed to the decking. A drifting ribbon of flaming silk settled on my sleeve.

Rolling to the side, I slapped at the fire and scrabbled forward, straining to recall the room's arrangement from my morning inspection. *Around the low tables, over a divan, shove the chair aside.*

New flames exploded before and behind. Searing, thundering, they drowned out the screams and wails that had guided me. Everyone on the barge could be dead for all I knew. *Father Creator, no air here.* My throat scorched; my eyes streamed and blurred. *Which way?*

Instinct clamored that my friends lay beyond the thickest battlements of white-hot flame. Near blind . . . panicked . . . I drove through the roaring wall. My feet stumbled on the aft steps. I scrabbled upward, and burst into the air, gasping and swatting at my smoldering hair.

The marqués and two deckboys were passing buckets of

water to Haile and his steward, battling the encroaching flames on the port side. The dowager, half her body seared like roasted meat, wailed piteously. Ilario, pale hair and fine garments blackened, had stretched his long body over her to shield her from fiery debris as the flames crept ever closer. His head jerked up and his eyes widened as a post and crossbeam crashed beside me. The blazing fountain catapulted me forward. I curled in a knot, my seared lungs fighting for air.

Calls for help from the starboard promenade spurred me to my feet again. I doused a cushion in the river and beat at a towering wall of flame, ever more frantic as the cries became screams of mortal pain and terror. I might as well have been trying to snuff the stars in a middle-night sky.

The barge lurched and wallowed. The horizon spun. My boots slipped and I crashed to the deck. Coughing, breathless, I clutched my wrapped hand to my breast and pressed my head to the planks. The flames flared higher, engulfing the entire center structure beam to beam. I was no hero who could defeat an inferno. The agonized cries became mindless bleats until the thunder of flames silenced them. *Please, saints and angels, let Maura . . . Philippe . . . Ilario . . . Dante . . . not be in there.*

Portier, get up! The stern voice of conscience lifted my head from the blistering deck, just as a wind gust cleared a hole in the heavy smoke. Philippe sat wedged against a bulwark, his head bleeding, a charred beam crushing his middle. An unknown man in tattered garments was attempting to shift it. I scrambled across the steaming deck. "Sire, are you well?"

"See to the others," mumbled Philippe, adding what strength he could muster as we hefted the beam and shoved it overboard. Wrapping his arms about his ribs, the king curled his head to his knees, coughing.

Another gust stirred the gray smoke. On the far side of the stern gallery, Orviene and Gaetana had laid out scraps of charred silk, a great deal of shattered glass, a palm-sized golden flask, a silver drinking cup, and a brass fitting from the ship. Using a rope, they had created a ritual enclosure about the particles and themselves. Gaetana knelt at one vertex of a triangle, the rope looped round her waist. Orviene stood at a second vertex, the rope wound about his arm. They had enlisted Maura, hair straggling, one shoulder bare and blistered, to support the third vertex of the enclosing triangle. I did not need to see Gaetana's grip on a string of rubies twined around her fingers or Orviene's focused concentration on the array to guess they had already infused a spell—something huge to require so elaborate a rite. The air crackled with more than fire.

Helpless rage consumed me. To charge into the middle of an ongoing ritual risked worse disaster. But Dante . . .

The mage, apparently unsinged, leaned against the stern rail between me and the other two, arms folded around his staff—doing nothing. Was he deaf? Blind?

"Dante!" I yelled. "The oarsmen are trapped. People are dying. The king is in *peril*."

I could not tell if he heard me over the thunderous fire. His dark brows shadowed his eyes at such a distance. But he did not move.

Another explosion ripped through the holocaust, and I threw myself atop Philippe, expecting a scourge of fire and splinters. But the droplets that spattered my head and back did not burn. Cold, wet, soothing; the spattering quickly became a gentle drumming, as enchantment riddled my innermost being, and the sky brought forth a deluge.

CHAPTER ELEVEN

Eight people died in the fire on the *Swan*: the two heralds, a botanist, one of the Fassid merchants, the bargemaster, and three oarsmen—one burned, two drowned. One rower was blinded by the explosion. The disfigured dowager was likely to die as well, sooner or later. Almost everyone suffered burns, many far worse than mine. The rain had saved our lives.

After the pleasure barge limped into port, King Philippe, the blood cleansed from his face, had proclaimed to the awestruck crowd that the Pantokrator himself had surely sent his blessed rain to douse the fires begun by a "faulty brazier" on Massimo Haile's vessel. The king reminded his subjects that the glory of the event must not be sullied by an accident that could happen on any common day. The *Destinne* and her noble crew were safely launched on their noble voyage, giving honor to Sabria and bearing the dead infant prince on his journey to Heaven.

Beloved and honored as Philippe had been since his defeat of Kadr—unlike the Blood Wars, the kind of wholesome conflict that creates heroes—he soon had his people cheering. He walked all the way up to Castelle Escalon, as if to show himself uninjured and unafraid. I suspected he had cracked ribs and could not bear the jostle of riding. Along the way he distributed another barrelful of memorial coins imprinted with his dead son's likeness on one side, and the words Honor, Remember, and Destinne scribed around a ship's emblem on the obverse.

It took no time at all for the rumors to begin—that the fire had been no accident, that the celebration banners had been enspelled with the white waxy substance known as *devil's firework*, that the queen's mages had worked terrible spells *before* the fire, and that the queen's absence meant— Some dared not complete their conclusion, but many others did, inside and outside the palace.

On the morning after the fire, a new chapbook showed up in Merona's markets—and in many a courtier's gloved hands. The story told of a Syan concubine who decided to burn her land's emperor to bring back the spirits of her former lovers. That afternoon, the queen's coach, transporting two of her ladies to the lace market, was battered by a barrage of rock-centered mudballs. Despite the crowded street, no witnesses to the incident could be found. If rumor and innuendo shadowed truth, the king would be able to stave off the hounds baying at his wife for very little longer.

Ilario summoned me to his apartment that evening. His barber had trimmed his scorched hair short, save for one fair lock that dangled over his right temple, hiding a raw red streak. Twirling an ivory-headed walking stick, he paced and fidgeted, entirely unlike himself, as we exchanged platitudes about the dreadful event.

"It is a grace the queen was not aboard the *Swan*," I said. Head muddled and stomach churning from the incessant pain of my hand, I offered this sentiment entirely without innuendo.

Ilario slammed his stick onto a table so hard, the maple cane broke away and flew across the room, shattering a mirror. "She fell ill!" he shouted, and launched the ivory elephant that remained in his hand clear through the open door and off his balcony. "For her to sail would have been torture."

"Certainly, Chevalier. Certainly." His vehemence shocked me out of my sleepless stupor.

"And everyone in Merona knows it is customary for the queen to supply celebration banners." Ilario's ferocious kick buckled the leg of a delicate chair that likely cost ten times my year's pay; then he snatched up a tasseled pillow and began ripping out its threads. "*Anyone* could have enspelled them. She herself stitched only the *Destinne* ensign. Others sewed and finished them."

Great Heaven! Grim certainty infused my heart, alongside sympathy and sorrow for both husband and brother.

"Perhaps . . ." Ilario's slender hands paused in their destructive agitation, and he made another circuit of his room. "Now Philippe has seen evidence of true sorcery, perhaps he will broaden his mind. Compromise. He and Michel forever scoffed at her requests for caelomancers or healers. That's why Geni took it on herself to find help when Desmond fell so ill. If some mages are corrupt and wicked, it is no fault of the magic . . . or of my sister."

"My lord, if you could persuade Her Majesty to allow us to question—"

"Don't ask it!" He swung his long body around. "By the sainted Reborn, she'll not do it for her husband; she's certainly not going to do it for me. Her household is her only pride, her only demesne. Deeds of honor that can further her family's progress through Ixtador must be her own. Not lent. Not granted by a husband. She will not yield control. And she will *not* be treated like a common thief."

Of all the prattle that had fallen from Ilario de Sylvae's lips in these past days, the sincerest and most sober were those that embraced his half sister. No matter his flighty ways, he cared deeply for her. And he was terribly afraid. Rightly so. No queen's crown or wedding vow was proof against a charge of treason. I did not point out how unlikely it was for Philippe to compromise with Eugenie about anything after this disaster. Had her husband been any but Philippe de Savin-Journia, she would already have been in custody. So might Ilario, as well. He had arranged our presence on the barge.

"Lord Ilario, look at me." I used the most commanding voice I could manage without splitting my skull.

He halted, startled, as if he'd already forgotten I was in the room.

"Tell me, lord chevalier, who prompted you to choose Massimo Haile's barge for the king's launch party?"

You'd have thought I'd just asked him why the Pantokrator created the world. "*You* did, Portier, or near enough. You said to do whatever I needed to keep the assassins off balance and ensure that you and the confounded Dante were near Philippe. No King of Sabria has ever graced a Fassid's barge, and no mage and no minor secretary have ever accompanied the king to any such event. You don't think Massimo—?"

The full import of my question struck him as a boot to the gut. He blanched and collapsed onto a silken divan that directly faced my own stool. "Merciful hosts . . . you think that *I* . . ."

"Certainly not. It's only I must have answers for the king." More ill by the moment, I could not answer further.

He peered closely at my face that felt as clammy as sweating cheese, then popped up from his seat. In moments he returned with restored composure, a small towel, and a vase stripped of its flowers.

"When I saw you burst from that hellish fire alive, I thought you must be one of the Saints Reborn, come to save us. Now you look as if we should cart you to the deadhouse." He dipped the towel in the vase and slopped the cool, wet thing over my head. "Go to bed, Portier. And think. If I want Philippe dead, and Geni and me hanged at Merona's gates, all I have to do is propose a game of stratagems and walk into his private study wearing a poison ring. His guards don't even search me anymore."

He tossed the emptied vase onto his silk divan, hauled me to my feet, and shoved me toward the door. "Philippe will never believe such scurrilous charges," he said, "especially now Orviene and Gaetana have been redeemed— and such a justification of Eugenie's wisdom *that* is. No, these events have been perpetrated by some rogue from Seravain. You must shift your inquiries there."

And so was *I* stymied, as well. For, indeed, our structure of ill-informed suppositions had collapsed the moment Orviene and Gaetana followed the cursed banners onto the *Swan* and raised a rainstorm. The queen might still be the enemy Philippe feared, but our only *magical* suspects had saved the king, not slain him.

ILARIO RETIRED TO HIS COUNTRY house for a few days to recover his spirits and grow out his hair, so he said, but insisted I stay behind and work on his scientific exposition. "I want it held on the Anniversary—to honor Prince Desmond as the launch was meant to do. Mayhap it will blot out the taint of this wickedness. Eugenie will be pleased. Philippe, too."

The Anniversary. Six-and-forty days away. Little more than a month to arrange a scientific and magical display "unequaled in this age." I could not even begin.

My attempts to address our more important business were equally futile. Plagued with persistent pain and nausea, a lingering cough from the smoke, and an internal storm of guilt and failure, I could neither follow the confusing trail of evidence nor devise any stratagem to further our investigation—assuming Philippe wished me to continue. Every hour I expected a summons and a dismissal.

The echoed screams of those dying on the *Swan* ruined what sleep my sickness allowed, and a pernicious dread grew in me every hour. On the third night from the fire, I huddled on the floor in the corner of my bedchamber, my head buried in my arms. A familiar, seductive inner voice insisted there was no use forcing myself to impossible tasks, no use striving to be something I was not, no use eating or drinking or sleeping or breathing. . . .

Nine years it had been since failure had so unraveled me, since the day I had killed my father in defense of my own life. On that occasion, illness, guilt, and despair had come near finishing what my father's knife had begun. Past, present, and future had faded to gray. My dreams of destiny had withered, replaced by blinding headaches and unfocused anxieties. A month it had been until I could speak my own name; two until I could engage in conversation; six until I could complete a simple task on my own; a year until I had relieved my mentor of his burden and resumed responsibility for my own life.

Not this time, I mumbled, as the sky lightened yet again. *You've sworn loyalty and perseverance to souls other than your own. If you cannot move forward, go back and start again.*

To begin, I drafted a letter to my solicitor, expressing a desire to locate the family of a disgraced guard captain and direct the paltry thread of my family allowance to its sustenance. It would be enough to stave off starvation. I sought out Verger Rinaldo and told him of a muddled "vision" of a family in danger, mentioning naught but Riverside and a girl child and a guardsman/father gone missing. He promised to investigate. If Gruchin's family were to be found, he would do it.

Then I returned to the more difficult task. The keys to Ophelie's torment and Michel de Vernase's fate must surely lie at Seravain. To travel there unremarked, I needed Dante's cooperation. Yet conscience demanded I tell him what I thought of a gifted man who could hear fellow humans suffer and die without so much as raising his hand. Such frankness would risk our partnership. But I could not stay silent.

Once resolved to the necessity, I shouldered my journal like a flimsy shield and pressed through the busy byways of the east wing. I had scarce lifted my hand to knock on the mage's door when it flew open. Dante yanked me inside by my belt.

"Gods, where have you been?" he said, before I could speak even one of my carefully rehearsed words. "I near fright the serving men out of their trousers every time they bring me a dinner tray. We need—" He grabbed the wrist of my bandaged hand. "Damn the vile creatures, are you burnt?"

With a grip kin to a mad dog's jaws, he dragged me to the sunny end of his apartment, shoved me roughly onto the couch, and kicked a stool into place so he could sit close. Fortunately, he took better care as he laid my hand on his lap and unwrapped the bandages.

"Stop," I said, pain scrambling my arguments. "There's no need—"

"*Never* bind a burn so tight. And *never* slather a burn with ointments like this. Burns need air. Joints need movement. Can you uncurl your fingers?"

"Somewhat. It's only— Aagh!" He had laid the back of my hand open to view, forcing my fingers out straight. The whole was swollen and seeping. Though smaller than warts, the fifteen or twenty angry wounds yet stung as if burning spikes had been driven through flesh and bone. My stomach heaved as had become its unfortunate habit. It was all I could do to hold back until he supplied a rag to catch the remnants of my breakfast.

Dante disposed of the foul mess, poured a slick, bitter potion down my throat, and took up exactly where he'd left off, wriggling each of my fingers in turn. "It's well that it hurts. You understand that much?" My sweat-beaded face must not have reassured him. "If the burn is too deep, it destroys the underlying nature of flesh—the very senses that give you pain or pleasure. The physicians washed your wounds with natron, as I told them?"

My left hand massaged my head, which prickled as if tiny brooms were sweeping away the cobwebs of fever and sleeplessness. "Natron . . . yes. *You* told them?"

"People assume that every mage knows healing." He jumped up and scrabbled through the paraphernalia on his worktable, returning with an amber flask and a wad of clean linen. "Unfortunately, the study of healing requires a patience I've only recently developed. At the time I had the chance to learn, I desired grander magic."

He dampened a square of linen and dabbed at the raw wounds. I strove for mental discipline, hoping to prevent further humiliation. One would think the particles had burned straight through my gut to the roots of my toenails.

"I can scarce distinguish bone from muscle or liver from heart," he said, "nor can I soothe so much as an itch out of mind, whether by conjury or practical wisdom." He patted all dry, then bound a length of fresh bandage loosely about each finger before rewrapping my whole hand in the same fashion. "Burns, though"—he snugged the trailing end of the bandage, then grimaced at his own scarred appendage—"burns I know. Now tell me, did we not judge these villains rightly? So very clever they are. I'd never have understood what they were up to had you not laid the very revelation in my lap. Well done." He jumped up and kicked the stool away in sheer exuberance.

Thrown completely out of mind, hand throbbing, stomach curdled at imagining a burn that could have caused so terrible a ruin as Dante's hand, I could not comprehend in the least what he was talking about. We had been entirely *wrong* about the mages.

Dante seemed to need no response from me. He circled the room, the fever of discovery propelling steps and speech.

"I'd never have thought you subtle enough to extract such secrets, but then I've no understanding of *talk*, as you've seen. Only the magic. An arrow that could penetrate iron, placed in the hands of an expert marksman. Caelomancy prepared in advance to douse a sudden conflagration."

Halfway through his second circuit of the room, he snatched up the flask, linens, and bandages and returned them to his worktable.

"So now, student, bend your mind to the villains' purpose. It's not just to lay suspicion on the lady queen—though her absence from the *Swan* fits that purpose like the popinjay fits his hose. That requires no such elaborate plotting. Nor can I think they were just looking to raise the reputation of sorcery, though Gaetana looked sour enough to gnaw her own arm when she heard the king speak of the 'Pantokrator's blessed gift of rain.' If His Majesty refuses to admit what saved him, then next time they might decide to actually kill the royal fool!"

My reviving faculties began to knit these rambling threads together. "You're saying they planned—they were not trying to kill Philippe at all!"

And then, of course, the revelation—the elusive mystery of Calvino de Santo's testimony—dropped into my own lap like an enchanted stone. Gruchin, the first mule, had been *an expert marksman.* He had aspired to be a sorcerer, but Gaetana had dismissed him from her service, accusing him of using transference. Yet she had not reported this offense. The threat of exposure and certain execution would ensure his silence about anything he'd seen or done . . . until the fool got drunk enough to babble about it to his captain. Only then did his accuracy with a bow begin to fail. And when de Santo dismissed him for his shaky hands, he had vanished with no one to notice save a wife and child. Gaetana . . . someone . . . had bled Gruchin for two years.

What if Gruchin's marksmanship had not truly failed, but had been only temporarily blocked? What if the mages had promised him redemption and healing if he placed the arrow exactly where they told him?

"Gruchin's arrow was *supposed* to miss," I said. "Supposed to penetrate the saddle and kill the horse and come ever so close to killing the king, making everyone believe that someone wanted the king dead—most likely his queen. Supposed to leave everyone afraid and suspicious. And then Orviene and Gaetana caused the fire on the *Swan,* but you believed—you knew—they intended all the while to bring on the rain to save Philippe."

Dante scooped up a flat box and several other items from the worktable and headed back toward me. "Gaetana is a calculating witch. She would hardly have come sailing with us without a way to undo whatever mischief they intended. Orviene is thick enough to go sailing in his own piss. It just took me damnably long to figure out the banners were the danger. I wasn't close enough to them until we stood talking to you, and I smelled the wax. If I'd discovered the truth sooner, I'd have found some less drastic way to warn you."

"You saved my life," I said, stupidly. And my eyes, a gift of no less value. Yet with eight dead souls screaming in my head, how could I thank him?

He tossed an open book aside and set the flat box, a ball of string, and a knife beside me on the couch. He didn't meet my gaze. "It has occurred to me I might need you to get me out of here someday. To vouch for my good purposes and all that."

"Too bad we couldn't have warned a few others, even if they were less useful to you."

Dante's face, body, and spirit froze. "Speak this accusation completely, Portier." His voice reverted to the soft, cool precision so much more menacing than heated fury. "And while you're about it, lay out the terms of our agreement. If you wish me to salvage every sorry dullwit who strays into the path of wicked sorcery, then state that right now. Or if you wish me to curry these mages' favor and allow myself to be drawn into their trusted circle, state *that*. But understand that I am not so talented as to do both."

"People were burning . . . dying. You did nothing."

"Great works of magic that thwart murderous nature—works that might shield a man from fire or pain or drowning—cannot be devised in a heartbeat like a mother's trick to divert a naughty child. And I claim no subtlety to tease men out of danger or in half a moment create an impregnable excuse to heave sixteen oarsmen overboard. You told me at the beginning that this was a dangerous undertaking. I thought you understood what that meant."

This naive misunderstanding was certainly the truth. I had aspired to service, to useful purpose, hoped to prove that an accident of birth need not condemn a man to a hollow life. Never had I imagined Philippe's charge would cause me to see a man's eyes seared to blindness or to hear a human mind disintegrate as fire consumed its living body. Perhaps I had allowed Dante's undeniable talents to impress me overmuch with confidence in his skills, and his enthusiasm for the hunt to induce me to forget that he despised his fellow men. Yet never could I have believed that the right course of my service must be to approve the choice Dante had made. What of simple mercy?

Furious with Dante, with myself, with circumstance that forced such choices, I could see naught but to go on. Allowing such crimes as had been done to Ophelie and Gruchin to continue was unthinkable, as well.

"Fair enough," I said, gritting my teeth. "Clearly I held

unreasonable expectations. Have the mages made over-
tures? Welcomed you into their secrets?"

"It has begun," he said, all his eager ferocity locked
away. "Gaetana informed me that certain members of the
queen's household were invited to the launch of the *Destinne* in company with the king. I assumed the arrangement was your work and agreed to come." As I had
demanded of him.

He strode to the window and threw open the casements.
"They have also asked if I would teach them how I worked
the little frippery at the lady's party. I refused. They'll ask
again."

"And is it both of them? You said Orviene is thick. I see
him as trivial."

"She leads. He follows. Whether he knows where he
goes or how, I cannot say."

The silence stretched. Questions, strategies, misunder-
standings swirled in my head, and I could not leave without addressing them.

The box he'd set beside me contained thirty or forty
small cloth bags filled with fragrant herbs. "What are
these?"

"I need them tied shut. It's a thing I can't do." Brittle
words; frigid. His maimed hand twitched, but he didn't
turn around.

I took up the task, more to give myself time to think
than to assist him. I had to gather the mouth of each bag
and grip it with my left hand, using my injured right to do
the tying—an awkward process that I could not accom-
plish without flexing my painful fingers. With every twinge,
I cursed him.

Yet, as the hour ticked away, whatever potion he had
used to bathe my wounds seemed to ease them. And I had
released my festering anger, no matter how unsatisfactory
the resolution. As a result, I was able to think more clearly
than at any time since the fire.

"This doesn't make sense," I said after a while. "Why
would Orviene and Gaetana work this weather marvel to
rescue the king, a wonder that could revive people's appreciation of sorcery, and then risk its association with the

worst blights of magical history—mules and transference?"

Dante snorted. "Gods, student, you are blind. Do you truly believe that collection of refuse they spread out on the deck drew the rain from the sky? The pattern was flimsy and absurd. No, the real caelomancy had already been worked and linked to a receptacle—some object they brought aboard. Not something picked up by chance to balance the magical elements. This enchantment was so huge and so complex, it required the strength of both mages to quicken it. I've never . . ." He tugged at his collar, a fretful move I'd come to think signaled uncertainty. "I am not skilled enough to dissect such spells as yet." His clipped words dripped scorn—for himself, not me.

I recalled Dante's still, focused posture in the stern of the *Swan*, as the fire raged. I had desired him to work some miracle to save the dying, because I had already tried and failed. Helpless, frightened, I had wanted him to pounce on the two mages and withhold a coming doom. He had not, because he believed their spellwork benign—as it had proved. He had been feeling, sensing, examining, using whatever was this talent that enabled him to see the very structure of spellwork, doing what I had engaged him to do.

"But no matter my incompetence." He turned slowly and settled himself on the window frame, staring at something far beyond his chamber, arms folded. "I'll swear on anything you care for that their gold flask drew forth the rain. The surge of power"— he closed his eyes as if to envision it again—"was as like the Camarilla's usual magic as a hurricane is to a baby's breath, as arsenic to mother's milk."

"Power fueled by Ophelie's blood infused into the spellworker's veins."

"Whoever has done this—their contempt is monumental." Dante ran his fingers through his untamed hair. "I believe the mule—the girl—was meant to be discovered. Not as she was—before the event and able to speak. But after, so she could be linked to the murderous 'magic' of the banners, which those few who understand the properties of the mineral phosphorus will understand to be no magic at all; a wax seal prevents its untimely combustion. Everyone would believe she ensorcelled the banners, and without her fingers, it could not be proved otherwise. Some well-laid trail would link the banners to the queen, whereupon we would be forbidden to search further. Another mystery unsatisfactorily 'solved.' And the lady of sorrows blamed."

He aimed his storm-hued gaze at me. "Now *you* tell *me*, great sympathizer with sorry humankind: Why did the girl believe she had to die before this happened? Whatever her captors would do with her blood had already been settled. She could not stop it. She spoke of betraying a 'good *man*,' not a 'good *queen*.' What would an aristo student of magic call *sin* or *betrayal*?"

I had assumed Ophelie's "betrayal" meant royal assassination—murder. But if they'd never planned to murder Philippe, then what?

"I've not a guess," I said after a fruitless few minutes. "The conspirators are taunting Philippe, forcing him to look the other way because elsewise he must blame his wife. A queen who champions sorcery accused of treason by a king already considered an enemy of the Camarilla—it would destroy the Concord; throw the kingdom into chaos. But they're taunting *us*, as well. They might not know who we are, but they suspect that *someone* is examining what they've done . . ."

"Perhaps."

". . . which means they're up to something that a persistent investigator *will* see if they don't distract him. Something that requires the kind of power they cannot draw from their innate talents. Ophelie was bled for near a year; Gruchin for almost two. Who knows how many other mules they've used. What else have they done?"

As if taking the cue from my conviction, Dante strode into his bedchamber and returned with two wads of fabric. Shoving the box of half-tied herb bags onto the floor, he sat beside me and unwrapped the smaller one—a kerchief containing the twisted shard of metal from the crypt—Ophelie's manacle.

"This piece teases," he said. "I've no doubt it bound the girl. The blood"—he showed me the dark residue in the jagged tear that had freed Ophelie—"matched the keirna of the samples I took from her body. But *she* didn't break it. I found no commonalities between her blood, or anything you've told me of her, and the magic that tore the metal. Nor did I discover any commonalities with the magic worked on the *Swan*. True, that was a very different spell, and a joint working, but I would judge . . ."

". . . that the magic that freed her was worked by someone else entirely." So easy to complete his logic—forcing an astonishing conclusion. "We've yet *another* sorcerer involved."

Dante rewrapped the shard and gave it to me. "The magic was not only tremendously explosive, but entirely undisciplined. Not even a spell as we think of it. It felt as random as a lightning strike, its pattern utterly simple, but as raw and dangerous as the torn edge of the metal."

As I fingered the wrapped manacle and marveled at the story it told, he unwrapped the larger bundle. The spyglass lay innocent in the folds of a cambric shirt. A bit of metal dropped to the floor and rolled to my feet. I picked up the silver coin.

"That's an oddment," said Dante. "Its keirna is very different from that of other coins, but then coins pass through so many hands for so many different purposes, they have quite a complex pattern to begin with. The oddities might come from its being a double strike or from being in a mule's pocket at the moment of his death. But whatever its history, it is now magically inert. It carries no spells. Stranger yet, none I've tried seem to affect it in any way."

The silver disk induced no odd sensations as I had experienced the first times I'd held it. "And the glass?"

He lifted the spyglass and shoved its wrappings aside. "I've taken it apart. Studied it a bit with no ill effects. I've no doubt you'll inform me if I take on an even more fiendish bent."

"I'll certainly speak out if I sniff brimstone in here again," I said, but no wry spark illumined his shuttered face.

"Is your royal cousin a devout man?"

I rolled the double-faced coin between my fingers as I considered the odd question. "I'd say not, though that's pure supposition. What other Savins I know keep private altars, but they live . . . heedless."

I glanced up to see if he understood. He inclined his head.

"You said the king saw dead men he knew, wandering in desolation, when he looked through the glass," he said. "What did *you* see? If I'm to explain this particular mystery, I need evidence."

His request made sense. But no sooner had I sketched out my vision than he began to pick at its threads, gathering intensity like a lowering storm. *What kind of gate?* Iron. *Was it embedded in a wall?* No, it stood alone. But the way—*no*, I didn't see an actual path—led through it. I just knew. *Was your father's attire familiar?* Yes. His favorite hunting coat. *Was the landscape known to you?* A dry hillside could be a thousand different places in Sabria, but the gate . . . *Did your father ever attempt sorcery?* Not that I ever saw or heard. He was weak in all ways. *Was there physical violence between your father and you when you were a boy?* No. *As a man?* Once. Only once. *Do you pray for your father?*

"That's quite enough," I said, jumping to my feet, trembling as the old scar on my left arm throbbed in time with my burns. I could not afford headaches or memories of daydreams that bled truth, or any of the turbulence these topics forever roused. "What does this have to do with the spyglass?"

He didn't answer. Didn't look up. Didn't speak at all for a while, as he carefully unscrewed the outer brass ring from the wide end of the spyglass and lifted out a second, this one with the glass lens fitted in it. With a small prying implement he removed five tiny brass fasteners from the rim, then pointed to a pattern scratched on the lens ring. "I think this might be the mark of the lens maker," he said. "Can you see it?"

Still flustered, I motioned him to turn the ring into the sunlight. A squint revealed the scribed image of an eye with three rays spreading out from it. "I'll find out whose mark it is," I said. "But what does my private business have to do with this? What have you learned about the glass?"

"Nothing certain, though I doubt it provides a window into some divine hunting ground. The spellwork pattern is erratic, like a quilt jointly made by a royal seamstress and a blacksmith. Some aspects are quite subtle, using properties of light and aether I've never conceived of; some are little more than acolyte's fumbling. The power that infused the spell is weak. And, as I told you at the beginning, the instrument's physical construction is uneven, as well. Like this . . ." He removed the brass rim and exposed the hidden edge of the lens. Bubblelike voids and tiny cracks marred the wavy edge of the glass. "Filled with flaws. Again, I believe, we have a different practitioner. Less skilled even than Orviene. Far less raw talent than the one who burst the manacle."

"If it doesn't penetrate the Veil, then what, in Heaven's name, does it do?"

He didn't seem to hear my question. "This guard captain, de Santo, he is not of the blood?"

I thought back to the way de Santo had spoken of Gruchin's blood ties, and my glimpses of his grimy hands . . . bare of family marks . . . covering his head. "I don't believe so."

"And you don't think he could be working for Orviene or Gaetana?"

"Definitely not. He believes the king has betrayed him—that Philippe sacrificed him and his family in order to shield the queen and the mages who work for her."

"I want to see the captain. Tonight."

I bristled at his demand. "Why? Was my interview flawed? My report incomplete? De Santo saw nothing of Gruchin's attack."

Dante, closed and cold, carefully reassembled the spyglass. Only when he had tightened the outer ring did he answer. "He may have seen more than he thinks."

Further questioning did naught but close him tighter. Eventually I yielded. "Tonight, then. Meet me at the temple minor at ninth hour. Meanwhile, I need you to make a fuss about your books. It's time to go to Serav—"

A rapping at the door sent both of us to our feet. Dante hurriedly rewrapped the spyglass and tossed it onto his jumbled worktable. "Enter."

As I crammed Gruchin's coin into my pocket, the door opened to Gaetana.

CHAPTER TWELVE

Gaetana's chilly gaze slid from me to Dante and back again.

Dante snatched up the book that yet lay open on the floor and thrust it into my arms. "Does no one in this wretched place heed a man's word? Keep this nursery tale, librarian, and bring me the books I asked for. I don't care if you must copy them yourself or crawl all the way to Seravain to find them."

I hunched my shoulders and gave a curt bow. "I just thought—"

"That's the problem, isn't it?" he said, taking up his staff. "I didn't ask you to think. Another delay and perhaps I'll prevent your thinking altogether. Now. Get. Out."

His staff blurted fire and I scurried out the door, not stopping until I reached the window gallery. Gaetana's derisive laughter followed me, scalding my ears as if I, too, could hear through walls.

I slid my journal into my doublet and smoothed the crumpled pages of the book Dante had shoved at me. Annoying to note my hands yet trembled, near an hour since his questioning. By all saints, why did any mention of my father throw me over? He couldn't spring a knife on me again. Onfroi Guillame de Savin-Duplais was nine years over and done with, no matter what the cursed spyglass showed.

When I noted the title of Dante's book, I almost laughed at the irony. Translated from the ritual language of the Kadr witchlords, its title *Rolfkhedri Muerge* meant *Manifestations of the Dead*.

As it happened, I had read the text before. It recounted a history of hauntings and phantasms, enumerating the distinctions between ghosts and spectres, spirits and souls. The writer had been the first to propose the idea that those we Sabrians called saints, the holy dead designated by the Pantokrator as his hand in the living world, actually walk among us reborn into bodily form—a manifestation he called a *biengasi*. The Cult of the Reborn had grown up around this theory.

Had Dante given me the tattered volume merely to support our diversion, or to keep the book from the woman's observation, or as material for study? Some day I would force the damnable mage to answer a question or two. I hiked the overlong distance to my apartments, stowed the book behind my armoire, and set out for the administrator's office to arrange my journey to Collegia Seravain.

THE SUPPLICANT BENCH SAT UNOCCUPIED when I reached Damoselle Maura's office. The lady herself sat at her writing table, her eyes focused somewhere distant, her tightly folded hands pressed to her mouth. A pen lay idle on her writing table beside an unstoppered ink bottle and a ledger book.

"Divine grace, damoselle," I said, tapping on her door, "are you well?"

The smudged eyes searched my face and promptly filled with tears.

I shut the door behind me. "Lady, may I be of some service? Fetch you wine . . . or some friend . . . a physician or apothecary, or"—it occurred to me that she might be of a religious bent—"perhaps a temple reader?"

"You still hear them, don't you, sonjeur? They break your sleep, as well?"

No need to ask whom she meant. "Aye, damoselle. I try to believe . . . There was naught we could have done differently to save them."

"I try that, too. Though I'm so afraid—" She quickly pressed fingertips to her lips, and a tremor racked her shoulders. Then she forced her features into something not quite a smile and picked up her pen. "What business brings you here this morning?"

That moment's break between grief and resignation revealed emotion more disquieting than our shared memory of horror. "Lady, what frightens you so?"

"As you said, some matters we cannot alter. Some promises we cannot undo." She tapped her pen on the table. "And now, please, sonjeur, your business . . ."

Without encouragement, I had no choice but to move on, yet I resolved to return to the question. "Two matters, damoselle. First, Mage Dante has become . . . um . . . insistent . . . about his books. I must travel to Collegia Seravain. My familiarity with the collegia's policies suggests that some official representation of his position in Her Majesty's household will facilitate his book borrowing. As to the second matter, you likely recall how Lord Ilario has tasked me to set up a scientific festival. . . ."

We spent the entire morning together laying out Ilario's exposition, making lists and sketching venues, laughing at the infinite possibilities of magical and scientific exhibits that could astound Merona's worldly citizens. The easy grace of her company, her bright mind and incisive wit, her consideration for the needs of guests and household only strengthened my growing admiration.

By midafternoon, she had obliged me with an official letter of request to the collegia for whatever materials I would specify, sealed with her authority as the queen's representative. She also provided me a letter of credit and an instruction for the steward's office to provide me a mount and expense money for my journey. And naturally, she offered referrals to a number of Merona's tradesmen who might craft the scientific displays. Among them were several lens makers who might also provide a pair of spectacles at a reasonable price to a private secretary who had not yet received an advance on his pay.

I blotted the page where my unburnt left hand had awkwardly scribed the list of tradesmen, closed my journal, and stood to go, Maura's letters in my grasp. "Damoselle, this day has been . . . exceptional. And now, please, will you not allow . . . Might I assist *you* in some more personal fashion? Or perhaps you have some other friend to confide in?"

I felt like a stammering fool. But throughout my worst days, the ready ear of my mentor, Kajetan, had coaxed me out of my skin's armor, allowing me to release grief and fear and burdens held close since childhood.

She walked me to the door. "Ah, kind sonjeur, you have not lived long at Castelle Escalon. Friends are rare enough for one who holds the queen's keys. Trustworthy confidants extremely so." At least I had prompted a smile, however forlorn. "For the present, I must attend my lady and report on the day's business."

"I'll be off, then. But good lady"—my hand rested on the door lever, still refusing to press it—"when I return from Seravain, would you consider—? I would deem it a great honor, and a great favor, if you would forego business and walk out with me some afternoon. I vow by my royal cousin's head to provide you a trustworthy ear. Or you could regale me wholly with nonsense, if you prefer, as my appreciation of that art has grown deeper with recent experience."

As the warmth from a morning fire sweeps quietly through a chamber to devour the night's chill, so did the lady's pleasure smooth her brow, soften her smile, and flush her cheeks to an even deeper hue. She dipped a knee and tilted her head most charmingly, causing my body to respond in ways it had near forgotten. "It would be my delight to engage in such a venture. Far too long has passed since I've spent an afternoon walk exchanging nonsense."

"Well. All right, then." I pulled open the door.

"Divine grace smooth thy journey, Portier," she said as

I stepped out, her voice enriching my name as clotted cream improves whatever sorry fruit it sits on.

It required the long, steep hike down to the lower city to replace unseemly distraction with my afternoon's purpose. But mind triumphed over flesh, and I spent the rest of the afternoon exploring Merona's craftsmen's district. After a start on exposition business, I turned to the lens makers.

With six scattered shops on the list, it would have been simpler merely to ask if someone knew which shop used the radiant eye as its crafter's mark. But Michel de Vernase might have pursued these same lines of inquiry, and I deemed it wise not to walk too obviously in his footsteps. Unfortunately, I completed my last interview at the last shop on the list without encountering any such mark on signboard, doorway, or lintel.

"Your spectacles will be ready tomorrow morning, son-jeur," said a lanky young man named Watt at a tidy work-shop called the *Glass House*.

I had not truly intended to buy spectacles, not being of an age to require such aids. Yet I had been astonished at the clarity of fine-printed text when reading through some of Watt's sample lenses. When he proffered a guess that I might suffer blurred vision and watery eyes after prolonged reading, especially in poor light—which was exactly true—I asked how he knew. On a slate he used to tally up costs, he sketched a diagram of the human eye, as presented in a lecture at the collegia medica, he told me. With deft strokes he showed how rays of light enter the eye's own lens at various angles from close and far objects, forcing the marvelous structure to alter its very shape.

I marveled at this knowledge and could have discussed the subject for another hour. The artistry of such a creation would surely convert a nonbeliever to the Pantokrator's service. But as Watt totted up what I owed him, his sketch prompted me to one last inquiry.

I tapped a finger beside the drawing. "I've seen this pattern before," I said. "An eye with rays of light streaming in or out. Simpler perhaps, but very like. I can't think where.

Has someone erected a copper plaque to memorialize this insightful scholar? I seem to recall it etched in metal."

Watt laughed and from a shelf on his wall pulled out a common magnifying lens, its scuffed ring of tarnished brass fastened to a yellowed ivory handle. He pointed to a scratch on the brass ring. "Was this the mark?"

My soul exulted at the chance so nearly missed. "That's it exactly. Is it your own?"

"Nay. 'Tis the mark of Reven Skye, a fellow artisan known more as a lampwright, who crafts both instruments and lenses to order. He's a decent sort who works cheap. Only two streets over. In confidence"—he leaned forward—"he's only a bargain if you don't care about finish or precision. I can refer you to three instrument makers will do you better for a lord's exhibition—and my lenses come second to no one's. You'll hear it said all over."

I asked no further details, insisting my master would not tolerate poor work. But I explored the area "two streets over" from the Glass House and found Reven Skye's grimy little shop down an alley. No one in such a place was going to believe I'd come to consult about a royal exhibit, so I presented the equally grimy Reven Skye a different story.

"A fellow from Castelle Escalon recommended you as one who could make *uncommon* instruments," I said, exposing my hand quickly, so he could not identify the family mark. His own left hand was bare. "Perhaps incorporating a particular lens I've made myself."

"Aye," he said, and licked his yellow-brown front teeth. "I've done specialty work for your like. What kind of instrument? And who's your friend?"

"He'd rather me not say, as he's employed high, you know," I said. "And the matter's confidential. I've a need to peep in a gent's window. See if my wife's visiting. He said you do a fine spyglass."

"Gruchin!" He leapt from his stool, sending tools and metal bits crashing to the floor. I was wholly unprepared when he barreled into me, his soft, heavy body crushing me against the table, fetid breath bathing my face and a rasp pointed at my eye. "Where is the whoreson villain?

Near three years and he's never paid me for the instrument. Sneaking belly-crawler, with his precious lenses and grand schemes. Claimed his luck had turned. Said the thing'd make us a fortune."

"He's dead ... honestly, Goodman Skye ... I've no money. ..." My babbling attempts to divert his wrath soon convinced him I wasn't worth a charge of murder.

"I don't believe Gruchin's dead," he grumbled, grinding his rasp on a lump of bronze. "Some said it when his house burnt. But they only found his wife and youngling in it, and maybe his *luck* is what had him away from home when it happened. For sure as I'm born, not a year ago, he stole that cursed spyglass right out of here. Thieving weasel. I spotted him running away with it."

A half hour and all the coins in my pocket save Gruchin's double strike silver—the dead man's luck charm, so I learned—and Reven Skye was back at work, mumbling of vengeance, thievery, and cheats. Climbing the hill to Castelle Escalon, I pieced together the story. After Gruchin was dismissed from the mages' service, he had fashioned lenses with spells he'd learned from them. Skye said the guardsman had decided to make himself a sensation by selling glimpses through his magic spyglass, "Though I never saw the use of a *miracle glass* that showed naught but a blur."

Verger Rinaldo would find no girl child to rescue. According to the lens maker, Gruchin's house had burned shortly after his dismissal from the Guard Royale, well before the fateful arrow shot. I added the child and her mother to the tally of murders. Perhaps Gruchin had learned what they'd done to his family and planned his revenge all the months they'd bled him. But, for certain, early on the very day Gruchin donned the armor of a royal guardsman and joined the Guard Royale's exercises, likely the only moment of freedom he'd had in almost two years, he had stolen the "useless" spyglass from Reven Skye's workshop. Once he had taken his not-quite-murderous aim at the king, the mule had grasped his unholy glass and stood where the fallen guardsman could not possibly fail to kill him. Though his captors had muted him, he had found a way to expose something of their work.

Nothing suggested the mages had come looking for the spyglass, either before or after Gruchin's death. An eager ferocity rushed through me. It seemed to me that unless a captive Michel de Vernase had told them, they didn't know it existed.

CALVINO DE SANTO UNHARNESSED HIMSELF from the coal cart in the pale glow of a watchlamp.

"Speak to him or leave him be," I murmured to Dante as we crouched in the alley watching. "Does it give you pleasure to spy on a good soldier's shame?"

The tarry night of the stale, filthy alley behind the Guard Royale barracks obscured my companion's face, though I doubted I could read any more answer there than usual. Dante had devoured my tale of Gruchin's spyglass like a starving dog cleans a bone, then insisted on searching out the disgraced guard captain immediately, while revealing naught in return. We had expended an hour of the unseasonably warm evening hunting de Santo, and three more following him about his night's drudgery. Every time I made a move to approach the man, Dante's iron hand had held me back.

"Will you just—keep—silent?" he snapped through gritted teeth. "I've worked a theory."

De Santo's yoke and straps clattered as he threw them into the cart. He left it standing beside the black hill of coal that fed the guardpost braziers throughout the palace, then disappeared into the barracks doorway.

Annoyed at the wasted evening and Dante's surly company, I stood, stretched out my aching legs and back, and cradled my throbbing hand. It was almost middle-night. "I'd like some sleep. I'm off to Seravain tomorrow early. We can test your theory when I get back."

Dante's cold grip encircled my ankle. De Santo had reappeared in a stream of yellow light spilling from the doorway, a blanket thrown over his shoulder and a pail in one hand. As the closing door shut off all but the pale watchlight, he turned away from us and trudged farther into the alley, where an iron fence barred the end, and the shadows were deep.

Metal clanked dully on stone. Water sloshed. The man coughed and spat. Silence fell, but Dante did not release his grip. Moments later, de Santo began to speak. "Holy angels, messengers of Father Creator"—the familiar prayer rose from the distant dark—"heed my petition for hearing and grace to ease the journey of Galtero de Santo, honored father, and Nicia, beloved mother, of Barela and Guilia, sisters fallen in their childhood, and Roland, son of my body. Let neither my dishonor nor my corruption taint their memorials or slow their steps. . . ."

His prayers were lengthier than those I dashed off each evening, and heartfelt as only a man who asked naught for himself could make them. I growled at Dante and dragged at his shoulder to come away. We had no right to hear this. But the mage would not budge. He gripped his staff and stared into the dark and whispered, "Discipline."

I closed my eyes and crushed my rising temper, and in that fathomless darkness behind my eyes appeared a snarled tangle of scarlet threads and purple barbs, and disjointed blots of shaded gray crossed with livid stripes. How could a pattern of color writ on the inside of my eyelids turn my knees to jelly?

"And for one other lost traveler, unmourned"—de Santo's voice quavered—"hear me, most gracious angels and holy saints. . . . No, no, no!"

Shifting air stirred the warm stink of piss and rot in the windless alleyway. The chill, dry intrusion spoke of earth and dusty leaves and cedar.

"By Heaven's grace, leave me be!"

When de Santo's panic wrenched my eyes open, I thought Dante's magical seeing had seared through my head. Faint silver flashes and purple flickering outlined the captain's kneeling form. Not lightning. Only the great bulk of the palace armory stood beyond the iron fence at de Santo's back. My stomach rolled.

"What do you want of me?" de Santo cried. "I pray for you. I can do no more than that."

The light crawled about de Santo, shooting out tendrils of livid green and purple, charging the air to bursting. De Santo's pleas disintegrated into a despairing moan.

I pressed my back to the brick and sank down beside Dante. "By the Creator's hand, what . . . ?"

The question died on my lips. The mage had pulled out the spyglass, propping the brass body in his clawed right hand while holding the eyepiece with his functioning fingers. When he tried to adjust the eyepiece, the wider end slipped out of his dead fingers. Swearing softly, he tried again, with the same result.

I slipped my shoulder underneath as a prop and steadied the glass with my unbandaged hand. Better to be the support than the one peering through that cursed lens.

Dante's breath caught; then he exhaled, long and slow. After a moment, he eased his grip on the glass and pressed it urgently into my hands. No mistaking his intent.

A sickly, wavering light now cocooned the wailing Calvino de Santo. Dread shriveled my skin like old grapes. But I raised the glass.

Sainted bones! I could not but recall Watt's sketched light, the straight rays bending as they passed through curved glass and again as they penetrated the textured eye. But the artisan's rendering had shown the object of vision clarified, unblurred, not wholly altered, not reshaped from green and purple lightning into a man's starved likeness. Protruding teeth. Receding jaw, bony and stubbled. Scars and mouthlike wounds gaping everywhere on knobbed gray limbs. Small, close eyes, blacker than a nouré's obsidian gaze, accusing and terrible.

You don't believe in ghosts, Portier. Dead is dead. I snatched the glass from my eye. My throat near clogged when I picked out Dante's dark shape creeping along the alley wall toward de Santo and the flickering light. Cursed idiot . . . as manic a fool as Ilario . . . to seek out horror . . .

Responsibility dragged me along the wall behind the mage. Someone who cared for the weeping soldier ought to be alongside. Yet, with every step forward, mind and body escalated their war. My skull ached as if crushed in an iron clamp. Despite the night's warmth, I could not stop shivering.

De Santo remained oblivious to our presence. Poised a

few paces behind him, Dante stretched his arms wide, as if to embrace the poisonous vision. Indeed, for a few moments the writhing fire flared brighter as if the mage were new kindling to feed on.

Like a virulent outwash of the encounter, bitter anger settled in my bones. Purulent hatred clung to my spirit like sap from broken cedars. Prayers of unseemly gratitude bubbled from my soul as I huddled to the clammy brick. Gracious angels be thanked, this horror was not mine.

When, after a fathomless time, the last purple wisps faded, Calvino de Santo slumped into a silent, shapeless blackness, and Dante withdrew. The mage nudged me down the passage and around a corner before sinking to the filthy cobbles, uncurling his broad back against the brick wall, and clutching his staff between drawn-up knees. His breath came in hard gasps, as if he'd run a footrace.

"Some might call blood-born power a curse when it refuses the summons of will, as yours has done," he said after a moment. "But I think it serves you." He removed the forgotten spyglass from my paralyzed grasp and weighed it in his own wide palm. With a grimace, he stuffed the instrument into his shirt.

"My blood serves me? How? Blessed saints, what did we just see?"

"I believe that when you first looked into this glass, it played on a particular guilt and horror you carry with you about your father's end. The same for your king, who saw friends and good servants he has led to their deaths. The factor you hold in common is your Savin blood, however ineffectual that may be in magical circles. When de Santo first looked through the glass, he glimpsed the mule at the moment he crossed the plane of death, and guilt left him vulnerable to the glass's spell, as it did for you. But the captain is not of the blood, and for him the enchantment did not resolve fully, as if his own spirit became caught in a trap of wire and broken glass and cannot get free of the unresolved vision of the mule. Whenever the captain opens his spirit, when he prays, for example, as a devout man does every night, he brings the mule's spectre to life again."

"The spyglass *bound* Gruchin's spirit to de Santo? His soul cannot pass beyond the Veil?"

Tales in every age spoke of sorrowful spirits who lingered after death, chained by vengeance, grief, or urgency to the earthly plane. Ghosts, shades, visible spirits . . . The implications of magic that could force a soul to such incomplete existence were beyond imagining.

"What we saw was *not* Gruchin's ghost, not anything you'd name a soul. Believe me, there was no intelligence, no person there." Dante shook himself as if to be rid of the encounter. "A spectre is only a splash of energies . . . a phantasm or seeming . . . a vivid memory. A nasty, vicious one in this case, no argument there. The mule died committing a purposeful act of vengeance, filled with malice and rage, and this spectre encompasses and inflicts that pain every moment of its manifestation."

"There must be more to it," I said. "Why guilt? De Santo didn't even realize who Gruchin was until later."

Dante shrugged. "Guilt knows little of truth. As far as the guard captain knew, the mule was an assassin who'd come a hairsbreadth from slaying the king he'd sworn his life to protect. And the king was shed of his armor by de Santo's act. Perhaps excitement or fear would do the same."

"But *I* never glimpsed the man, living or dead, and I know as well as I know anything in this life that the face I just saw was Gruchin."

"Aye. The consolidation of the spectre, the accuracy of the likeness, that's a considerable wonder. But perhaps not so much as when one with a bent for magic spies through the glass. De Santo experiences a fragment. You and your king see something wholly real. We just don't know what."

"Reven Skye saw naught but a blur."

"Perhaps the key to the spell had not been spoken. Perhaps the lens maker was never affected by anyone's death. I don't know. But the lenses seem to focus these overpowering emotions and metaphysical realities connected to death, fix the resulting energies to physical memory, and so create a phantasm. A considerable accomplishment.

Yet—think about this—not at all what the *queen* has in mind."

Of course. It was so easy to get caught up in the moment's wonders and forget the driving force behind Dante's investigation. The queen did not desire phantasms.

My grateful fingers clung to the rough edges of the solid, mundane brick behind my back. "Then the spyglass enchantment was a failed experiment," I said.

Dante sighed and hauled himself up with his staff. "That's my belief. As the fop told us—as the lady herself expressed to me at my interview—the queen wishes to speak to her mother and have the dead lady answer back. She desires neither spectres nor ghosts, but *engasi*— embodied spirits, returned from the dead to walk the earth. An entirely different matter."

"True necromancy."

"I've never seen it done," he said, almost speaking to himself. "Of all my teachers— I don't know if it's even possible. That's why I need the books. *All* of them I asked for."

Teachers—it was Dante's first mention of his schooling, and curiosity near overwhelmed my sense. But it came to me that I might be more likely to get an answer if I *didn't* pounce this time. Odd and testy as Dante was, I liked him. And I respected him beyond my wonder at his considerable gifts, and I believed he must have good reason for the bitterness that drove him, as my own peculiar history drove me. That's why I'd been so angry at what I'd seen as his failure in compassion. I'd been angry at myself for failure in judgment. Someday I would learn.

I sighed and rubbed my tired eyes. "I still don't see what necromancy has to do with Philippe. He has long turned a blind eye to the queen's illicit desires. The Temple is too weak to contradict his judgment. The Camarilla won't; they've never condemned necromancy, only its abuse, bending to the Temple's rule in the matter only to ensure their own survival after the Blood Wars. Philippe's subjects love him well enough that *they'll* not be prompted to rebellion by rumors of his unlucky wife's grieving. So these distractions of feigned assassinations, mules, and transference are hiding . . . what?"

"I don't know."

He offered me a hand, dragging me to my feet as if I were but a stripling. We set out through the warm night, neither of us able to answer this most critical question. A dog barked in the distance. A flurry of invisible wings greeted us as we passed through a deserted garden. A fountain rippled and gurgled. Peaceable sounds to contrast with what we'd seen.

"Michel de Vernase must have trod close to the answer," said Dante after a while. "The king has received no ransom demands? No encouragement to change . . . anything . . . in exchange for the conte's life?"

"No. I hope to pick up Michel's trail at Seravain."

Dante paused between the two arched gates that led into the more traveled pathways of the palace. He was little more than an angular shape in the dark. "This morning Gaetana asked if I could translate a treatise on the divine elements, written in her family's private cipher. They seem to have lost the spellkey to the code. I accepted the task."

Heat rushed through my limbs and fluttered my belly. After a day that seemed to have wrung every possible emotion out of me, it took me a moment to recognize sheer excitement. My eyes met Dante's. Their feral brightness near blinded me.

"Good," I said, matching his ferocity. "Excellent."

He nodded. "I should make my own way from here. You're off tomorrow, you said?"

"Yes. I'll be gone three days. Four at most. If you need something right away, Ilario returns to Merona in the morning."

He turned to go, but hesitated halfway round. "You oughtn't trust the peacock. His untruth is seated so deep, it is scarce detectable. Your king trusts him at his peril."

"Lies about what?"

"If I knew, I'd hardly keep it secret, now would I?"

"I've questioned Ilario," I said. "I've had my own reservations about him, especially after the *Swan*. But I see naught but a good-hearted, ridiculous man, who loves his half sister inordinately. He's made a place for himself in this world—not one you or I would want, but one that seems to suit him. Give me evidence of something else, and I'll take it to the king."

Dante shrugged. "I've no source you'd credit."

"Tell me when you do. And by the bye"—I raised my bandaged hand, ignoring the barbed spikes that shot up my arm with every movement—"thank you for this. It feels better already."

He snorted rudely. "Lies do not become you, student. Tend the hand. Use it. You'll be glad."

He started for the gate, a strange, lonely figure, his white staff marking his passage. Where, in the Father's creation, had he come from? "Master," I called after him. "Does *your* blood shield you from the spectres of the spyglass?"

His answer drifted backward as his shape merged into the dark of the garden arch. "I don't pray."

CHAPTER THIRTEEN

The sultry breeze ruffled the pages of five years' worth of logbooks heaped on the library table. Nidallo, the soft-bodied adept temporarily assigned to my position as Collegia Seravain's curator of archives, hovered at my shoulder, disapproving. "You must allow me to close the casement, Acolyte Duplais. Constant temperature and gentle handling are critical to preservation. And I don't understand why you need so many logbooks out at once."

The sun-sweetened airs of Seravain's rocky vale had cleansed the musty odors of deadhouses, royal crypts, and haunted alleyways from my head. I wasn't about to shut them out. How had I borne fifteen years in these stifling precincts—nine of them closeted in this dusty labyrinth of book cupboards, lamp-grimed walls, and age-darkened study tables?

"Note the dryness of the parchments in the older journals," I said. "Experience informs us that more water would improve the balance of elements in the preservation spells. The moisture in the air will suffice. Surely you don't suggest immersing the books in water, Nidallo?" My recent practice at fabricating lies served many circumstances on this journey.

"Certainly not!" He shook his head sharply, as if trying to extract sense from my logic.

"Then keep the windows open. And if you could give me a better idea who might have borrowed *A Treatise on Heaven and Earth*, I would not need so many volumes. Visiting scholars borrow books every week. You must keep a running tally, compiled monthly at the very least. I've a notion it was Ydraga de Farnese who last requested this work, but have no idea when the good woman last visited. If you had to deal with this new mage at Castelle Escalon, you would understand my determination! He is the most unreasonable, crude, demanding . . ."

Angels protect me, I babbled like Ilario. The torrent of words poured from my mouth, each whorl and eddy leading poor Nidallo farther from espying my purpose—or so I hoped.

The adept retreated to his search for the missing treatise. He had not seen me slip the exquisite little volume into my pocket within a half hour of my arrival at my old haunts.

I stretched out my newly unbandaged fingers and settled back to work in the quiet niche. Nidallo's irritated mumbling at the disappearance of a valuable text kept me apprised of his location.

Switching logbooks frequently enough to prevent anyone from noting which most interested me, I jotted more entries in my journal. The gate warden's log confirmed that Michel de Vernase had indeed visited Seravain twice the previous year, the first time shortly after the assassination attempt, the second a tenday after his letter to the king hinting at new information and an extended journey. He had met with six senior mages on the first occasion, and only two on the second. Both times he had spoken with Kajetan, as well. That was only to be expected. Seravain's chancellor received every high-ranking visitor.

As I recorded Michel de Vernase's visits and appointments, I encoded them with shifted notation, even within my usual cipher. I shifted times, dates, and other names in a similar fashion. The need to mask my inquiries wrenched my soul. Collegia Seravain had been my haven from family upsets and an unwelcoming world, a serene community of the mind where I could explore and contemplate the wonders of a mystical universe. Yet its genteelly crumbling walls enfolded ugly secrets, tainting my memories as if mold had crept out of its corners. A sorcerer associated with the collegia had vilely abused Ophelie de Marangel right under our noses for *months*. How could those of us entrusted with children's minds—myself included—have been so inexcusably blind?

I recorded and encoded every reference to Ophelie, as well. In the early days of her residency, the girl had made occasional day visits to Seravain village, usually in company with the same few students—names duly noted. She had spent short holidays with the families of these same girls, only returning to her home in Challyat for the month-long harvest recess.

Library records scribed in my own hand indicated that three years ago, against all earlier indications, Ophelie had advanced to the rank of adept. That is, she had daemonstrated sufficient talent and skill to study serious magic. The timing jibed with Dante's estimate of when she had begun bleeding herself. Only lunatics and desperate children could find logic in bleeding away one's soul to unblock the wellsprings of magic. Ironically, only an innately talented child could derive benefit from the attempt.

Sometime in the next year—long before she had been moved to the crypt at Castelle Escalon—a more experienced hand had begun taking her blood. Certainly in the months after her advancement, Ophelie's habits had changed dramatically. She left the school only rarely, at first alone, later in company with a different girl, a younger student named Lianelle ney Cazar.

Everyone knew the Cazar girl. Tutors considered her talented but erratic, and were forever chastising her lack of discipline. I recalled her as unremittingly annoying. She would demand to read every work in the library, even the most advanced texts, on obscure topics such as animal summoning or bone reading, rather than choosing a broader selection of materials suited to her age and level. And she had plagued me with endless questions about impossibilities, such as invisibility or altering time. I had never realized she and Ophelie were friends.

I jotted another date . . . then jerked my pen from the page. "But that's the same—" The words slipped out before I knew it.

"Is something wrong, Portier?" Nidallo imposed his beaky face into my light again as I flapped a page of my journal back and forth and back again to verify what I had just noticed.

"No, no. I just thought I had found Ydraga's name in Mage Gadevron's appointment list for the thirty-first of last Ocet, but my eyes played tricks on me. I'm not yet accustomed to these spectacles."

But the surprise had nothing to do with Ydraga, and there was no mistake. As I had encoded the last instance of Ophelie and Lianelle visiting the village, it struck me that I had encoded the same date on a previous page. It was the exact day of Michel de Vernase's first visit to Collegia Seravain.

I quickly scanned the gate log for additional references to Lianelle ney Cazar. The younger girl had gone out on her own early that same morning of Michel's visit, noting her intended destination as *the fields,* and her purpose as *to collect fresh herbs for a formulary project.* She had returned an hour later.

Flipping through the wide pages, I skipped to the occasion of Michel's second visit. A scrawled notation glared up at me. Lianelle had left the school on *that* morning, as well, with destination *Tigano* and purpose *to return a stray dog.* She had returned to the collegia less than an hour before Michel de Vernase's arrival. I gave no credence to coincidence.

Not daring to feel excitement, I spent the next hour retrieving all the information I could glean about the Cazar girl from the archives. She returned to the Cazar demesne for school recesses, but otherwise left the collegia only on class outings. She took no more of the "village market" excursions she had taken with Ophelie. She had appeared before disciplinary boards at least twelve times in three years, and had been placed on probation twice.

It would be awkward to find the girl. Classes were already completed for the day. Only specialized tutorials went on in the hour before supper. For students not involved, it would be free time. . . .

I pushed away from the desk enough to spy around a corner to Nidallo's desk. The handwritten paper posted on a nail beside it provided a possibility.

"Adept Nidallo!" I called. "I need assistance retrieving some additional materials for Master Dante. Have you this month's restriction list?" Lianelle ney Cazar had spent half her time on the restriction list since she had arrived at Seravain.

I smothered a smile as I perused the notice. Indeed the girl's name appeared along with those of six other students available for extra work during their free hours due to disciplinary infractions. Nidallo roused a student from a corner table to fetch the two malefactors I selected.

As I waited, I occupied my twitching fingers by reshelving logbooks. On a whim, I flipped the student log to Maura's records, thinking to discover some common bent that might lead to conversation outside palace business. I'd spent much of the two-day journey to Seravain reliving our pleasant hours working on the Exposition and planning what I might say when we next met. Unpracticed at casual conversation and with so much of my present life secret and my past dull or melancholy, I felt as nervous as an acolyte.

The record provided only one interesting tidbit. I had assumed Maura abandoned her studies for the same reasons I had, but indeed she had passed the intermediate examinations for adept's rank with high recommendations in all disciplines. Her claim that sheer boredom had sent her to court must be the truth. The reason was certainly not lack of talent.

Shuffling footsteps rounded the corner into my niche. I shoved the logbook back into its place.

"Divine grace, Benat, Lianelle," I said, exposing my hand to a fidgeting, spotty youth of about fifteen and a wiry, sun-browned girl a little younger.

"And w-with you, Ac-c-colyte..." The stammering boy exposed the back of his hand.

"Sonjeur de Duplais," said the girl, scarce dabbing her small hand on her shoulder. Her gray eyes raked me from head to boot. "Are you come back to Seravain, then, Curator? Everyone says you gave up and left because you couldn't read your way past the examinations."

Lianelle was exactly as I remembered her. Dark green student's gown stained and wrinkled. Hair escaped from two braids and frizzed about a smudged face. Speech neither belittling nor sarcastic, but merely uncomfortably frank for a girl of thirteen.

"I am now attached to Queen Eugenie's household," I said. "And I require assistance obtaining materials for Her Majesty's mages. As you may remember, I like to ensure that students on restriction make good use of their time." To be sure, I had called on the quiet Benat, continually disciplined for his inability to speak clearly, more often than the brittle-edged Lianelle.

I whipped out my transcriptions of Dante's odd requests, items ranging from crystals of blue-white antimonium to several types of exotic feathers to shards of Fassid pottery and Syan porcelain, many of which were difficult to obtain outside a sorcerer's supply room. The requirements were so numerous and so varied, requiring trips to the aviary, the metallurgical store, and several individual mages in addition to the general supply cupboards, it should take the students several hours to fetch them all—longer, in truth, as I had split the list most unfairly, leaving all the most difficult acquisitions to poor Benat.

Once the two were dispatched on their errands, I began packing a stack of borrowed volumes into crates destined for Dante. Inevitably my mind turned to the Mondragoni texts. Since the day I had refused his demands to acquire them, our mystery had spiraled deeper into a darkness where innocents died in fire and a conjured spectre drove a decent man to despair. Illicit power for sorcery and transgressing the boundaries of death were exactly the specialties of the Mondragoni, who had named their family the Brotherhood of Malevolent Spirits. How could I deny Dante any resource that might lead to understanding our quarries' aims?

Acquiring the texts would not be easy. Assuming I could find an excuse to visit the vault and abscond with forbidden materials, in no way could I take them all. The collection comprised more than fifty bound manuscripts and scrolls—far too many to escape notice were anyone to come looking and find them missing.

"Adept," I called, "could someone have shelved our missing treatise in the vault by mistake?" The short downward stair to the library vault began in an alcove just past the curator's desk. Impossible to pass without Nidallo's noticing.

"No," he snapped, slamming a large herbal on my book stack. "Every visit to the vault is supervised. Just because you no longer serve as curator does not mean the library has fallen to ruin."

"No, no. Certainly not. But you see, I myself might have put the book there a few months ago. I seem to recall hearing that the Challyat copy had been destroyed in a fire. I was concerned that our original would be the only remaining version. Perhaps we could take a look." As I had done frequently during the day, I tapped my fingers idly on Maura's document authorizing my access to all Seravain's resources.

Huffing in profound offense, Nidallo retrieved the keys from his desk. The vault door swung open with a dull clang. The adept hung a lamp from the drop chain in the center of the small stone room, then planted his back against the door frame and waved a hand at the two small cupboards and three chests—one of wood, one of leather, and one of iron. "Quickly, if you please."

The cool, windowless chamber housed what few magical texts had survived the Blood Wars. I touched the brittle volumes reverently, noting a threadbare cloth cover that had split, and a gilded title that had tarnished to unreadability. Few people ever looked at the fragile, fading texts. Many, like the Mondragoni collection, were encrypted. A few appeared entirely blank, their information beyond our current skills to retrieve, though age, wear, and the presence of encrypting enchantments bespoke certain significance. Some texts had been composed in obscure dialects or comprised little more than extensive references to even older works we did not possess. The essential knowledge from the readable texts had long been distilled into the *Encyclopaediae of Workable Formulae*, ten volumes filled with detailed instructions that students were required to memorize and practice. What spells responded to a particular student's talents might take a lifetime to master. It left little time for browsing.

A librarian, on the other hand, had plenty of time for study. Nine years had I scoured these source works for explanation of my failure. Though providing no answers, the effort had taught me a great deal about the deterioration of our art. Page after page referred to magic unknown to our experience—control of earth movements, protective wards reliable enough to prevent the spread of diseases, techniques to address afflictions of the mind. . . .

What had the Bardeu villagers said of Dante? *'E fixes them as is cursed in the mind.* I had assumed the mage worked such standard remedies as sleeping potions or sedating enchantments. But back then I'd not yet experienced the strength of his will, the compulsions he could induce, the explosive energies of his magic. Could he truly address aberrant reason? What a blessing such an ability would be, and what terrible risk, too, if such power belonged to one without scruple or moderation. We knew so little about him.

But then again . . . I flexed my fingers, pocked with healing burns. Perhaps my experience of the man spoke more of his true nature than his own words did. For better or worse, I trusted him.

My survey of the cupboards complete, I rummaged through a heap of leather scroll cases in the wooden chest. "No books at all in here," I said, as if unfamiliar with the contents.

Nidallo rolled his eyes and fondled his keys.

Whispering the spellkey to release the locks and wards, I thumbed the slight indentation on the side of the iron chest. As I opened the lid, a stench of black mold rolled out. I pressed the back of my hand to my nose, aghast.

Four or five mold-ravaged texts, each marked with the scorpion device of the Mondragoni family, all that remained of thirty-three bound volumes, lay half submerged in a sea of green-black slime. Only three of nineteen leather scroll cases had survived, soggy parchment protruding from long cracks in their sides.

My thumb brushed one of the sodden pages. For one seemingly endless moment, the bones of my hand screamed with a cracking pressure. Then scroll and case slumped into a formless mass as would a lead slug thrown into a smithy furnace.

Was I meant to believe that ordinary mold and rot had so completely devoured these manuscripts in the two years since I'd brought them to the vault? Did someone think my senses too dull to recognize such powerful, corrosive spellwork?

Scrambling for explanations, I shut the lid and sensed nature's sigh as the magical wards settled back into place. The chest's magical protections remained intact—unforced. Even if Kajetan had changed his mind and chosen to destroy the documents, he'd never have destroyed them in place. The Gautieri, a powerful blood family, had encrypted all Mondragoni works as unfit for common readership, and then themselves been wiped out in the Blood Wars. Perhaps they had sealed the pages with destructive spells, as well, and we had triggered them by moving the documents here. I could not recall the last time I had inspected the chest.

"Mold's got in here," I said, tapping the iron box. "Best purge the entire chest, lest the blight spread to other books."

"When I have time," said Nidallo with a yawn. "I've more important things to do than play charwoman." Either he knew very well what had happened to the collection or he had no idea of its significance.

"You'd best make time to clean it up," I snapped. "These were incredibly rare. Master Kajetan will pillory you for this—and likely me, as well! Is your logbook complete?"

He frowned, blinking rapidly, thinking. "No one's come in here without signing the book. I'm sure of it."

The vault log lay open on its lectern. The open page covered two years. In the month since my departure, only two people had visited—Mage Samiel, a healer who frequently found an ancient herbal to be of use, and Mage Eliana, who studied family bloodlines. But Gaetana's tight signature glared from earlier on the page.

I had opened the vault for Gaetana many times. She had never daemonstrated any interest in the Mondragoni chest, but then her frequent visits would have left her familiar with the drawer where I kept the vault keys. Perhaps she had removed some of the works—or most of them—before destroying the rest. As ever, I cursed my inability to identify magical imprints.

"No luck," I said, frustration finding an outlet as I slammed the last chest shut. "Is the *Heaven and Earth* treatise lost to mold, as well?"

"Honestly, Portier, I've taken good care of everything. I'm working here only until the chancellor appoints a proper curator." Nidallo had sloughed off his self-important hurry and seemed genuinely concerned. "You'll not report me?"

I slapped him on the shoulder. "No. Maybe you'd best leave the mess locked up after all. If there's a scandal, I'll do what I can."

Nidallo huffed as we climbed the short stair. Awaiting us at the top was Lianelle ney Cazar. The girl hefted a basket half her height, heaped with packets, vials, and boxes. "I've got these things you wanted. May I go now?"

Nidallo returned to his desk, and the girl and I returned to my niche. "Empty the basket."

I surveyed her acquisitions. "Not at all correct or complete," I said, flipping through the contents of three leather packets. "Someday, Acolyte Cazar, you will learn to examine your work with a careful eye. Come along, let us try again."

"What are you talking about? I did everything just as—"

Grabbing the girl's arm, I hauled her past Nidallo and down the library stair. Clanging bells summoned students to supper. Thus, rather than exiting the main doors into the crush of people in the collegia's central yard, I drew her downward to the library cellar.

"Where are we going?" she croaked. "I fetched you everything on that ridiculous list."

"We need to discuss that," I said, moving even faster as she started wriggling.

A winding trip through deserted binding and copying rooms led us to the back exit and into a weedy enclosure. Around and above us, throughout the sprawl of collegia buildings, lights winked on one after another, like stars in the darkening sky.

"You're hurting me." Her voice rose, and her free hand flailed at my face. "What's wrong with you? Let me go."

She jerked away with strength enough that I needed both hands to keep her. I halted and gave her a firm shake. "Keep silent or I'll see you on restriction for the next seven years."

That at least gave her pause. I propelled her across the uneven bricks and through a gate into the long-neglected outer gardens. Honeysuckle vines tangled in the arched trellises of an old pergola would shield us nicely from view.

"My regrets for the rough handling, Lianelle," I said. "I needed privacy to speak with you on a matter of grave importance. Will you listen?"

"I've nothing to tell you or anyone," she said.

Her belligerent stance only confirmed my suspicions. This was as stubborn a child as any at Seravain. "Your friend Ophelie de Marangel is dead."

Her small body stilled instantly.

"Cruelly dead from sorcery so wicked and terrible, I'll not speak of it unless you force me."

"Ophelie was *not* wicked." A child of thirteen ought to be more surprised at such news. She certainly knew what had killed Ophelie. Elsewise, nothing in the world would have prevented Lianelle ney Cazar from insisting I tell her.

"No, she was not," I said. "She was immensely brave and determined to expose the villains who hurt her so dreadfully. Unfortunately, I found her too late to help her."

"How—where did you find her?" Her voice quavered only slightly.

"At Castelle Escalon. She broke free of her captors. Just too late to survive."

"*Captors?* But they were supposed—but she went home!" Lianelle was not fast enough to cover her slip. She expected Ophelie to be somewhere else. Not home, but safe. "She was sick."

"Here's what I believe. Ophelie was bleeding herself to empower her magic. Someone here discovered it and began taking her blood for themselves. Lianelle, who was bleeding her? Did she see their faces?"

"I don't know what you're talking about. Ophelie never told me anything." No wavering this time. She was stubborn and angry, as only a child on the verge of adulthood could be. "She helped me with schoolwork, that's all. You've no cause to question me."

She tried again to wriggle away. I needed another tack.

"I've every right and reason to question you. Murder—this kind of murder—is more serious than friendship or promises. No one who believes in justice can let it pass." Retaining a hold on her arm, I sat on a peeling bench and drew her close. "Let's start again. A simple exchange. Facts won't hurt anyone or betray confidences. I can discover facts in many ways, but asking you is easiest, because you were Ophelie's friend. When did you last see her? Last year, I know. Sometime after midsummer."

If I was right, the girls' meeting with Michel had occurred on 13 Siece. Michel's last letter to Philippe had been dated 17 Siece, and the conte had visited Seravain for the second time on the thirty-fourth day of that month.

"Sometime in Siece," she said after a long stare, as if to plumb the depths of my nefarious questioning. "Or maybe it was later in Nieba. Ophelie helped me with schoolwork. I'm terrible at memorizing. She had been sick all spring. She got worse and worse, but the adepts in the infirmary couldn't make her well. So she ran away home." The answer marched out of her as perfect and unnatural as a tutorial recitation.

"But just today I've checked the infirmary log and it

shows no entries for Ophelie in the month of Siece or Nieba or at any time last year."

"Oh!" That surprised her, or at least set her thinking. "Why ask, if you already know?"

"In Siece of last year, a nobleman came here to question the mages about a crime in Merona—about someone who suffered the same injury as Ophelie. I'm thinking you might have heard about the man and his inquiries. Maybe you sneaked out early one morning to meet him, before taking Ophelie to see him. He returned here some days later. Was Ophelie still at the collegia when he came that second time? It can't hurt her to tell me that, and I can surely search the archives and find out. Give me the truth, and I'll tell you something important about that man."

Something in my patchwork of facts and guesses had struck home. She'd gone rigid as a post. Her pulse pounded like that of a frighted deer, choosing whether to run or stand her ground.

"Help me, Lianelle. The truth can't hurt her. Not anymore."

"She was still here." She near swallowed the words.

"All right. Good. Now I'll give *you* something. You may or may not know that the man's name was Michel de Vernase, Conte Ruggiere. He is a great friend of King Philippe. I need to know what you and Ophelie told him. I believe he's held captive by these same villains."

She jerked free of my grasp. I cursed the deepening dark that obscured her face, for I would have sworn she swallowed a cry. In any case, this answer came promptly. "We didn't meet any gentleman. No one took her." Quiet. Solid. Certain. Stubborn. "I can't tell you anything. I won't. I don't know you."

She was right to be cautious, no matter that we had seen each other on hundreds of occasions in the three years of her residency at Seravain. And yet—I rubbed my aching temple—her very assertion that she didn't know me was a deviation from her steadfast testimony . . . as if she might be able to tell me something if she *did* know me. If she trusted me.

That led me to examine the facts again . . . and they

fell into perfect alignment. "Michel *took* her! He came back here that second time to fetch Ophelie. And you . . . you promised to keep it secret and helped confuse the days so no one would realize he'd taken her. *You* spread the rumor that she'd been sick and wanted to go home. That she'd run away. No one denied it. Those who had hurt Ophelie certainly wouldn't, and the collegia staff would be embarrassed that an ailing student had left without their knowing. But the villains guessed what Michel had done, caught up with them, and took them both. And if so . . . Child, you are in terrible danger. If anyone suspects you know what happened to her, who was hurting her . . ."

"Ophelie ran away. She just wanted to go home. Everyone heard us talking about it. Why would I stay here if I knew anything dangerous? I'm not stupid." The faintest tinge of panic colored her bravado.

"Listen to me, Lianelle. Go home to your family." The Cazars were a very old blood family, descendants of ferocious marauders who had holed up in the mountains of Nivanne before even the Fassid had invaded southwestern Sabria. They could protect her. "Feign your own sickness. Fail your classes. Just get away from Seravain. You've no reason to trust me, else I'd take you myself. But you *must* go."

"Fail my classes?" Even afraid and angry, the girl trumpeted scorn. "Do you think I'm a loony? I've talent leaking out my ears, could the old cods here bear to admit it. I should already be studying for an adept's level. There's nowhere else I can earn my collar or stay in the Camarilla's grace. No one can make me give up my place here. *No one.*"

Souleater, spare me; how could I, of all men, argue that? What right had I to steal her future? She had survived for almost a year. And yet . . .

"Do you understand what these leeches do, child? Every day they pierce your veins and attach their cups and tubes and pumps. *Only a few millilitres today,* they say. *Only a thimbleful.* But over the months, as the blood drains away, your flesh withers until you cannot tolerate food or drink. Your soul withers until you're incapable of reason. They leave you nothing."

"I don't know what you're talking about." Her face but a pale blotch, she backed away to the end of the pergola. "I don't need you. Stay away from me."

Indeed, this very conversation dragged her deeper into danger. Why hadn't Michel de Vernase taken both girls? Had this one convinced him so easily, or was he simply careless of her safety? Blessed angels, the girls had trusted him. Yet I'd seen naught to evidence him as sympathetic to the wreckage he'd left in the wake of his investigation. First Calvino de Santo, then Ophelie . . . Perhaps Ilario's opinion of Michel was not so far off the mark.

"Lianelle, just tell me one more thing: Why did he wait? The conte? Why didn't he take Ophelie that first day, when he saw what they were doing to her? It was cruel . . . despicable . . . to leave her in such circumstances."

"He was *not* cruel!" she cried, her armored silence cracked.

As ruthless as any villain, I plunged my fist into that crack. "The conte *killed* Ophelie, Lianelle. Waiting . . . leaving her here those extra days . . . killed her."

"No! Ophelie agreed to go back. He *had* to know where to find what he was looking for; the place where everything started. As soon as she learned the name, I wrote him a letter, and he came for her. Only, I guess"—a sob escaped her—"I guess it was too late." Her presence fluttered like that of a bird poised to take flight.

"What was the name, child? I swear on everything good and worthy in this world, I mean no harm to you or the conte. What did your brave, beautiful friend tell him? *What* was the place he was looking for?"

She bolted as she spoke, leaving the answer hanging in the thick air: "Altevierre."

CHAPTER FOURTEEN

*A*ltevierre. The word scratched on the crypt wall. The word Ophelie de Marangel had spoken with her last breath. The mystery Michel de Vernase had pursued to his doom. The *place* where everything started. I held the name close as I scurried back to the library and stomped up the stair, grumbling loudly about recalcitrant students. Was it a town, a village, a crossroads, a house?

Nidallo sat at his high desk near the library entrance, reading a volume of the *Encyclopaediae of Workable Formulae.* He broke off pieces of a steamed bun as he read, dabbing his fingers on a kerchief before turning each page. The *Catalog Geographia,* a bloated volume that purported to list all place names in the kingdom, sat enticingly nearby on a book stand. But its size made it impossible to disguise amid my lists and books, and my purported mission provided me no cause to consult it. Nidallo's presence put me back to work, sorting and packing the materials Lianelle and Benat had gathered.

As ninth hour of the evening watch boomed from the clock tower, I stuffed the last packet into Dante's crates.

The last student had scurried off to his bed. Nidallo was dozing.

I had no sooner opened the *Catalog*, excited at the prospect of enlightenment, than a rangy, silver-haired man burst through the library door, his blue robes flying, his long arms spread in welcome. "Portier! Bless my heart, it is good to see you. I squeeze in a long-delayed sabbatical to visit my family—a short few months only—and what happens? My prized curator takes a whim to abandon his outpost of sanity and take up residence at Castelle Escalon! Do tell me you've come to reclaim your seat."

"Master Kajetan!" The room felt excessively hot of a sudden, as guilt robbed a long-delayed reunion of its pleasure.

"No pouting, Nidallo!" The mage waved an eloquent hand at the groggy adept, stumbling to his feet. "You know Portier has ever been my goodson. Absent yourself for half an hour."

I crossed to my worktable before the chancellor's exuberant survey of my turnout could take in the open *Catalog*. "It's fine to see you, sir. No one told me you were expected back any time soon." In fact I had rejoiced that my long-time mentor remained on leave. Far easier to tell him lies in prose than while facing his iron gray gaze.

"I'm not actually returned." Kajetan paused as a sullen Nidallo gathered bun and book and left us. "To speak truth, I was visiting my sister in Tigano," he said, silver collar flashing in the lamplight, "debating whether to extend my leave a while longer. But Charica sends me a daily report on collegia business, and there at the top is your name. So I needs must come and demand explanation." He spun and surveyed the open crates, stacked books, and my journal, ink, and scattered lists. "Are you truly reduced to groveling for your cousin's favor? I believed I had instilled in you some sense of your own worth."

"It's very complicated, Master. I . . . needed to move on. Or rather, to come to some resolution about my father. I'd like to get the past out of my head once and for all. You know the conflicts it has caused me. . . ." I embellished those points of motivation and uncertainty that jibed with what he knew of me—likely more than anyone in the world, including my mother.

Philippe could not know what hardship he had imposed when compelling me to deceive this man. As a new student at Seravain, I had lived in awe of Kajetan's magic, skills that allowed me to explore cities while sitting in a forest or to stroke a purring cat in my lap when only a block of wood lay there. But as I grew more sophisticated in analyzing spellwork, I came to see that his illusions resembled pretty paintings on silk more than fully fleshed sculptures. His greater gifts were incisive intellect and devotion to a world enriched and strengthened by our glorious art. Inspired by his eloquence and demand for excellence, every student at Seravain held strong against the winds of popular scorn.

The chancellor had personally assumed my tutorial when a broken leg forced me to spend my first harvest holiday at Seravain. Unlike most of the collegia's mages, he had never chastised me as I repeatedly failed at the magical tasks he set, nor had he offered maudlin sympathy when I recognized my defeat. Rather, with unyielding candor, he forced me to confront the truth of my failed magic and confess it aloud, so that I might hear the verdict in both ear and heart, and then he guided me through the storm that followed. He had saved my life both in metaphor and in literal truth. For on that terrible night when I confessed my failure to my father and became a father-slayer, Kajetan had stanched the bleeding. Once I had recovered, he gave me a refuge among these books, a position ordinarily forbidden to incapable sorcerers. I could never repay such debts.

"I don't understand this need to humiliate yourself to enhance Onfroi's afterlife," he said, resting his backside on my worktable. "You despised your father—and rightly so. Weak and willfully blind, he allowed an insignificant detail of birth to consume his life. He turned his back as his only son came near destroying himself to prove himself a man of substance, and then laid his own hand to complete that destruction. Onfroi deserves to languish in Ixtador and endure whatever unpleasantness that entails. Let the Souleater take him on the Last Day."

"Master, please don't. . . ."

He clapped me on the shoulder. "But then, you've always had a tender heart. No matter that I've tried to stiffen it a bit."

He had hammered honesty into me, and honesty stripped away any argument that might rebut his disrespectful logic. So I let the matter drop. When he picked up the spectacles I'd set aside and waved them in the air, I yielded to his good humor and returned his teasing grin. "You forced me to study too much, Master. My eyes are old before their time."

But I near choked as he set the spectacles aside and fluttered the pages of my journal. And I relaxed only slightly when he picked up Dante's scrawled list of materials. I truly did *not* want to explain my day's work. Kajetan was intimately familiar with my record keeping and knew how unlikely I was to forget the very details I'd used to confuse Nidallo.

As much as Kajetan was my friend and mentor, he was a prefect of the Camarilla. The mages I pursued lived under the aegis of the Camarilla, as well. In no way could I imagine Kajetan a partner in horrors, but, as I had oft told Ilario, personal feelings could not chart our course. Our success and safety as *agentes confide* mandated absolute secrecy.

"So this mage who can dispatch you on errands like a mindless lackey is our mysterious *Exsanguin*?" he said.

"It seems he is."

I deliberately released my fingers that were clenched in nail-digging knots. Dante had earned his rank legitimately. He served at the queen's pleasure, under her protection, and had done nothing to draw Camarilla censure. It was only natural Kajetan would be curious.

"My current employer, the queen's foster brother who is addicted to charms and luck spells, ran across this Dante practicing in some village in southern Louvel, the very demesne *Exsanguin* claimed as residence. His collar is properly sealed with the Seravain mark; yet the woman who administers the consilium told me he submitted no references and refused to claim even a birthplace as a surname.

Master Dante told her the Camarilla wouldn't know him, save by 'the annoyance of his collaring.'"

"I don't like it," said Kajetan, his lean face skewed to a frown. "Naturally, the Camarilla requires regular communications from Orviene and Gaetana, but their work has so little commonality with what we do here, their reports are quite arid and dismissive. I think those two are something jealous of their privileges." His brows lifted and his full lips stretched wide in good humor. "So tell me about our extraordinary mage. Have you witnessed his work?"

"Some." Knowing with what severity the Camarilla viewed uncanonical teaching, I was inclined to minimize the truly startling aspects of Dante's practice. Yet our plans required that Dante tread the boundaries of legality close enough to avoid Camarilla indictment, while daemonstrating power of the kind valuable to rogues. Kajetan communicated with everyone in the Camarilla and his rumor could only further our aims. Thus, I set about filtering the truth. Omitting all mention of spyglasses and strange patterns written inside my eyelids, I reported my experience of Dante. "He is ill-mannered and has an unwholesome affinity for violent behavior, but I'll say I've rarely sensed such power as he wields. . . ."

The chancellor did not interrupt as I told of the strangely composed circumoccule, the fiery display in the deadhouse, the shattered gaud, the rumors of mind healing, and the extraordinary, lingering virility of Dante's public magic.

When I'd done, Kajetan's fingers combed his close-trimmed silver beard. "Hearing of such strength in an unknown of such erratic temper. We've heard rumor of transference revived—"

"No, no, Master!" My explosive dismay sharpened Kajetan's attention, leaving me fumbling to recover. "I mean, I can't believe *any* mage would be mad enough to start that up again. Even Dante, disagreeable as he is."

But how could I defend him? A mage so driven to discovery and so little grounded by family, society, or moral persuasion as Dante was certainly *capable*.

Kajetan fingered the scattered pages on my table.

"Portier, would you feel it unseemly to leave me a copy of these lists? We live in a delicate balance. Should our art be dragged into evil yet again, I cannot imagine we would survive it."

Our art. *We.* The Camarilla. My kind mentor had never overdrawn the line that excluded me from his fraternity. Yet Kajetan's quiet request, spoken with such sincere concern, exposed that boundary for an uncomfortable fracture. My mentor and I did not, and would never, share a position in life, or experience the "delicate balance" of sorcerous power and political governance in the same way. But I dared not challenge him on it, lest it suggest some personal investment in Dante's concerns.

"I understand, sir. I see no harm in leaving you Dante's lists. He never claimed them private. I'll leave copies with Nidallo."

Kajetan smiled and clasped my hand, his smooth thumb tracing the Savin mark on the back of my hand and the knife scar that scored my wrist and vanished under my sleeve. "I could not persuade you to come back here, my son? Nidallo, for all his gifts, has not your good mind or your love for the art, both of which have been left stronger, I believe, by your deficiency in practice. I feel better trusting all this"—he waved his hand to encompass library and archives—"to one who has actually *read* our history."

I drew my hand away, and my gaze dropped to the region of his hem lest he observe my guilt. "Someday, Master, perhaps. The world remains an uncomfortable place."

"Indeed so. Have you found acquaintances in Merona? Here, alas, you seemed caught between students and staff. I hoped your new situation might provide you companionship at least."

"Not many at court deem a fool's private secretary worth cultivating, though I've met a few friendly sorts— the steward's third secretary, a guardsman or two."

"Your blush betrays you, lad. Could you have found a woman undaunted by your awkward connections?" Though his own wife chose to reside with her wealthy family in Tallemant, Kajetan had ever urged me to ensure my future beyond the Veil by contracting marriage—through a marriage agent, if naught else. "Tell me, who is she?"

"I've met someone amiable. Likely no more will come of it than usual." No matter my disclaimer, thoughts of Maura induced a most pleasurable anticipation. She was so different from anyone I'd met—so sensible, so lacking in artifice.

He laughed heartily and jumped up. "Forget the past, Portier, and forge ahead. I'll be awaiting happy news. Now, I must be off. If I wish to continue my sabbatical, I must be away again before Charica hears I've come."

"Good night, Master."

He paused in the doorway, sobriety erasing good humor. "I must insist, Portier: Anything you learn of this Dante, send it to me. Particles that fit no known formulas, mind healing, extraordinary power—his practice feels most disturbing."

Had my old friend made this request a month before, I would have acceded instantly. I'd have agreed that a prefect of the Camarilla could not but draw on every resource to ensure magic's purity. But no matter urgency or righteousness, my newfound understanding of spying made his demand distasteful. Unlike Philippe, whose position gave him authority to demand such uncomfortable service, and with whom I had no personal bond but common ancestry, Kajetan compelled my obedience with ties of respect, affection, and gratitude. Transference—the worst perversion of sorcery—had occurred here, under his own watch. Did he suspect? How could he have missed it?

I could speak none of these arguments, nor question him. Sure as I stood there, he would prod and poke for explanation. I rubbed my arm, where the ragged scar yet pricked from his touch, an indelicate reminder of debts unpaid.

"Certainly, Master. As you wish." It was the only answer possible. "Though I fully intend to avoid the man, now I've satisfied his requirements. As ever, I am an abject coward at confrontation."

"Nay, lad. Speak not so slighting of my best work." His

elegant hand touched my cheek, and with his usual wink and flourish, he hurried away.

Unsettled with these conflicts, propelled with a heightened urgency to complete my mission before Nidallo returned, I sped to the lectern and leafed quickly to the alphabetical listing of the *Catalog Geographia*. No entry corresponded with the name Ophelie had bled to discover.

The royal geographers who assembled the *Catalog* were known for their prejudices. They listed locales in Louvel, Aubine, Nivanne, and Tallemant in detail. But they frequently left out much from the less-prosperous demesnes-major, or places that lay in the demesne-minor of a personal or family rival. To find the most accurate information, of which the *Catalog* was but an organized extract, one had to look to the unwieldy volumes of the Survey, the census taken at the outset of each Sabrian king's reign.

Hastening into the Survey Room, I pulled out the index volume of the *Survey Philippi*. Even more than before, the painful sense that I must not expose my purposes consumed me.

Altevierre did not appear in the Survey's summary list of great houses, nor anywhere in its sparse index. I removed my spectacles and pressed the heels of my hands into my gritty eyes, forcing myself to concentrate. I had no time to read the entire Survey. The spelling of *Altevierre* rooted the word in central Louvel, whose lexicon had become standard as printed books spread throughout the kingdom. But Ophelie might have misspelled an overheard name. Perhaps the word drew from an older tradition. . . .

Altevierre could be interpreted as *highest view*. I pulled out the Survey volume devoted to Grenville, the rugged demesne to the north, where local dialects had evolved from the same invaders who had populated Dante's Coverge. I scoured every entry—every farmstead, house, village, and crossroads—and found nothing.

Growling in frustration, I tore through the slim collection of pages devoted to mountainous Coverge, but Sabria's poorest demesne-major had no great houses, farms, or towns, only scattered mining settlements, none of which came anything close. I ran my fingers over the remaining volumes. As a fish hooked and drawn, my finger halted on the slender volume entitled *Demesnes-major: Arabasca*. I snatched the book from the stack.

A door slammed. Measured footsteps echoed on the library stair. I dared not stop. Who knew when I might get another chance?

My finger sped through the pages, pausing at any name remotely similar. And there it was.

Eltevire: Seven-and-thirty residents. Nine men of arms-bearing age. A hundred eleven goats. Eight stone houses. A temple ruin and watchtower, ca 450 SE, both scavenged for building stones. Watering hole. Dry well. Thirteen knives. Two axes. Access by goat track and stone bridge, three kilometres due north of the shrine at Canfreg Spring.

A goat track to access a watchtower—a highest view. I shoved the Arabascan volume into the stack and slammed the book cupboard shut. Then I snatched up the lamp and turned to go. Nidallo loomed in the archway opposite.

"Your lists made no mention of Survey volumes," he said, glaring at my hands, as if expecting evidence of theft. "They do not leave the library."

Emboldened by discovery and fueled by an unfocused anger, I had no trouble with this play. "I've taken no Survey volumes. Count them, if you wish. You are not privy to every matter my mentor and I discuss. Now, I've closed Mage Dante's crates with tamper seals. If you could provide rope . . ."

I oversaw the delivery of Dante's crates to a local drayman and left Collegia Seravain without another word to anyone.

Altevierre. Eltevire. I should have known to look to Arabasca first. Some two years before, I had retrieved a cache of books unearthed from the ruins of a once-fortified Arabascan town called Xarles. Before and during the Blood Wars, Xarles and that entire corner of Sabria's eastern borderlands—crags and stony tablelands pocked with wildcat dens, hermits' caves, and robbers' lairs—had been the demesne of the Mondragoni necromancers.

HAD IT NOT BEEN MIDDLE-NIGHT at the dark of the moon, I would have set out for Arabasca immediately; yet simple wisdom insisted that investigating Eltevire on my own would be a fool's gambit. Despite my youthful dreams that had repeatedly anointed me the boldest of knights, I lacked the weapons to dispatch even a single despicable mage. Trained awareness of enchantments, paper knowledge, and a borrowed courret could scarce stand against magic bolstered by transference. And the manly art of righteous combat was as alien to me as the practices of sculpture or painting. The only "gentleman's swordmaster" my father could afford had been a drunken tavern brawler. I needed Dante.

A dreadful night in the local hostelry affirmed the sensible course. In the dark wakings between my own nightmares of glaring spectres and fleshless mules, and the mumbling, snoring, wind-ridden sleep of my companions in the bachelor's loft, I resolved to save Lianelle ney Cazar. I would not force myself on the girl, but neither would I follow Michel's example and abandon her. Ilario would know her family. Somehow, in his odd way, he could devise a scheme to remove the girl from Seravain. Once that was settled, I'd devise some ruse to roust Dante and ride for Eltevire.

Even such resolution did not ease me into sleep. I spent the last hours of darkness huddled over a corner table in the inn's common room. Meg, the yawning, drop-shouldered woman who kept the shabby establishment, brought me ale and cold steamed buns left from the previous day.

"Yer back to Merona with first light, then," she said as she spitted a slab of bacon over her newly stoked fire.

"Aye. The great wicked city, all fish and sour wine, with evils round every corner." My mirthless humor echoed the common local opinions.

Meg bobbed her head, knowingly. "There was a lad from out near Oncet what went to Merona and near got hisself starved. . . ."

Citizens of Tigano prided themselves on exchanging lurid tales. Living in the shadow of the collegia magica seemed to expand everyone's imagination into the realms of the fantastic. This common room witnessed many a night of competitive tale-spinning. Yet made-up stories paled beside a plotted web that linked royal assassination and transference, Merona and Collegia Seravain, the living and the dead.

Of a sudden, my sluggish curiosity woke. What had people seen roundabout Seravain and Tigano? One sure way to prompt more stories . . .

"Your Oncet boy fared lucky even so," I said, issuing my challenge as soon as the woman's story wound to a bittersweet end. "Fellow in my lodging house at Merona was found murdered not long since. Ears, nose, and fingers cut off. Corpus dropped in an alley near the docks, emptied entire of his blood. The whore who lives upstairs says the man's ghost lingers in the lane. Scared three customers away. Dreadful things like *that* don't happen in Tigano."

Meg, dusted with flour and smelling of smoke, scooped up my emptied mug and refilled it from the tap. "Nah, boy. 'Tis not only in the city ghosts are walking. Every morn Bets the Seamer spies her gammy what was hanged a'dangling beside her washing line, and Dame Fanny herself says her dead sons creep about their old rooms in the manse. None dares go to our deadhouse save in best daylight. But it's true, we've seen no grueish murders such as you're telling of."

"Be thankful," I said.

When she issued no new attack in our lurid joust, I drained my cup and gathered my traveling case to go. Too much to hope that evidence lay about the countryside awaiting my eye. I'd had a moment's thought that if Gaetana or someone else was practicing transference at the collegia, some evidence of a mule might have turned up here. They'd not dare use a second student.

"But then . . ." The woman's hand slowly turned her bacon. "I've not seen a man so staggered as Adept Coperno when Constable called him down from Seravain and he declared Grafer Wheelwright three times dead. Emptied half my tun afore he spake a word."

Meg blotted her sweaty brow with her sleeve, and she did not look up to make sure her tale had created the proper state of horrified amazement on my face. This tale frightened *her,* as well.

I lowered myself to the stool. For a constable to call in aid from Seravain was not uncommon. For an adept to be frightened by a corpse was something else again. And for that adept to be a cocky former classmate who had left Seravain abruptly a few years previous mandated a hearing. "Three times dead? I never heard such."

Though her complexion took on the color of soured milk, she could not resist the telling. "Grafer got drunk and beat his wife. As was his common way, he run 'ta the wood to sleep it out. But a trimonth passed and he never come home."

She filled herself a mug and dragged a stool up to my table. "Then it happ'd one night a crate was left in my own yard to be shipped off to Merona. No one spake me, but only left the proper coin with it. Come daylight, the drayman and his helper, loading their wain, dropped the crate"—she leaned close until I smelled the ale and garlic on her breath—"and 'twas Grafer curled up inside—dead. Constable called the coroner. But the coroner couldn't say what killed Grafer, as the lad had marks of strangling on his neck, and yet had green scum lodged in his throat as though he were breathing and fell into Breek's Ditch."

She drank deep of her ale. "Adept Coperno come down from Seravain and worked his magic to seek which way Grafer died, so they could name the murderer. Three . . . four . . . five times over he worked it, till he puked all over the deadhouse floor, for he'd no magic left in his blood to fire his spellmaking. Once he drunk up my ale, all Coperno said was, 'Three times dead. Strangled and died. Stabbed and died. Drowned at the last. And maybe more besides, but my seeing failed me.' And then he stumbled out and's ne'er again come down the hill."

A story to make anyone blanch. A story that teased and nagged and roused a certainty that this was no exaggeration, but very much a part of the exact same story I lived. "That's a cruel, wicked tale, mistress. This happened when? Six . . . seven . . . years ago?"

" 'Twas exactly three years past, come midsummer, as it

happened when my daughter was confined with her youngest, and we had a charm-singer in to ward her house from—" The innkeeper flushed and jumped up, as if she'd just recalled that I, too, was a follower of the Camarilla, who lashed or fined such unsanctioned practitioners as charm-singers. "Best get to my baking. Everyone will be up soon."

She stuck out her hand for payment. I rummaged in my belt purse, and the first coin I pulled out was the double-strike silver—Gruchin's luck charm. I'd never returned it to Dante. No reason not to spend it; silver was silver. But I slid the coin into my boot, then pulled out twenty copper kivrae and tossed them on the table.

"One more thing, Mistress Meg," I said, snagging her apron as she scooped up the coins. "Did the constable send after the one who was to receive the crate? Surely that person would have knowledge of the crime. I'd like to think such mystery simply explained—and well punished."

She downed her ale and shook color back into her sagging cheeks. "Constable thought same as you, but my lads had already broke up the crate and thrown it in their morning fire, and none recalled what was writ. Some say Grafer haunts Breek's Ditch. I've not seen him, but I don't go down there no more. 'Tis a wicked age we live in. Temples deserted. Disbelievers growing bold. Folk forget their ancestors and make daemonish devices that steal the stars from the heavens, and prison time itself in jewel cases. My mam said the dead rise to give us warning of evil times, and so I believe." She jerked her apron from my hand.

I rousted the stable lad, preferring to lead my mount until the light grew than to remain in Tigano one more moment. As I trudged along the rutted road, I could not shake the notion that Adept Coperno had met a fate no fairer than Grafer Wheelwright. Had the frightened adept gone back to Seravain and asked one question too many? For I would swear on my hope of Heaven that he had left the collegia exactly three years ago at midsummer without a word to anyone.

The rare physician could retrieve a life whose spark had dimmed past common detection. But only a sorcerer of uncommon power—only three I'd read of—had ever reclaimed a dying person from the very folds of the Veil. Only a sorcerer exploring the unholy might see use in repeatedly driving a man to that brink and snatching him back again.

The light grew, tinting the scant clouds with vermillion and rose. Old Meg's story had raised such dread in me that I felt near drowning in it. I retrieved a flask from a saddlebag and drew down a long pull of ale, then pressed my face against my horse's flank. And in that moment of warm, living darkness, memory raised an image of freshly splintered wood . . . not Grafer Wheelwright's crate, broken and thrown in a fire, but long strips scattered in Ophelie's cell in the royal crypt. Great Heaven, had someone transported *her* to Castelle Escalon in a crate? And Michel—

My heart near stopped its beating. I had *seen* such a crate as could hold a tightly bound man, not two days after Ophelie de Marangel had escaped her prison. A crate exuding the stink of "mushrooms growing in dirt and dung" had sat in Castelle Escalon's steward's office. Had it held a dead man or . . . the god save us all . . . a living one?

I threw myself on my horse and pushed the poor beast unmercifully all the way to Merona.

CHAPTER FIFTEEN

23 QAT
38 DAYS UNTIL THE ANNIVERSARY

The morning air hung heavy and damp in the bustling passages and courtyards of Castelle Escalon. I ducked my head as I forged through the ever-moving river of courtiers and servants. The sense would not leave me that anyone I *noticed* would turn up dead.

I had arrived the previous evening after two long days on the road, only to find the tally of the fallen grown to yet more dire proportions. Waiting in my apartments was a message from a devastated Ilario. Mage Orviene's adept Fedrigo, Ilario's favored maker of crocodile charms and stomach elixirs, was reported knifed in a tavern brawl near the docks and thrown dead into the river. And beside Ilario's scented paper lay a letter scribed in my own hand, still sealed, returned along with a message informing me that the Marqués and Marquesa de Marangel and their two young sons had met an unfortunate fate. An *explosion of devil's firework* had devoured Ophelie's home and family not a tenday past. Someone felt us on the trail of discovery. Every hour since learning this news had been filled with a creeping dread, the first tremors of an earthshaking that set birds and beasts to flight.

My morning's first task was to settle the matter that had gnawed at my vitals all the way from Seravain. Henri de Sain, third secretary to the palace steward, was my quarry of the moment. Assuming *he* lived.

Henri was sweeping his private office, which was not at all private and very unlike an office, being little more than a closet off the stone-floored, north-wing undercroft. Casks, trunks, and teetering stacks of crates shared the vast undercroft with a legion of undersecretaries, paymasters, footmen, draymen, and ladies' maids.

"Divine grace, Henri," I said, as if our two brief encounters had made us personal friends, "I just wanted to thank you again for the recommendation of your tailor. As soon as I've pay in hand, I'm determined to give him fair custom."

"Oh, very good," he said, looking a bit surprised as I occupied his stool, drawing up my knees and wrapping my arms round as if set to stay awhile. He set his broom in the corner and brushed off his sleeves. "Is there something I can do for you, Sonjeur de"—his eyes darted to my exposed left hand—"Savin-Duplais, is it? Portier?"

I bobbed my head. "Honestly, you're the only person in the palace who's been civil, so I didn't think you'd mind another inquiry. I've just returned from Collegia Seravain whence I shipped three book crates back here for this wolfhound of a mage, Dante." I screwed up my face in disgust. "The taverner told me a dreadful story about a crate that had been dropped in her yard, only to find a *dead man* in it. A *corpus* . . . to be shipped *here* to Castelle Escalon, she said! And not respectfully in a decent coffin as a family might do, with a verger's blessings and proper pall over all, but curled up tight in a nailed-up box as one would never suspect. Have you ever heard of such wickedness?"

"Nay." His nostrils flared in distaste. "Such a violation would be—"

"Exactly so. But you see"—I dropped my voice, drawing him nearer with every word—"I recalled that stinking crate you had in here not a tenday ago, just before the fire on the *Swan*, and it gives me the frights to think it might have been a corpse, as well. And I'm wondering— This

Dante has already laid threats on me, you see. I'm bound by my duties to deal with him, but if he's the one shipping corpses about the kingdom or having them sent, I'm thinking to resign my post and hie me back to academe."

Henri's knotted brow softened. "You needn't fear, good Portier. He's neither sent nor received any parcel whatsoever. That particular nasty crate—living mushrooms as I recall, destined for an apothecary in Mattefriese—originated with the least likely person to be engaged in abominations of any kind, Damoselle ney Billard herself."

The sunlight pouring into the dusty hall dimmed to gray. I heard myself laughing and prating about foolish anxieties and country superstitions. But all the time Maura's own words crowded my memory. "Some matters we cannot alter. Some promises we cannot undo." Eugenie herself had stitched only the new DESTINNE ensign on the celebration banners. Who but Maura would have seen to the ordering of linen and hiring of seamstresses and the delivery of the finished rolls? Maura, the queen's trusted household administrator, who had been unstrung since the fire on the *Swan*. And Mattefriese lay on the Louvel-Arabascan border, the last town of any size between Merona and Eltevire. Blessed angels . . .

My spirit recoiled. Rebelled. Yet, as if I had split into two persons at once, Portier, *agente confide,* nattered with Henri about his busy life in the palace, and all the crates and bundles that came through the palace, exclaiming how easy it must be to get them confused.

"As do you, I keep a journal," he said. "Everyone says I can recall names and dates and sizes as some recall their children's birth stars and lineage." Flushed, he waved off my feigned amazement. "I'll send notice when your boxes arrive. Then you'll be finished with this fearsome Dante. A footman I know saw the mage set fire to his food with his eyes. He was at table with the queen's ladies and claimed the meat was off. And the maid who washes his linen swears he can see through walls, as he forever opens the door before she knocks! Could that be true?"

"I'd put no outlandish talent past him," I said, truthfully. "But I'd best hush. What if he finds out I've spoken ill of him?"

Henri blanched.

"One more small thing," I said. "You've surely heard about this event Lord Ilario plans for Prince Desmond's deathday? I'll need banners to be made. . . ."

Numb already, I was scarce surprised to hear that the palace seamstress who had sewn the banners for the *Swan* had slit her wrists, horrified that her faithful work had been used to endanger her king.

The third secretary would make a fine, credible witness, said I, the king's chosen *agente*, a lunatic who had dared imagine that out of this snarl of ghosts and murders something new and good might take root in his own sorry life. I made it as far as the wide steps of whorled marble that led into the queen's wing of the palace before I dived into a small fragrance garden to be sick.

The heaving seemed to purge my head as well as my stomach. Maura could *not* be involved in these crimes. I did not question my growing certainty that Henri's crate had held a living prisoner, but any of two hundred people could have attached Maura's name to it. She did favors for everyone in the queen's household. And surely fifty other people had been involved with the delivery of the banners to the *Swan*. Unlike her mistress, Maura had boarded the ship.

Questioned outright, she could surely provide an explanation for everything . . . only I could not ask. Secrecy must be maintained. Exoneration was not my prerogative. My charge was to gather evidence, make linkages, investigate, deduce.

I wiped my mouth on my sleeve and plucked mint leaves from a spreading plant. Chewing the pungent leaves, I headed for the east wing and Ilario's apartments, speeding through the curved window gallery that displayed the ruddy rooftops of Merona. I would task Ilario with saving Lianelle ney Cazar, and then persuade Dante to come with me to Eltevire. Unmask the true conspiracy, find the murderers, and all would be clear.

"Duplais!"

I near jumped out of my skin. A firm hand on my sleeve drew me out of the stream of footmen and maidservants to the window wall. "I've been hoping to speak with you, and here you manifest in my own haunts."

"Mage Orviene!" Every distraction receded as I bestowed my entire attention on the neat little man with pomaded hair, silver collar, and pleasant smile. I inclined my back. "Divine grace, sir. How may I serve you?"

His wide, soft features drew into a focused concern. "Excuse my abruptness, Sonjeur de Duplais, but I hoped you might be able to enlighten a grievous darkness."

"Whatever I can." Curiosity scorched my mouth dry.

"My assistant, Fedrigo, has gone missing for more than a tenday. A reliable report says he's been stabbed in a brawl and drowned, but I"—a nervous finger rubbed his rounded chin—"I cannot accept it. Drigo was an abstemious man, not at all inclined to gaming or rowdiness. I'm extremely worried about him."

Had I charms or amulets or enchanted swords to defend myself, every one would have been raised. Why would Orviene come to *me* with this?

"A grievous matter indeed," I said carefully, "but I scarce see how I can help you. Though my employer ever sings Adept Fedrigo's praises, I've met the fellow only once."

Orviene propped himself on the window seat and examined me with a sharp, wry glance. He cleared his throat. "Well, this *is* about your employer. Lord Ilario frequently hires Fedrigo for private spellworking, so I thought perhaps he might know why the lad might have gone down to Riverside or whom he might have met there. But your chevalier forever behaves as if I am a goblin lurking in his closet and refuses to speak with me beyond formalities. If *you* could enlighten me, I'd need not bother your master. And truly . . ." Of a sudden, the mage's whole posture shifted, as if a mask had dropped away. "My apprentices are as sons to me, Acolyte Portier. Drigo has no family save his mother in Delourre. How can I write her of his death, offering no more explanation than drunken foolery? She cannot even claim his remains."

The world stilled. "His body's not been found, then," I said.

The mage motioned me to bend my head closer. "You'll have heard whispers of the resurgent evil abroad in Merona, and that the practice might even be linked to the events on the *Swan*. I wish I could declare such rumor false. Any with a marked hand is at risk. I've urged my aides to stay wary, and so you should, as well. I fear greatly for Drigo's fate."

No trace of the bantering courtier remained, but only a sincerely troubled man afraid his missing apprentice might face a death more terrible than a tavern rowdy's blade in his craw. Dared I believe him?

"I can try to find out, sir mage," I said, slowly. "Naturally, I could not betray Lord Ilario's confidence."

"I'd never presume that."

"But if he knows aught of your assistant, I'll let you know."

"I would be most grateful." He offered his hand, palm up, requesting a trust bond—an old-fashioned custom among magical practitioners. Though I had no magic to forego, I laid my palm on his without qualm. Warm and steady, his hand conveyed no ill.

"Mage," I said, seizing an opportunity unexpected, "if you've evidence . . . or suspicion . . . that the fire on the *Swan* was linked to illicit practice, should not the Camarilla be warned? So many died."

One small hand flew to his mouth; the other jittered in a vigorous denial. "Merciful saints," he whispered, eyeing the passing maidservants and courtiers. "Forget the ravings of a loose tongue. Of all men, you should understand my position. Do I speak my suspicions, all will name it jealousy and ambition, an attempt to divert attention from my own . . . limitations. Even so, if the murderous fire *itself* gave me pause, I would speak out. But, it was not in the crime but in the remedy I felt the stirring of strength . . . extraordinary."

"In the caelomancy, then," I said. "You believe transference enhanced the magic wielded to bring the rain?" That jibed with Dante's experience.

He winced at the word spoken aloud. "We all reached for strength beyond our own that day. That was likely what I felt. If you hear aught of Fedrigo . . ."

"I'll inform you right away, of course."

Orviene could certainly be accused of jealousy and ambition. Gaetana was a master mage and the queen's First Counselor, privy to the queen's secrets, always first to be consulted, always at her right hand. No matter Orviene's popularity with courtiers and servants, it must appear impossible to gain ground on her. Was this only a play for sympathy or did he suspect my role? I could get no firm sense of the man.

I watched the mage hurry up the queen's stair, then turned into the passage where the three mages had their apartments. Morning light revealed naught but dancing dust motes. When I rapped on Dante's door, enchantment grazed my knuckles like broken glass.

"He'll not answer."

I lurched around and slammed my back to the door. Truly, the morning had my nerves shredded.

A dark young man in adept's gray lugged a desk toward me, a stool upended on its top. His sharp features and trim beard looked vaguely familiar, which could likely be said of every young male adept in Sabria. Every one of them had passed through Seravain's library at some time or other. And every one of them grew a manly beard once he escaped the collegia's strictures.

"Is the mage away, then?" I asked, lending him a hand with the heavy table.

"Not that I know. He's only given up answering the door." He bobbed his head toward the stretch of wall beside Dante's door. "Just there, if you would."

We placed the desk as he wished, and he unstacked the stool, setting himself on it to catch his breath. "If the door is locked and warded, even I can't get in, which is why I've commandeered this desk. I'm hopeful that if I daemonstrate a resolute spirit, my new master will decide he can use me after all."

"You're Master Dante's new assistant." Curse my distracted mind, where had I seen him?

He entwined his long fingers and rested them on the desk. "I confess it. Assigned three days ago. I've hopes of learning a great deal once he allows me into his chamber. You're the librarian from Seravain, the royal cousin. I'm greatly reassured that you survived your fiery resignation."

The deadhouse! This was Conte Bianci's adept. Recalling my craven posturing on that night set my complexion ablaze. "Aye, that's me," I said. "My temperament is ill suited to violence."

"Mine, as well," he said, grinning, "but the magic is incomparable." He flicked coal-dark eyes to Dante's door. "I'd sell my gammy to learn how he does it."

"I just know my gullet clamps shut whenever he points that staff at me," I said, resisting the temptation to compare experiences of Dante's wonders. The poorer the common assessment of my capabilities, the better. "Paper knowledge feeds the soul and intellect, but provides little defense against fire spouts that char your clothes." I exposed my hand and bowed. "Portier de Duplais."

He returned the courtesy. "Jacard de Viole. I never thought to see you outside your archives, Curator. You were as imposing as the library facade. I believed you must have lived there unaging all the centuries since it was built and had accumulated all the knowledge to be found there. Your direction helped me through many an examination."

But not the final examination as yet. He wore no collar.

Many adepts left the collegia to apprentice with master mages, hoping to make the leaps of talent and insight that would carry them through mage testing. Most never made those leaps and never returned, remaining minor practitioners of the art under strict Camarilla supervision.

"Glad to hear I was useful," I said, unable to recall Jacard or his talents. "This new direction my life has taken . . . I'm not sure it suits as well. Which leads to business: I must inform Master Dante about the errands I've run for him—my last, as it seems."

"We can try."

Jacard popped up from his stool, tapped on the door, and pressed the latch. He did not flinch, nor did he examine his fingers as I did every time I touched one of Dante's wards. Nor did he seem to sense the flood of magical energy that rushed through the open doorway like a herd of newborn lambs. The whorls and eddies of power made me feel sixteen again, full of vigor and unsullied hopes.

"Master," said Jacard, as he stepped through the doorway, "Sonjeur de Duplais wishes to speak with you."

When I stepped out from behind the adept, shock stole my tongue. Illness or exhaustion had rewritten Dante's body in the five days since we'd visited Calvino de Santo and his spectre. He stood in the center of his circumoccule, leaning heavily on his staff. His eyes, circled in gray, had sunk deeper under his already-heavy brows. His gaunt cheeks were faded, as if these weeks of palace life had not just paled the sundarkening of his skin, but sucked out its natural coloring, as well. His thick, wide shoulders bent as if holding up the vault of the sky. Great Heaven, what had he been up to?

"I'll see no visitors today. No flea-wit assistants. And no failed cowards *ever*. Weakness offends me."

Cursing Jacard's presence, I stammered, "Master, I've only a brief—"

"I said *not ever*!" Blue and purple lightning belched from his staff. Gleaming spicules scored exposed flesh and pierced garments, flesh, and bone, stinging like frozen needles. Throat and lungs were seared with frost and my mind with a ferocious repudiation. Only a determined observer would have noticed how Dante's hand trembled as he extended the staff.

Jacard hurriedly dragged me back over the threshold. The door flew shut behind us.

The adept rubbed his arms, as if to make sure his skin remained whole. "Why did he leave the god-blasted door unlocked if he didn't want company?" he mumbled, kicking his stool against the wall so hard it bounced into the middle of the corridor, causing a passing maidservant to squeal and scuttle past.

I knew why. Dante had wanted to warn me off. *Don't come here ever.* Something had changed. My glance flicked to Jacard, reappraising. Did the danger lie in the new assistant himself or some other threat?

"Who can explain one like him?" I said. "When he allows you inside again, inform him that the materials he requested are on their way from Seravain. Father Creator, I'm pleased to leave him to one younger than I. May you learn enough to make your difficulties worthwhile."

"I'll give it a little time," he said. Heaving a sigh, he retrieved the stool, and settled himself on it, feet propped on the desk. As I rounded the corner into the window gallery, he pulled a book from the folds of his gown and began to read. He seemed ordinary enough.

Frustrated and concerned, I set out for Ilario's apartments. My imagining faltered at any *magic* which could cause so great a change. And what could induce Dante to refuse this one last meeting for which I had a reasonable excuse? I needed to tell him all I'd learned.

As I hurried up the broad curved stair to the royal level that housed the elite of the queen's household, a cluster of ladies in cream-colored silks started down it. They twittered and buzzed softly like moths, the luminous Eugenie de Sylvae at their center. I moved to the side and bowed deeply as they passed.

As I straightened, the queen glanced over her shoulder and smiled ever so slightly. A tweaked corner of her mouth, crinkles at the corners of dark, sad eyes . . . I could not have said exactly how she framed an expression that left me awash in the knees. How could such ethereal beauty be tainted with the vileness of this conspiracy?

But then, I thought, as I moved on down the passage, Ophelie de Marangel might have grown into such a graceful woman. Who was left to weep for Ophelie but Lianelle ney Cazar and I? And if I didn't see to it, Lianelle's fate might mirror her friend's. I rapped on Ilario's elaborately carved door harder than I might have otherwise.

Oddly, the door opened but a crack.

"Lord?" I said, recognizing the pale blue eye that peered out at me.

"Heaven's mercy!" breathed Ilario as he opened the door just enough I could squeeze into his private sitting room. "I am not at all suited to hidings and sneakings."

As Ilario threw the latch, I watched in astonishment as

another visitor stepped through a narrow gap in the red brocade wall, then shut a hinged panel, quickly rendering the wall whole again. Dante leaned his back against the hidden door and slid slowly to the floor.

"I JUST NEED SLEEP," SAID the mage, once Ilario and I had hauled him up and over to a couch. "Stop fussing."

"You look like death," I said, "or near enough. And you're not so fine as all that, if your legs'll not hold you up. When did you last eat?"

"Can't remember." He brushed his shaggy hair from his face and scrubbed his sunken eyes. "What did you want to see me about? I need to get back. Gaetana might come for me."

Ilario held a glass of wine under Dante's nose. "Start with this. I'll send for food."

Dante hesitated.

"Shall I sip from it first?" snapped Ilario. He slammed the glass onto the table he'd shoved next to Dante's knees, slopping the dark liquid over the rosy marble.

"I just . . ." The mage reached for the glass. His hand trembled so violently, he could scarce get it to his mouth without spilling it over himself. "Gods."

Making any plans or decisions in his state would be unlikely to serve us. "If you would, Chevalier, food is an excellent idea," I said. "I've not eaten since I got back last night. And you must partake, Master. I'd not like to waste my time on a corpse."

Ilario marched off to the next room to ring for a servant, slamming the door behind him.

"What is this about?" I said.

"Naught to concern you."

"Not so. We cannot afford you to be incapable. If you're ill, we'll fetch a healer. If it's something else, I want to know. We're nearing the crux of this mystery. I need you fit."

"I am not ill."

He would not meet my eye. Rather, his gaze traveled Ilario's apartment, as if to make sure no one lurked behind drape or statue. Certain marvels, like the Syan silk hanging of human-sized dancers, the elephantine urns trimmed in gold and bursting with flowers, and the round tabletop of pink marble supported by intricately worked castings of fanciful beasts, caused his gaze to linger. Each time, he wrenched his attention away and fixed it on his staff for a moment before returning to his inspection. His color deepened when he noticed me watching.

Odd how that simple reaction forced me to look at him with new eyes. Curious, yet embarrassed to be caught gawking, he'd likely never been inside a wealthy man's private apartment. No matter his formidable talents, or his unique and powerful insights into magic, he was only a man, still young in countless ways. I needed to remember that.

"If not ill, then what?"

"There is a thing I can do . . . that I am learning to do . . . to read another mage's spellwork from a distance and draw it into myself. So I can see the exact pattern of the enchantment—its keirna—even as it's being shaped." He gripped his staff and shifted uncomfortably on the thick blue cushions, as if he were eighty years old with grinding joints. "All sorcery requires certain expenditures. This requires more. That's all. I can manage it."

"To see into a living enchantment . . ." So casually he spoke of it. To make his mind an opticum that could see the invisible cells, not of stems and leaves and crystals, but of spells. He would be able to understand a spell's composition and intent far more completely than by analyzing its residue. He might be able to devise magic to counter it. Not even in the vault texts had I heard a glimmer of such a possibility. "Gates of Heaven, man, have you accomplished this?"

Counterspells, as I knew them, required endless trial and error and an assumption that a particular enchantment would be repeated to an exactitude. If we could know what the other mages were doing, we'd not have to insinuate Dante into their trust, and hope to make them spill their secrets in words.

He grimaced and ground the heel of his staff into Ilario's fine carpet. "I'm no good at it yet. But the last few attempts . . ." He glanced up, and I caught the feral gleam I'd espied in him so often. "Orviene has all the magical skills of a tool grinder, but he's careful. His poison wards are clean and meticulous. His sleep spells follow common practice and work as well as any. But Gaetana brings far more talent and a sharper will. Her work is complex; things like honing the fighting skills of the queen's bodyguards; sharpening their awareness. I've yet to pattern one of her works completely."

But he would. I could read it in him. Though it might kill him, he would.

Fed by his fever, ideas bloomed in my head like night lilies. "Perhaps we've been mistaken, assuming Orviene and Gaetana work together. Just an hour since . . ." I told him of the missing Fedrigo and Orviene's hesitation to report his suspicions of Gaetana. "He seemed sincere. Perhaps Gaetana's worked the transference alone or partnered with someone else."

"Mayhap." He considered for a long moment. "Orviene craves to be more than he is. But his magic doesn't *reach*. I'm no good to judge more than that. But the woman . . ."

Dante shifted again, and downed the remainder of his wine, wiping his mouth on his sleeve. Then he stared at the heel of his staff without speaking. I refilled his glass and summoned patience.

"I completed Gaetana's little translation task," he said, after a while. "A simple magical cipher. It was no treatise on the divine elements, but a few pages of a mage's scribblings. He was trying to prove that animals have souls by teaching them to understand human words, exploring techniques to disrupt their natural behaviors with regard to hunting, mating, pain, and the like. Some very unpleasant techniques." His lip curled. "I think Gaetana wanted to see if I balked at such practice. When I didn't, she said she had another text for me to unlock and translate, a manuscript buried deep in layers of wards and ciphers. Even less savory, but carrying knowledge of the uses of magic that have been lost for generations. She prates that a practitioner of 'exceptional talents and proper ethics' can convert any knowledge to good purpose. I've yet to see that text."

The fever of the hunt rose in *me* then. "Was this why you warned me off today?"

"I'm watched closer every hour," he said. "Gaetana walks in at odd times, often without leave. Adepts and acolytes trot over with messages or requests for information. Orviene pesters me to collaborate on his puling little projects. Now I've this fool adept lurking about, thinking he's the god's own son, and he was once their lackey. I'm attempting to discourage visitors. We need to—"

Dante broke off when Ilario returned with a tray of cold roast lamb, sugared oranges, and hot cider. While the mage dug in, and Ilario propped himself at the doorway in a sulk, I inspected the brocade wall. No enchantment, seam, or mechanism marked the secret entry.

"Oh, here, Portier," snapped Ilario, after I had fumbled about for a while. He marched across the carpet, tapped a brass gargoyle tucked into the corner beside his marble hearth, and slid the ugly little visage to the side. The panel in the wall swung open, revealing a gap that might have been a coal chute at middle-night.

"How long have the two of you shared this little connection?" I said, recalling Ilario's prattlings of hidden passages, trapdoors, and spelled closets that he and Eugenie had explored as children.

"When I heard about Dante's new assistant, it seemed reasonable that the two of you would be less free to talk together from now on in *his* rooms . . . which I know you do, though you never tell me half of what you discuss. So I found occasion to inform the mage about the route between here and there." Ilario hooked a thumb in his belt and returned to his aloof stance by the door. "Never imagined he'd actually use it. Has not my fool's wit exposed our every secret?"

"It will be most useful, lord chevalier," I said, fully sincere.

A glare seemed enough to move Dante to speech, or perhaps the rapidly vanishing food and wine had soothed his brittle edge as well as his exhaustion. He cleared his throat with a growl. "You have shown . . . resources, Chevalier. And the food is welcome."

"Have you a response, my lord?" Truly I felt like one of the women who minded the youngest students at Seravain, settling their fights when they dropped mice into one another's boots or dumped cold tea on one another's sheets.

Ilario fondled his lace and fluffed his ruffles while gazing at the ceiling. "Shall you provide an exhibit for my exposition, mage?"

Dante swallowed the last bite of meat with a grateful sigh. "Aye. It's another thing I've been working at. I aim to shock the twittering birds around this palace, including some murk-headed beginners not so far from here. Did you bring my other books and materials, student?"

I took what peace I could and resisted falling prey to his taunt. "Most. And I learned a bit. . . ."

As Dante devoured the last of the bread and oranges, I launched my tale of Lianelle, Ophelie, Michel de Vernase, and bodies in crates.

"The Cazars are an old-fashioned lot," said Ilario, who now sat on an exotic footstool, tapping his fingers thoughtfully on his chin. "They build on clifftops and keep close behind their walls, playing knife games and dancing until dawn. But something tweaks me about the name. One of Philippe's envoys might be a Cazar or related to one. I'll inquire about it . . . yes, *discreetly*, sir mage! But Damoselle Maura a villain? That seems unlikely. She is so . . . ordinary."

Ordinary. Unlikely. The very qualities I brought to Philippe's clandestine service.

No. I could not be so wrong about Maura.

Dante's demeanor had hardened as I spoke of Seravain. "This Kajetan," he said, "your *friend* who asks you to spy on me . . . Should I be expecting visits from Camarilla inquisitors?"

"Certainly not. The transference worries him, and the consequences should relations between the Camarilla and the king break down further. He's the only surviving mage in his bloodline. I wish we dared ask his help."

"Keep your friends *out* of my business," Dante snapped,

wiping sticky fingers on his sleeve. "You'd do well to consider what kind of mentor locks his student in a tomb when he fails. If he can't teach, he should find someone who can."

"You know nothing about him," I riposted, anger flared all out of proportion to his jab. "Or me."

The green eyes burned. "I know what it is to believe life's dropped you in a shaft you can't crawl out of. And I know what the hand that reaches down to you looks like. I'd wager my eyes 'tis not the hand of this mentor of yours."

Dante, gifted with talent beyond imagining, could never understand. Kajetan's library had saved my sanity. "Your interpretation of my life is irrelevant to our task, mage," I said, "and I'll thank you not to speculate on my personal situation. Kajetan will not have occasion to query you unless you do something to warrant it. On the other hand, I think this mystery of Eltevire must be followed without delay. The Marangels, the dead seamstress, the cell in the crypt . . . The murderers are cleaning up after themselves. They know someone's after them."

"I agree," said Dante, tapping his staff on the carpet. His head was cocked my way in a most annoying manner, as if his mouth were engaged with the present conversation while his mind yet dealt with the last. "We oughtn't be seen leaving Merona together. I'll meet the two of you at the shrine at Canfreg Spring, what . . . seven days hence?"

"Both?" Ilario straightened his back. "Yes, I could possibly make the time to accompany you. You may have need of a knight. I'll spread it about that I've gone back to the country for a cleanse, as I do every summer, but I'll tell John Deune I've a liaison with a lady. He's quite discreet for a valet, but none too clever, so someone will wheedle the news from him. I'm attentive to so many ladies, some will think it's one and that one will think it's another, until everyone is in a merry muddle and won't know where I've gone."

Dante wiped his mouth and rolled his eyes.

On another day I would have laughed, but on that morning, I felt only urgency. "Canfreg Spring," I said. "Midday of the seventh from this. Then on to Eltevire."

CHAPTER SIXTEEN

"He'll come," I murmured, dribbling wine onto the stained rock and passing the pewter cup to Ilario. "He's a man of his word. We'll finish our prayers, leave him some kind of token, then ride out. He'll catch up. We cannot remain here."

I bowed to the tarnished ikon and moved toward the round door of the little stone shrine, one of a hundred such shrines that lined a pilgrim way stretching from the western sea to the city of Abidaijar in Aroth—the home of the Cult of the Reborn. We had arrived at this barren holy place well before midday of the seventh day out of Merona, and had lingered through a blistering afternoon and a devilishly cold night awaiting Dante. Now the sunlight had again begun its crawl up the jumbled crags to the east.

Ilario made a quick oblation and hurried after me, the low ceiling forcing him to hunch as if his neck were broken. The soot from centuries of smoldering herbs had already soiled his soft gray hat and its soft gray cryte's feather. "But what if his horse has pitched him in a ditch or he's gotten himself sick again with his sorcery?"

"We can't help him by dawdling," I said, pausing at the

doorway. I felt exposed here. Every birdcall raised the hair on my neck. The dry breeze whispered of treachery. The chevalier and I were too conspicuous even for the small traffic that traveled this red-rock wasteland.

I should never have brought Ilario. At my insistence he had traded his satin and lace for canvas breeches, plain shirts, and buff jerkin, and his horse for a pilgrim's donkey. But Father Creator had surely designed the fop to fit in Castelle Escalon's halls like the gilded caryatids and fluted columns. In places like this wayside shrine, where one met few but goatherds, pilgrims, and scoundrels or adventurers bound overland for the exotic lands of Aroth and Syan, Ilario stood out like a magpie among sparrows.

A nosy tinker had spent the night near our encampment. A trio of surly pilgrims—a balding, fleshy fellow of thrice Ilario's girth, his gap-toothed brother, and a wan, flat-eyed woman—had ridden in at dawn to fill their waterskins at the muddy Canfreg Spring. For pilgrims they were exceedingly well armed. Dirks at belt and boot. The big man carried a war ax and a looped chain. They had stared at us for an hour before moving on east.

A temple reader had arrived at midmorning in a heavily laden donkey cart. The reader, a thickset provincial with a profusion of black, wiry hair, and his red-haired manservant, a hungry-looking, agitated sort of man with a wolflike jutting nose and chin, set up a small booth and altar across the road from the shrine. Temple servitors disdained the Cult of the Reborn, yet the bluff, friendly reader invited Ilario and me to join him for devotions. He had exposed his left hand. A man of the blood, then. Though my own gesture was quick, his keen-eyed manservant took full note of my own family mark. The two settled in for the day.

We needed to move on.

As we stepped into the heat-blasted afternoon, Ilario returned the offering cup to a niche above the doorway. I clutched our wine flask.

"Your lengthy devotions send a fair odor to Sante Marko," said the leather-skulled mendicant brother squatting just outside the shrine. "The sweet smokes will lure our beloved saint back through the Veil to stand stalwart in our earthly battles."

"We await the day," said Ilario, crossing his arms over his heart in pious fashion. Ilario's familiarity with Cult customs made me suspect him a believer.

Relentless sun and wind and the incessant inhalation of "sweet smokes" had withered the mendicant brother to a husk and left his mind adrift somewhere between the barren landscape and Heaven. His ragged garments—the cast-off donations of myriad travelers—flapped in the dry breeze. Dangling from his neck was the same green pilgrim badge Ilario and I wore, marked with the red phoenix insignia of the Cult.

As if of their own accord, the mendicant's bony fingers tapped the side of his rusted cup, reminding us of our obligation to make a more solid offering to keep his herb basket full. Ilario dropped a silver kivra in the cup and one of our bread rolls in the old man's lap, then strolled across the dusty ground toward our tethered donkeys.

I tossed a few coins after Ilario's and followed, studying the rock-lined path, the hivelike shrine, and the rubble walls of the sacred enclosure for some way to leave a sign, so Dante would know we'd come and gone. Gruchin's silver coin, tucked into my boot since Tigano, would be too tempting to any passerby. We'd need my compass to locate Eltevire. I had no scarf or gloves. . . .

"Sweet Heaven, it's a ruin," Ilario grumbled, brushing at his hat. His efforts had succeeded only in spreading the thick soot from his hat to his favorite leather riding gloves.

Inspired, I snatched the modestly feathered hat from Ilario's grasp and returned to the mendicant brother. "My master especially reveres Sante Marko," I said, dropping my voice. "He holds a belief that he once met Sante Marko Reborn, the elderly swordmaster who taught him all his knightly skills. But in the shrine yestereve, he experienced a revelation that he should bare himself to the elements to mellow his pride in that encounter. It's why we've stayed to proffer additional devotions. As his prayers provided no relief from the saint's geas, he offers you this fine hat."

The mendicant brother spread his arms as if to embrace

the sky, then reverently brought his fingertips to heart, forehead, and lips. "Sante Marko ever fills our needs," he said, his voice as arid as the wind across the stony landscape. "Warn your master to heed the letter of the saint's instruction. Where the Veil is thin, the Saints Awaiting view us clearly."

"Where the Veil is thin, brother? What does that mean?"

"'Twas in these lands first blood was shed in anger between human and human."

"The Lay of Goram and Vichkar?" I said. The tale of two friends who battled to the death over a bronze knife had been told since long before the rise of the Sabrian kingdom, before cities, before vineyards, before writing. "You believe it occurred near here."

"Aye. Their battle is our blessing and curse, as is all of creation save Heaven. The saints draw back the Veil to witness such terrible deeds."

Certain places on the earth provided a potent venue for spellwork: deep caves where ancients had painted beast images on the walls, an ancient vineyard in Louvel, a desolate plain in the heart of verdant Challyat. Devout Sabrians claimed such extraordinary magical places to be the actual venues for the creation stories—the cave where humankind first mastered fire, the plain where we first shaped a wheel, or the field where the Pantokrator planted the first grapevine—inevitably linking magic and holiness. They believed the tales collected in the *Book of Creation* to be history as true as the founding of our kingdom, their lessons a message from the divine.

The Camarilla deprecated such factual interpretation, insisting that each "location of magical significance" exemplified but a fortuitous confluence of the five divine elements. Such a site would inevitably attract those who practiced sorcery, imbuing the places with history alongside the layered residue of their magics. This position made more sense to me.

A few mages who lived before the Blood Wars had proposed a truth somewhere in between—that stories of such longevity must hold some secrets of gods or nature that we ought to be able to decipher. However, even they had never hinted that the tales might witness to a *physical* proximity of the human and divine worlds.

"What have you seen, brother?" I said, crouching beside him, my hands flexing as if to wrest his knowledge from inside his bald head. "What witness do you bear of Goram and Vichkar's blood in this land? Or the thinning of the Veil?" It was easy to believe this dry, red wasteland had witnessed humankind's first murder.

The mendicant brother clasped his hands before his breast. "I have witnessed marvels and terrors: the Stone That Does Not Fall, the Stream That Runs Uphill, the Shadow That Burns. The Pantokrator's Aurora shines through the Veil from time to time, and I've seen the Souleater's servants fly from the god in terror, drenched in blood, passing so close as to freeze my soul."

These marvels he spoke of came from no lore I knew. But what if the conspirators had heeded such rumor and had chosen to pursue their magics here, thinking to find the area a potent field for spellwork? Perhaps, the Mondragons, preoccupied with necromancy and daemonology, had claimed this region for their demesne based on such stories.

I pressed the brother to tell me how and where these strange things manifested themselves, but he rambled on of holy mystery and Sante Marko's blessings. My questions made no more sense to him than asking how did the earth manifest its solidity or the Arch of Heaven—the Tenth Gate—position itself in the night sky. Some things just were. The perpetual smokes of Sante Marko's shrine took him wandering the land. Whether in his mind or in his body, today or twenty years past, it was all one to him.

Jittery and frustrated, I bowed and bade him farewell. "Until Sante Marko comes."

"We await the day." His lips widened over broken teeth, and he plopped Ilario's smudged hat atop his sun-scalded head. Dante could not miss it.

"NO MATTER MY POOR LOST hat, the mage will never find us." Ilario planted his backside on a boulder and blotted his forehead, as I examined another thread of hard-packed dirt and gravel in search of tracks, hair, or droppings. "And we'll never find the way back to our beasts. Holy saints, Portier, we'll languish on this wretched rock forever—starving, filthy, mad like that cult brother. Were there ever any two more useless wilderness travelers?"

A chukar, flushed from the scattered rocks, clucked and squawked, mocking us.

We had ridden eastward from the shrine on the pilgrim road until well out of sight of the mendicant brother and curious travelers. Tethering our donkeys where clumps of blue-green wheatgrass sprouted thickly in the shade of an overhang, we had scrabbled up the tilted slabs and scree as best we could to reach the higher ground. Once above the scarp, we circled back westward across a stony tableland, hunting the elusive goat track that should lead us up the jagged ridge where the Survey said Eltevire must lie, straight north of Canfreg Spring.

"My compass keeps our heading true, lord. Besides, a simple snare could take yon partridge; I've read how to make them. And your sword could skewer it. We'd not starve."

Ilario scowled and stripped off his jerkin, stuffing it into his already crammed rucksack. "'Tis ungentle to patronize me, Portier. I already feel like a sheep being driven to the slaughterhouse."

My search futile, I waved him onward. "Consider yourself fortunate," I said, as we struggled up the mountain of stone shards that pulsed with afternoon heat. "The cult brother would have you shed *all* your garments on this journey as an offering of humility."

"*All?* What saint could see merit in fried bones? I've scarce meat enough to cover them all as it is, and surely even . . . *everything* would shrivel away. Sweet patroness of love, defend me!"

My deeper coloring prevented much scalding from the incessant barrage of sun and wind. Fair-skinned Ilario's forehead, ears, and long nose were going to pain him fiercely.

Despite a monologue of complaints and fervid intercessions over the eight days since we'd left Merona, Ilario had shown himself more resilient than I could have imagined. Better than me in the rough. Able to sleep on rock, and as nimble as a goat on these treacherous slopes. More than once his hand had hauled me up steps where my cheaply made boots found no purchase. I was glad he'd come.

Two hours after leaving the donkeys, a clump of coarse hair, snagged on a clump of thistle, hinted we'd found the way. A few more precarious steps, and we climbed onto a well-beaten path that hairpinned up the rubble slope, invisible to all but those who stood upon it. Surely, this was the route to Eltevire. Power . . . magic . . . I could see no other reason to settle in such desolation.

I waved my hand at Ilario and he pulled a small, elegantly engraved spyglass from his belt pouch. As it had all day, the little glass—a "gift from a lady"—revealed no telltale puff of dust or movement behind us.

An hour later, we thought we'd gone wrong again. No sign of goat, house, or ruin was to be found in the forest of sandstone rock spires atop the ridge. The path ended abruptly at two massive boulder stacks standing outlined against the indigo sky like one of Ixtador's Gates. Between them naught was visible but a lip of downsloping ground and the expansive sky. But our next step forward stole our breath.

Beyond the pillars and a few crumbling downward steps, the land took a precipitous plunge into a chasm so deep, its bottom was already lost in night. Only a narrow span of rock, perhaps one and one-half metres wide and fifty long, bridged the chasm. At its far end lay a sun-drenched plateau of crumbled stone and scrubby grass.

"Saints Awaiting!" Ilario's outburst was no less explosive for its being whispered.

I peered eagerly into the glare. The plateau's elevation was enough lower than our own that we could pinpoint the features listed in the Survey. Eight stone houses, built in the same beehive style as Sante Marko's shrine, clustered about a stone ring that must mark the dry well. A splotch of richer green near the center of the plateau evidenced the watering pond. Ilario's little spyglass revealed the ruined temple and watchtower as little more than a square of broken steps and fractured paving, almost lost in the golden haze.

The eighteen-year-old Survey had listed a population of seven-and-thirty people and one hundred eleven goats. We saw no sign of either. Save for its dramatic setting, nothing appeared at all extraordinary about the place.

Fighting off disappointment, I tried to be sensible. If this village was Eltevire, and Eltevire was the heart of our mystery—*the place where everything began*—we needed to be wary before blundering in.

Ilario grumbled when I insisted we sit for a quarter of an hour before proceeding. "Are you so tired, Portier?" he said, damping his voice when I scowled at him. "Honestly, you must get out more. And if you wish to see yonder ruin any closer, we'd best go now. The Souleater himself could not persuade me to cross that ridiculous sliver of rock in the dark."

Indeed, though deep gold light yet mantled Eltevire, our position already lay in shadow. But I wouldn't budge. "We need to listen," I whispered. "Our own footsteps and hard breathing mask sounds. If someone's following, I want to hear it."

Afternoon waned quietly. Dry gusts ruffled our hair and clothing. A scuttling vole rattled pebbles beyond the gate, rousing a cloud of swallows from the cliffs below us. No sounds of life emanated from the village across the bridge or behind us. I desperately wished Dante at my side.

Soon, I could put it off no longer. Dante might never come. "Have you your crocodile charm, lord chevalier?"

Ilario near dropped his rucksack into the chasm. "You don't think . . ."

I summoned patience. "No, lord. No crocodiles here. But we may need a light later on."

Reluctantly, he pulled the charm from his jerkin. "The key to the light spell is *crassica*."

A most unlikely grin forced itself through the foreboding that had weighed on me all day. Ilario's spellkey meant *large teeth*. "It is good you are here, Chevalier," I said.

"Tuck yourself behind one of these rocks where you can still watch. Stay hidden until I signal."

"I ought to go with you," he said, face screwed into a grimace and hand tapping his sword hilt. "You've no weapons. But I immensely dislike bridges; we should wait for the mage."

"From the look of the place, I doubt I'll need defending. But we don't know for sure. If you see the least hint of something awry, get away. Don't stop. Don't speak to anyone. Don't let anyone delay you. If you can't find Dante, go straight to the king." After a moment's hesitation, I passed him my journal. "Give him this. The cipher is not magic."

Ilario glanced at the worn little book and back at me, swallowed hard, then tucked it inside his shirt. "You'll have a care, Portier, yes?"

"Absolutely." More excited than fearful, I hopped and skidded down the unstable gravel and dirt steps. As I stepped onto the stone span, a humming cloud of gnats and sand fleas descended on me. Brushing at my skin, I took a second step. . . .

The world reeled. The chasm yawned. The cliff walls writhed, expanded, contracted, braiding the sunlight and shadow. My skin flushed hot, then cold, then hot again, and my belly heaved. Enchantments!

I dropped into a crouch, planting elbows on my knees and spinning head on my fists before I could topple into the chasm. In the moment I closed my eyes, the sensations vanished.

A visual ward, then—simple and indeed deadly, considering the narrow span of the bridge.

"Great Heaven, Portier, are you well?"

I winced as my name bounced repeatedly between the cliffs and Eltevire's plateau. Why did he have to shout?

Raising my hand to reassure him, I opened my eyes and fixed them on the mottled stone surface of the bridge. Cautiously, I stood. The world and my stomach remained calm. I took one step forward. The world sloshed only slightly, like the liquid in a carefully moved cup. I took another step.

Much as I hated to waste progress already made, I reversed course. Ilario's shout had likely alerted any lurkers. Nonetheless, my tongue refused to call out from such a distance.

"The bridge is warded, lord," I said when I stepped back onto the land. "When I signal you to come over, keep your eyes fixed on the span itself. Look neither right nor left nor up nor down, and pay no mind to anything beyond it. If you feel dizzy or your skin begins to itch, do as I did: Get low and close your eyes. Let the sensations ease; then try again. Do you understand?"

Ilario edged backward. "Perhaps you'll not need me. I'm no use around enchantments. I've no idea why the mage wanted me to come. He'd as soon push me over this edge."

"He'd never do that, lord. You are just very different from anyone he's known. He does not trust easily." Though truthfully, Dante's insistence on Ilario's company on this venture mystified me, as well. "When I'm sure all is clear, I'll call out or shine the light from your charm."

Blood thumping, I turned back to the bridge. No ordinary ruin would be so viciously warded. I crossed the rock span without further difficulty and strolled down the path into Eltevire and late-afternoon sunlight. The gusty breeze shifted dust about my boots, whipping it into small whirlwinds.

Two of the stone houses in the circle had collapsed. Tattered scraps of leather flapped in several doorways. The rest gaped open or were blocked with rubble, tangled peashrub, or gangly stems of asphodel, thick with white flowers. A peek inside evidenced soot, dust, and a few oddments: shards of pottery; a great deal of goat hair; three broken bone needles; a splintered piece of wood with closely spaced holes, which might have been a piece of a loom.

Bones lay in heaps, inside and outside—the fine bones of chukars and other fowl, of voles, rock pigs, and other scuttering creatures, the larger bones of goats and foxes. A stained stone tub, numerous worn-out tools, and bone pegs bore witness to a village tannery. Had not the Survey contradicted me, I'd have said no one had inhabited Eltevire for centuries, and no magic ever had been worked here. Why had Michel risked Ophelie's life to learn its name?

Crossing the field toward the temple ruin, I strained for some hint of magic. The rocks and grass and blowing dust almost glittered in the ocher light, as if ground glass infused the air. The breeze smelled of dry grass touched with pungent herbs I could neither locate nor identify. But I sensed no spellwork. None.

The temple ruin, situated at the far end of the plateau, revealed no more than the village itself. Sun and scouring wind had faded the temple floor mosaics, obliterating any meaningful design or inscription. What few dressed stones had not been carted off to build the beehive houses displayed no carving or painted surface, nothing to link the place to the story of Goram and Vichkar or to the Veil, to conspiracy or torment or to magic itself, come to that.

I squatted in the center of the temple floor. Broken bits of once-colored tile, sand, pebbles, and grit sifted through my fingers, scattering on the paving whence I'd gathered them. I was flummoxed.

Spluttering in frustration, I strode down the temple steps and across the rock-strewn field of tufted hare's tail and gray-green stipweed to the pond. The sun, bloated and wavering in the dust haze, settled toward the jagged horizon.

The watering pond was no gritty mudhole like the shrine spring. The clear, bottomless pool lay in a snail-like shell of rock, a catch basin gouged from a knob of the plateau bedrock by centuries of wind and rain. Examination revealed naught unusual.

Swearing, I threw in the temple debris yet clenched in my fist. The obstinate bits and pieces floated atop the dark water, circling slowly, as if a giant's spoon stirred the pool.

One side of the hollowed basin formed an overhang. Trampling the green onion grass that grew on the bank, I circled the pond and climbed atop the protruding rock, sighting back toward the bridge. Ilario might as well come and see the *nothing* we'd traveled so far to find.

A haze drifted across the plateau like mist or smoke in

a direction wholly opposite the direction of the wind. I squinted, but Ilario had hid himself well. Still stupidly reluctant to yell, I spoke the key to trigger his charm. *"Crassica."*

Light flamed from my hand like a blue sunrise.

Sainted ancestors! I released my grip on the shells, and the light vanished. But it took moments for my vision to clear, and longer yet for the spell's residue to settle over my spirit like silken sheets. I'd felt no such vigorous energy when Ilario triggered the charm in the crypt.

Without waiting for Ilario's response, I trotted back to the temple ruin. If the nature of Eltevire—its confluence of divine elements or inherited holiness—could so enhance worked spells, what might it do for spellmaking? Selfish. Foolish. My sudden hunger had naught to do with assassination plots or cruel hauntings, but solely with magic. *My* magic. *Please, gods . . .*

Dropping to my knees on the faded mosaic, I laid out my compass and whispered the key to a spell I had created when I first bought the little instrument. *Locuti.* Locate.

The bulging sun touched the horizon. My eyes near stretched from their sockets as I tried to detect the wisp of white smoke that should indicate the compass's location— and my spell's successful execution. But all I sensed was a shiver that passed through me to settle on the paving like spilled wine ready to stick to my shoes—the residue of failure.

Perhaps a weak spell bound so long ago would never work, even in a place of magical potency. But something new . . .

Manic, I stripped leaves from a stalk of asphodel that poked through the broken paving and laid them beside my compass. I added my handkerchief, and a pebble fetched from the crumbled temple steps, encircling my chosen particles with a thread ripped from my snagged hose. The brass of the compass supplied the elements of base metal and spark. The pebble brought the steadiness of its composite elements—base metal and wood. The leaves added the element of water into the balance, needed for transparency and sinuous movement. The kerchief supplied wood and air, essential for combustion. My mind raced, estimating, adding, and subtracting. Perhaps a smaller stone, lest the working grow too large.

I near cackled at the ridiculous image of uncontrollable fire coming from any work of mine.

The particles appeared correct, their arrangement as prescribed. My will stood ready. Yet instinct would not allow me to begin. I recalculated. Without tinder or kindling, the spell would require a great deal of spark. Brass did not provide enough. I needed silver.

I ripped open my belt purse, cursing as I sorted only twelve silver kentae. But Gruchin's silver double strike was larger and heavier, bearing my royal cousin's raised likeness on both faces. I extracted the coin from my boot and laid it atop the stack inside the loop of string. Another quick calculation. Ten thousand times had I worked this spell, always failing, and ten thousand times had I imagined it, always succeeding. Trained instinct called the balance perfect. Ready.

Mustering every scrap of will inside me, every remnant of longing, belief, and desire, I called on the magic of my blood and spoke the proper words to complete the formula for fire, the most fundamental of spells.

Faint as a snake's heartbeat in winter, cold as a dead man's nose, a rill of power threaded my veins. Gold sparks burst from the center of the looped thread like grains of sunlight scattered in the encroaching dark, promising warmth and safety. My heart swelled to bursting . . .

. . . and shriveled again, as one-by-one the sparks winked out, my veins warmed, and the heartbeat of my magic stilled. As ever.

The sky dulled to ocher, streaked with purple. The land lay silent and empty.

I could not swear. Could not weep. Could not allow myself to feel this yet again.

And so I did as I had always done. Forced my lungs to pump. Forced myself to move. I folded the handkerchief and tucked it away with my compass. I brushed the leaves, the stone, and the thread aside, lest someone notice their particular arrangement. Certainly the balance of elements had been inexpert. Rushed. So many untried particles. Just because Adept Fedrigo's crocodile charm had worked so explosively, it didn't follow that this place would enhance *new* spellwork. Excuses. Explanations. Anything but admitting the unshakable truth.

"Aaaagh!" Irrational, uncontrollable, a lifetime's disappointment exploded from my every pore. I snatched up the piled silver and flung the coins across the temple floor. The kentae scattered, bouncing and rolling. The double strike coin flew farther, spinning in the air, catching the last stray beam of the vanishing sun. Then, like a hummingbird feeding, the coin paused in its flight and hung suspended in the air . . .

And hung.

Moments passed. I blinked. Squinted. Surely this was some trick of evening light. Tired limbs propelled me to my feet. The breeze of dying day wafted over the plateau. Mesmerized, I moved to stand beneath the coin, scarce an arm's reach above my head. It remained stalwart in its defiance of de Vouger's acclaimed treatise, *Principles of Falling Objects*. It gleamed as if it were the first star awaiting a blackening sky.

I plucked it from its hovering, and it sat heavy in my hand; ice cold, not warm as it should have been from its recent housing in my boot. Dante had declared the thing magically inert, and even yet, I detected not the slightest trace of enchantment about it. I launched it again. It bounced across the paving as any coin would do.

Accuracy. Precision. Repeatability. Without them, you've naught but accidents and happenstance. Dante's teaching echoed as if he stood at my shoulder. I threw the coin again.

It hung in the air, spinning slowly like a gear wheel in a mill. I reined in soul, body, and mind, not daring to feel, not daring to admit, even by wondering, that an object could so violate the simplest, clearest laws of nature without aid of enchantment.

Again, I threw the coin, Gruchin's luck charm, the sole object found in the assassin's pocket. And again . . . Never did it behave the same way twice running.

I tucked the double strike into my boot, gathered the scattered kentae, and repeated the tests. The silver coins behaved properly. I tried copper kivrae, a gold kesole, the crocodile charm, a button, a buckle cut from my boot. No oddity. What was different about the two-faced coin?

I snatched up a shard of mosaic half the size of my palm and tossed it across the temple floor. It rolled lazily, end over end, drifted to the floor, bounced higher than my head in an entirely unlikely direction, and landed back at my feet. A pebble flew ten centimetres, then plummeted to the ground as if it had slammed into a wall, though I used the same motion, the same strength for its launch. A handful of dirt tossed into the air drifted slowly onto my shirt, as if the grains were dandelion cotton. Merciful angels, this was madness.

Recalling the debris I'd thrown into the pond, I gathered a handful of variously sized stones and ran across the field, trying to outrace the settling dark. I threw one of my coppers into the water. It sank as I would expect. Another, and it did the same. Then I tossed the stones into the pond. Some sank. Some floated. I knelt on the bank, the scent of onion grass sitting like thickened paste on my tongue, and retrieved three of the floating stones as they circled past. They weighed solidly, one near the size of an egg. I tossed them in again. One sank. One bounced off the surface of the water and onto the shore beside me. The egg-shaped one settled to the surface as gracefully as a black swan.

Footsteps crunched on the weedy field behind me. "Lord chevalier, hurry! Come look at this!" I called over my shoulder. "By the Creator, you'll never believe it!"

But this time, *I* fell. A bludgeon slammed into my back, just between the shoulder blades. My face met the ground with all expected force.

CHAPTER SEVENTEEN

31 QAT
30 DAYS UNTIL THE ANNIVERSARY

"Now who exactly might you be?" said the owner of the boot grinding my nose and cheek into the crushed onion grass and the rocky soil beneath. "And where bides your pretty, sneaking *lord* who carries such a fine sword?"

"Ow! Stop!" I said, though the words came out somewhat garbled. "I'm Damiano de Sacre Vaerre. Pilgrim. Ho—pthew—holy place." I spat out the words along with dirt and grit, and grabbed on to the ankle attached to the offending boot, determined to remove it from my cheekbone. And perhaps break it.

Pain exploded in my side. Yet another boot. My breath seized, and my arms flopped to the ground, limp as a dead bird's wings.

A huge, warm weight settled on my back, pressing the remaining air from my lungs, and then a hand snarled my hair and wrenched my head backward. Wiry hair pressed against my cheek, accompanied by warm, beery breath. "What common pilgrim ventures a warded bridge?"

"Or travels with a lord knight dressed common? They've secrets, Quernay. Secrets. He's blood born sure."

This voice, more excited than the first, came from in front of me, though my watering eyes revealed only a black blur. Two men. At least two. Friendly as jackals.

"The holy brother told us—aagh!" My scalp threatened to rip. "Please, let me spea—"

The one on my back—Quernay—jerked and twisted my neck into an impossible angle and spat on my cheek. "Answer our questions. Where be the noble swordsman?"

"Out east, waiting for me at Fe-hikal. He dresses poor to discourage thieves. Please, he'll travel on without me."

"Are you so worthless? Why are you here?"

"Awaiting the Reborn."

This time the boot landed on my chin. Blood spurted from my lips and chin. Pain lanced through my jaw, trebling the strained agony of my neck.

"Try again," said Quernay's overeager friend with the boots, mashing his gritty sole into my face.

"Back off, Merle," growled the one at my ear. My stomach churned at the stink of him and the onion grass and the strained posture. "You've been working spells, oddments. To what purpose?"

My prepared story thinned like wafting smoke. I needed something better, perhaps closer to the truth lest I be tested worse; dizziness already clouded my thinking. "I am a failed acolyte," I said. "The mendicant's tales . . . thought I might succeed up here."

"And your pretty lord?"

"Despises me. Calls me lackwit. Dunce. Wanted to show him. Please, take what you will and let me go. Master said he'd leave me behind did I not join him by sunrise."

"Mmm," wheezed Quernay. "Methinks you've seen a bit too much to let you go." The heavy man slammed my face to the ground as he climbed off my back, then snagged my clothing when I attempted to scramble away.

Without wasted word or breath, the two immobilized my legs with cords wrapped from ankles to knees. They bound my wrists behind my back and wound the rope all the way to my elbows, pinching my arms together so tightly they near left their sockets. I could not inhale a full breath.

Blessed angels, keep Ilario hidden. These two were no

common bandits. They'd not touched my purse or scattered silver, and, certainly, they themselves had crossed a
warded bridge. At least one of them must have some
trained sensitivity to magic.

"Get him through the trap," said Quernay. "I'll take a
look around."

As the bigger man strode away, his excitable partner
looped a rope around my chest and under my cramping
shoulders and dragged me across the field. Sharp-edged
grass slashed my face. Rocks ripped my clothes and gouged
my chest and thighs. I fought to keep my head up, so as not
to have it bashed against the rocks. Oblivion would have
suited better.

Once he had bumped me up the steps, my captor
dropped me on the faded mosaic like a goat brought for
sacrifice. The world drifted lazily, like the water in the
pool.

"*Aberta,*" he spat.

A great whipcrack of magic split the air, trembling the
ground beneath my cheek. I tried to press myself into
the stone.

Grunts of effort, mumbles, thumps, and creaks located
the brutish Merle to my left. "Why the frigging saint did
you have to show up here at sunset?" he grumbled.
"Oughta slit your throat just for the trouble. Quernay's,
too. *Get 'im through the trap. I'll take a look around.*
Dung-eating goatherd thinks I'm his slavey. Thinks he's
aristo 'cause he can conjure a spell or two."

Accepting that a mountain was not about to fall on me,
I drew my bound legs toward my belly and rocked onto my
side to get a look. My captor's black shape was outlined
against the violet afterglow. The temple reader's red-haired
manservant from the shrine—Merle—was wrestling
with . . . I blinked dirt away. Everything looked wrong.

No matter my blinking and squinting, the view did not
change. The slight, wolfish Merle was raising a rectangular
slab that must surely weigh ten times his body's total.
Grunting, he gave a prodigious shove, and the slab . . .
drifted . . . to the pavement. Yet it landed with a teeth-

rattling thud. Then he reached *through the floor* and withdrew a paned lantern. My stomach heaved.

I blinked again, and my perceptions shifted. A layer of illusion masked a rectangular gap in the temple floor. But was the slab that had closed it granite or silk? Experience and estimation no longer sufficed.

Merle set the lantern on solid ground, then stepped back a few paces. *"Illuminatio."*

Ah, not fair at all that a brutish thug should key a fire spell so soon after my abortive attempt to create one. But indeed, flame blossomed atop the thick white candle inside the lantern. Yet its light entirely contradicted Watt the lens maker's tidy diagrams and explanations. My eyes did *see* the light, but not a beam illumined anything beyond the glass. The night, deeper black than before, snugged up around the lantern panes and trapped the fiery glow inside the glass walls.

"Illuminatio."

This time, flame engulfed the lantern, a wind-whipped bonfire of gold and yellow that could likely be viewed as far west as Tallemant. Merle stood well away from it, his outstretched hand held flat against the flame as if to shield himself. The light beams curled about his outlined fingers.

"Illuminatio, you daemon-cursed bit of wax."

The third invocation of the key quenched the bonfire instantly. But a new flame sprouted like an eager weed from the blackened wick and burned brightly within the lantern's confines. The beams spread softly across the paving, clean and straight as they ought.

The wolfish man bellowed laughter. "Guess you're fuddled, eh?" He swung the lantern at my bruised face. I jerked my head back, the glare near blinding me. "We'll fuddle you all."

Truly my senses were entirely fuddled. The first two attempts to key the spell had not satisfied him, yet, had my eyes been closed, I would have been unable to distinguish their residue from the third, successful attempt. Impossible, I would have said a day before, yet perhaps no more extraordinary than coins that flew, stones that floated or sank as if by whim, or light beams that cast no reflection save in a human eye.

My captor gave me little time to sort it out. He lowered the bright lantern back through the hidden gap in the floor, then took up my leash and hauled me toward the same location. Gods . . .

Though the sharp edge between *floor* and *no floor* was not wholly unexpected, the gut-plummeting drop near sliced my arms off when the rope reached its abrupt limit. Gasping for air, I spewed curses as I had never in my life produced. I hadn't realized I knew so many.

After three or four jerky lowerings, my toes touched ground, slackening the rope. I toppled like the stone slab onto the very hard, very cold floor.

Lamplight spun. The world blurred and bent. Harsh whoops dragged air into my burning chest. "Souleater's servant!" I spoke in true conviction of Merle's identity.

The heavy leash rope smacked the back of my head.

Boots ground on steps. Merle's warm body stank as he bent over me. Quivering fingers pried at my pockets, unbuttoned my shirt collar, pawed my neck, tugged at my sleeves . . . searching. He crowed when he snapped the courret from its slender chain about my neck and stuffed it in his pocket. Everything else—purse, knife sheath, spall pouch, compass, crocodile charm, Gruchin's coin, and the boots from my feet—he lobbed into the corner. I didn't regret the wardstone's loss. It hadn't warned me about him.

"The Aspirant will be quite interested in your mark." Somewhere beyond the red-hot skewers inside my shoulders, he shook my needling-numb left hand. "You'll keep no secrets from *him*."

Damnable incautious fool! I swore at myself, not at Merle. All our efforts would be wasted if the conspirators learned my identity or, angels defend us, Ilario's or Dante's. Who were these people? An aspirant was a magical apprentice, not even a student of my own rank.

"I've no secrets," I mumbled into the floor. "Blood's sour. Can't conjure a dewdrop."

"We'll see to that." Somewhere behind my back a blade left a stinging track across my palm.

"Sante Marko, defend!" I bucked and twisted.

"Merle! Get off him!" The voice came from above my head. Heavy boots pounded the steps, skipping the last few to drop hard on the floor close by. "We want a body left to question."

"Look at his mark, Quernay. See what's fallen into our lap."

The bigger man's noisy breathing soon placed him close. Cool, hard hands forced my clenched fist open. Belying any implication that his object was mercy, he twisted my hand to expose its back, then gripped my bloody chin, and used it to wrench my face up into the lantern light. My tight-bound arms prevented my body following all the way.

"So, who is he?" Quernay's broad face swam in the glare—wiry black hair, wide brow, chin like an anvil. He was none but the temple reader from the shrine, not so friendly anymore. Above him a rectangle of night marked the entry through the temple floor. No illusion masked the opening from below.

"Don't know the mark exactly, but I'm sure I've seen it. It's a good mark, I know. He's blood, for certain, and we need—" A vicious thwack of flesh on bony flesh silenced Merle's views.

"The Aspirant will decide what we need," growled Quernay. "While I fetch the supplies, you get this one into the hole and yourself off to the bridge. Wouldn't want that swordsman to lack a proper welcome should he come looking for his sorcerer."

"Told you, I'm no confounded sorcerer," I croaked. "And my master won't come for me. He's off to Abidaijar to vow himself to the Saints Awaiting. He'll ne'er be back to Sabria. *I'll* ne'er be back do you let me go. Please, I'd no intent to trespass or blaspheme. I didn't know. . . ."

Quernay shoved me into an awkward heap. A better view did naught to soothe a rising panic. A few metres away, between me and a whitewashed wall lined with cluttered benches and shelves, a wooden armchair had been bolted to the floor. Leather straps were affixed to its flat arms and the thick, narrow plank that served as its back. Black splatters stained chair, straps, and floor, as well as a fire-glazed urn that stood next the thing. Old blood. Everywhere. Blessed saints . . .

The excitable Merle did not argue. He just watched and quivered as Quernay clambered up the stair and through the entry. Then, exposing his pointed teeth in a grin that made my skin creep, he lashed an arm-length truncheon to his wrist with a leather thong. "Need some practice," he said, raising the club. "Need to make you tender for the blades."

I thrashed and yelled, trying to dodge his precisely placed blows. I butted my head and shoulders against his ankles and slammed my bound legs into his, hoping to trip up his dancing steps. My antics only made him laugh the louder.

Logic screamed that Merle's virulence made no sense. Such reasoned brutality arose from fanatical dispositions, as with the Kadr witchlords who viewed those without their particular power for magic as prey. Or it stemmed from personal bias, passion-wrought grudges over property or family, or overstretched fathers whose profound disappointments prompted them to slay their failed sons. Merle didn't even know me.

Trussed as I was, defensive postures were futile. All too soon, I lay limp as a dead fish, logic as impossible as resistance. At one distinctive instant, my temple slammed against the bolted legs of the chair, and the world went dark. . . .

"I am no one," I whispered as he slapped me awake again. Spittle and blood had pooled under my cheek. "Nothing. My blood is weak. Please—"

Merle didn't seem to hear. Or perhaps he didn't care. Sweating, roaring in high spirits, he took his brutal pleasure. To my sorrow he did not kill me.

Eventually he dragged me into a small, dark room, redolent with pungent scent, and shoved me to my knees. By the time he had fixed my wrist bindings to an overhead loop, drawing my cinched arms so high and tight behind my back as to bend my head near the floor, I could not have told him my true name, much less where I was or why I'd come.

ABSOLUTE DARKNESS. A PUNGENT SCENT that roiled my stomach. A shearing, lacerating agony in my skull. The viciously cramped rack of my upper body that left every breath a struggle. A paralyzing terror of what was to come.

As the lightless hours flowed one into the other, indistinguishable, a bitter litany beat in time with my stuttering heart. *Inexcusable to let them take you. Blind. Inattentive. Caught up in selfish dreams. Unworthy.* Eventually, inevitably, a warm flood soaked my breeches, firing my skin with shame and my soul with humiliation.

Unable to sit or recline, I tried once to ease the strain of my position by standing, but my wobbling knees refused to hold me. The resulting collapse dropped my entire weight on my overstrained shoulders, near wrenching my arms from their sockets. My cry reflected sharply from the enclosing walls, a knife blade prying at my cracked skull. Sobbing, desperate, I scrabbled aching knees back under me, and there I remained, vowing to every divine being never to move again.

Blackness swelled and flowed, puddled and pooled. Overwhelming. Enveloping. Cocooned in silence, my mind had difficulty holding to any sensible course. Incapable of sleep, I dreamed of faces: my dead father, whom I did not mourn; Kajetan, living, whom I did; Philippe, who had graced me with his confidence; kind, graceful, intelligent Maura, whom I had determined to trust. Ideas, imaginings, and a few small threads of logic floated past me in the dark, like coins and stones on Eltevire's strange pond. And from time to time, a clearly formed conclusion would waggle its tail, troutlike, and attract my notice.

Materials native to this place refused obedience to the prescriptions of natural science; materials brought from elsewhere behaved themselves, the sole exception being Gruchin's coin. Perhaps Gruchin, the not-assassin, the mule, had been bled here. Perhaps his lucky coin had been in his pocket or his boot when he was subjected to the torments of Eltevire. What kind of spellwork could ensorcel silver—the perfect amalgam of the five elements—beyond the bounds of nature, yet leave no residue? *The place where it all began.*

These people were going to bleed me until my soul and body shriveled like a grape left too long in the sun. Another strained inhalation. Another deluge of cold sweats. I shivered uncontrollably.

A small victory when I identified the aroma exuded by the walls. Camphor bespoke the rare whitebud laurel. Whitebud laurel, and walls so close I could feel the reflections of my own breath, bespoke a sorcerer's hole. Lined with cypress, inlaid with camphor laurel, the exterior locked and banded with iron, such windowless closets were the single enclosure ever discovered that could completely frustrate the use of magic. If my posture had allowed me a full breath, I might have laughed at the irony of such a space wasted on me.

Another fish twitched its tail: Perhaps Merle and Quernay were actually Goram and Vichkar, the bloodthirsty companions of holy legend who had blighted history by perpetrating its first joint and mutual murder. Perhaps daemonic spirits could be reborn to do mischief, just as the saints sacrificed their heavenly sojourn to come back and aid sorry humankind.

I dismissed this fishy theory quickly. I could not imagine these two as bosom friends who loved their mothers, as legend bespoke.

Father Creator, how had I come to this? What fool's illusions of purpose had led me so beyond my safe library? Not mother's love. My mother doused herself with lavender scent and tormented her serving girl. Since my father's death, she would dissolve into hysterics whenever she saw me.

A scraping noise heralded a thin, vertical band of gray light that split the wall in front of me. Despite its painful brilliance, I inhaled the light, longing to be a lumenfish, able to drink in the sun's rays, only to release them again in the long dark of sea nights. "D-did you love your m-mother, Quernay?" I croaked through chattering teeth, feeling madly brave. "Are you a f-fish?"

When he failed to answer, I ventured a glance upward, and near pissed myself again. The black-gowned form was not Quernay. Taller, surely, but less bulky overall, the newcomer wore a leather mask formed to a male's likeness. Severe in its perfectly proportioned beauty, serene in its superiority, the walnut-hued face might have been that of the Pantokrator himself or one of his warrior angels . . . or perhaps the Pantokrator's chief adversary. The *Book of Creation* named the Souleater the most beautiful of the fallen. Ophelie's leech had worn a mask.

"Daemon get! Merle's left him pulp!" So Quernay was here, too. "Best send the lackwit back to the city, lord, else he'll have us all dead in our beds."

Back to the city . . . Visions of imprisonment in a crate near stilled my heart until I sorted out that he spoke of mad, wolfish Merle, not me.

The silent visitor squeezed through the slotlike doorway, built purposefully narrow to slow an imprisoned sorcerer's escape.

"I've a guess this one will be too stubborn to die on us." The throaty whisper crawled into my soul, quiet like a spider. Gloved fingers lifted my chin. With the light behind, the mask's eye slits revealed naught but tarry voids. The thought came to me that a daemon returned to the world might wear such a mask to hide his corruption. "How did you find me?"

Chilled and sick, I could summon no mettle to control my shaking. I clung to my tale. "I am nothing," I mumbled through swollen lips. "No one. Failed. A pilgrim."

"Let me be more specific," said the Aspirant, low and harsh. "I believe I am addressing a very particular *no one.* Did your royal kinsman send you here, librarian?"

I had thought I could get no colder or sicker. "R-royal? N-not even my m-master—"

He allowed my head to drop, launching new bolts of lightning through my neck and shoulders and catapulting my head into such throbbing agony as could obliterate reason.

"Hear me, failure." He ground the whispers into my ear, into my skull, into my soul. "I am Philippe de Savin-

Journia's worst nightmare, and I *will* know his purposes. And lest you maintain some hope that you'll not be required to answer, know that we have eliminated your lordly companion—not much of a swordsman after all."

Eliminated? Dead? Ilario?

"Alas, our eager Merle dispatched him before he could tell us all we wished to know."

He might have been telling me the Souleater had launched his legions against a dragonfly, a mosquito, or a luminous moth flitting about a lamp. For one eternal instant I teetered on the precipice, refusing to believe it.

A sodden lump dropped to the floor beneath my drooping head—a fine leather glove, stained with soot and blood. Unmistakably Ilario's glove. Unmistakable, too, that a severed hand remained inside it. My spirit plummeted into the vastness of horror.

"You are quite alone, Portier de Savin-Duplais. You are nothing. Failed. And we have all the time in the world to learn your secrets."

CHAPTER EIGHTEEN

31 QAT
30 DAYS UNTIL THE ANNIVERSARY

The Aspirant and his henchman left me alone, suspended in the silent dark, to contemplate their promises. The walls of a sorcerer's hole were purposely built thick, lest magical keywords penetrate and quicken a prisoner's balked spellwork. And the hole was purposely left dark. Spark was the single element required for every spell; thus a prisoned sorcerer was stripped of anything that carried spark and was allowed no glimmer of light.

Yet even the painful void in which I existed could not compare to that within—guilt and anger and a sadness that left my spirit aching beyond any physical hurt. Ilario: illogical, foolish, preening, silly, but clever in his way, and generous and honorable, and so earnestly devoted. A man of scarlet finery, ruffled lace, and silly charms and elixirs, of incessant babbling, now forever stilled, leaving a sorry, sober vacancy in the converse of the world. Even the dread of bleeding could not divert my grieving.

Hours passed. My extremities lost all sensation. Back, neck, shoulders, and head felt riven by hot irons. Pain and grief festered, and as the press bears down on the vineyard's harvest, so did the waste and wrongness of Ilario's death render a familiar liquor—disappointment, failure, guilt, and self-loathing—as if my father had taken his knife to me again. Back then, despair had flavored death with sweetness, and at three-and-twenty, with half my blood left puddled on my parents' floor beside my father's corpse and my dreams of magic, its intoxication had near made an end of me. Now, as then, its seductive aroma promised release.

But this time, the stakes were higher than my incapable self. *Focus, Portier, or you're going to betray them all— Ophelie, Lianelle, Calvino de Santo, Gruchin, Michel de Vernase, Philippe and his vision for Sabria's glory, Ilario and his determination to seek truth. You have no leave to despair. The first lesson of your schooling: Put aside distraction. Make a plan. . . .*

Escape. I had to persuade them to unbind me. That was the extent of my strategizing. Quernay arrived. Agony obliterated thought as he unhitched my arms and dragged me out.

They had lit torches in the great chamber. Firelight danced on the stone floor. I could not lift my forehead from the gritty stone. It felt as if nails had pierced my temples. I could not stop shivering. "P-please. M-my hands are numb. D-damaged, they'll be useless. My livelihood . . ."

"Who told you how to find me?" Leather muted and distorted the soft words spoken so high above me.

"No one. I came here to test my—"

A boot, not Merle's, nudged my bruised groin. Lightning speared my gut. The floor squirmed underneath my face, as I drew up my knees. Summoning my last modicum of pride, I did not vomit on the Aspirant's boot.

"Who told you?" His toe tapped not five centimetres from my nose. "You are not clever enough to discover us on your own."

Gritting my teeth and forcing my wits into order, I glared at that damnable boot and dared it to reveal its wearer. Indeed, it was no countryman's cocker like Merle's, nor was it a peasant's nailed brogue, nor an elaborately stitched, wide-toed boot of current fashion as Ilario had worn. This was a horseman's knee-high boot of good leather, rubbed thin on the inside of the leg, the plain, double stitching well waxed to keep out sand and water. Worn leather spur stops protruded from the heel. A well-loved boot. A knight's boot.

Think. Who is this man? Lord, Quernay had called him. A knight, it seemed. A sorcerer, I presumed, though his assumed title said not. *Aspirant*—what did that signify? One like Dante, not of the blood? Someone who knew me or knew *of* me. I could think of no one to fit the shape. Not yet. But on my hope of life, I would.

"Be assured, librarian, you've done no mischief that I cannot undo."

But I *had* done mischief . . . if I could keep Dante unknown. More, if I could get free. The thought of my partners, one living, one lost, infused a remnant of strength. Let this devil think me cowed.

"Please loose my hands," I mumbled, wincing as speech ground the cracks in my skull one edge against the other. "I'll tell you whatever you want."

"Indeed, you will." The knight's boot nudged my swollen lips and forced its gritty leather way inside, crushing my cheek, shoving my tongue aside, inevitably stretching and filling my bruised mouth until I gagged repeatedly. "The answers will . . . *leak* . . . out of you . . . *drip* . . . *flow*. What a pitiful thing you are. I will make you more useful than you could ever be to the King of Sabria."

Abruptly he removed his foot. I spat, coughed, and swallowed repeatedly to clear the foul taste, my skin ablaze. Shame fueled my risen determination into fury. I would babble like poor dead Ilario and twist my tale into such knots, the leather-faced villain would never find the end of them.

"Get him in the chair," snarled the Aspirant. "His Savin blood is not so sour as he claims. The blood of failures has fed our best work."

The blood of failures . . . Ophelie? Gruchin? As if I needed more fodder for my hatred.

Quernay unwrapped my arms and legs, and sensation returned to my cramped muscles in a fiery flood. Before I could claim any use from them, he hauled my carcass to the chair and strapped down my awakening limbs with the wide strips of supple leather. An extra strap bound my neck to the tall, narrow slat of the chair back.

Above the stair, the doorway to the night remained open. I could not go anywhere trussed like a goose and locked in a sorcerer's hole, but in the chair . . . if I could stay sensible . . . recover some use of my extremities . . . break the damnable straps . . .

A bronze tray sat atop a wheeled trolley next to my chair. Quernay laid out thin tubes of silver on it, alongside a porcelain bowl, pots of herbs, flasks of oils and liquids, and glass cups and tubes, some fitted with brass or ivory handles. The Aspirant opened a flat wood case containing neatly arranged lancets of every size, but he picked out a small brass block and flicked a lever on its top. Ten or more small blades popped out of its polished base.

Saints defend . . . Horror shivered my skin. I had seen sketches of scarificators in histories of the Blood Wars. I clamped my jaw tight.

"Clean him up and we'll draw a sample."

As the masked man watched, Quernay snatched a dagger from his waist and sliced through my ripped and filthy shirt. Grinning, he traced his blade lightly across the bloodied bruises his red-haired friend had left me. "Pity for you we can't use what's already let," he said. "But the Aspirant likes it clean. Fresh."

I shrank into the unyielding chair, needing no player's skill to convey my fear. "This is forbidden, p-perverse."

"You'll learn. We've many a lesson to teach."

With a rag doused in pungent oil from one of his flasks, Quernay wiped dried blood and dirt from my chest. Then he plunged the fiery wick of a lit candle into a bulbous glass cup from the tray. So quick I could scarce follow, he removed the flame and laid the mouth of the cup on my chest. The smooth rim, not so hot as I feared, clung to the skin, and I watched in dread fascination as the circle of flesh purpled and swelled into the cooling cup.

Quernay's finger under the edge of the glass loosened the cup, and he tossed it aside. Before I could speak or think, the Aspirant laid his chilly block of brass over the dark circle of swollen flesh and flicked its triggering lever.

The searing shock set me hard against the leather straps.

"And for good measure," the masked man whispered, "because you have set my plans askew . . ." A precise click and he set the metal block askew in the same spot, cool against the fiery wounding. The lever snapped again. Ten blades bit again. My skull threatened to explode.

"Father Creator," I mumbled, weakness radiating from the spot in scalding waves.

Quernay pressed a tubular glass fitted with a brass plunger over the wound, ensuring the oil on my skin sealed its heated mouth. He twisted the plunger's ivory handle and tugged it slowly outward. Blood surged into the glass. I thought my gut might be drawn out with it.

"It's time I looked in on our other friend," said the Aspirant, tossing his nasty implement onto the tray. "The adept's ready. Bring Portier's offering when you've milked enough for a trial." The masked man moved behind me into the passage that led to the sorcerer's hole.

"Aye, lord." Quernay removed the glass tube, deposited my blood into a porcelain jar, and picked up his glass cup and candle to begin again.

The Aspirant's footsteps halted. Locks snapped, and a heavy door scraped open. Then rose a keening as spoke of eternities of misery, of despair so cold and dark I felt the firelight dim, of suffering so profound my soul quailed. Not *friend*. Victim.

"Legions of Heaven bring you mercy." I had scarce breath enough to speak it, scarce mind enough to think who, in the name of holiness, the poor soul might be. *Michel de Vernase?* The Aspirant had mentioned an adept—so the *missing Fedrigo, perhaps, who might have seen too much of Gaetana's work? Please gods, let it not be Dante.*

Quernay pressed his cup to my chest. I wrestled the cursed straps, until the lout struck me so forcefully, the sand-hued light blurred and spun, smearing his dark face and my blood-striped skin with gleaming glass and fire. Though my head screamed agony, I clung to sense.

Quernay picked up the gleaming scarificator and cocked its blades. *Snick*. And it bit again. . . .

Such shallow cuts give up blood more slowly than a lanced vein. The day could stretch interminably, and I needed to act while I yet retained some wit. Only one thing was sure to halt a leech using a mule. He wouldn't want that mule to die until he was ready.

As Quernay suctioned blood from the fourth or fifth cupping circle, I took a lesson from Dante's discipline. With every scrap of will I could muster, I sent my mind voyaging into a cave darker than the sorcerer's hole, conjuring the sound of ocean, the rhythmic crashing of implacable wave on resistant rock. I immersed myself in stillness. Retreated, until my head sagged against the neck strap.

Quernay lifted my head by my hair. Shook my chin. Threw water in my face. But failure had prompted me to work diligently at denying feeling. Sensation remained remote, and I remained limp.

"Weak-livered dolt," he grumbled. "Can't have your heart seizing up. Not yet." He pried the suction loose with a thick finger. After depositing the blood-filled instrument on the bench, he unbuckled the neck strap, allowing my head to droop without risk of strangulation. His heavy footsteps faded down the passage.

Raising a fervent prayer to whatever bright angels might frequent this daemonish place, I shook off my trance, bent to the right hand wrist strap, and worried the buckle with my teeth.

As in every circumstance since giving up my studies, a spell formula popped to mind. The spell for breaking was not complex. It required base metal, unadulterated by water or air, and proportioned according to the material to be broken—less for paper or thread, more for wood or rope or leather, monumental amounts for thick stone or metal. The metal must be balanced with spark, proportioned as to the metal particle's hardness, as if—gods, I'd begun thinking like Dante—as if to make the spell's edge keen.

Idiot. I needed to bend my mind to escape, not dream of magic. I worked the leather tongue free and yanked the

buckle loose, only to realize that freeing one wrist bene-
fited me nothing. A second strap at the elbow held my arm
in place. My freed right hand could not reach my other
arm to loose either wrist or elbow. Nor could it reach the
buckle on my side that held the strap across my waist or
the straps across my thighs.

As I swallowed screaming frustration and rejected the
impossibilities of gnawing leather straps in twain or bursting them with main strength, magical calculations continued running in my head. The chair's thick bolts were surely
dense enough to supply the needed proportion and quality
of base metal. But spark . . . My scattered coppers would
compromise the metal without supplying enough spark. The
torches—their flame pure spark—were stuck in mounted
sconces too far away.

In frantic foolishness, my eyes roved the long chamber's
furnishings. In one corner stood a water butt, tin cups
stacked atop it. The long, low bench was piled with metal
basins, towels, flasks, and a thick, leather-bound ledger,
propped on a stack of other books. Beside the stack sat
Merle's lantern.

Had not my face felt as battered as a tin pot fallen off a
mountainside, I would have grinned. A man incapable of
creating magic could still invoke a key. Anyone with half a
mind kept spellkeys secret. Clearly, damnable, murderous
Merle had less than half a mind.

Without touch to access the spell, I had to focus carefully. Quenching fear and frustration, I considered the lantern and mumbled, *"Illuminatio."* Nothing happened. I
breathed deep and tried again.

"Illuminatio." The candle winked out. Curls of smoke
filled the lantern.

"Illuminatio." The wick sparked into a small steady
flame. *"Illuminatio . . ."*

On the seventh invocation of the spellkey, the lantern
exploded into a storm of fire, shooting flames and smoke
plumes all the way through the rectangular opening above
the stair.

Imprisoned in the bleeding-chair, I laughed as the oiled
leather binding of the ledger book burst into flame, quickly

charring its pages. And I felt no librarian's qualm as the rapacious fire caught the other books and burst the glass flasks of oils and herbs. Nor did I quake when the spilled oils fueled a burning of the bench itself or when a gout of flame caught the tangles of rope so lately used to bind my limbs.

If the spark traversed the ropes all the way to my chair, I would infuse my will into the flame and the other particles bound within the compass of the chair, attempting once again to create magic. But even did I fail, as was certain, my captors must surely note the conflagration and set me loose. Once free of ropes and straps, once dragged up the steps and into open air, then we'd see.

Foolishly, I hadn't counted on smoke filling the chamber so quickly. Gray and yellow plumes billowed and curled. My eyes flooded. Coughing threatened to splinter my broken head. It took all the mind I could muster to hold the spellwork ready, awaiting the arrival of the flame. My hands clawed the wooden arms in the very grooves and gouges left by those who'd been bled in this cursed chamber. As I gasped for air, a door deep in the passageway behind me crashed open.

"I'll take care of this one," shouted the Aspirant. "You get Portier out!"

Footsteps pounded toward me, Quernay cursing with a production and artistry that made my own pale. He set to my bindings. "Is this fire *your* doing, sniveler?"

He'd loosed only one ankle when a boulder plummeted straight through the thickening murk, near landing on my head. The moment's terror screamed that Heaven was caving the roof to make an end of us all.

But naught else fell. And Quernay shot to his feet, lurched backward, and drew his sword. Soon weapons clanged and hammered amid the growing din of fire and Quernay's roaring curses. I could see naught but two bodies clad in writhing smoke.

I bared my teeth and crowed. This was Dante, surely. Now we would put an end to these devils.

The sound of the unseen combat measured its progress. The scrape and clash of weapons . . . fast, vicious. Harsh breathing, grunts of effort, edged now and again with the keen timbre of pain.

"Obscuré!" Quernay bellowed. The firelight dimmed and smoke darkened.

Dante did not counter with magic. Odd. Surely his potent sorcery overmatched his combat skills. I'd spied no sword ever in the mage's rooms, and he had only one useful hand. Families in Coverge, slaveys in the quarries or mines, could not afford swordmasters.

A body crashed into the bench. Glass shattered. The dulled flames spiked, and smoke billowed thicker, reeking of scorched herbs. The figure lunged back into the fray. Flailing bodies bumped my back, my arms, my scorching knees. The raw wounding on my chest screamed as if with its own voice.

A sweating back pressed to my shoulder. "How many are they?" The voice was none I knew. Certainly not Dante's.

"Two here," I croaked between gasps. "One outside. Another prisoner, deeper in."

He darted away, shouting a question back at me. But I could not comprehend it, for rising flames licked the legs of my chair and singed my bare feet, surrounding me. The air became unbearably hot, and my breath came hard . . . hot, too . . . and I could not fill my lungs for the racking cough and the agony of my head, and the fire thundering ever louder and ever closer . . . and I needed to *break* these cursed straps and be *out* of this cursed chair . . . and I wanted to jump overboard, but the *agente confide* within reported I was not on the *Swan* this time and there would be no such easy escape and certainly no magic. . . .

Blind, coughing, sure my skull must crack, I did not feel him slash the leather straps. But someone hefted me across a set of bony shoulders, and hauled me up the steps toward the blessed air. Whether my rescuer was villain or savior, I near wept with gratitude I could not speak. Then my head whacked the edge of the trap. The smoky world wavered between charcoal and black, between stillness and movement, riven by lightning bolts that rendered me wholly speechless and lost in a midnight of misery.

CHAPTER NINETEEN

The wet cloth tied across my eyes might have been dampened in Journia's snowmelt. Water droplets dribbled down my nose like pearls of ice. As far as I could remember, I had been shivering, puking, and head-splintered forever. If I only knew why . . .

Cobweb memories floated in the dark. Held captive. Beaten. Bled. There'd been a fire. Flame yet raged in proximity to my lungs, within and without. Now I sat on stony ground in the open air, back propped against a rock wall, and my head felt as if the Pantokrator's own mace was bashing it. But I had no idea where I was or who had brought me here. I needed to be careful. I needed to *know*. I needed to *see*.

"Who's there?" Even such a raw whisper started me coughing, but at least my hands were free to clamp the bones of my skull together. While there, my fingers tested the knot of my blindfold. I tugged one tail and felt it loosen.

Firm footsteps crossed a bit of rough ground, halted, and a body knelt down beside me. "None you know. Stay still until we discover who's about."

A hand cupped the back of my head.

I jerked away, which launched fiery spears from skull

through spine, setting me gasping through fire-seared lungs and barking like a maddened hound. . . .

Arms wrapped my shoulders and buried my face in a man's chest, holding me tight and still until the paroxysm quieted. My head did not quite shatter.

"Let us try this again," he said, soft and urgent. "I am not going to hurt you. I'm going to give you a tisane to soothe your throat and clear your lungs. Might make you a bit drowsy, too."

Gently he held my head and poured a litre or more of lukewarm liquid down my gullet. It tasted of anise and the scrapings from a stable floor. I choked and burbled a feeble protest, while pressing the heel of my hand to my throbbing forehead.

Lacking a voice or nerve enough to move again, I could not rebel when he snugged the wet blindfold tighter. "Your eyes are smoke-scalded, and you've clearly broken your head, so you'd best leave this in place for a time. If you *please*." The recommendation sounded very like a command. "You really ought to be dead."

My companion rose, then moved away. His walk bespoke a trained swordsman, sure of himself, light on his feet, but rooted firmly to the ground, one might say. He paused, took a few steps, paused, took a few more, circling from my right to my left before returning to settle beside me. I smelled smoke and death blood on him, at least until he raised another stinking cup under my nose.

I waved it off. But liquid slopped and spattered on the ground beside me. The next thing I knew, he was gently blotting the raw wounding on my chest with a scalding cloth that stank of his tisane. My body near seized with the hurt of it and my stomach with the smell.

"Sorry," he said. "I thought it had cooled."

Cloth ripped. He dabbed at the scorched cuts and tied strips around my torso. I worked at keeping still. At listening. At remembering. At staying awake.

"How many in their party? Use your hand to tell me."

Surely, if he asked, he was not one of them: not the wolfish one who'd kicked me half to death, nor the brute who'd strapped me in the chair, nor the masked one . . .

The incoming tide of memory and urgency charged my aching body with fury. Ophelie's murderer, I was sure of it . . . and Gruchin's . . . and Ilario's. For certain the Aspirant had caused a man to emit a cry of torment that might have come from the Souleater's caverns.

"The man in the mask," I croaked, struggling to sit up. *Philippe de Savin-Journia's worst nightmare.* A knight. A sorcerer. I ought to know him.

"Hush." The hand with the warm cloth rested heavy on my rapidly pumping chest, while the other touched my mouth. "Use fingers. I can account for only two men. A scrawny one at the bridge. The big hairy fellow down below. How many more?"

I raised one finger. "He wore—"

"Yes, yes, the third wore a mask. Are you sure there were no more? That makes no sense if they were guarding secrets."

"Maybe an adept. And a prisoner," I whispered. "Desperate, dying. Go!" I shoved at him and waved him away.

He remained solidly in place. "Sante Marko himself could not send me back into that inferno. Smoke's still pouring out the hole. But I looked about before I hauled you up. None remained in the cells, and none's come out since. Either they're dead, or there's another way out, or . . . you were confused. There's not a sign of anyone hereabouts."

Coughing racked me again, threatening to turn my raw lungs inside out, and he muzzled me again and held me still, which was a mercy on my head. When I next opened my mouth, he poured another litre of anise-and-barnstraw tea down me, now rimed with ice. It tasted even nastier when cold.

"I've no yearning to stay here, but I'd rather drag you across that devilish bridge with this cough better settled." He laid something over me—a blanket or cloak that reeked of smoke. "And I'd like some notion of how many others might be waiting for us over there. Sleep easy. I'll watch."

The man's voice bled weariness. He rose and walked away again, making the same pattern: a few steps . . . a pause . . . a few steps. A patrol, only this time he halted halfway round.

"Damn and blast." The quiet oath sounded more in the line of annoyance—a banged shin or snagged hair—than emergency. Even so, it raised another brush of cold sweat.

The wind blustered, tainted with smoke and dust. The harsh screech of a hunting bird echoed from the nearby cliffs. Still shivering, I snugged the blanket round chin and neck. As my breathing eased, the head pounding settled to a duller rhythm, and my cobwebby thoughts collected themselves. I slipped my hands behind my head and untied the damp knots. Slowly, I tugged the cloth down and peered through slitted eyelids.

The wall supporting my back was the well enclosure in the center of the ruined village. Just inside one of the beehive houses burned a small, smokeless fire. Leaning gracefully against the doorpost, frowning at the little spyglass in his two uninjured hands, stood Ilario.

He must have glimpsed the movement of the cloth, or heard as much as I could make of a gasp or a laugh. I myself could not have said which. Or perhaps he'd been slammed by the sheer force of my astonishment, pleasure, and relief, for he glanced over at me, his lips pursed in rue, then looked back at his lady's gift. "Should have known you weren't so addled as you seemed. You'll not mention this to anyone, I trust."

"That you're not dead?" I croaked, choking back a cough with all my will. "That you saved my life? That you leapt through an illusion into a holocaust, freed me from that chair, and fought—"

"Just the one down there. The twitchy fellow's at the bottom of the chasm. Hoped nobody would notice he'd been stuck before he fell. Till the fire bloomed out of that cursed hole like sunrise, I'd come to think *you* must have fallen, too. Now stop talking. I don't like it here."

The fire. Resting the back of my head on the wall, I grinned at the thought of the "Pantokrator's Aurora" that had saved my life. Ilario's knightly sword dangled from his belt. I'd thought it naught but show.

"They showed me your riding glove with a severed hand in it," I whispered.

"The little ferret snagged my rucksack as he fell," he said, with a choked laugh. "My best gloves!"

The man peering through his exquisite little instrument, twisting and shaking it, *looked* like Ilario de Sylvae: the earring, the fair hair cut fashionably ragged since that other fire, the long nose, unblemished skin, and lithe physique. And yet he was someone else entirely. "*Untruth seated so deep, it is scarce detectable*," so Dante had said, as if such untruth must ever be dangerous and wicked. Which it could be, I supposed.

Sobered, I waggled my hand to catch his attention. "Tell me who you are, lord chevalier."

His complexion took on the tint of firelight. "One who learned very young that elders pay no mind to idiot children. They don't lock them away. They don't murder them in their beds and call it *childhood flux*. They allow them to stay close to those they care about."

Close to Eugenie. "Does even your sister know you?"

He scrubbed tiredly at his forehead. "She sees as she wills. Beyond that, she does not care."

I interpreted this as *no*. "But Philippe . . ."

He stuffed the spyglass inside his jerkin and moved away from the fire and the house, until he was but a darker silhouette against the starry night. "Truly, Portier, I beg you put this out of your mind. You must have the constitution of an ox. The tisane should have put you to sleep three times over. If I'd thought you'd see . . ."

He would have donned his fool's mask. No, far more than a mask. He would have reverted to that other person, a man as vividly real as anyone I'd ever met. Philippe surely knew. It explained why my cousin had such faith in Ilario. Their friendship expressed itself in private games of stratagems, played out over many years.

"You need to sleep," he said again. "We've maybe two hours until first light. Once we're well away from here and Fedrigo's tisane has done its work, you can tell me what you've learned between getting bashed and burnt—or not, as you choose. But I'd prefer not to fight any more of these lunatics. They don't tire." He drifted to the next house. And the next.

Sleep was impossible. My head throbbed. My chest stung. Every portion of my cursed body hurt, and I had to flex my fingers repeatedly to keep them from going numb. The wind moaned about the beehive houses, swirling dust and grit into my face. My mind leapt from one puzzle to the next without resolution.

Eventually Ilario interrupted my grumbling with more tea. "Eugenie was only eight when Soren chose her to wed," he said as I drank. "Three months she cried. He didn't touch her—not even Soren was so vile as that—but she'd never been from home. She just missed us all, her papa and mama, and her dolls and dogs. And me. We'd always got on. She is so loving—"

He straightened, dropped three weights in my lap, and strolled off to take up his watch. The weights were my journal, my scratched and dented compass, and Gruchin's double strike coin.

"Antonia suggested Papa send one of the dogs to soothe her. On the very day he received her letter, he called me into his study and told me he'd decided to send me instead. Amid all the lessons and warnings one would expect before sending a boy into fostering, he told me how he'd tried to discourage the marriage until Eugenie was older, and how he had petitioned the Temple to have it nullified on the grounds of Eugenie's misery. But King Soren insisted on an alliance with the House of Sylvae, and that was that. Papa charged me to stay close to Geni no matter what. To protect her as he could no longer do.

"And so I went, happy in Papa's trust, happy for the adventure, and happy to be with Eugenie. The moment I arrived at Castelle Escalon, she stopped crying. Ten days after, a fire destroyed our home. Papa, and Geni's mother whom I adored as my own, and all their servants died in the fire, along with our dogs and cats and birds."

"Angel's comfort, did you ever learn who was responsible?"

"I was eleven, Portier," he said, dry as the Arabascan landscape. "Soren's court comprised a thousand people and thrice that many plots and schemes. Even yet I can't swear whether it was murder or no. Antonia was kind and tried to mother Eugenie, though she has no more instinct for mothering than a berry bush. But I remembered how somber Papa had been, and how his hands had trembled as he spoke to me that last morning. And I thought how if he hadn't sent me, I'd be dead, too, and how the people at the palace had wanted a stupid pet. So I became what was wanted. I've stayed close to Eugenie, and for better or worse, I've stayed alive."

"And somehow Philippe learned the truth."

"That is a private matter. We—hsst!"

Ilario whisked his sword from its scabbard. Without taking his eyes from the direction of the bridge, he extended his left hand and hauled up my creaking bones. He snatched a poniard from his left boot and pressed it into my hand, motioning me into the house where the little fire burned. He himself dissolved into the night.

I scooped dirt over the fire. Telltales of smoke would be less noticeable than live flame on a night when the air was smoke-laced, anyway. Then I wrapped myself in Ilario's dark cloak and huddled, dizzy, by the low doorway.

Quiet, hurrying footsteps crunched the stony ground. A shapeless figure entered the village circle. "Sheathe your weapon, fool of a lord. The both of you come with me if you favor living an hour more." Faint scarlet light flowed up Dante's white staff like warmed honey, twining his maimed hand and illuminating naught else of him but a billowing black cowl.

"Where in Heaven's demesne have you been, mage?" My voice was much too loud, unfortunate for several reasons. The subsequent lung spasm near shattered my head, and it would not stop.

Before my watering eyes could quite make him out, the mage was beside me, wrapping a string round my throat and his luminous stick. As I coughed and clutched my head, he dragged a finger along the string and snapped, *"Kiné sentia."*

A leaden blanket enfolded my chest, silencing me in midspasm. I could breathe, albeit I had to think about it.

Dante's hand caught my elbow just as my knees buckled. "Over here, lordling," he snapped quietly. "Put your hand to Portier."

"Saints Awaiting, mage, you've no idea the dreadful

frights we've encountered!" Ilario—the more familiar Ilario—stumbled out of the inky shadows, fumbling sword and dagger as he tried to sheathe them. "That wretched bridge was near the death of me. If Portier hadn't got himself free of that chair and found me, I'd be a quivering—"

"Keep him on his feet, peacock. We *must* move."

Ilario stowed his weapons, including the knife he'd loaned me. As I struggled to draw breath, he thrust a long arm under my shoulders. "How the devil are we to get him across the bridge? It's nowhere wide enough for two. And there may be more villains than the ones Portier bashed with the lantern."

Ilario could not have imagined how unlikely I was to remember these fabrications. Dante's spell pressed me inevitably earthward.

"By all you name holy, keep silent, fool," said Dante. "And hurry. This rock is riddled with unstable enchantments. We do *not* want to be here."

The mage led us out of the village, the gleam of his staff reduced to a puddle of scarlet on the path. His urgency seemed reflected in the night air. The stars had vanished. Wind gusts threatened to knock us from our feet. A wingspread owl swooped over our heads, shrieking.

Instead of venturing onto the worrisome bridge, we clambered down a rock shelf . . . and then another . . . and another . . . each shallower and narrower than the one before, until we were descending a crude, even-more-worrisome stair, hacked from the plateau's rocky flank. Each step took shape in the scarlet pool of light that slopped underneath Dante's billowing hem to settle about our feet.

I dared not take my eyes from the light. Some shallower steps could support only our heels. Some were but broken stubs, so that Ilario had to go before and help me down to the next. Some crumbled ominously beneath us. Jagged edges and sharp gravel tormented my feet, yet I was almost grateful for the lack of boots. Bare feet gave me better purchase.

The chevalier alone kept me upright. Knees like porridge, I could scarce move air in and out.

It was a madman's descent into the abyss. Only the grazed evidence of my fumbling knuckles proved a solid wall existed on our left. On our right, the air churned like boiling tar.

Ilario jerked and waved his hand, as a shadowy shape, far too big for leaves or birds, flew in front of us. Revulsion fluttered my spirit. An icy whirlwind whipped another dark shape past and sent it howling into a gaping darkness vaster than the chasm below. My senses—who could imagine they reported faithfully?—insisted they scented dry cedar on the wind and tasted mouldering leaves of trees that had never grown on desert rock. Whisperings that were not quite words raised the hair on neck and arms, speaking hatred . . . anger . . . a gleeful fury. . . . I blessed Ilario for taking our exposed flank, and I thanked all gods that he was not the ninny he professed.

A great rumbling shivered the stair. Rocks and pebbles skittered around our feet. "Hurry!" shouted Dante above the din. "The dawn comes! Dawn is the danger."

Though I could not understand his concern—I yearned for dawn and light—I clung to Ilario and stumbled downward. The cliff wall bulged and split. A hail of rocks bounced across the path. But no longer was it only my lungs needed forcing. My heart's lumbering pace hobbled my feet.

When we reached a step so broad that Dante's light did not drip off its edge, extra arms grabbed me, and the two men together dragged me through a tangle of trees— fragrant myrtle and prickling juniper, cracking limbs sticky with resin. Leafy wands slapped face and torso, as my bare feet squelched in mud and slipped on moss-slicked stones shuddering with the world's upheaval.

"Here," said Dante, even *his* substantial voice gone breathless. "Stow him here. We're at the boundary. That will have to do."

My back grazed earth and stone. I slid downward, near dissolution from the crushing weight of the world's end. Everywhere in or on me hurt. I could not so much as twitch a finger.

In air lightened to charcoal, my bleared vision picked

out the soaring bastions of Eltevire two hundred metres in front of me. "Boundary?" I wheezed, laboring to push air out as well as to draw it in. "What—?"

"Aagh!" Face twisted, Dante clapped his hands to his head. . . .

Eltevire's heights erupted in orange, red, yellow, and green flame, a thundering, unnatural dawn that cast cliffs and weedy thicket into high relief, sounding a din of Dimios's battle against Heaven. The earth before, beneath, and behind me heaved and bucked. Sharp reports of cracking rock heralded cascades of earth and stone. My stomach lurched. The lurid light illumined the impossible steps we had descended in the night, just in time for an avalanche to sweep them away.

Ilario dived to the earth, arms flung over his head. But Dante stood between the both of us and the disintegrating cliff, his dark hair flying in a wild wind, staff upraised. Rocks and earth rained from the sky, causing silvery glints in the air before falling short or bouncing harmlessly away, as if the mage held out a silver shield visible only when it served.

The quake stemmed from naught of nature's work in sky or earth. Deafening, ruinous, its violence pummeled, crumbled, shattered soul and spirit, earth and flesh and bone. Such frigid fury, such visceral hatred lashed about the peripheries of Dante's trembling shield arm that I believed Merle's truncheon pounded me again.

After a small eternity, the rumbling quieted. One last heave, and the earth shuddered and stilled, and the residue of sorcery began to settle, an invisible dusting that stank of scorched bones.

Dante yet held, his every muscle quivering, staff gripped in a bleeding hand. "Let it go, mage," I whispered, dragging air into my starving lungs. My head felt like rubble. "You've done enough, both of you. I thank—"

My weary body could not force another breath. As the rising sun blazed through the dusty length of the abyss, my senses slid back into night.

CHAPTER TWENTY

" . . . don't know how he survived it. Besides all this lot, and the hatchwork of his chest where they bled him, I think his skull is broken. He has this lump on his head the size of an ostrich egg, and I tried to put wet compresses on it as my old nurse taught me, but there was blood everywhere, and I scarce knew where to start. Makes me queasy."

"It was my quieting spell near killed him. Gods, why didn't the damnable prig tell me he couldn't breathe?"

Propped up by a boulder amid clumps of sage and nettle, I could not see the two behind me. But my ears were working well enough to hear this not-quite-whispered exchange. It sparked an extraordinary good humor. To hear Dante confess a mistake always raised a grin. Or perhaps it was merely that I was alive and in the company of exceptional friends.

We had descended into the abyssal ravine that separated Eltevire—or the broken heights where Eltevire once existed—from the highlands we'd traveled to get here. Plumes of smoke and dust drifted across the silvered sky, while fog and shadow hung thick in the bottomland. The stone bridge was gone. Not far beyond my toes, the rubble of the mountaintop had buried a forest of locust and juniper.

I carefully inflated my chest to its fullest capacity, ignoring the scabs that stretched and broke and stung under the scratchy remnants of someone's scratchy cloak, and then sighed all that delicious air out again in thorough appreciation. My catalog of miseries had subsided. The exceptionally cold desert dawn had me shivering. A spring bubbling noisily through a tangle of marshwort roused thirst to a fever. And I had learned not to move in an untimely fashion. My head . . . gods . . . every twitch set off its hammering. But my heart paced an easy rhythm, and the cough had eased.

"You warned me you'd no healing skills, mage," I croaked, teeth chattering. "I b-believe now."

"You're awake!" Ilario scrambled into view on hands and knees, bellowing his delight. "What a fright you gave us! The mage had to strip his spell away and blow into your lungs to start them up again. I feared you were dead and whatever would we tell the k—?"

"Hush, lord!" I said, flinching. Relief at living had not made me forget our circumstances.

Dante loomed over the both of us, his haggard mien little improved from my last view of him at Castelle Escalon. "None's within hearing. And I doubt any's coming back here."

More evidence destroyed before we knew what it meant. But at least we had seen it.

Ilario, apparently none the worse for a night spent with the Earthshaker, leapt to his feet and spread his arms like spindly wings. "Truly, I thought the Last Day had come and the earth would disgorge the Souleater. And you did *something* to save us, mage, for which I must profoundly thank you, but I'm not sure I can bear thinking of it again, as I've never been so frighted. I've thought since then that perhaps you caused the whole thing."

"No, you blighted idiot, I did not cause it." Dante's ferocious gaze raked me stem to stern. "Portier, you must move as soon as you can. They've gone, but I cannot— We need to be away from here." His agitation was profound, as was the tremor in his hands and the shadowed exhaustion that leached the life and color from his skin.

I had no wish to linger in a place where cliffs could be launched at my head. And if Dante was nervous, I most assuredly wished to be gone. "Now I can breathe, I feel like a new man," I said, holding out my hands for assistance. "Or at least the better parts of the old one."

My skull did not actually explode when they hauled me up. But its grinding bones seemed connected straight to my gut, which promptly revolted in humiliating fashion.

"More?" Ilario pointed at the blessed waterskin I had just drained.

"I could do with three more and a bath in yon spring," I said, dumping the gritty dregs over my head. I smeared the droplets around my face and enjoyed the illusion of cleanliness.

"Do either of you understand what *haste* means?" Dante thrust a straight, slender branch into my hand. It was smoothed at the grip and cut to a reasonable length for a walking stick. "They *must not* see us."

"You said they were gone!" I resisted the temptation to swing around to look back at Eltevire's crumbled remains. Thoughts of the man in the leather mask roused a deep-rooted panic that the deep, cool shadows of the chasm did naught to soothe. "Whatever comes, he mustn't find you with me."

Dante's quivering hand pushed back his hair, resting on his temple as if he suffered the same wretched head as I did. "You *heard* them? Were you able—did you recognize a voice?"

"He wore a mask and a knight's boots. Called himself the Aspirant. But he knew Philippe had sent me."

Dante shook his head dismissively. "Fool of a student. There are no *men* here. Now, move."

Before I gathered his meaning, the mage was ten metres downstream. Tentatively, reluctantly, I reached out with the senses I used to detect enchantments. The much-too-cold ravine seemed to buckle and twist. The malevolent presence I had sensed on our descent the previous night was entwined with the mist, its hissing anger blended with the rill's gurgling. Beyond the deep, cold crevices in rock and rubble yawned the deeper void I'd thought morning had dismissed. "Chevalier, please . . ."

Ilario lent me his strong shoulder again. His brow creased in question, but I devoted strength and concentration to movement. Silent, desperate, Dante swept us down the gorge like a springtime flood. I could not go as fast as he wished. The mage would race ahead, then double back to help Ilario hand me over fallen trees or boulders. Shamefully weak and wobbly at the knees, I had to fight off repeated bouts of nausea. My flesh felt riddled with maggots. The tumbled boulders seemed to crawl alongside us.

Once Ilario and I came upon Dante, shaking violently, forehead pressed to a rock, his arms flung around his head as if to block out the sights and sounds of battle. "Mage," I whispered, not touching him, "can we help you?"

"Keep moving," he rasped. A pocket of frigid air brushed my skin. Naught was visible, but when I blinked, a blur of color streaked through the haze like a darting fish. We moved. Eventually, Dante passed by us, leaning heavily on his staff.

By midday, Dante awaited Ilario and me in the glaring slot of sunlight that signaled the eastern end of the gorge. The shadows had paled, the fog dispersed. My senses no longer detected anything unnatural.

"Portier," said Ilario quietly, while we were yet a goodly distance from the mage. A tortoise could have outrun me just then. "Our story. We need to agree."

"You heard me call and blundered into the hole. Despite my injuries and bindings, I freed myself of the chair and felled Quernay with the lantern. Is that right?"

He nodded. "I merely helped you up the steps and out. Simple enough."

"I dislike lying to Dante," I said. "My mind's a sieve where he is concerned. Besides, he's our partner. I believe him honorable." He had saved our lives the previous night, and just now shielded us from . . . something.

For the five-hundredth time, I stumbled and Ilario's

strong hand kept me upright. "This is my *life*, Portier. I beg you honor my choice."

"If the mage somehow got into that cellar and saw the chair, he'll catch us out. He'll know I could never have loosed the straps."

"But certainly you managed it. By the time I had done for the hairy brute, checked the cells, and retrieved my crocodile charm, you had broken free of the straps. You were just out of your head."

"All right, all right. I'll play." Naught could ever repay his help. But who'd have thought he could slip so effortlessly back into his idiot self after the journey we'd just experienced? "I owe you my life, lord. You needn't fear my loose tongue."

Eyes fixed on the rocky path, he inclined his head. "Now will you tell me what in the name of Heaven just happened? I've a notion I just crawled out of a dung heap."

"Honestly, I've no idea." Only that something had near unraveled Dante. Whether he'd been protecting us or probing mystery, my mind balked at imagining what it might be. My bones yet quaked, and I flinched with every blink.

A careful survey of the bleak country spread out beyond the gorge revealed not the slightest movement, no stirred dust, no whinny, no glint of metal, no untoward scent of man or beast. Half a kilometre into the open country, Dante relented and let me be still for a while in the shelter of a turpentine tree. As Ilario and I shared a waterskin, the mage propped his back on the tree and stared into the wasteland. I wondered if he was afraid to blink, as well.

"These bandages should be tended," said Ilario, dabbing a dainty finger at the blood- and dirt-encrusted rags bound to my chest. "My physician insists we cleanse wounds every day. A disgusting task . . ." Which he took up right away.

I resisted searching Ilario's pruned expression for evidence of the swordsman or probing his babble for hints of the man I had met at Eltevire. I would honor my promise. Besides, I doubted any flaw was to be found.

As Ilario worked, Dante shook off his reverie and joined us. The mage was no longer shaking. He inspected the lacerated purple circles on my chest for several uncomfortable moments, then nudged my ruined shirt aside to expose several older scars—my father's legacy. He reached out as if to touch them, then hesitated and glanced up.

"If you must." I didn't understand his interest.

His finger, firm, sure, and cold—thrumming with magical energies—traced the long scar that creased my left side and the short one just above my navel. The careful scrutiny recalled his inspection of Gruchin's spyglass, and I wondered if he was building the ragged marks into one of his runelike patterns in his head. I shifted uneasily.

"Killing strikes, these," he said, withdrawing his hand.

"Near enough." So Kajetan had told me when I regained consciousness, weak, nauseated, and bathed in blood and cold sweat. "It was a long time ago."

"Maybe nearer than you think. What happened to the one who did it?"

"He travels Ixtador, I suppose."

"Your father. Gods, he bears a fearsome grudge."

Cold iron lodged in my belly. He did not speak in the past. "How would you know that, mage?"

My demand bounced off his impenetrable stubbornness. "That bandage is filthy." He stood and tossed a clean kerchief of cheap linen into Ilario's lap. "Tell us about this Aspirant, student."

After Ilario folded the kerchief and tied it up for me, he forced me to accept the meager supply of cheese and ale from Dante's pack. Once begun eating, I couldn't stop, despite the profoundly unsettling morning and my annoyance with Dante. Likely a good sign that I was ravenous. Mules lost their appetite as their blood was repeatedly drained. As I ate, I told them the story of Merle and Quernay and their master.

Dante sat cross-legged, as intent in his listening as in everything else. "So this Aspirant worked no enchantments as his assistant drew the blood. Did he inject it directly into himself or distill it?"

"I didn't see. He took it back to where the other prisoner was kept. I was glad enough they didn't try to fill their entire urn in that one hour. They took half a litre, more or less. That's not enough to do much with, do you think?" I paused between bites. I hadn't yet considered the part of me I'd left behind, now taken who knew where.

Dante's long speculation gave me no reassurance. "If you start with odd dreams or unusual behaviors, you might want to tell me. To trigger what we saw this morn, destroying half a mountain in the hour Eltevire was compromised . . . The spellwork makes the doings on the *Swan* look like acolyte's play. It means someone has a talent beyond—"

"Beyond the level of a minimally talented hod-carrier?" I could not resist the jab.

His head jerked in assent. "Aye. Even allowing for transference to enhance inborn skills. Even allowing that the worst of this day and night was worked two hundred years past. We've a foe I didn't think existed."

This trace of humility on Dante's part frightened me more than anything we'd encountered.

"What was so mysterious about a cursed ruin?" asked Ilario, giving me a hand up. "They had a bleeding cell in the royal crypt and didn't see it necessary to explode the temple to hide it. What *began* here?"

"The whole place was enchanted," I said. "Objects in motion, light, fire, water . . . nothing behaved properly or consistently. At least nothing that originated in Eltevire. . . ."

As we plodded along a faint cart path that skirted the end of the ridge, I told them of my experiments—not of my attempts at magic, which proved naught but that "place" could not make an incapable sorcerer capable, but of the coins, Gruchin's silver, and the pool, the crocodile charm, and the lantern. ". . . think of your tisane that was lukewarm one moment, boiling the next, and felt like glacial ice but a moment later. Nothing behaved."

We retrieved Dante's donkey, left tethered beside a shady spring where we could fill our waterskins. "I arrived early at Canfreg Spring," said the mage, as we set out again, faster now with me astride. "When I heard the old man's tales—" He shrugged, and I understood. His hunger for knowledge had driven him to Eltevire ahead of us. "I intended to rejoin you, but three men rode in behind me and I dared not counter the bridge ward or its trip signal."

He slowed his steps and waved his staff at me. "You should have more care, student. You sense enchantments and residues. To disentangle a trip signal from a common ward is only one step more. It could have saved you this thrashing."

"Then *teach* me, if magic is so damnably easy," I mumbled. The donkey's jarring gait had my head pounding too awfully to yell at him. Despite his air of hard-won wisdom, the mage's brittle arrogance surely named him far younger than only six years my junior. Naturally, he didn't answer.

"So you were in the village while Portier was tortured?" Ilario burst out. "Ill done, mage! Unkind!"

"I never crossed the bridge, never went up to the village until I came for you. I let them pass and came around here. The mendicant had told me of the chasm stair."

"But if you kept away, how did you know they were going to explode the mountain?" spluttered Ilario. "Mage-work cannot predict the future, no matter what's said, else I'd have never come on this nasty trek! And why didn't the wards along *this* path bring them down on you?"

"I learned what I needed in the chasm. The destruction was writ in Eltevire's bedrock. A very long time ago, I think. Last night the rock's pattern shifted, and I could see a danger building. And just then, three men descended the stair in a hurry—though one was slow and weak—your prisoner, I'd say. Magic takes on extra potency at sunrise and sunset, so I expected the blow at dawn. Fortunately for you, peacock, I guessed right."

Three men had arrived at Eltevire: Quernay, Merle, and the Aspirant. And three men departed: the Aspirant, the prisoner, and who? The prisoner's guard, perhaps. Or perhaps "the adept" was not a prisoner, but another guard. I blotted the sweat from my bruised temples and squinted into midday.

"Over a day and a night I explored these physical anomalies," Dante continued, "though not so systematically as with your coins and pebbles. But it's the *mechanism* of Eltevire's madness that bears most significance." He halted the donkey for a moment and made sure I was listening. "To leave the gorge we had to travel along a boundary—a separation of two natural entities as distinctive as sea and land, or stem and leaf, or wing and air. Even as we walked that boundary, it was disintegrating, soon to be gone entirely. Until this morning, it completely encircled Eltevire's plateau."

"Separating *what*?" I said. "The two sides appear the same—land, vegetation, rock, wind. You're saying these villains enchanted *everything* within this boundary, creating some new kind of natural separation."

"No, Portier. Much more than that. Eltevire was not enchanted. Yes, the boundary was created with sorcery, but within the boundaries of that rock, nature itself was altered, *including* magic, for magic is *of* nature." Dante might have been a once-blind man explaining the wonder of his first sunrise. "A stone behaves like a stone, or a sparrow like a sparrow, because the pattern of natural law is written into the pattern of its being—its keirna. If you toss your coins into the air in Castelle Escalon, they behave according to their keirna. When a Merona sparrow takes wing, its flight reflects the physical laws we know. I believe that when the natural laws of bounded Eltevire were altered, the pattern of natural law written into the keirna of every object within that boundary was revised, as well. Did you find any spelled object in Eltevire?"

"None," I said, my mind racing to keep up with him.

"Aye, because your methods of detection are based upon the nature that you know, on the *magic* that you know. What if Gruchin's coin were brought to Eltevire and enspelled with a locator charm so he couldn't escape them? Its keirna, once solely of the world we know, would have been altered. But you or I would never detect the spell, because we don't know how to detect *Eltevire's* magic."

"And what of the crocodile charm?" I said. "It was enspelled in Merona, not Eltevire, yet its behavior changed when I invoked it in there."

A ruddy heat suffused Dante as from a lathered horse nearing its home ground. "The light charm worked exactly as its keirna was laid down. When the keyword is spoken, the spell is triggered and the charm emits blue light. But in Eltevire, the properties of *light* are not immutable as our natural philosophers daemonstrate. Use the charm fifty times in Merona, and it will always trigger blue light of a certain quality, but do the same in Eltevire and the manifestation could vary every time."

Ilario pulled his spyglass from his shirt and stared at it as if it were a daemon's trinket. "I don't understand half of what you say. But I'm thinking perhaps my glass is not broken after all. In Eltevire, sometimes it would show me my own feet, sometimes the stars, sometimes nothing."

Dante extended a hand, and Ilario passed him the glass. The mage's long fingers caressed the engraved case. He sighted through it up the slope we had to climb to retrieve our mounts, then passed it back to Ilario.

"It's not spelled. And it functions as it should. Light passes through its lenses and is bent, allowing our eyes to see what is directly in front of us, only drawn close. But in Eltevire, light beams do not always follow the rules. Our glass lenses would never work reliably there. Nor our eyes, I'd guess. Nor our magic."

"Father Creator," I said, as my own mind grasped his conclusions: a land where nature itself was altered, where neither physics nor magic could be predicted. *Guess you're fuddled*, Merle had said. *We'll fuddle you all.* "Such a place would be chaos."

"Aye," said Dante. "Chaos. Especially when you add in that there was more inside that boundary than the land you walked. Voices that had no right to be there. Sights you couldn't quite see. More than you know. Naught that I can explain . . . yet. But it's no mystery why they're wanting a handy necromancer."

Father Creator, send your angels. I could not speak. I could not think in aught but prayer, though instinct had whispered it all morning, and Dante had told me, *Your father . . . bears a fearsome grudge.*

The day was heating rapidly. Dante threw his dark cloak back over his wide shoulders, clicked his tongue at the donkey, and planted his white staff on an upward path. "I'll tell you one more thing, my partner *agentes*. The keirna of that boundary was far older than our conspiracy. Think about it: The cult brother's stories of this region have existed for centuries; the Mondragoni settled here well before the Blood Wars. Neither your Aspirant, whoever he is, nor Gaetana nor Orviene *worked* the enchantments that created Eltevire's aberrant nature. They don't know how."

He glanced over his shoulder at me, his green eyes flashing. The beginnings of a smile transformed his gaunt face into something younger and less haunted. "So now I know what they want me for."

WE DIDN'T TALK MUCH THROUGH that long afternoon. Even Ilario's determined idiocy found little outlet. The path was too steep, the day too hot. We moved carefully, scanning the landscape in every direction, but we saw no sign of human or beast . . . or anything else. The lump on my head belonged in a smithy.

Dante had implied that some connection with Ixtador lay beyond Eltevire's boundary. I tried to comprehend what that meant, but exhaustion had its way, and for the first time in nine years, I slipped into my vivid dreaming. I was wielding lightning to hold a mountain pass against a barbarian horde, while a fleeing populace reached safety. Fire threaded my arms and the heated charge of sorcery stank like seared stone. When my magic failed and the enemy bludgeons began to crack my bones, I blinked awake to the wastes of Arabasca and honest bruises and mysteries too deep for comprehension. Then the cursed donkey missed its footing, and in my distraction, I failed to brace. The pain in my head caused me to waste everything I'd eaten.

Vowing not to sleep again, I spent the next miserable hours contemplating everything we had learned from the day Philippe led me into Lady Susanna's dungeon until Dante's fierce conclusion. Perhaps the feigned assassination of Sabria's king had not been a mere distraction, but a first skirmish in a new war, a feint designed to test their plan. The conspirators were gathering power through transference, and if Dante was correct, exploring ways to upend the rule of reason. Chaos. Discord. Fear. So who would benefit from chaos?

Some two hours later, we stopped to drink and rest on the stepped tableland above Sante Marko's shrine. Only then did I speak to a disturbing possibility that had presented itself.

"Chevalier," I said, "what does Michel de Vernase look like?"

Ilario frowned and blotted his sun-scalded forehead with a filthy kerchief. "He's a big man. Near tall as I, but built for a fight. Muscled like a bull, head as well as body. Darker complected than Philippe, gold-brown hair starting to gray. Rough as a battlefield, but ladies fall all over him, which I've never understood."

"Knightly," I said. "Horseman, swordsman, all that. No grandiose reports hiding poor truth?"

Ilario rolled his eyes. "No false reports. Whatever a man can do, Michel de Vernase can do better. Rides like the Arothi. Fights like the warrior angel. Drinks like a sailor. Carries himself like a Linguan stallion."

I persisted, seeking to escape my logic. "But common, you said. Who are his people? Vernase village is the seat of the Ruggiere demesne. Was he born there? Educated?"

Dante looked up from relacing his dusty boots, his face sharp with curiosity.

Ilario draped the filthy kerchief over his forehead. "No family. I've heard he was a basket child, found and raised by an unlanded knight at a military outpost in . . . Grenville, I think it was. No doubt he's clever, and supposedly he's remedied the lack of education since Philippe raised him up. His wife gentled him enough to come to court. Mayhap she set him to his books, as well. Madeleine's worth a hundred of him. Old family . . ." He paused, his hands still for a moment. Then he peered over his kerchief.

"What does all this matter?" Eyes widening, he caught his breath. "Was he the Aspirant's prisoner?"

"I thought so," I said, "but now . . . Listen to me. Michel de Vernase was raised up to First Counselor, the highest post in Sabria, short of her sovereign. He was granted a demesne that had ever been reserved for the nobility. How many resentments has he faced on those accounts, as well as for his bullish manner? Yours, Chevalier, and others, I'm sure. He owns Philippe's implicit trust, yet knows he will forever be seen as a product of Philippe's favor. A second part: When the infant prince died, Philippe named a new heir, a secret no one in this kingdom shares—save perhaps Michel, the friend of his youth, closer than a brother, closer even than the estranged wife Philippe loves so dearly. As you put it, lord, Philippe and Michel have always covered each other's sins and drunk each other's wine. One month after the new heir's name was scribed in stone, Philippe's horse went mad and threw him."

Ilario scowled and shook his head, but I hushed him with a gesture. Perhaps he sensed where I was headed.

"Michel publicly scorns magic, as does his friend and liege. The spyglass implicated sorcerers, as did Gruchin's body, mutilated by transference. Yet Michel had Philippe's horse and saddle burned, and he neglected to have a mage examine the arrow. He bullied the Camarilla and the mages at Seravain. Ham-handed we called him, yet Philippe considers him a skilled, successful diplomat. And Michel instantly accused, not a sorcerer, but Calvino de Santo."

As I reconstructed my chain of reasoning, a certain fury took fire within me, from embers left smoldering since witnessing Calvino de Santo's testimony. Michel de Vernase had brutalized the guard captain, making him a public scapegoat when Queen Eugenie, the one witness who could aid him, had stubbornly refused to testify. Yet Michel had never extracted Gruchin's name from de Santo—which could have led the investigation back to Gaetana. And Michel had used two young girls, persuading—coercing?— one to return to terrible danger to discover the name of Eltevire. At the least his actions had killed Ophelie and left her young friend at equal risk. But there were other ways to interpret his course.

"What if Michel de Vernase had his own motive for prying the name of Eltevire from the mage who bled Ophelie? All along we've seen clues thrown in for confusion's sake, the trail of evidence obscured almost as quickly as it was laid. What if he wanted to make Eltevire his own?"

"But his name was scribed on the crypt wall," Ilario insisted. "Ophelie spoke it as she died. *Michel . . . captive . . .*"

The more I voiced my theory, the more I was convinced—possessed—of it. "Perhaps she didn't mean that Michel *was* captive, but that Michel had *taken* her captive. The *good man* she hoped to save from the fire could have been someone else altogether. Someone whose name she didn't know, but who possessed magic enough to break her manacles. Perhaps your charm maker, Adept Fedrigo. I don't know that anyone has seen him since Ophelie's escape. Perhaps Fedrigo scratched the Ruggiere symbol on the crypt wall because Michel was there, not as a prisoner, but as captor."

"Well reasoned, student," said Dante softly, his chin propped on his staff. "Very well reasoned."

"Michel de Vernase is this Aspirant? The leader of this conspiracy?" Ilario's shocked face had paled under his sunburn. "True, I never liked him, but many do. And Philippe . . . He'll never accept it. How could you possibly come to this?"

"Boots," I said. "The Aspirant's boots belonged to a knight, not a mage. They belonged to someone who guessed my identity easily and assumed Philippe had sent me. My cousin said he has been gathering reports of me for years. Who else but Michel would have been assigned such a delicate family task for his king? Who else might guess what *agente confide* Philippe might tap should his good friend vanish? Perhaps, before he went away, Michel himself suggested my name." Perhaps he suggested Portier de Duplais should head an investigation which a dull, failed student of magic could not possibly unravel.

"It would explain why he didn't worry about leaving that Cazar girl at Seravain," Ilario mumbled, wilted by distress. "She's likely in no danger at all. You see, I finally remember about the name. Michel's wife is Madeleine de *Cazar* y Vernase-Ruggiere."

And so did another link snap into place. Lianelle ney Cazar was Michel de Vernase's daughter. As I had done, she had dropped a father's name that would see her scorned or snubbed among a society of mages. I did not believe the child herself involved in transference and murder. When I had accused Michel of callous disregard of Ophelie's safety, Lianelle's distress had been unfeigned. But the father . . .

I could not deny my lust at the prospect of justice for crimes of such magnitude. And amid my sympathy for those like Lianelle, cruelly used by a father's ambition, lay hope for Maura. If the queen herself was innocent, then surely Maura's involvement was but another diversion.

Reasons, motives, the sorcerers who most assuredly had abetted the traitor, the methods to be used to create a kingdom of chaos—the precise construction of this plot could align in a thousand different ways. More than ever we needed Dante to pursue the magic. But the most difficult part would be to convince the king of the danger—that Philippe de Savin-Journia's worst nightmare was not his wife, but his beloved friend.

CHAPTER TWENTY-ONE

4 CINQ
21 DAYS UNTIL THE ANNIVERSARY

"His Majesty will see you now." The satin-garbed undersecretary's lips squeezed to a fleshy knot as he called me from the waiting chamber. Whether his disapproval addressed my cheap, ill-fitting garb, the massed green and purple of my healing bruises, or the king's overgenerosity in granting a coveted private audience to an embarrassment of a fifteenth cousin, I did not care. Too much else weighed on my mind on the first morning of my return to Castelle Escalon.

The undersecretary led me down a soft-lit passageway, his velvet slippers whispering on the cool travertine. Others glided by—a footman bearing a tray of sliced fruit, a perfumed woman herding a swaggering youth of an age to be squired, a lesser temple reader juggling a box. As my escort gestured toward an unpresuming door at the end of the hall, I bowed and exposed my hand to the portly, bearded man who had just come out of it. Baldwin de Germile, a man whose expansive girth and genial manner often saw his intellect underestimated, had yielded his position as First Counselor to Michel de Vernase gracefully, only to reclaim it after the Conte Ruggiere's disappearance. He flicked forefinger to temple in a cheery greeting, though he clearly did not recognize me.

Angels defend, what would such honorable men as Baldwin make of my tale? Every night of the return journey from Eltevire, I had labored over my journal, recording every detail of our experience in Arabasca, every connection I had drawn to events already described, every assumption, every unanswered question. On the previous night, newly arrived, I had foraged the palace library for historical details that might give background to the story. More and more I believed that Michel de Vernase had conspired with an unknown sorcerer not to murder, but to destroy his king.

Michel's personal history with my cousin must surely outweigh any single bit of evidence I brought in, no matter how damning. Philippe, no blind simpleton, had named Michel his infant son's goodfather. Even those Sabrians who maintained a casual distance from temples and tessilae would entrust guardianship of their children's education, estate, and marriage, and the welfare of those children's soul beyond death, *only* to a person of proven honor. Someone closer than blood kin. Which meant the chain of my story must be unbreakable, each link, in its turn, able to withstand hostile scrutiny.

The door swung open. "Your Majesty, Portier de Savin-Duplais."

The undersecretary stepped aside for me to pass into a map-lined study. Then he retired, closing the door soundlessly behind me.

I sank to one knee, my eyes on the jewel-hued Syan rug. Though I had caught but a glimpse of the man standing across the room, I sensed a fierce appraisal. The bruise on my temple was fairly horrible and the cuts on my lip scabbed over. My hair, never luxuriant, had been clotted with blood and singed into ragged ugliness by the Eltevire fires. Heurot's fussing attention and skillful knife could do naught but whack it off—a convict's shearing.

"Cousin Portier, I believed our understanding precluded any direct encounter." Though this greeting held none of the familial warmth of our first meeting, I did not permit my resolve to waver. My cousin likely feared what I might tell him. Rightly so.

Given no leave to stand, I remained on my knee, eyes down. "Circumstances have changed, sire. I am known to your enemies, though my fellow *agentes* remain hidden in place, ready to pursue these matters until they are resolved. Both have brought exceptional courage and skill to your service."

"And you have news for me?"

A scarlet thread in the carpet might have been an image of the story I must tell, twisting upon itself, hiding behind the lapis-hued warp threads, only to emerge somewhere altogether unexpected. "We have uncovered much that is dire and terrible, and I would give my arm not to speak the painful words I must. Will you hear me out, Majesty, all the way to the conclusion?"

I felt, more than heard, him move toward me, thus did not startle when he touched my bruised temple. "It appears you have suffered your own hurts to bring me answers. How can I refuse mere words?" His ringed hand brushed my shoulder, but did not pause for me to kiss it.

I rose and took the straight-backed seat he indicated, while he settled in a deep armchair, cushioned with maroon velvet.

"To the conclusion," he said, propping elbows on the chair arms and his chin on tented fingers. "I shall not interrupt."

I inclined my head. "I know you have received some intermediate reports of our investigation, courtesy of Chevalier Ilario, but I would ask you to forget all you've heard, imagined, or assumed about these plots. The story truly begins long before the Blood Wars, when the Mondragoni clan laid claim to an ugly little corner of Arabasca and made it their hereditary demesne. . . ."

An hour I spoke without pause, first outlining the disturbing nature of the magic the Mondragoni had worked at Eltevire. My hour in the palace library had confirmed that no other family had ever held that corner of Arabasca. Then I laid out the threads of our investigation—brave Ophelie and old Audric; Gruchin and his spyglass and an arrow that was never meant to kill; de Santo and his haunting; the fire on the *Swan*.

When I spoke of Lianelle and Ophelie, and Michel de Vernase's visits to Seravain, Philippe closed his eyes as if he could not bear to hear more. But his stony expression did not change, and I continued without pause to tell of Ophelie's family dead, and Gruchin's family dead, and suicidal seamstresses and missing adepts. I explained how Gaetana's approaches to Dante, the nature of the spyglass, the missing Mondragoni texts, and the mysteries of Eltevire hinted at sorcery so disturbing, he dared not fail to pursue and understand it.

"We cannot ignore the congruence of your enemy's work and the Veil—the natural boundary between life and death—and this unnatural boundary created at Eltevire, where natural law, as we know it, borders on a chaotic otherness. But the most significant question to be answered is the identity of your enemy—the leader of this conspiracy. Who dares use your safety, your wife's grief, and relentless murder to hide this exploration of death and chaos? And why?"

Dante himself could not impose such pressure of will upon me as did my cousin, sitting expressionless in his chair.

I inhaled deeply. "From the beginning, I believed one or both mages of the queen's household stood at the center of these events. That may yet be true. I see now that in my deepest self, I also assumed your wife responsible. But an investigator must not blind himself to possibility. Dante and I have come to believe that the queen's yearning to comfort her dead children has provided a smoke screen for those who pursue an interest in profound and unnatural mysteries. Yet it was only at Eltevire that a glimpse of a man's boots forced me to shift my eyes. This masked man who called himself *Aspirant* never worked magic in my presence. . . ."

As I recounted my tale of beatings, bleeding, and boots, Philippe grew rigid in his chair. And when I reported the Aspirant's claim that he was *Philippe de Savin-Journia's worst nightmare*, the king shot from his seat and strode to the window.

I paused, heart hammering. I had not yet spoken Michel's name.

His back to me, my silent cousin motioned me to continue.

"It is only in assembling all these bits and pieces, and imbuing them with . . . aspirations . . . that we see a larger story. Let us return to the day that Gruchin, near madness from two years' bleeding and compelled by unknown torments to loft an arrow at his king, stole his crude spyglass from his old partner's shop. Hoping to direct attention to the nefarious activities of his masters, and thus avenge his family's murder, he brought his spyglass and his coin to the field and made sure his own corpus would be left alongside them as evidence. You assigned your friend and counselor the Conte Ruggiere to investigate the matter. . . ."

Never did Philippe interrupt my account. I did not offer my interpretations of Michel's state of mind, as I had to Dante and Ilario, nor did I dare ask whose name my cousin had scribed on the Heir's Tablet in the royal crypt or what Michel de Vernase had thought of his choice. I did not soften my telling with apologies or implied excuses designed to flatter the king or his friend. Philippe would accept what I said or not. He knew the conte better than anyone.

"Majesty, you told me at the beginning of this journey that Michel de Vernase is either dead or hostage to those who wish you harm. Yet, in most of a year, you have received no request for ransom or favor. I say, either he is dead, or he is one of them."

I did not beg pardon or forbearance. I merely stopped speaking and waited. Any number of reactions seemed likely: denial, argument, imprisonment, interrogation, accusation.

For interminable moments, Philippe remained motionless. Then he whirled about, snagged my arm, yanked open the door, and propelled me through the halls of his palace.

My eyes refused to meet those of the myriad curious courtiers and servants who stepped aside, bowing, to let us pass. My skin burned. I was unsurprised when Philippe burst through a door on the second level of the northwest tower—the headquarters of the Guard Royale—but my spirit quailed, nonetheless. House arrest? Or Spindle Prison, the desolate finger of stone thrust up from the river Ley? My heated skin broke into a cold sweat.

A mustachioed captain, built like a bridge piling despite modest height, leapt up from behind a scarred table and dropped to his knee, alongside several officers and orderlies. "Majesty!"

Philippe twitched his hand to get them up, and his head to clear the room of all but the sturdy captain. "Captain de Segur, since fifteen Cinq of last year, the Conte Ruggiere has been away from Merona on a diplomatic mission. I have just received information that on thirty-four Siece last, he was taken captive. By midday today, you will dispatch the fifth gardia to find him, beginning the search at Collegia Seravain and working outward in every direction, questioning every man, woman, and child in the demesne if needs must. You will dispatch the seventh gardia to Challyat. I will draw up orders for the Challyat's chief magistrate to investigate the recent fire that killed the Marqués de Marangel and his family. It was no accident. As Magistrate Polleu looks into the murders, the gardia will conduct a search for Conte Ruggiere from Marangel outward. You will dispatch the eighth gardia to search— Tell him where, Portier."

My gaping mouth had already closed, but I could scarce control a stammer. "Ah—Arabasca. Begin at Mattefriese and work both east and west along the pilgrim road. Suspect any man of more than middling size, especially one who carries a finely sculpted leather mask."

Philippe believed me, at least so far as to act upon my word. I should be pleased. Yet I could not shake the sense that I saw but the outliers of this royal storm and might still end up drowned.

"The ninth gardia will proceed immediately to Vernase," snapped the king. "They shall maintain a cordon two hundred fifty metres distant from the estate of Montclaire. The contessa and her children will be treated with respect, but no one else is to be allowed in or out without identity vouched by three local citizens or an order sealed by this ring." The royal signet of Sabria glinted from his clenched fist.

"Understand, Captain, and make this clear to every officer and man: Michel de Vernase has been the captive of sorcerers and tortured to break his mind. He *must* be apprehended, controlled, and kept in isolation until he stands in my presence. But no matter *what* he says or does not say, he is my First Counselor, a peer of the realm, and my friend. He will be offered every consideration and treated with the full honors of his rank. Have you any question?"

The captain did not waver from his stance. "No, Majesty. All shall be done as you say."

Did Philippe believe what he said? Did he truly believe Michel a pawn? I could not guess.

"Nothing shall serve as excuse for failure."

De Segur bowed. Philippe's grip on my arm tightened, and we were out of the tower and forging yet another path through Castelle Escalon before the captain could have straightened up again. I could only brace for the unexpected.

Our destination became apparent as we barged through gawking crowds in the curved window gallery and on the broad stair leading to the queen's household wing. My cousin bypassed Ilario's apartments and charged through a small atrium, adorned with alabaster statues of dancers and horses. Even the pair of opalescent doors centering the curved wall did not slow us. Philippe slammed through them as if they were a leather swag over a peasant's shanty.

Jeweled ladies in cream-colored silk covered their mouths or halted their embroidery in midstitch. Lady Antonia, plucked eyebrows exacerbating her shocked expression, stared up from a tête-à-tête conversation with Maura. Maura's face clouded with concern as she took in my bruised face and the shoulder of my doublet wadded in the king's fist.

Though I longed to reassure her, I dared not. My feet stood too near a chasm . . . as did hers. I looked away.

Near an open window, eight or ten ladies clustered on a plush couch and the floor cushions in front of it. Eugenie de Sylvae sat in the center of them, holding an open book, a soft flush draining rapidly from her cheeks.

Stiff and controlled, the king inclined his back to his wife. "A private word with you, madam." No one would mistake this politeness for a request.

In a wave of shining hair and billowing skirts, the queen's friends and attendants dropped into deep curtsies. Eugenie herself rose from her cushion. Tall—but a handsbreadth less than Ilario—and regal, she waited just long enough, and then sank, perfectly composed, into her own obeisance.

The queen did not wait for the king's permission to rise. Her ladies followed her up in practiced unison. Most of them scurried immediately for adjacent chambers. A few, older women for the most part, awaited the queen's gesture of dismissal. Even then, Lady Antonia went to Eugenie and kissed her on the cheek before sweeping from the room.

The last door snicked shut. Eugenie's dark eyes fixed on her husband. Her chin, at once firm and fragile, lifted.

Philippe released my arm. "All these months I have yielded to your determination to rule your household as you desire and daemonstrate your confidence in your servants. No matter that my every counselor has entreated me to set you aside, I have trusted that you hold this kingdom's welfare paramount and would allow no grievance with me to change that. And whether or not you deem me fit as sovereign or husband, I could not—and cannot—believe you wish me dead. No longer can I afford forbearance."

Though the queen maintained her silence, the stretched emotions in that room made my forced posture in Eltevire's sorcerer's hole seem comfortable.

"Sit." Philippe waved at her couch.

The lady's entire demeanor stiffened like setting plaster, as if the matter of her sitting was a skirmish in their private war. The king waited, immovable as the palace wall.

Eventually, with a small shrug, the queen settled, graceful and dignified, to the edge of the cushioned seat. Yet she did not yield as might some bullied child, but as a mature woman who made her own choices.

Philippe acknowledged her acquiescence with a stiff nod. Then he shook a finger at me. "This man, Savin-Duplais, is a distant kinsman, a fawning favor-seeker who aspires above his place. In some fevered campaign to *protect* me, he chose to take up the question of last year's attempted assassination where Michel left off. . . ."

So did I come to understand my punishment for bringing the king such news. I had hardly expected thanks, and logic must approve my cousin's play. Yet, for my humiliating ruse to become the definition of my character was an ugly sentence.

As Philippe gave an abbreviated, remarkable, and almost entirely truthful rendition of my morning's recital, the queen's defensive posture yielded to intense listening and growing horror. While omitting all mention of Dante, Ilario, hauntings, the Veil, or his own cooperation, he revealed how my efforts had uncovered a conspiracy to revive transference and possibly destabilize the Concord de Praesta, the peace between the Camarilla and the crown.

I listened carefully, beginning to think he intended me to play some further role. Why else allow me to witness this painful encounter?

"Michel?" Eugenie's first word burst forth with full shock. "Working with sorcerers to destroy you? Philippe, how can you bear it? It's even worse"—the momentary gap in her self-possession closed quickly—"worse than believing your wife a dupe. Or a traitor. Or a traitorous dupe incapable of keeping her children alive. Or do you believe I have been seduced into *this* conspiracy, as well? Perhaps wife and friend are not such bitter enemies as everyone believes!"

Philippe acknowledged neither her moment's sympathy nor its bitter afterword. "Portier fears that one Adept Fedrigo may be another victim of these conspirators. If we could trace the young man's movements, we might save him before he suffers the Marangel girl's fate. Thus, we must and will question your mage Orviene. And you, lady, must tell me anything you know that might bear on this tale. Firstly, why, in the name of the Pantokrator, did you suggest to Calvino de Santo that I might wish to wrestle on that day?"

She shot to her feet, confronting him squarely. Fire had returned to her cheeks. "Is it so inconceivable that I should care for your pleasure, husband?"

"On *that* day? When a poisoned arrow lay in wait for me? When my *pleasure* ensured unarmored flesh would await its strike?" The few paces of soft carpet that separated them yawned as an indescribable gulf. "I do not believe in such coincidence. How can I?"

For a moment I believed she might yield her secrets, so deep did her gaze search the man. And truly I wanted to remind them both that the arrow was never meant to strike him.

Eugenie folded her arms across her breast. "You have my permission to question Orviene about his missing adept. Nothing more, though, as always, my liege may do as he wills. As to the wrestling: Earlier that day I engaged in conversation with several friends. Our discussion ran to the manly arts, and it reminded me of things you told me in days when we did not know each other so well. Do not ask me names. My judgment names my friends trustworthy, and I will not have persons like your sly kinsman subject them to demeaning interrogation. I cannot possibly enlighten you further. Now, if that's all . . ." She extended a hand toward the door.

"I will ask you to consider *this*, lady," said the king, unchastened. "Was it you or your 'trustworthy friends' who raised the subject of *manly arts* that day? And if it was you, then why did it strike you on that particular day, when our personal pleasures had not been a matter between us for so very long? I will not believe Michel my enemy until I hear it from his own mouth. But if such a friend as he can turn traitor and murderer, then no person in this world is above suspicion." *No wife, either*, he did not say.

He snapped a hand toward the door. I bowed to the queen and followed him out. He could not have seen her hands clenched fiercely to her breast or her grief-filled eyes locked to his back.

The king did not manhandle me as we hiked through the corridors. Neither did he dismiss me. Like a bruised duckling, I trailed after him to the study where we had begun. He sat down at a small writing desk and pulled out several sheets of paper, pen, and ink.

"Sit," he said. Without looking at me, he waved at a side table. "Drink if you wish."

I sat, gazing lornly at the decanter and cups, but could not imagine swallowing anything.

My cousin's pen moved in bold strokes. When three papers were written, signed, and sealed with his ring, he rang for the pinch-mouthed undersecretary and dispatched one missive to the Grand Magistrate of Challyat, and one to the commander of the garrison nearest Vernase. The king dropped the third letter into my lap. It bore my name.

I clutched the sealed parchment as he moved to the sideboard, poured wine for each of us, then settled in his armchair. "I apologize for forcing you into that most awkward interview," he said, quite unapologetically. "You needed to be there."

"What would you have me do now, sire?"

"Go to Montclaire and continue your investigation publicly. That letter is your commission. You can be sure Madeleine will demand to see it."

I swallowed my astonishment. "The Conte Ruggiere's home? His family . . ." Philippe's own goodchildren.

"It will be impossible to silence the news that I am searching for Michel or to hide the particular nature of my orders to the Guard Royale. Suspicions will swarm this palace as insects swarm the maquis in high summer." He drained his cup and set it aside. Distaste hardened his fair visage. "When he is found—alive, I pray—and proved innocent—which I believe absolutely—then the worst thing I could have done for him is feed ill rumor with the perception of indulgence. As with my wife, I cannot and will not express anything less than full faith in Michel de Vernase. Your theory demands investigation, cousin, and the court and the kingdom must see it pursued diligently, but *against* my personal inclinations. This lays the awkward burden squarely on you. You must continue serving as the efficient *agente* you are, while playing the diligent fool we have made you."

"I understand, sire."

I had resigned myself to the role of Portier the Sycophant, the overeager kinsman who aspired above his place, when I first took it on. Though my notions of destiny had never involved public humiliations, I should have been relieved that playacting was the worst penalty I reaped. Yet Philippe's scarcely concealed contempt pained me, even as I came to understand it. The king viewed sorcery as lies, trickery, and subterfuge, and the belief had fueled his disdain for the mystic art. Now lies and subterfuge—the province of spies—had entangled his heart and limbs, as well. And we were not done yet. Not by half.

"Before you go, you will question this Mage Orviene." Philippe's lips thinned and hardened. "I give you leave to extend that questioning beyond my lady's bounds, even to the woman mage if you judge it needful. Some sorcerer or other is a part of these works you describe. Michel has no connection to a blood family. Over twenty years, I've seen no hint of magical talent."

"I'll certainly question Orviene," I said, mulling the tangles ahead. "But I don't think . . . It's not yet time to wring out the mages. Dante is yet in play to observe them. Perhaps—" How far would his tolerance extend? "You have already acknowledged to Her Majesty that sorcery is involved in this case. Perhaps you could confess you need her help. You could suggest that the overreaching Portier, a failed sorcerer, is clearly incompetent to judge the signs of nefarious sorcery. As you employ no sorcerers of your own, she might provide one to . . . supervise me on the journey to Vernase."

Philippe's knuckles glared white against the dark wood of his chair as he considered this. His gaze fixed on the cold hearth across the room.

"My wife is ever eager to impress her belief in magic on me," he said after a few moments. "But she might choose any of the three. Which would you want—this Dante or one you suspect?"

"If she chooses Orviene or Gaetana, I'll have a chance to observe that one closer," I said. "A fool is easily discounted, as we well know."

His darting glance at me, as quickly returned to the hearth, removed all doubt that he was privy to Ilario's long deception.

"But I could use Dante better," I said. "Sire, would your lady not respond to your suggestion that selecting the mage who was *not* in her employ on the day of the attempted assassination might lead you to a more objective view of her servants? Might she not think such a partnership could lead even you to appreciate magical talents?"

He pressed his fingers to his forehead that could not possibly be throbbing more wretchedly than my own. The shredded remnants of dignity that I'd preserved so carefully these past years lay scattered from his court to the rubble of Eltevire. Perhaps it was that which impelled me to bait a powerful man as he wrestled the maddening truth that he could not trust either of the people he loved most; or perhaps it was only my tired, foolish attempt to raise his better humor.

"Indeed, cousin," I said, "one might argue that your views shifted on the day you summoned a 'kinsman sorcerer' from Seravain. Surely, admitting faulty judgment in a marital dispute could not be received amiss."

In a move so swift as to blur my vision, the king sprang from his seat, hefted his chair, and smashed it onto the writing desk, splintering the delicate furnishings in a storm of falling cushions, breaking glass, and splattering ink.

"Get out," he yelled, reaching for the broken chair, as if to ready it for a new target. "Do your vile business and crawl back into your hole."

CHAPTER TWENTY-TWO

"Will that be all, lord sir?"

Heurot shut the clothes chest after storing my clean linen. It was the first he'd spoken that evening, which was entirely unlike the chatty young manservant. Before I'd gone to Elteviire, he'd habitually come to attend me in the evenings only after his other gentlemen were satisfied, lingering in my chamber to speak of such matters as his brothers and sisters in service, his latest reading from the chapbooks he picked up in the markets, and the progress of the giant pendulum the king was having constructed in the palace Rotunda. Perhaps he'd sensed my dismal mood.

"Not quite." I handed him a sealed note and sixty kivrae. "Deliver this message to Secretary de Sain in the steward's office right away. And I'd be most grateful if you'd have my new boots picked up from Tick the Cobbler before morning. I'll be leaving Merona tomorrow early, and these bought on my last journey would better fit a twelve-year-old maiden with square feet."

"Certainly, lord sir." The youth accepted my missive for Henri, finalizing arrangements for the journey to Vernase, and slipped the coins into his tunic's voluminous pocket. Then he bowed, as he'd never found necessary before, and backed awkwardly toward the door. But he bumped into the clothes chest, then stumbled over the horrid boots Ilario had bought me in Mattefriese to replace those lost at Eltevire. "I can fetch your new boots right now. Tick works late. Divine grace shine upon you, sir, sonjeur."

"Divine grace, Heurot. Are you quite all right?" His behavior was altogether odd.

"Aye, lord sir. Definitely. Thank you for asking, lord . . . Sonjeur de Duplais." After another jerky bow, he backed out of the door into the passage.

Amused and puzzled, I returned attention to my journal. Dipped my pen.

The door slammed shut, but tight breathing raised my eyes again.

"Will ye be back this time, sir, lord sir, sonjeur?" Heurot pressed his back to the closed door.

"Barring misfortune. Why? Are you sure you're all right, lad? Speak up. And *sir* or *sonjeur* is quite enough."

He stared down at the ugly Arabascan boots. "It's just, I've heard . . . this disgrace . . . that the king's so angry with ye, and dullard me didn't even know ye were his kin, and I've been so free, joking and not acting properly respectful all these days. But I wanted to say, if I wasn't to see ye again, that ye've been kind to me and ye don't seem a lackwit or craven or mercenary at all. Only I didn't know whether it was proper to speak of such."

I suppressed a smile and a sigh of regret. Rumor progressed rapidly, as the king had foretold. More so after his destructive outburst of the morning. Yet rumor served.

"Ah, Heurot, my blood is so remotely related to His Majesty that his wolfhounds are more familiar to him, and more valued. Indeed, my efforts to remedy our distance have put him in a foul temper, and he's sent me off on a wild errand, subordinate to the worst possible taskmaster." I grimaced and shuddered.

Few would understand my early-evening pleasure at hearing that Dante would accompany me to Vernase. Where had I learned how to move a king to bend his neck to his wife's whims? Sometimes I felt far older than two-and-thirty years.

"Yet I am at little personal risk, and ever hopeful to serve the crown honorably to forward my father's Veil journey. Though it were well"—I beckoned the lad close and whispered—"if perhaps you did not proclaim my better qualities aloud. I'd not have you tainted should I fail to satisfy the royal pleasure."

The lad tossed his yellow hair out of his widened eyes. "Aye, I see what ye mean. I'll pray the holy saints to serve your honor and your . . . satisfyin'."

"I could ask no more."

Smiling, I returned to recording the results of my interview with Mage Orviene. I'd questioned him shortly after leaving the king's study. The mage had offered me little new. Evidently, Adept Fedrigo was perpetually short of money, a matter Orviene did not wish to overemphasize, but feared might have sent the young man to the docks to gamble on the day of his purported murder. And no, the mage could not recall who had told him the story of the ill-fated tavern brawl. One of the palace servants, he thought. He would inquire and let me know. The city magistrate's written report had portrayed the brawl as no different from any other in the history of Riverside taverns.

As before, Orviene impressed me as sincerely grieved about his assistant's fate. He had not himself seen Fedrigo since shortly after I had first arrived at Castelle Escalon. When I mentioned our earlier encounter, and the suspicions he had voiced with regard to the *Swan* fire, he reiterated that he had no evidence of improprieties. But his eyes pointedly told me that his beliefs had not wavered. And that was that.

I hoped writing the details of the interview would grant me some marvelous insight, but not long after the palace bells rang eighth hour of evening watch, a footman delivered me a note, sealed without any device. Unsigned, its blockish characters set down ungracefully one by one, it comprised but one line: *Friend, I await you in the heart of Escalon. Please.*

"Hold!" I caught the messenger before he could disappear down the passage. "Who sent this?"

"Don't know, sir. A lamp boy caught me as I was coming from supper. Said he was given it to be delivered to Sonjeur de Duplais. The donkey hadn't asked on whose authority."

I sent the fellow on his way and scoured the message as if the sparse words hid something I could not see. For a blood-marked man to venture out in answer to so enigmatic a request in these dangerous times was idiocy. Yet the sender could be Ilario, returned early from the country, or Dante, whom I had not seen since we parted ways on the road from Eltevire. Our meetings must be conducted with redoubled caution now I was so exposed. I had to go.

Hoping to arrive while the dusky light yet held, I sped through the north wing and down the back stair to the underground labyrinth that delivered servants speedily to the principal areas of the palace. The branch under the south wing and a damp slanting tunnel delivered me to the south gardens. *The heart of Escalon* was not found within the palace proper.

Before the current residence was built, and long before the current fashion of elaborate, precisely laid-out gardens and follies, some Sabrian queen had grown the *escalon* or garden maze for which the palace was named. Instead of common boxwood or privet, she had chosen colorful plantings of the wildlands—gorse and flowering broom, brilliant yellow nestled amid the budding scarlet of hibiscus, and thick growths of purple-flowered bougainvillea—to disguise those who trod the maze paths. In the center of it all she had built a fair summerhouse of rustic floors and latticed arches, rotted and replaced a dozen times through the decades.

Scents of damp earth, sweet gorse, and freshly trimmed grass hung thick as I hurried through the narrow paths, increasingly anxious. Neither Ilario or Dante would have written *please*.

Holding quiet at the edge of the clearing, I peered through the advancing gloom. A solitary figure, mostly obscured by the latticed walls and deeper twilight inside the elliptical summerhouse, moved slowly back and forth between the peaked ends, pausing at each terminus as if to stare outward through its open arch. When I estimated the person's stature as considerably less than my own, I perused the note again and my heart leapt. *Friend.* Maura.

She halted her pacing the moment I raced up the steps. "Portier! Thank all angels you've come." Anxiety and relief twined together like the flowering vines.

I longed to answer as my own self and not the creature of conspiracy's invention. But the risks were far too high. Maura stood too near the quaking center of this earth tremor.

"Divine grace, damoselle," I said, bowing and exposing my hand, keeping my distance, even as heart and conscience clamored to soothe her trouble. "So secret a summons, lady?"

"I just couldn't— But I needed to find out: All these rumors about Michel de Vernase, about you. These dreadful events: the fire on the *Swan*; Filamena, the sewing woman, found dead in her bed; Adept Fedrigo gone missing. This morning, Henri de Sain tells me you've been asking about shipping crates and—and corpses. This afternoon I see your awful bruises, and I hear you've driven the king to violence. And this evening I'm tasked to arrange transport for you and that vile mage to Vernase. Friend Portier, what is happening?" She sank onto a circular bench, as if spilling her worries had emptied her of strength. "You're the only person I trust."

Her quiet sob near broke my resolution. But caution shaped more lies and kept me away.

"I cannot imagine any reason for you to be afraid." Hands clasped behind my back, I sauntered along the peripheries, underneath the gargoyles carved in the latticed arches. "Though you were wise to meet me in secret. My fool's quest is like to get me hanged. I've uncovered some distinct coincidences that shine unfortunate light on the king's friend, Conte Ruggiere, forcing His Majesty to decisions he detests. Not a path to royal favor. Forgive me for not revealing my—"

"Michel de Vernase would never betray his king." My words had infused iron in her spine. "He is honorable, compassionate, devoted entirely to His Majesty's service and to his family. This evidence cannot be credible. Tell me of it, Portier. Perhaps the answer's somewhat of common knowledge that I could easily provide."

This poorly disguised probing wormed its way beneath my skin like a glass splinter. I riposted. Lies came easy now. "A taverner at Seravain told me she posted a letter for the conte to a woman here at court. After so long, she couldn't remember the name, but the conte had teased her that this woman 'aided him in secret work.'"

Were I not listening with senses raised, I might have missed Maura's sharp breath. The splinter speared deeper, chilling my heart.

I lowered my voice and tightened the snare. "As I came to consider that Michel might not be so much a friend to His Majesty as everyone assumed, this report turned my thoughts to Mage Gaetana, as it is well-known that sorcerers instigated last year's assault on the king. Do you think it possible *she* is Michel's female accomplice?"

"None of this is possible," Maura said, in growing desperation. "How can circumstances appear so awful—so wicked—when no shred of ill intent lies back of them?"

I did not sense that she was answering my question. *Press harder, Portier.*

"What circumstances, lady? What do you know of the conte's activities?" And then I played my vilest trump. "Should I fail to daemonstrate some confirmation of my accusations soon . . . Damoselle, I do fear for my life. I had not reckoned on such staunch friendship between the king and a low-birthed warrior like Michel de Vernase."

Maura's cloak rustled. She moved as if to rise . . . but rocked back again . . . and forward . . . again and again. Her fear burgeoned to fill the summerhouse, and her mouth moved soundlessly, as if words battled to escape her control. Gods, what did she know? I held silent, afraid to remind her of my presence, lest she hold back.

"Gaetana asked me to send that crate to Mattefriese," she said, the hoarse phrases scarce more than a whisper. "It never occurred to me to refuse. Members of the household send things all the time. But who ever will believe that? Because last year, in the month of Siece, I *did* receive a letter from Conte Ruggiere. He asked me to have some girls' clothing made to specification and sent to Tigano in a large crate along with supplies for a tenday journey. Not two months past, I received two similar crates to be delivered to the temple. I did not question who the sender was or what the contents might be. I've always done favors for the conte. I believed—I still believe the conte is in hiding for good reason. I did not mention these incidents to anyone, as I had pledged him secrecy. I owe him— Sante Ianne! *I* ordered the banners made for the launch of the *Destinne* and arranged for their delivery to the *Swan*. It was my duty to relieve my mistress's burden. But who will believe that?" Her rocking stilled and she pressed her fist to her heart. "Merciful saints, Portier, I suggested the wrestl—"

"Silence!" I blurted. Dismay tore through my layered deceptions like the Aspirant's scarifying blades through flesh. "Say not one more word to me."

No sooner had I spoken than my arms gathered her to my breast. Somehow feet, hands, and heart had taken me where reason forbade me go. Her hair smelled of dusk roses. Her throat fluttered under my stroking fingers like a captive bird's heart.

"Easy, easy, sweet lady." The ragged edge of caution slipped from my grasp. "I will see you through this. But I am surely a sworn witness in this matter. Say naught to me that I cannot report." Her next word would have linked her with treason . . . regicide. I could *not* hear it.

"I did not conspire to evil, Portier. I swear it. Those poor people on the *Swan* . . . murder . . . I could never . . ."

"I believe you."

And I did—utterly and completely—which was wholly unexplainable save by some conviction passed between her body and mine. Was I so experienced with subterfuge that I could recognize truth and lies, so experienced with women that I could untangle wishing belief from desire and sympathy?

"Go back to your apartments and back to your work.

Be yourself. Speak nothing of this night. Nothing of me, save ordinary converse about these rumors. And by your hope of Heaven, lady, go nowhere alone until these matters are settled. Even during the day, keep constantly in company." Murder had dogged my footsteps. "If you receive letters, messages, packages . . . anything from Michel, anything related to him, anything from Gaetana . . . get them to me. You are exceptional—clever, efficient, trusted. Of all people, you can do these things without suspicion."

"I'll *not* compromise Michel de Vernase," she said, pulling away.

"Do not speak of him again," I said. "Neither defend nor condemn him." My hands slipped down her arms until they grasped her cold fingers. I gathered them and brought them to my lips. "It is not our place to choose what we will or will not see. We must have faith that unfolding truth will expose your actions in their proper proportion and his as worthy of your beliefs. Trust me"—I kissed her fingers, which tasted faintly of honey and springtime—"and don't be afraid."

"You make me believe that's possible," she said softly. "I've never—Who are you, who can bring me such comfort?"

"As you said, damoselle, I am your friend." Her lips tasted sweeter than her fingers.

Idiot! What kind of agente *confide kisses his witness? Or, angels defend us, his quarry?* As I waited for lovely Maura and her rose-scented hair to leave the maze well behind, I longed for a time when I did not have to consider such things as duplicity after a kiss of such blessedly enveloping heat as could melt a man's boots. The records at Seravain named Maura ney Billard a talented, accomplished sorceress of adept's level. *She* could be Michel de Vernase's magical accomplice, the woman who had tormented Ophelie, playing on my inexperience and pity to learn what I knew.

My soul refused to accept it. Or was it only my body

telling my soul what to believe? Why had I not asked what she *owed* Michel?

These circular musings halted upon my return to my apartments. Another message waited.

Sonjeur Duplais:

Regarding my promised inquiries: My valet reminded me that it was Mage Gaetana who brought me the story of poor Drigo's fatal night at the docks. In the spirit of completest candor, as urged by my lady queen, I must add that Mage Gaetana strongly disapproved of Fedrigo and had repeatedly urged me to dismiss him, complaining that he had invaded her private laboratorium a number of times unasked. I apologize for not mentioning this before. Scruple struggles at passing on such trivia. But conscience cannot permit silence. Fedrigo would have been collared by autumn, and his loss to our community and his family cannot be measured by petty scruple.

Regretfully,
Orviene de Cie, Mage of
the Camarilla Magica

Gaetana. Gruchin had been her creature, her adept, nurtured, discarded, and bled dry. Gaetana had frequent access to the missing Mondragoni manuscripts, as well as to the royal crypt and Maura's services. News of Ophelie's exposure had infuriated her. She had invited Dante onto the *Swan* and approached him with unsavory "translation projects." She had wielded sophisticated magic to douse the *Swan* fire. Most telling, Ophelie had named a *woman* as her tormentor. Gaetana had ordered the "mushroom crate" shipped to Mattefriese.

All of these things could be innocent circumstance, as could Adept Fedrigo's disappearance in the face of her displeasure. Orviene's "suspicions" could be opportunistic lies or spiteful gossip. Yet in their accumulation, the reports cast an aura of conspiracy over the formidable sorceress. We just needed direct evidence that she had engaged in transference.

My battered body and mind begged for sleep. I pressed the heels of my hands to my eyes as if I might squeeze out some plan to make the sorceress speak. Perhaps it was time to compose my own letter.

Over the next hour, I wrote a brief explanation of my search for evidence to prove Michel de Vernase responsible for the attempt on the king's life. To this, I appended an account of a horrifying incident, wherein I had been waylaid in the alleyways of Castelle Escalon, dragged to a subterranean laboratorium, and leeched by a tall, masked woman wearing a silver collar, who threatened to drain every drop of my "royal blood." Lies flowed as fluently from my pen as from my mouth. I described my scarified wounds, and her implements and techniques, and finished with the tale of my harrowing escape by way of an exploding lantern and a passing guardsman.

Shortly before middle-night, I roused a palace messenger and posted copies of this great fiction to Kajetan, my mentor, who had solicited news of transference, and to Angloria, a methodical, painstakingly honest, former instructor of mine, newly raised to the Camarilla prefecture. As guardians of the Concord de Praesta, they could not fail to investigate. Gaetana, the only female mage at Castelle Escalon, would find Angloria's inquisitors at her door by midday. The story was near enough the truth that they would ask her the right questions. Unlike me, they had means to judge the truth of her answers.

My instincts claimed I had done right. At some point I

had to take action, lest we swirl in evidence until we were all dead by fire and chaos. I would apologize for the deception later.

"Portier! Come, wake up." A hand rattled my bruised shoulder bones.

"Heaven's gates, what is it?"

A candle burned on my bedside table. Ilario's anxious face loomed near. "Come along, Portier, he wants to see you."

"The damnable mage?" I scraped the grit from my eyes and blotted my chin with my sleeve.

Ilario shook his head and tossed my crumpled shirt at me. "Philippe."

That woke me. Mayhap my cousin had reconsidered having a poor relation dictate the course of his marriage, friendships, and sovereignty.

The air from the open window spoke of lapsing night as I laced my traveling breeches and buttoned my shirt. By the time this errand was done, Dante would be waiting for me in the stableyard, ready to set out for Vernase. Unless I wasn't available.

"I didn't know you were come back to Merona, lord," I said as I pulled on my new boots and made to follow Ilario.

"Eugenie sent to me," he said, peeking out of the outer door before pulling it open. "Seems she had a wretched day and needed diversion."

I could well imagine Eugenie's need for comfort.

We tiptoed down the householders' hall, rounded into the northwest tower, and slipped into an abandoned stool closet. Alert now, I noticed Ilario shift the brick in the upper corner. Thus I was not surprised when a narrow panel swung out of the scuffed wooden wall. Once the door clicked shut behind us, Ilario unshuttered a lamp. A quarter of an hour, six turnings, two halts to scurry across public passages and through more hidden panels, and we ended in a capacious wardrobe closet.

"Portier," whispered Ilario, the lamp exposing lines of worry on his boyish face, "I don't like all this, people knowing you're on the hunt. You're awfully . . . exposed. And Philippe—" He puffed his cheeks and blew an unhappy note, shaking his head until his fair hair fell over his eyes. "I've not seen him so angry. So uncertain."

"I appreciate your concern, lord." Truly it warmed me more than I could say, even if he could only express it in the King of Sabria's closet. "But I can't exactly have a bodyguard trailing me around, can I? Not if we're going to find the answers we need. As for my cousin . . . none of us is immune to royal displeasure. At least I've blood kinship on my side."

He grunted a quiet laugh. "That's served *me* well. I'll be waiting here to take you back." He rapped on the wall and shoved open a panel, allowing me to enter the very study I'd been tossed out of half a day earlier.

The damaged desk and chair had been cleared away and the ruined carpet removed to expose patterns of dark and light wood. A small, bright blaze illumined the tiled hearth. Philippe, gowned in fur-lined silk, hunched in a chair beside it, as if he were eight-and-seventy years and not eight-and-thirty.

I dropped to one knee beside his chair. Before I could rise, he thrust a paper into my hand. Sitting back upon my heels, I read it by the light of the flames.

⌒

Sire:

I must assume that your battered cousin has limped back to Merona and whispered dreadful tales in your ear. If his story is at all coherent, then you, my friend, my liege, have surely guessed his tormentor's identity and are engulfed in rightful fury.

You must believe me. Things are not at all what they seem. Something extraordinary happened when your servant went searching for your enemies. He found them. And then he discovered things about himself, about magic and power, about the truth of the world. We have been wrong, Philippe. Terribly, blindly wrong.

There is too much to write, and our enemies are ever close. I am forced into hiding. As poor Portier experienced, the dangers are very real. Convey my apologies that I could not protect him better. Good fortune that he had a doughty companion to salvage him!

I do not expect you to meet with me yourself nor dare I trust just any messenger. Your court is riddled with treachers. In honor of our long friendship, the debts we have owned and paid, I beg you send the bearer of this letter—a noble heart well-known to both of us, utterly trustworthy and capable of defending himself—to meet with me, one to one. He will be met at Vigne Caelo at next moonrise and brought to my hiding place. I will send him back on my goodson's deathday with clear evidence of my discoveries.

Ever your servant, M.

"You'll not send anyone, sire?" I said, appalled. "Certainly not alone? This is but a lure." The high, open ground of Vigne Caelo, Heaven's Vineyard, was completely surrounded by rugged hills, notched with verdant vales—a thousand escape routes and a thousand hiding places.

My cousin's face might have been chiseled in coldest marble. "Is the letter magicked? Do I see what is not there?"

"There's nothing. No enchantment. No residue."

"The hand is Michel's. How can I refuse?" Yet clearly Philippe was torn. He was asking, quite explicitly, for a reason not to acquiesce, a shocking reverse from the morning's stalwart faith.

The wrongness of the words on that page seemed clear to me. Not only had the Aspirant not *protected* me, but he had helped extract my blood, which he yet held. His harsh voice still sounded clearly in my ears: arrogant, lustful, resentful. He had relished my groveling, exploited my history of despair against me, stuck his filthy boot in my mouth. Even discounting personal humiliation, I could summon no belief that he had only *feigned* cruelty.

"The screams I heard in Eltevire allow me no grace for the Aspirant, sire, be he Michel de Vernase or any other. Even now, he makes you doubt yourself. Heed your instincts, lord."

"We cannot fail to collect this evidence he offers. If he is villain and sends us lies, even that would provide grist for your mill of logic, would it not?"

He'd thrown my own words back in my face. "True, but—"

"Will you swear to me upon your life that the danger we face is of greater moment than my own safety? Greater than the normal consequence of a sovereign falling before his time?"

An odd swearing, but easy. Philippe himself had stated this condition when he recruited me. What passing doubts I might have harbored in those early days were long dismissed.

"Your enemies"—I purposely did not mention the Aspirant—"pursued forbidden magic in a place where nature itself is maimed. I swear upon my ancestors that your death is not their sole object and may never have been their object at all. Think what would have been the outcome of the Blood Wars, if those who battled the savagery had been unable to loft an arrow that would reliably hit its mark, or if those who wielded magic in the cause of right could not predict the outcome of their spellwork?"

Even I, who yearned for magic, could not imagine nature wholly unbound by law and logic. What would sway the balance of sovereignty in such a world? *Fear*, I thought. The power to outwit nature, to compose illogic and harness chaos. Sorcery.

After one moment resting his head on coupled fists, Philippe pulled a sealed dispatch from his lap and waved it and me to the outer door. "Give this to the one who waits outside."

I bowed, forced to swallow the questions and arguments his face forbade me speak.

The moment I opened the door to the anteroom, a rangy young officer in the colors of the Guard Royale jumped up from a waiting bench. "Sonjeur de Duplais! Divine grace." He bowed crisply. "Edmond de Roble-Margeroux. Do you remember me, sonjeur?" A ready grin illumined the young man's dark eyes and well-hewn features that surely sapped the knees of every young lady he encountered.

"Certainly, Greville Margeroux," I said. His thick black hair and cinnamon-hued complexion must instantly recall the luminous Lady Susanna to any who had ever met her—along with old Conte Olivier, and this, their striking son. The king's dear and trusted friends. No wonder, then, at Philippe's reluctance to send him into danger.

"How does my testy pupil?" said Edmond, leaning down from his height in cheery confidence. "Truly that was the most terrifying sevenday of my life. Never have I been threatened with dismemberment, transmutation, disordering, accelerated aging, scabs, leprosy, and worms all in one hour, and all over the matter of learning to use a fork. Is he here? Has he transmuted anyone into vermin as yet?"

"You did well, lord. The mage has made a place for himself in the queen's household, though he dines alone.

Everyone in the palace, including me, is terrified of him."
I glanced at the three doors that led to adjacent rooms and
passages. No one lurked, so late at night. "You've never
mentioned your venture into mage-schooling?"

"On my mother's back," he said, his smile vanishing as
he uttered a soldier's most solemn swearing. For this young
man, that particular bond would be formidable.

"I've brought your orders," I said, handing over the
sealed document. The return of his good cheer did not dismiss my wish that I could withhold the page.

His eyes sparked with excitement, flicking over my
shoulder into the near-dark study. "Am I to go, then?" he
whispered. "The letter was delivered to my barracks
sealed. But the note delivered with it warned me to ask
extended leave, as I'd likely be sent on a critical mission for
the king."

"I've not read these orders," I said, dread and warning
near deafening me. "But if so . . . Young lord, be on your
guard every moment. *Every* moment."

He sobered properly. "Naturally, sonjeur. This is my
first mission for my liege, who has ever shown my family
kindness and favor. I shall not fail him."

"There are things worse than failure, Lord Edmond."
Hearing myself blurt this platitude, I felt a righteous ass,
and though the young man bowed politely, his demeanor
spoke disbelief and a youthful assurance of immortality.

I grimaced and shook my head. "His Majesty has set
you free to go. Yet, hold . . ."

"Sonjeur?"

"Do you carry the note that brought you here tonight?"

"Indeed. I thought it might be wanted." He pulled a
folded page from his pocket.

The brief message reflected exactly what he'd said.
Though the hand appeared the same that scribed Philippe's
letter, Edmond's note was not signed and the broken seal
was plain. "What made you believe an anonymous message to be of such import that you sought leave from your
post and rode through the night to deliver it to the King of
Sabria?"

"Certain references in the message revealed the sender's

identity. I've known him all my life and knew the king would welcome word from him."

"Ah. The conte is a friend of yours, then."

He flushed. "Taskmaster more than friend. He sponsored my appointment to the Guard and trained me to be worthy of it. I was inclined to . . . withhold . . . in confrontation, not a useful quality in soldier or lord. Lord Michel taught me otherwise—a lesson neither easy nor pleasant."

"Indeed. But your families were friendly?"

"Not at all." He blurted this quite vehemently, then attempted to remedy it. "My parents, as you saw, do not go much in company. But I visited Montclaire once. The conte's family is most generous and welcoming, all of them so different from one another and so . . . astonishing. On one evening, the younger girl gathered every cat from the neighborhood into the house using sorcery, while Ambrose, spouting verse, dueled with a manservant in the drawing room. The contessa cajoled servants, family, and guests alike to dance a pateen, while Anne—Damoselle Anne—argued the movement of the planets with her father in three languages at once. I've always wanted to go back. This year past must have been awful for them—not knowing."

"Aye. Awful." But not the worst it could be. By far, not the worst. "Divine grace, Edmond, and godspeed."

He inclined his back briskly and left. Fraught with misgivings, I returned to the study. Philippe's gaze did not shift from the fire. Dismissed already, I bowed, slipped through the hidden panel, and threaded the dark passage in search of Ilario. Michel's two missives sat safely tucked inside my doublet.

CHAPTER TWENTY-THREE

5 CINQ
20 DAYS UNTIL THE ANNIVERSARY

"Get tha gone, sonjeur! I've four mounts come in early need to be tended, all the mornin' usual to be done for our own, and you demanding this 'n that on the skimmy. The upset's took Wek from his duties, when I've my two best lads puking from overmuch ale. The beasts *know*. . . ."

"What about *my* upset?" I grumbled, once old Guillam had limped away. If the grizzled dotard planted his feet in front of me once more, sucking his toothless gums, whacking a cane on his breeches, and blaming me for his unruly stable, my teeth would be ground to nubs.

Our delayed departure from Castelle Escalon could not be unnerving the king's horses any more than it was unsettling me. Just when my cracked head seemed to be healing itself, the cursed Dante had set it hammering again by failing to meet me as arranged. I did *not* want to be here when the Camarilla came for Gaetana. By the time we returned from Vernase, they would know something—the truth of her activities, I hoped—and I could apologize for my fabrications.

For an hour, I'd resisted the urge to go rip the mage

from whatever was keeping him. The arrogant devil was probably working on some new line of inquiry that he could not be bothered to tell me. And yet . . .

I peered yet again through the stableyard arch. Rosy dawn light bathed the palace's eastern portico, the logical route for a man leaving the queen's household wing for the stables. The doors remained firmly shut.

What if Dante lay in a heap on his floor, collapsed again?

Unable to dismiss this image, once it settled, I set out to roust the mage. Midway across the carriageway, a flash of color from behind the fluted columns caught my eye. Crimson and olive green—Camarilla colors. Anxiety swelled to panic, the certainty of danger a drover's whip, as real as the boots on my feet, as vivid as the out-of-time hero dreams of my youth.

God's teeth, how could inquisitors be here so quickly? Never had I known Prefect Angloria to make a decision in less than a tenday—especially one of such import. And Dante . . . One hint of suspicion, a single unpleasant encounter, and he would himself become the focus of an inquisition. They'd never forgo an opportunity to examine the legendary *Exsanguin*. Not only did I fear for our investigation, which already felt balanced on a hair, but for Dante himself. He would not bend well to Camarilla questioning. I had to get him away.

Though heart and mind galloped, I maintained my steady pace toward the portico. Nothing attracts a watcher's attention so much as reversing course or speed at first glimpse. I mounted the steps, inclining my head to the balding man and the square-jawed woman who flanked the doors, as if I were any common courtier out to enjoy the fair morning.

Neither responded. Bless the saints, neither looked familiar. I hoped my newly shorn hair, my mottled bruising, and the fringe of beard let grow where it was too painful to scrape would keep me unrecognized. Prefect Angloria, once my formulary instructor, would be somewhere inside.

Fierce urgency propelled me through the east wing passages. But as I arrived in the queen's household, I slowed my steps and smoothed my clothes. Courtiers huddled in conversation or ambled along the window gallery, enjoying the air and the view and gleaning gossip to fuel the day's conversations. More had come than usual today, titillated by mages' mysteries.

A craggy-faced, red-haired woman stood at the intersection of the gallery and the passage to the mages' apartments. Entirely unaffected by the attention she garnered, the scarlet-mantled Prefect Angloria waited like a rock in the confluence of streams. Her gaze roved the gallery and its denizens, the mages' passage, the royal staircase, and the bright scenery beyond the windows with equal disinterest.

Philippe's First Counselor, Lord Baldwin, no longer cheery, hovered at her elbow. From time to time he flicked a commanding dismissal at some lordling drawn too near or servant grown too bold with gawking. The gold-tied scroll in his hand would be the Camarilla warrant.

As specified by the Concord de Praesta, the warrant secured the Camarilla's right of entry, their privilege to enter any home to fetch Witnesses—suspected magical transgressors or potential informants. No civil authority was permitted to intervene.

I hung back, choked by frustration. No one seemed willing to pass by the prefect to access the stair to the queen's residence. I dared not be the first, thwarting my intent to use Ilario and his secret passages to smuggle Dante away.

"Portier!" My heart stuttered when Jacard, Dante's sharp-featured adept, snatched at my sleeve. His skin was flushed and damp. His blood pulsed at a gallop, noticeable even through my sleeve as he drew me into a window niche. "Have you heard the news?"

"I see Camarilla."

"Inquisitors have come for Gaetana," he said, scarce able to contain himself. "Broached her door an hour since, and her yet in her nightdress! Is this something to do with the mess you've dug up? What a paladin you are, out investigating on your own! Everyone's aflutter with the story.

I've heard rumor of unholy practice, bleeding. Corpses, even."

"It's no secret that sorcery caused the fire on the *Swan*," I said, keeping my voice low and my back to the strolling courtiers. "I've only pointed out that others must be involved as well. Are the inquisitors questioning anyone else?" I rubbed the mark on my hand. "They wouldn't be rounding up just anyone of the blood, would they?"

Jacard's color deepened. "To say truth, I tiptoed away as soon as they arrived. I didn't want them deciding they'd drag me along if Dante chose not to be at home."

"I feel quite the same."

Danger drummed in my veins. Camarilla inquisitors could use whatever techniques they deemed necessary to get answers. Rumor spoke of spelled artifacts created before the Blood Wars—effective things, uncomfortable things. The arrogant, impatient Dante's heretical teachings could get him branded and hung up in a cage.

"Jacard, I'm desperate to get to Dante's chambers. The king has charged me to follow the damnable mage on some ghost chase this morning. If we get delayed by inquisitors, it's *my* backside will be aflame. I'd be forever grateful if you could distract the prefect and Lord Baldwin long enough for me to creep past them."

"Fiddle a prefect? Are you mad?"

Ilario would have done it, but he wasn't there, and I knew no one else to ask. "I was mad to begin this holy venture, yes. Now I'm reaping havoc. So, never again. But for now, I'd give you—" Only one thing I knew might buy Jacard's aid. "Help me and I'll tell you the composition of Dante's circumoccule."

In an instant Jacard's nervous excitement was supplanted by calculation. "You saw it made?"

"He had me sear the trough in the floor and build the ring with no fewer than fifteen distinct particles. I can tell you at least twelve of them, and how they were laid."

"He works marvels there." Jacard's hunger echoed my own. "All right, all right. Give me a moment. Don't want the prefect imagining I'm trouble. Be ready to move."

Garbed in sober shirt and breeches rather than an academic gown, the sharp-chinned adept easily merged into a passing group of gentlemen and vanished down the gallery. Meanwhile, I slipped closer to the passage, gliding from one window niche to the next whenever a passing body shielded me from the prefect's view.

I'd almost given up on Jacard, when a sharp popping noise heralded a spray of tinkling glass scattering on the tile floor. The crystal lamp mounted above the intersecting passages had shattered. Moments later another lamp, a short span from the first, did the same. Passersby ducked and shouted, and everyone, including the prefect and the First Counselor, spun to watch the lamps, bursting one and then another, each farther down the gallery in the direction Jacard had gone. I stepped out of my niche and slid round the corner not two metres from Prefect Angloria's back.

Chest heaving entirely out of proportion to effort, I flattened myself into a niche alongside a tall, cedar cupboard. No one cried out the trespass. No boots pounded after me. A man's conversational tone emanated from deeper in the passage.

". . . entirely understand, Mage Inquisitor. I've no fear of questioning, though I would certainly have appreciated some forewarning. I could have come to the Bastionne on my own." Orviene's clear tenor carried down the way. "Allow me to don more seemly garb, while you examine my laboratorium. Do have a care with that box, Adept. . . ." The voice receded.

So they were taking Orviene as well. No time to dawdle. My only hope was to act as if I belonged here. The cupboard held a collection of refuse—a dented brass pitcher, a soiled towel, a cracked night jar, broken fans, and a torn pillow leaking feathers. I grabbed enough items to make a pile sufficiently tall to obscure my face.

Courage flagged as I stepped into the passage. The two mages outside Gaetana's door wore close-fitting, dull green caps that covered their hair and ears. Sewn with long jowl strips that buttoned over the wearer's mouth, an inquisitor's cap left only eyes, nose, and cheeks exposed above the mage's collar. The caps served as a reminder that inquisitors would neither hear pleas or testimony, nor speak comfort, reasons, or bargains, until their selected Witnesses were secure inside the Bastionne Camarilla, the fortress of the prefects.

Between the two inquisitors and two Camarilla adepts stood one such Witness, shrouded in a dark blue mantle and a thick, all-encompassing hood. Both mantle and hood had been sewn with iron rings to damp the effects of spellwork. Tradition mandated that none should know the Witnesses put to question by the Camarilla, lest rumor forever taint their works. Yet this particular Witness, taller than any other magical practitioner in the palace, could only be Gaetana.

I had always accepted strict, unbending inquisitors as necessary to ameliorate the risks of dangerous or reckless magic, dismissing rumors of cruelly forced testimony as the protestations of the guilty. But, somehow, witnessing this grotesque solemnity in the flesh upended my certainties. And I had brought it down on these people with lies. Holy saints, what had I been thinking?

Juggling my awkward armful of oddities, I strode down the passage past the somber group, as if well accustomed to macabre invaders. Without hesitation, I pushed through the charged enchantments of the door ward and into Dante's apartments.

The mage's great chamber was even more cluttered than usual. The man himself was nowhere to be seen, yet the air quivered with magical energies. Something was very odd. I spun slowly in place. Worktables, heaped with materials. Locking cupboards, doors hanging open. The amber circumoccule fixed in the scuffed mahogany floor. The couch, bathed in rosy light from the great east windows, unhindered by draperies. Ceiling, walls, plain and unbroken.

I blinked. Where was his bedchamber?

Memory insisted the doorway to the adjacent room ought to be midway along the west wall. I ran my hands over the smooth plaster. No mistaking when I found the doorway; the jolt of enchantment near set me on my backside. But only as long as my fingers touched the door frame did the spell allow me to see into the lesser chamber.

Dante sat at his desk, as I had seen him on my first visit so long ago—head bowed, eyes closed, white staff in the rigid grip of his maimed hand. His left hand rested on a small book, forefinger traversing a line of hand-scribed text on a yellowed page. Naught so extraordinary, save that purple sparks sprayed from the blackened tip of his finger, and plumes of frosty air billowed from his staff. The man himself trembled with such violence, his bones must have been near shattering.

I could spare no time for wonder. "Dante, we must get you away."

He daemonstrated no sign that he'd heard me.

One step past the threshold immersed me in a maelstrom of discordant energies—as if the sun and moon tried to shine at once in that chamber or the tide ebbed and flowed in confluence. I squatted at his side. His eyes remained fixed on the page. "Can you hear me? Stop this and listen."

His brow creased, and his finger slowed, but more in the way of pushing on through a disturbance than deciphering my speech.

"Dante!" Gingerly I laid my hand on his shoulder.

He reared backward, near rising bodily into the air. His staff clattered to the floor.

"The Camarilla's come for—"

The mage burst roaring from his chair, shoved me across the room, and slammed me to the wall, his formidable shoulders proving themselves no mere decorative accident of nature. Heat poured from his twisted face, darkened to the color of dried blood.

It took both my hands and all my strength to pry his forearm from my neck. "Let. Me. Go."

In an instant, he released me and stumbled backward. A moment's frantic search and he snatched up his staff and pressed his forehead to the wood, clinging to it as a seaman to his lifeline. "Did you ever consider that what I'm doing outside your presence might have *some* importance?" he said, tight jawed and breathless.

"Father Creator, how could I not know that?" I said, forcing equanimity. "But the Camarilla's come for Gaetana.

They're taking Orviene as a Witness. You'll be next . . . and perhaps me. You remember we were traveling to Vernase this morning?"

"Yes." He bit off the word, the storm of violence scarce under his control.

"Our journey's even more important now. The king's had a letter from Michel de Vernase, all but admitting he's the Aspirant. The conte claims innocence and promises to send evidence of his 'discoveries' by Prince Desmond's deathday. We cannot let the Camarilla delay us."

As I forced myself to patience, his breathing slowed and his back straightened. Eventually he looked up, and only the familiar hauteur was written on him. "Never touch me when I'm in trance, fool of a student," he said. "I could have killed you. Without intent."

"So I've learned," I said, appreciating the concession, while yet rubbing my overbruised throat. Someday I would know the roots of this violence that lay so close to his skin. Only a fool wielded a blade without understanding the irregularities in its tempering. "Now can we leave here before you're hauled off to the Bastionne? They'll be scratching at your door any moment."

"Certainly, I know the officious little pricks are closing in. What took you so blasted long to get here?" It was as if the blazing orange sun had retreated below the eastern horizon, only to bounce back up again arrayed in soft green or lilac. And as it shone so peaceably, the overpowering dread that had driven me since waking dissipated. I was left speechless and limp as old linen.

He tapped the end of his staff on his desk. "I couldn't afford to stop working. This could be my last chance to glean aught from this cursed book. *Gaetana*'s book."

My breath halted, interrupting my rising fury at his manipulation. Gaetana's book: *a manuscript buried deep in layers of wards and ciphers. Perhaps even less savory, but carrying knowledge of the uses of magic that have been lost for generations.* A manuscript that people of ethics might have difficulty with.

"Aye, the one I spoke of after Eltevire. If they've taken her, they'll learn of it, too, yes? And when they take me as

Witness, I must offer to yield it without coercion. But if I leave it here among my other reading material and fail to reset my flimsy and easily detectable chamber wards, it might not be here when they come back to search for it. Hardly my fault."

"You want me to hide it." We certainly could not allow them to confiscate the book before we knew what it was. "Better we both take it and go."

Dante twisted and stretched his shoulders as if he'd been hunched over the book for a very long time. "Better I get this encounter over with. It has to come sometime, and I'd rather inquisitors not dog our steps as we go forward. Besides"—he twisted his mouth in his wry semblance of a smile—"we can always hope I'll learn something of interest in the Bastionne Camarilla. The prefects have either deliberately overlooked these episodes of transference or kept their own investigation very close."

"They'll dig deep," I said. "They've old magic that even you—"

"Be sure, I shall yield the butchers only what I wish them to have." The mage's brittle edge reasserted itself, like keen lancets snapped out of a shiny brass block.

"The Camarilla is pledged to preserve the art from those who would pervert it," I said, hating this defensiveness his prejudices roused. "They *must* be strict, and they must keep their counsels, just as we do, to make their work effective. But Edmond de Roble is on his way to meet with Michel de Vernase. Every instinct and every reasoning bone in me is convinced that some piece of this conspiracy will come to a head twenty days from now—whether or not Gaetana is guilty. Someday the prefects need to hear what you can teach, but not today. I need you free. Alive."

The mage looked at me askance, as might a healer observing a hopeless patient. "I promise to watch my mouth, student."

Shifting uncomfortably inside my skin, I pointed at the book. Surely it pointed the way to Gaetana's deeper purposes. To her guilt. "So what is it? What have you learned?"

He scooped it up and waggled his dark brows, his best humor peeking out like sunglints through breaking storm clouds. "A beginning. I've scarce unlocked ten pages and the language is as murky as a pond choked with algae. But the title is *Diel Revienne—The Book of Return*—and we're not speaking of returning from a day's outing to Vernase. It's one of three. I'll tell you more once we're traveling. When the time is right, I'll astonish you!"

A thunderous knock set off a searing whine almost beyond hearing.

Dante shoved me against a stretch of blank wall opposite the door between the chambers. "Stay exactly here. I've set a barrier to hide you—far better than the wall closure. And heed this, student: These barriers inside you are ridiculously strong. *Anger* stiffens them."

I had no idea what he meant. Fingers of enchantment snugged me against the bedchamber wall like a well-fitted jacket, though naught hindered my view into the adjoining room. Dante stuffed the book inside my shirt. "Best keep still," he said with a sidewise grin, then grabbed his staff and stepped into his great chamber. Bellowing, *"Eximas!"* he stretched the staff toward the outer door.

The whine of the wards ceased. The door flew open. An adept, thick folds of dark fabric draped over his arm, crossed the threshold and intoned, "Master Dante of unknown family and demesne, the Camarilla Magica summons thee to Witness."

Though the man's elongated face wore the habitually haughty expression of Camarilla adepts, his eyes circled quickly, as if to determine whether the ceiling might fall or furniture start flying. He passed Dante a rolled paper, which would be the personal warrant, indicating whether the mage was to be taken as a violator or informant.

Dante tossed the scroll unread onto one of his worktables. He did not respond to the adept's greeting, nor did he bow to the inquisitor who followed the adept inside and began a cursory examination of the great chamber.

The inquisitor—whether man or woman was impossible to judge—brushed fingertips on the circumoccule, then moved on quickly to the cluttered worktables. The fleshy hands touched only one or two items, lifted a few lids, opened a book or two. Ripples of enchantment flowed through the room, splashing on me even where I sat. Dante, wreathed in disdain, remained near the door.

I swore under my breath when the inquisitor drew a flat leather case the length of my arm from a cabinet. Dante had assured me the spyglass and arrow were safely hidden. But the opened case revealed only three wicked-looking knives. I breathed again. Dante's mouth twitched, and I would have sworn by all I held holy that he winked. Father Creator, he was enjoying this!

From then on, I observed Dante's reactions, not solely the inquisitor's. Even when the eyes peering out of the green cap heated at discovering the masked door, Dante remained cool. The hooded mage entered the bedchamber, but, astonishingly, took no note of me. A quick perusal of bed, desk, cupboard, and chest, and it was done. As I exhaled slowly, the inquisitor returned to the great chamber and waved a finger.

The adept held out his hand for Dante's staff. Dante thumped his staff on the floor, and flame burped from its head. "My ancille goes where I do, Mage Inquisitor. If I'm forbid to carry it into the Bastionne, then you must do so yourself. 'Tis less stable than I would like. My finer skills remain imperfect." No one would mistake his statement for either apology or humility.

"The inquisitor will carry it, Master," said the adept. The inquisitor, naturally, did not speak.

Dante propped the staff against the wall and did not protest as the adept draped him in the shapeless gown of deepest blue, weighted with iron rings. Nor did he lash out as the adept dropped the heavy hood over his head. He wanted to, though. As clearly as blood pulsed in my veins, I experienced a smothered rage—a desire to break the cocky underling who led him, blind and suffocating, into the passage—and something else. . . .

I shook off the fancy. Dante would not fear the Camarilla.

The inquisitor spent a goodly time examining the markings on Dante's staff, before laying a tentative finger on it. First one, then another; then he lifted it gingerly and departed. The door slammed behind him.

Not overeager to venture out of my hiding place, I pulled out the little book. Its binding of faded, brittle leather was crudely stitched, its lettering unreadable, the fore-edge of the pages ragged and stained. An oily residue of spent enchantment made me grip it fiercely. Yet it remained enspelled. I opened to the first thin page. Though scribed in familiar characters—Sabrian script of approximately two centuries earlier—the words formed no familiar language. Indeed, all characters but the few fixed at a time by my eyes' focus shifted their order at random.

Magical encryption, then. But I needed no magic to unravel the book's origin. Inked on the opening page was a pair of dueling scorpions, the blazon of the Mondragoni.

Of a sudden, Dante's good humor and promises of revelation lost flavor, as will tender shoots and leaves left too long in summer sun. Always in my life, I had desired to know everything of magic. Yet for days after we first stored the Mondragoni texts in Seravain's vault, squeamish sensibility had prevented me pulling them out. Eventually I had yielded to temptation. Finding the pages locked away by the Gautieri wards, I'd convinced myself I was relieved. Now I saw the truth. I wanted to learn everything, even from the decadent masters of Eltevire.

Stuffing the little volume back into my doublet, I crossed to the window, careful not to be seen. On the carriageway, Guillam, the stableman, had brought up four horses. The Camarilla adepts aided the three shrouded Witnesses to mount. Prefect Angloria rode the fourth beast, and the inquisitors and adepts formed up marching ranks behind her. A wave from Angloria, and the bizarre procession moved around the corner of the palace, out of view.

The Camarilla warrant named Dante as informant, not accused. A relief, that. Unless they provoked him to some revelation of his ideas or his true power, he should be held only a short time.

I had not asked Dante what I should do to avoid being killed were I to find him "in trance" again, nor why an interruption should cause such rage. Nor had I inquired how, in Heaven's truth, he had summoned me to his side. . . .

barriers inside you . . . anger stiffens them. Certainly I had been angry that morning, with Dante, with Philippe, with Michel de Vernase, with the world that used such people as Maura and Edmond de Roble-Margeroux as pawns in terrible, dangerous games. It had taken the mage more than an hour to fetch me to protect this little book.

But how had he done it? I stared at my hand, pocked with the burn scars he had soothed and dressed after the fire on the *Swan*, as if it had taken on a wholly unfamiliar shape. Never in all my studies had I come upon a formula to embed enchantment into a man's very blood and flesh. Into his mind.

CHAPTER TWENTY-FOUR

6 CINQ
19 DAYS UNTIL THE ANNIVERSARY

"You said twelve of fifteen elements." Jacard frowned at my sketch of Dante's circumoccule. We sat beside the tall casements at the end of the mages' passage on the morning after the Camarilla had taken the three away. "It's none of my doing that Dante was hauled off before you could get him out. I risked my career."

"Sorry. Ten are all I can remember. Truly I appreciate your help, Adept, and as soon as I've a chance to consult my journal pages, I'll let you know the rest." Not that better instructions would do him any good without Dante's power to seal and charge the thing. So deeply shaken were my magical certainties, I could no longer assert that any particle embedded in the ring affected the mage's enchantments in any fashion whatsoever.

My skin buzzed with lack of sleep. I had not dared return to my apartments or be seen in public lest someone decide to enshroud me in dark wool and iron and haul me off to the Bastionne. I'd spent the entire previous day in a rose arbor, watching the carriageway for Dante's return. The night I'd spent huddled in the summerhouse, hoping to see a light in his window and trying to decide if the thoughts and fears and urgencies in my head were my own or a product of his enchantment. No enlightenment had been forthcoming. At dawn, rabid for news, I had given up and set out for the east wing. On my way to Dante's apartments, I had run straight into Jacard.

He folded the page and slipped it into his sleeve. "Acolyte Nadine's uncle is a house mage at the Bastionne. He hasn't been home since yesterday, but he sent her father a message that Gaetana's assistants are not to be summoned. And if hers aren't, the rest of us aren't likely. You're something of a special case I suppose, with this 'holy mission' to root out treachery, but I've not heard your name mentioned. They'd surely have come for you already if they thought you had something useful to say."

"That seems good news," I said. "Perhaps none of this is as serious as it seems." But it was, of course. Too many hours had passed. Camarilla inquisitors did not indulge in drawing room chatter with their held Witnesses.

"Head up," whispered Jacard. "Someone's coming."

"Let me pass. Let me pass." A disheveled Mage Orviene swept down the passage toward his grandly carved door, drawing acolytes and adepts behind him as a comet leads its tail of stars. "I must sit in my own chair. But follow me in, all of you. You must hear what I've to report. And by your hope of Heaven, recall that your lips are sealed by the oaths you have sworn to the Camarilla."

"I'll find you later." Jacard jumped up and joined his fellows, eight or nine of them crowding through the doorway after Orviene.

I slipped onto the back of the group as if I belonged, remaining nearest the door.

Orviene's expansive great chamber vied with Ilario's in overblown elegance, if not so obviously in cost. The mage sagged into a cushioned chair, carved in the shape of a rampant lion, motioning for one of his acolytes to light a man-high lamp of fluted brass. Though the hour was early on a bright day, thick draperies covered the chamber's sole window.

The lamplight only clarified the mage's out-of-character

turnout. His chin-length hair, customarily pomaded and combed, straggled on a soiled collar. His skirted doublet hung unbuttoned; his meticulously tailored sleeves flapped about his wrists. But his round face carried worse news, his complexion gray, his eyes dull and uncertain.

"Mage Gaetana was beheaded by the Camarilla Magica at the first hour of morning watch . . ."

The news slammed my chest like a battering ram. Warning, denial, horror, guilt exploded in my head and heart. Only with difficulty could I follow the rest of his words.

". . . unholy practice . . . transference . . . a former adept in her charge . . . and an innocent girl . . . murder . . . confession after intensive questioning . . ."

I had killed her, as clearly as day followed night. As coldly heedless as a child who burns an insect to see how it reacts, I had set the Camarilla on her. *Intensive questioning.* Holy angels, Father Creator . . . I'd never have written the letter had I truly doubted the woman's involvement in terrible crimes. I'd wanted her out of play, prevented from tormenting anyone else. Yet I had expected a prolonged investigation, time to be certain. And what of Dante? Saints defend him.

". . . shock . . . dismay . . . private quest for arcane knowledge . . . thankfully, no evidence of collaboration . . ."

No sense. No sense. No sense. Even amid this nauseating self-reproach, the *agente confide* in my head bullied me with reason. Why had they not come for the lunatic who had written the accusing letter? Great gods, I had signed my name. And these young colleagues were inexperienced, yes, most of them new to court, overawed at their privilege to study with the queen's own. Those I recognized were not Seravain's elite, to be sure, but capable. Yet they had not been asked for their own observations. That must mean the Camarilla possessed other evidence implicating Gaetana.

". . . who worked for her are dismissed without prejudice. I shall personally write recommendations. For my own self and my staff, we must wait to see how Her Majesty reacts to the news as the prefects present it to her. Information may be curtailed or held entirely in confidence. Such scandal so near her royal person! Truth be told, I am tempted to resign."

Her Majesty. When the world learned the queen's mage had been executed for illicit magic, Philippe would be forced to act—to declare his support or arrest her. And if he declared his wife innocent of murder and corruption, he must have the truth to offer his people instead.

The Concord de Praesta had been wrought to prevent civil and magical life from swallowing each other. It ensured that magical practitioners were subject to a law that took into account the particular demands, requirements, and possibilities of their deeds, and it ensured that those lacking magical talents would never be judged by those with talents so alien to their own. Only the Camarilla could judge matters of magical practice. Only the crown could judge civil matters. On the day I had been admitted to the study of magic's secrets, I had sworn the oath to uphold the Camarilla's prerogatives as set by the Concord, believing fully in their value. No argument had yet convinced me otherwise. I had to pursue my own part of this investigation, trusting Philippe to give me time to bring him the truth.

Shaken to the marrow, bursting with questions to which I had no answers, I slid round the door frame into the passage before anyone noticed me. With such alarm and upheaval, none present were looking beyond their own futures. I sped lightly to Dante's door and slipped inside, only to receive another jolt. One might imagine a herd of elephants had arrived before me.

The contents of the worktables had been scattered from one end of the room to the other. Every box had been opened. Every bottle emptied. Every book unstacked. Every paper . . . I spun in place. Not a paper was to be seen. Dante had predicted the Camarilla would come looking for the book. Better they than Michel de Vernase.

It was tempting to run to Ilario. More than four-and-twenty hours Dante had been held. Yet even were we willing to risk our partnership, Ilario, a man outside the magical community, could not intervene with Camarilla business, even to ask for news, nor could his half sister or the king. And I was oath-sworn not to speak of Camarilla business to an outsider.

And so I sat for a while in the midst of the destruction, worried, guilty, and wholly unsure what to do next. I did not so much doubt Gaetana's guilt, as wonder at the circumstances of her "confession." Haste implied a wish to avoid probing too deep, a wish to hide unpleasant truth, a wish to contain and conceal. What if someone in the Camarilla itself wanted Gaetana's testimony cut short? How likely was it that Gaetana and Michel de Vernase worked alone? And why, why, why did they keep Dante so long?

Near midday, unable to sit still any longer, I began to tidy up the mess, blotting oils and inks, stacking books, and gathering the scattered leaves and scraps, the beads of coral, jade, and lapis, and slips of varied metals onto a sheet. As the afternoon waned, I collected the emptied bottles and jars, settled on the floor beside the heaped sheet, and began to sort the materials into their proper containers. The sun slid westward. . . .

"So when do we ride?"

I jerked upright to the chinking clatter of glass and stone. The world had gone black, save for the soft glow of a white staff.

"Dante! God's teeth!" I jumped to my feet, the sorting debris showering to the floor. "Are you all right? Is it true about Gaetana? What, in the god's creation, did they do to you? What did they ask? So many hours . . ."

I could not slow the spill of questions, even as he moved away, raising his staff high enough to cast its soft light on the jumbled cupboards and filthy floor.

"A blighted mess here. I presume you did not cause it."

"Certainly not." How could he speak of such trivialities? "Dante, tell me about Gaetana."

"The Camarilla killed her for bleeding the girl. She confessed to it."

A statement of fact, entirely dispassionate. I expected rage—or gloating, perhaps—anything but glassy calm.

"And what of you, Master? What did they ask? Did they use . . . extraordinary methods?"

"I am neither dead nor accused." He nudged the broken night jar with his toe, then strolled across the room and touched his staff to the wall. A spike of red light split the dark, and the bedchamber doorway stood revealed. He picked up an emptied rucksack from a worktable and carried it into the bedchamber.

"Shall we get a start on the morning?" he called through the opened doorway. "I've no wish to field idiot questions from slobbering ladies-in-waiting or devious assistants. The moon's just past full, and I've been told the road to Vernase is a good one."

The suggestion surprised me. Dante hated riding, and night travel could be slow and unsettling. But, then, perhaps he was as anxious to be away as I was. Perhaps he dared not speak of the Bastionne inside the palace, where listening ears were everywhere.

"Certainly. Yes, of course, we should go. I'll roust the stableman and meet you in the yard."

"I've a few things to gather; then I'll be down." As I touched the door latch, he called after me. "You do still have my book, yes?"

His will nudged my hands and tongue, subtler than his earlier attempts to influence me, but unmistakable now I knew to watch. Yet even so small a move unleashed a fury in me. I no longer even questioned that he was capable of magic my studies deemed impossible, but that did not mean I would ignore this crude manipulation.

"So tell me, Master, do you still not trust me, or is it you believe me a pure dullard? Would it make a difference if I repeat that these spell tricks are unnecessary? Or that I prefer us to deal with each other as honest men? Or if I told you that an armed assassin would not have kept me from your side once I saw Camarilla in the palace?"

He appeared in the doorway, the rucksack on his shoulder. To my astonishment, he had donned a mage's formal blue gown instead of his favored russet tunic and scuffed trousers. Though his silver collar gleamed in the light of his staff, his face remained shadowed. I could imagine its ascetic arrogance well enough.

"I don't know what to make of you, student. On the one hand, I never met a man who understood himself so little as you. Your own excessively rigid mind plays more tricks on you than I ever could. But on the other hand . . . So tell me, honest man, where is my book?"

"I've put it away, as I presumed you wished." Underneath a bench in the summerhouse, to be precise, as my "excessively rigid mind" had not completely failed me.

"Exactly so. But if I'm to discover anything of interest in it, I'll need it back, won't I?"

I bit back a useless retort. We were not children, and the past two days had surely overstretched him as well as me. I'd known from the first he was subject to this choler. "I'll fetch it with us, certainly. And as we ride, you'll tell me what you've learned from it."

He stooped to rummage through the heaped contents fallen from a gaping cupboard. "Little enough. A few tricks. Some tedious history. The Mondragoni had no use for this other family, the Gautieri, I'll say. Evidently the other way round, as well, as the encryption is hideously complex, doubly so for what puling spellwork is written in it. I doubt I'll ever be able to finish reading the thing, much less grasp its full meaning." He picked a few items from the heap, carried them into his bedchamber, and stuffed them into his leather satchel.

I gaped for a moment, not sure what I was hearing. Dante, suggesting a magical task he could not perform? A conclusion that wholly contradicted his statement of a day earlier that he would "astonish" me with what he learned from the Mondragoni text. "What foolery is this? You said—"

Caution aborted my retort. Did he speak this way for my benefit or for some other listener—perhaps someone who also knew of Gaetana's book? His deliberate preoccupation offered no prospect of immediate enlightenment. I would challenge him again, once we were on the road.

So I left him at his packing. It would not pain me to

rouse the stableman, Guillam, from a sound sleep. Perhaps with a cannon.

OTHERS WERE AWAKE IN THE middle-night hours of Castelle Escalon. As I awaited the mage in an unlit corner of the carriageway, an increasing number of footmen and guards raced in and out of the east wing doors. Extra torches were brought out to light the portico steps. Before very long, old Guillam himself led out two palfreys, one white, one sleek bay, both saddled for ladies.

"We'd best be off before we get caught in this lot. The house is in an uproar." Engrossed in the activity, I near shed my skin when Dante spoke from behind me. He snatched his mount's reins from my hand.

A troop of guardsmen marched round the corner from the direction of the barracks, just as a knot of people emerged from the east wing: guards, ladies, court officials. Lady Antonia, unmistakable in a yellow cloak, hair piled in billowing curls, descended the steps and was assisted into her saddle. Her voice carried, but not her words. Two more followed her—a tall, slender figure, draped head to toe in black and leaning on Ilario's arm. It could be no one but Eugenie de Sylvae.

"He's sending her away," I whispered. It was the only conclusion that made sense. But was my cousin dispatching his wife to her family's home in Aubine or his own mountain fortress Journia, or had Gaetana's treachery pushed him past patience?

The answer came swiftly. The queen and Ilario were bustled down the steps and wrenched apart, amid a flurry of sharply announced commands. The lady, surrounded by a bristling forest of spears, was aided to mount. No coach. No baggage. No attendants but her foster mother. A snapped order moved the party forward, and the milling courtiers dissipated like smoke in wind, leaving the pale-haired Ilario alone in the carriageway.

One other watched alone from the east portico as the queen's party vanished into the dark. Ilario marched up the steps and past my royal cousin without so much as a word. When the king slowly followed the chevalier inside, footmen stepped out and doused the extra torches. A sense of utter failure settled over me like a leaden mantle.

The yard quiet again, Dante and I rode out into a restless city. Lamps blazed. Doors stood open. Knots of citizens had gathered in the streets. Many an eye glared at Dante as we rode by. "Ought to burn 'em all," yelled a burly taverner, just after we'd passed his doorway.

A crowd of boys and rowdies surged across the road, heading down toward the river. When I asked where they were headed, a boy yelled back, "Sorcerer's whore is headed to the Spindle."

I was relieved when we left Merona behind without further incident. For beyond all this, we had still to determine if Michel de Vernase, king's friend and confidant, who called himself the Aspirant, was trying to drive Sabria into chaos with Mondragoni sorcery or save her from those who were. If any clues were to be found in Michel de Vernase's house, we needed to get there before his family or co-conspirators thought to remove them.

Surely Philippe would wait for my report from Vernase before he judged Eugenie—surely.

THE GIBBOUS MOON HUNG HUGE and yellow in the cloudless void, bathing the quiet vineyards south of Merona in ocher and gold. As the road led us into the soft hills, the shadows of clustered hornbeams and downy oaks mottled the roadway, requiring a rider to keep alert for pits and obstacles as well as the ever-present possibility of thieves. Fortunately the horses could see better than either of us.

Dante continued to put off my questions, claiming the concentration required to stay on his horse quite consumed him. When I persisted, he insisted I shut my mouth unless I had something useful to tell him. We had scarce exited Merona's gates when he had demanded the Mondragoni book. Perhaps if I'd been clever enough to hold it back, I could have pried a few answers from him in exchange.

Well along in the night, the road dipped into a thickly

wooded vale creased by a shallow river. "The moon's too low to do us good," I said, weary to the bone. "We should halt until sunrise and rest the horses here by the water."

"Can't say an hour's sleep would go amiss," said the mage, yawning. "Inquisitors don't heed day or night. They pursue what clues they're given." A white glow swelled from his staff, and he urged his mount ahead of mine.

Using his muted, steady light, we found a clearing by the water, a few hundred metres down a side path. Old dung, wheel tracks, and scattered ash evidenced that other travelers had used the clearing. We tended the horses and set them to graze, matters for which the inexperienced mage needed constant direction.

As I wiped sweat and dirt from our saddles, Dante touched his staff to a blackened ash ring and murmured, *"Incendio, confinium a circumna."* Sparks snapped and flew from the heel of the white stick—and inside my skin. The mage tossed in twigs and bits of dry moss he'd gathered from the trampled ground, and in moments flames had sprouted. The bright enchantment devoured me, a surge of cold fire from feet to head that shivered my bones. The questions I'd prepared for him along the way, the arguments, the appeals to his agreement and our effective partnership, all fled before my longing.

"Creator's Hand, what makes the difference?" I said. No urgency gripped me more than this most fundamental one. "Your enchantments live and breathe. Beside them, every other I've known seems but an image of an image."

Instead of answering, Dante walked. A quarter of an hour . . . half an hour . . . he strode the perimeter of the clearing: thick trees, tangled underbrush, the river, broad and swift-flowing, aglint with the beams of the sinking moon. I could not see his face. He had cleanly and purposefully chosen reticence about the past night's encounter, but *this* silence seemed a struggle.

When he returned to the fire, he crouched and planted his staff between his knees, gripping it so tightly that his knuckles gleamed pale. Poised on edge, I sensed revelation but a decision away.

"Magic must rise unhindered from one's own depths,"

he said at last. "Only then can it encompass and magnify the entwined keirna of its objects. As I told you, your mind is riddled with barriers solid as mortared walls. And you maintain this stubborn belief in elements, particles, and formulas, as do all those taught at Seravain. Here . . ."

Near spitting with impatience, now he'd sloughed off indecision, he jumped to his feet and beckoned me after him. He halted at the path that had brought us into the clearing. "Learn this path," he said, brightening the glow of his staff, scooping a handful of the black dirt and cramming it into my hand. "Squeeze this. Smell it. Examine its color and composition. Dark and rich here by the river. Mixed with old dung, bark, the rot of fallen leaves and decaying trunks, and all that's washed in from the river in flood."

He scuffed his boots in the rutted track. "See how worn the path is, this wide trough. Consider its uses—tired travelers, maybe fearful ones, scavengers, wheels, horses, mules. This camp is decently protected by the water and the tangled trees, but we ought to build a ward that will warn us if any approach by the path. Where do you begin?"

"Wards require impermeability—base metal. . . ." Rote memory spat out the answer.

"Use your mind, Portier! Think not of divine elements, but of what's here before you." Dante crouched down and tapped a pale knot protruding from the dark soil of the path. "The path is laced with roots. Hornbeam clearly, from the color, and the branches hanging over your head. So, examine the tree roots with your fingers. Then look up, recalling everything you know of hornbeam—modest in height, its wood pale as birch but hard as iron, seeds winged like insects. Feel these leaves, crimped like women's hair."

He swept his arm back the way we'd come. "Someone's coppiced most of the hornbeam in this wood, as the shoots make good poles. But the wood has been ill tended, left to grow for a long time—perhaps the Blood Wars wiped out those who minded it. My staff is hornbeam. The wood is strong, almost impossible to work. It binds magic well. Now wait. . . ."

He crashed off into the tangled underbrush. I studied the path and the dirt in my hand, not at all sure what I was doing. Questions and mysteries and sleeplessness nagged at me, yet magic lay at the heart of our mystery. I had to understand it. And Dante was the only mentor I wanted.

The mage emerged from the thicket and thrust a slender limb into my hand. "Here. Use this to scribe your enclosure about the snarl of roots and the dirt from your hand. Encircle them in your mind, as well."

"Ow!" The hornbeam shoot was approximately the length of my arm, the diameter of a finger, and smooth, straight, and pale, save for one blackened end —still hot, where he'd burned through to cut it.

As commanded, I dumped my handful of dirt atop the exposed roots and used the shoot to draw an elliptical pattern around the pile. Before closing the oval, I hesitated. "Perhaps it's not wide enough. If I need to block the entire path, or if there are more parti—more objects to contain."

"The size of the enclosure does not matter," said Dante. "Stretch it as you work if need be."

I took his word that this would eventually make sense.

"Now fashion a simple crossing ward: You're to be wakened when a warm body passes the barrier. Build the spell pattern in your mind. Your hand can serve as the warmth needed. Surely you know your own hand better than anything in the world, just as you know best what warning can wake you from sleep. So, lay your hand atop the roots and dirt within your enclosure. When the pattern is prepared, seek the power that exists in it already, joining it with what lives in you."

Spell pattern—not so easy as it sounded. As I had learned magic, particles enclosed by a physical boundary— rope or string or circumoccule—provided both the physical and mental structure for spellwork. Formulas prescribed the placement, as well as the balance, of particles—the metal used for spark must sit beside the fabric used for wood and air in the fire spell, for example. I had been taught to hold that exact physical arrangement in my mind as I infused it with will and magic. I'd never been required to create a pattern in my head, a structure of understanding, of random ideas like *crossing* or of properties like *warmth*, provided by physical objects that could be stretched, arranged, molded solely by force of will and inner vision.

But I recalled the runelike structures Dante had shown me, and I worked at creating something similar. Carefully, precisely, as if nurturing the last flame that might keep me living in a tempest, I considered *warmth*, *crossing*, *strength*, *barriers*, *waking* . . . and I imagined each of them as an abstraction of shape and color. My creation looked something like a gate. And then I reached for what magic might live in hornbeam and soil and the night and the warmth of my own hand, as well as that born in my blood. . . .

As a blizzard wind, enchantment rushed upon me, billowing, thrumming, slamming, sweeping through my heart and soul and mind in a sere glory . . . and vanished two heartbeats after.

Gutted, bereft, I crouched in the dirt in the dark of a woodland after moonset. My skin could not sense the night damp, much less any enchantment. The river's burbling slop sounded a thousand miles distant. Dante had gone off again, taking his staff and its quiet glow.

Gods, fool. What were you thinking? That nature would relent because you've had a difficult few days? That Dante would lend you the keys to Heaven's gates? He's off laughing at you.

I tromped back to the fire, rolled up in my cloak, and closed my eyes in search of sleep. Dante did not return. Sleep was a long time coming. . . .

WHEN THE TRUMPET FANFARE SOUNDED inside my skull, I leapt out of the tangle of sleep as if bit by a viper. Dante leaned on his glowing staff, standing in the path just on the near side of the lumpy hornbeam roots. "Decently done, student. Naught to raise you into the Camarilla, but decently done."

CHAPTER TWENTY-FIVE

Magic! Half-giddy, disbelieving, I made Dante step back and cross the ward thrice over. I insisted he leave his staff behind and do it three times more. When I shamelessly implored him yet again to swear he had not himself sounded the warning trump in my head, he glowered and waved his stick to move me out of his path. "Enough. I would like an hour of sleep before the sun rises. We've three days on the road ahead."

As I squatted in the path and gazed fondly on the gnarled hornbeam roots, he wrapped himself entirely in his cloak. Sitting with his back to the tree nearest the fire, he appeared naught but a shapeless appendage of night. When I gave in and returned to my own resting place, his muffled breathing had already taken on the shallow regularity of sleep.

Though sorely tempted, I did not attempt to create another spell. Depleted as I was, I would surely fail. It seemed more important to relive every moment of the ward's creation, etching each word of Dante's instruction upon my bones. My soul ached at the implications of his teaching. Every spell of a kind could be different—every ward, every bending of light, every cleansing spell, every weather charm—differing not only in quality, but in its very creation. Blind . . . holy Creator, it was as if sorcerers had lived with senses chained these many years, and no twisting of logic or drawing down of history could explain to me why that was so.

Eventually even the satiety of a lifetime's yearning must yield to exhaustion, and I fell into vivid dreaming—of a bloody battlefield where my arm strained to breaking as my luminous staff held off a ravening multitude, of rescuing a besieged caravan in high mountains, of conjuring a floodwall for a city threatened with annihilation, of being chained to a bleak and barren rock through season upon agonized season as penance for some brave deed long past remembrance. Every dream story I had glimpsed throughout my youth came full-blown upon me in that waning night. Surely I smiled in my sleep. If my hand could conjure enchantment, then even the wildest fantasies of heroic service might take on true life.

I WOKE TO THE SOUND of rain . . . or the river . . . or . . . I propped myself on my elbows. Bleared eyes noted Dante standing in the path, relieving himself on my treasured hornbeam roots. No trumpet sounded in my head. No magical residue settled on my spirit.

"The sun's been up an hour," he said, when he was done. "Could I saddle a beast one-handed, I'd have headed for Vernase without you." Cold as a marble tomb, he stepped over me and kicked dirt over his fire that had burned through the night without feeding.

Lurching to my feet, I chose to douse my head in the river before thinking too deeply. It served. Not only did the cool water cleanse me of road dust, sleep grit, and Dante's sour greeting, but of naive hopes and childish dreams.

Gaetana was dead. Dante had spent six-and-thirty hours in the Bastionne Camarilla and had chosen to tell me exactly nothing more than that, diverting my attention with the one thing he knew would erase all other concerns. He had played me like a dulcian.

As I saddled the horses, the mage sat on a log, eating a dried fig. The Mondragoni book lay beside him. "Did *you* work the ward?" I rasped, swollen anger and humiliation lodged in throat and chest. "Or did it ever exist at all?"

He accepted the reins and climbed into the saddle, as out of comfort with the horse as a fish in a barnyard. Yet his arrogance remained unyielding. "Did you not sense the spell binding, then? Pity. Even if a slattern despises her bastard, she cannot fail to recognize it as her own."

His vehement ugliness stunned me speechless.

Naturally, I examined the roots. Though I brought every inner sense to bear, no bound enchantment existed on the path or anywhere in the camp. Slight residue of spent magic hung about the defiled hornbeam roots, like morning fog in a hollow, but even if I'd had the skill to disentangle it, it was masked quite effectively by the physical residue Dante had left there.

And naturally, I spent a painstaking half hour attempting to reproduce the pattern I'd created in the night. Nature did not so much as sputter in contempt.

When I caught up to Dante, I passed right on by without a word. I could not bear to look at him. Serving a pitiful vengeance, I raised the pace too high for his inexperienced horsemanship. Stiff as starched sheets, he bounced and jostled, jerking on the reins so that he repeatedly had to coax his confused mount to keep moving at all. By nightfall the mage would think he'd been beaten with Merle's truncheon. Perhaps by then I could put grief and humiliation aside and put him to the question yet again.

The road took us through the grand estates of southern Louvel. Budding vineyards teemed with laborers hauling away weeds and winter's trimmings, or dredging ground limestone and dung into the soil. Farther south, a few tenant farms and freeholds appeared, squeezed between the endless ranks of vines. Here and there a laborer shouted as we passed. I could not hear what they called, and Dante did not say, but the rude gestures were easily interpreted, as well as their pointed reference to Dante's collar. Dante paid them no mind.

The Camarilla's diligence in eliminating false practitioners had left bitter resentments in the countryside. Villagers deprived of their wise women and potion makers could not afford trained mages or adepts. Yet the penalties for purveying false spellwork could be anything from lashes to branding to ruinous fines. The penalties for practicing magework without a collar or adept's work without Camarilla supervision were far more severe.

As the morning waned, rage leaked away, swallowed by profound misgiving. The inquisitors would have questioned what Dante knew of Gaetana, of transference, perhaps of necromancy or other kinds of unholy magic. They might have pushed to know of his training or his methods. If he had spoken his beliefs about magic, they would never have let him go. If he had exposed his role in our investigation, the prefects would have complained so vociferously that the king was violating their authority as laid down in the Concord, everyone in Merona would have heard the uproar. Neither had transpired.

Ever had the mage been blunt and inconsiderate, but never had he been cruel in our private dealings. And never once in our partnership had he told me an untruth, until he allowed me to believe I had worked magic. Something in his hours at the Bastionne had aimed his deepest rage straight at me.

Two more days—one, if we pushed hard—would take us into Aubine. The Ruggiere demesne lay just inside its boundaries. Dante and I needed a plan to approach our investigation, which meant I had to clear the fouled air between us.

As we neared the market town of Sciarra, the traffic picked up. Forced to a walking pace, we had to thread a path between bawling pack mules laden with early vegetables, dung carts bound for the vineyards, and a youthful swineherd and his unruly charges. A roadside fruit seller spat in our wake. "Cheat! Conniver! Camarilla whore!"

Sciarra's town gates had rusted open and were overgrown with chickweed and trailers of black bryony. I nudged my mount alongside Dante as we rode through. "We are partner *agentes confide*, Master," I said, sucking in my tattered pride. "What have I done to earn your despite?"

Stone-faced, he stared straight ahead, ignoring the stares of townsmen unused to seeing a collared mage guiding his horse through a sea of pigs. His gloved hand tightened on the reins and his nostrils flared. "I warned you to keep your Camarilla friends out of my business. So you promised. I warned you I detested liars. But it seems I've you to thank for my visit to the Bastionne. And you persist in the lie by pestering me for information. Surely you know your mentor is a skilled and ruthless interrogator. Has he not given you the full report?"

The Camarilla letter. I'd never had a chance to tell him of it. He thought I'd set the inquisitors on him apurpose. And Kajetan . . .

"Father Creator, Dante, I never intended you to be taken. We should have been well away by the time they came for Gaetana. And I'd no idea Kajetan was in Merona. I swear—"

"No more swearing. Better we make an end to this demeaning confederacy. Sooner will please me best."

It was as if a gate had been slammed in my face. This was no afternoon's offense, as when I had challenged his actions on the *Swan*, no playacting, no testy independence that would eventually yield to shared purpose, as our every dispute had done. Though my accusations had not named him, my thoughtless, careless, desperate play had risked his freedom to practice sorcery—the one thing he held more valuable than life. Naturally, he would see it as betrayal. And forgiveness was not a word in Dante's vocabulary.

Eyes darting hither and yon, the mage shifted in his saddle and loosed the strap on his staff. The town's tall houses throttled the road, crowding travelers, carts, and beasts. The pigs had toppled an onion cart, and the onion seller screamed at the swineherd to keep his charges from eating what was spilled.

I felt as incapable as the hapless swineherd. Certainly no words would repair this breach. Yet, at the least, I had to know how it would affect our work. "Was Gaetana guilty?" I blurted.

"I told you, they executed—"

"But was she guilty? Did she bleed Gruchin? Do *you* believe it?"

"Yes." The answer struck square as hammer to nail.

"And Ophelie?"

"Yes."

Every instinct at my command testified that his conviction was not feigned. This eased my conscience somewhat, but not my regret. "You agreed to the terms of our partnership," I said. "But, altogether without intention, I've betrayed your trust. I understand that will be difficult to mend, though I will do my best. Master, do we finish this or not?"

"Eltevire is destroyed," he said, cold as spring frost. "Gaetana did not know how to formulate such magic, nor did she know anyone who could. None of them know. Camarilla hounds can dig out her confederates. But I will witness to any who listen that her interests did not extend beyond the magic. Once we identify this Aspirant, the instigator of this plot, the matters of *our* investigation will be closed, and we can each return to our own business. The sooner I'm out of that nest of aristos—"

A thump caused Dante to jerk and grunt. A second caused him to throw up a hand protectively. A third projectile bounced off his back and struck my knee. Stones.

"False! Liar! Cheat! Souleater's tool!" Shouts and more missiles flew from a yawning upper window, peopled by shadowed faces. I covered my head, but the sudden barrage caused a squealing riot among the meandering swine that now filled the road side to side hunting onions. My mare jinked and whinnied, and it required all my skill to keep her from panic.

Thank the Creator, a few excited pigs did not rattle Dante's stolid carthorse. A thudding impact on the mage's shoulder had him growling and yanking his staff from its straps.

"Master, no!" I snapped. "No magic! Just get out of here." A hostile magistrate could cause us days of trouble. We could afford no more delays.

Dante did not call up lightning, but only whacked a sow or two on the nose with the staff, then squeezed out of the press into a side lane. Swept past the same turning, I guided my nervous mare through the melee. By the time I left the squealing mass of pork behind, the mage had emerged half a kilometre down the road. Before I could catch up to him, he had vanished through a rickety gate that sported a peeling signboard labeled THE ARBOR.

Swearing at pigs and troublemakers and recalcitrant mages, I followed him into a close, stinking innyard. My jaw dropped.

Dante had already dismounted. He stood between a ramshackle hostelry and its dung-fouled stable, yelling at Adept Jacard. ". . . incompetent lout. I told you to bring the kit I'd left on the bench. Before we arrive at Vernase, I'll expect to have at least the bergamot, juniper, cedar, vetiver, and hyssop oils in hand. The artemesia, as well."

Jacard, filmed with sweat and road dust, frowned as if Dante had handed him a snake. "But, Master, you stressed promptness above all. Surely we can acquire these on our way to Vernase."

"Vetiver is near unobtainable outside a seaport. You can sell your body to a whoremaster or your soul to the devil to get it for all I care, but *get* it."

I dropped to the filthy ground beside them. "What, in the Souleater's demesne, is Jacard doing here?" Invited, apparently. Intended to accompany us, though to take the ambitious, curious adept along as we searched Michel de Vernase's home was idiocy.

"I'll not be questioned by a mewling secretary," snapped Dante, "no matter who his relatives are. Nor will I hear excuses from a lead-wit who cannot seem to follow the simplest instruction."

Surely a mage in full regalia had never graced this yard. He had lowered his voice at the least, frustrating the curiosity of two gawking drovers, a blowsy tap girl peering through a skewed doorway, and the pair of piggy eyes squinting over her shoulder from the dark interior of the inn.

Dante spun to glare at the drovers, who quickly busied themselves with loading a pair of mangy hounds into a cage on their wagon. The piggy eyes blinked, and a fat, pale hand drew the tap girl deeper into the inn.

"Hold, girl!" Dante's shout near startled her out of her overfull bodice. "I'll have a stoup. Out here."

"A w-what?" She gawped at the wooden steps at her feet, then back at Dante. "I can't give—"

"A *cup* of your best ale or cider," I called to her, as Dante's color deepened. "An ordinary tasset. I'll have one, as well." No tap girl south of Merona would recognize the peculiar terminology of Coverge's mining settlements.

"Nasty inside there," Dante mumbled as he secured his staff in its leather straps. His eyes did not leave the doorway. "More's gone in than out that door."

Jacard shrugged and rolled his eyes at me. I grimaced in return, less concerned with disreputable hostelries than with this convoluted mess. The mage knew how fiercely I would object to Jacard's company. Though pleasant enough, Jacard was yet a stranger who had once worked for Gaetana. The adept's presence must quench all honest talk between us. Dante would undoubtedly laugh at the idea of *honest* talk. Gods, how could I have been so stupid?

The tap girl brought out two dripping tassets, the cleanliness of both girl and cups justifying the mage's reluctance to enter the inn. Running his thumb along the cup's rim, Dante mumbled an incantation. The dirty vessel began to glow. The drovers' hounds howled. The gaping girl bobbed a knee and scrambled backward.

"*Mine's* safe to drink now," Dante said when the dogs quieted. He downed it in one long pull and wiped his mouth on the sleeve of his blue gown. "Shall we go?"

More's gone in than gone out . . . My attention snapped to the piggy eyes still watching us, relishing decently dressed travelers, silver collars, and imaginings of a mage's reputed wealth. Cursing under my breath, I emptied my tasset into the muck and tossed the cup to the girl.

JACARD WAS NOT A TERRIBLE companion when it came to tending horses, fetching supplies, or the other tedious necessities of travel, and he maintained an admirable good humor in the face of Dante's unmitigated contempt. But his presence had me entirely on edge for two very long days.

He chattered like Ilario, boasting a great deal of his studies with this or that master at Seravain. He had naught but scorn for Orviene. "His spells are flimsier than paper, Portier, and wholly unreliable. How he earned his collar is a mystery for the ages!"

"Gaetana was better?" I said.

As ever when her name was mentioned, Jacard shuddered. "Praise the saints, she hated adepts and gave us naught but bits and pieces to work on: deriving a formula for warming feet or making a ball roll uphill—which is impossible, I can tell you—or producing a potion to liquefy a particular bit of charmed paper she owned. Such trivialities chafed a bit after training with Elgin and Corrusco! Worse, she'd never tell us the use of our tasks, nor daemonstrate any but the most mundane magic. Then she would scream that we never met her requirements, though she'd not show us why, either. She pawned me off on Conte Bianci two months after I arrived in Merona, and I was glad of it." He dropped his voice. "Dante's even less agreeable or talkative, but his magic . . . Sante Moritzio! . . . at least there's meat to it. I'm sure to learn something if I stay close. Mage Elgin says I've exceptional skills at disentangulation. . . ."

Though interested to hear of Gaetana's work that explained disintegrated manuscripts and revealed her interest in upended physics, I wished Jacard gone. His unending curiosity led inevitably to my own history, to my peculiar quest to serve the king, and to my relations with my royal cousin, with Dante, and even Maura. It required my best wits to keep ahead of him and guide the subject elsewhere. By afternoon of the second day, I was babbling the tales of my youthful dreaming, anything to avoid more tales of his education or the risky topics of transference and forbidden books. I went on longer than I intended about the dreams, as Jacard was so clearly bored by it. Perhaps boredom would still his tongue.

Dante rode behind us, unspeaking. At every stop, he pulled out Gaetana's book and wandered off by himself.

To interrupt him was to call down Heaven's wrath. And he knew very well that I would not wish Jacard to take note of a Mondragoni text.

When we passed through the market town of Florien, and the mage dispatched Jacard to find the supplies he required, Dante insisted I go, as well. I could not defy him without breaking role. Clearly the mage did not wish to be alone with me. Our arrival at Vernase, the village nearest Michel's home at Montclaire, came as a divine mercy.

AFTER THE ONE NIGHT SPENT with Dante on hard ground, and a second sharing a dampish pallet with Jacard at a hostelry little better than The Arbor, the little crossroads tavern in Vernase seemed a paradise. The Cask was clean, genteel, and in possession of an efficient stove and a most excellent bathing tub. Jacard and I shared one of the tavern's two rooms, kept for wine merchants, royal messengers, and other respectable sorts who came to do business with the Conte Ruggiere or his lady. Dante contrived to arrive later and took the other room.

That evening I sat alone in the taproom. The mage took supper in his room, and Jacard spent the evening in the outhouse, complaining of a turbulent belly. As a hearty portion of Mistress Constanza's well-roasted lamb soothed what aches the bath had left, I engaged the taverner in talk of the countryside and my purported mission to offer my services to the conte as a private secretary. "My former employer recommended the Conte Ruggiere as a noble lord who treats his employees fairly."

"Oh, aye, he does that," said the hearty Constanza, a woman of robust appetites, good cheer, and oft misappropriated verbiage. "Them as work for the lord are loyal to the bonesprits. A nobler collaboration'll not be found than the family at Montclaire—lord, lady, and their youngers that's mostly grown now—always generous and lively about the house and countryside, but close and companionable with one another, you know, as you'd want your own family to be. At least that's what we here in Vernase have circumspected these years since the king, divine grace to his name, give him the manor, though Lord Michel weren't even a noble born."

"Good folk, then. I'm glad to hear it," I said, tweaking a finger to bring the woman's broad face closer. "Some few in Merona name the lord more bull than lamb, if you know what I mean."

She gave my rumor due consideration, drawing her mouth and her opinions up tight. "The conte's firm, no doubt, and determined, but any man can drink a dozen tassets in a night while he holds his quarterlies, yet kccp a fair good humor with the common dunderheads that happen by to puke their grievlings in his lap, has a good heart beneath, to my mind. But then again, I've got to pass the direful news that the king's own soldiery has set up a line, tight as a tinker's purse, about the manse. The soldiers say the conte is suspicioned of treason, which is wholesomely outlandish to anyone knows a gnat's brow about him."

"Treason!" Appropriately shocked, I begged the good Constanza to forget all I'd said, and asked her about other families and businesses round the area that might have need of a secretary.

She knew no locals with such needs. "But you might try the mage what's rented my other room. He's a dour sort. Slammed Remy into a straw bale for naught but trying to unload his horse. The lad near broke his wing bone from it. Course, I've a vile temper for sorcerers as I was conflicted with a rheumy eye for a year by a rogue mage. But what high and mighty parsonage like a mage wouldn't need a man of business, eh?"

This news struck me with a chilly bite. It was one thing to erupt when startled out of spellworking in dangerous circumstances, as the mage had done in his chambers. But to let fly at a stable lad seemed out of character as well as foolish. Dante played the simmering volcano for our public purposes, but why put on a show for no witness but a boy and a horse? Unless it was no show.

THE CINCH STRAP OF THE Guard Royale encircled Montclaire at a discreet but firm distance. Each soldier stood

within hailing distance of the next, so none could pass between without proper identification. My official orders
from the king gave Dante and me passage, and, at Dante's
glaring insistence, Jacard as well.

I had dispatched a young officer up to the manse that
morning to inform Lady Madeleine that a master mage of
Queen Eugenie's household and a special envoy of King
Philippe would be pleased to wait upon her and her children. We had not waited for an answer, but followed the
messenger up the long swell in the green landscape to a
hilltop prospect rivaling any in Louvel or Aubine.

Montclaire. The crystalline morning etched the hori-
zons with the snowcapped peaks of Journia far to the
northeast and the sultry green crags of Nivanne to the
southwest. And beyond the dry, wildflower-mottled ridges
to the south shimmered the sea, scarce but a silvered imagining. In between, the sun-splashed fields and vineyards of
Aubine spread over gentle hills, encircled with vines and
notched with red-roofed villages. Everywhere bloomed
the flowers of early summer—anemones, crown daisies,
marigolds, and scarlet pimpernel—amid healthy groves of
olive, almond, and lemon trees. If Louvel was Sabria's
pumping heart, Tallemant her industrious arm, and thin-
aired, pristine Journia her ethereal soul, then Aubine was
surely her fertile womb. Philippe had granted Michel de
Vernase a prize, indeed.

A broad lane took us through the outer wall into the
sunny precincts of the manor. Cascades of purple and pink
bougainvillea draped the rambling stone-walled house
and gardens. On a flagged terrace, beneath the spreading
branches of a walnut tree, the young soldier held a polite
distance as a small woman read my note and Philippe's
order.

In the yard, a balding man supervised a boy walking
our messenger's horse. As we three rode in, the man, his
plain black breeches and hose, collarless white shirt, and
dark jerkin naming him a servant, drew his spiky gray
brows into a knot and stepped forward, as if to bar us from
closer approach.

"We're the visitors announced by yon messenger," I said. "All is in order."

"I doubt that, sonjeur," he said, politely holding my horse as I dismounted. "Will you be long?"

"Most of the day, I should think," I said, glancing at Dante, who was no help at all. His brooding gaze roamed the windows that overlooked the terrace and the yard, and his fingers were already loosing the straps that held his staff and the bag of oils and herbs Jacard had filled in the Florien market.

"I'll see the beasts tended," said the stableman, assisting Dante and Jacard to dismount. "You can wait—"

"We'll wait right here," I said, clasping my hands at my back as if I'd all the time in the world.

As he led the horses away, the man raised a decisive finger and another boy came running from the tile-roofed stable to take charge of the three animals. Once his instructions were conveyed, the man lounged against a flower-decked wall, observing us.

"Why don't we just set to?" whispered Jacard, standing at my shoulder. "It's not as if the contessa can refuse us. And she's naught but a slip of a thing." Indeed the messenger towered over the slender woman whose long dark hair fell over one shoulder.

"Manners," I said. It seemed reasonable that diplomacy would gain us more answers than a frontal assault, though truly I had no basis for such a notion. "Lady Madeleine comes from an old and influential family. Her husband is the king's dearest friend—as yet—and her children the king's goodchildren. Even if my suspicions are proved true, we've no reason to believe the conte's family involved in any misdeed." Happily, Sabrian law did not hold blood kin forfeit for a relative's treachery. Society and custom were other matters entirely.

The lady folded the papers and spoke to the soldier, who bowed, pivoted crisply, and joined us. "The contessa agrees to speak with one person. Her children, the young lord Ambrose and Damoselle Anne, are not to be approached outside her hearing."

"But she has no say in the matter," said Jacard, altogether too excited about this interview to my mind.

I ignored the adept. "Thank you, Greville. Please to remain at the lower gate lest we need messages taken."

The young officer snapped a bow and departed. I turned to Dante, measuring my words. "We seek evidence of illicit sorcery, specifically transference, evidence of dealings with assassins or other suspicious persons, links with the fire on the *Swan*, and whatever insights the family can provide as to Michel de Vernase's ambitions and state of mind. Shall I speak to the contessa or shall you?"

It was risky—giving the mage an opportunity to shut me out of the most significant interview of this investigation thus far, but if he was bound to thwart me, best to know straightaway.

Dante had tossed his black bag to Jacard. His hands had vanished into his flowing sleeves, and he had raised the hood of his gown, so that the merest arc of his chin was the only flesh showing above his silver collar.

"I must meet the woman briefly, no matter her wishes," he said. "But then I will examine house and grounds. The adept will follow me, keeping at least ten paces behind and following my instructions exactly. You may have the pleasure of questioning the treacher's kin."

I breathed a little easier. That Dante planned to keep Jacard at arm's length was reassuring. Had he only brought the adept along to distance himself from me?

"As you wish," I said. "I'll join you when I can."

I straightened my doublet and set out for the terrace, where the Contessa Ruggiere waited beneath the walnut tree.

CHAPTER TWENTY-SIX

"**D**ivine grace shine upon thee and thy ancestors, my lady," I said, bowing deeply and exposing my hand. "I am Portier de Duplais. My sincerest apologies for this intrusion."

"You may choke on your apologies, sonjeur." The contessa exposed her left hand in passing as she returned the king's warrant to me. Voice and glare mimed flint and steel as Dante joined us under the walnut tree, Jacard ten steps away. "Only a cretin would believe you and your brethren have come merely to *locate Conte Ruggiere*. Not after a year. Not with an entire gardia camped round our home, choosing who will or will not enter our gates."

I had not expected the contessa to be welcoming, but neither did I expect her to so clearly reflect the ferocity of her bandit ancestry. Cazar nobles held to clannish customs, so I had read, and kept their women . . . tame.

"As my message stated, we have come at the king's behest to gather information. Master Dante, a mage of Queen Eugenie's household, and his assistant, Adept Jacard"—I extended a hand toward each—"must necessarily examine your house and grounds. They will not interview your children, but will leave that to me . . . in your presence, as you have requested. If you would like to inform your children of these arrangements . . ."

"Our servants will see to that."

"Lady—"

"Let me make this clear to you, sir. My husband has ever been Philippe de Savin-Journia's friend, devoted subject, and loyal servant. I will not help you or your king brand him a traitor, even if it might soothe Philippe's guilt at imprisoning poor, confused Eugenie. And if you make the least attempt to taint my children with this folly, or use this mage to seduce any of us into some confessional, your blood will feed our grapes for next year's harvest."

It had not escaped my notice that the sylphlike contessa wore a slim leather belt around her layered draperies of crinkled white gauze, nor that a sheathed zahkri hung from that belt. The angled Fassid knife was as suitable for gutting an enemy as for gouging a furrow in stony ground or harvesting a cluster of grapes. Nor had I failed to note that the contrast of the white garments with the lady's dusky skin, dark eyes, and dark hair—not black but deepest brown, burnished with copper—was as breathtaking as the view from her hilltop home. Wars had been fought over less treasure than Madeleine de Cazar y Vernase-Ruggiere.

Dante stepped forward, formidable in his shrouded mystery. He extended his hand—his healthy left—palm up, asking for a trust bond, an obsolete custom foreswearing use of magical coercion. "I swear to truth, lady. Will you?"

She did not quail at his forbidding appearance or at the unusual request, delivered as it was without shred of warmth or emotion, but readily laid her slender hand atop his wide, rough one. "That you would ask tells me that lies fester in your heart," she said. "No finding of yours will alter my beliefs."

Startled at Dante's gesture, it took me a moment to register the surge of enchantment at the moment of their touch. By their very nature, trust bonds rarely involved magic, and never of a quality that left an *observer's* fingers tingling. Yet I had felt this before, whenever Dante took the measure of something new—be it human, stone, or magical spyglass.

The contessa did not seem to notice. Her expression was all contempt as Dante departed the terrace in a swirl of robes, Jacard trailing behind. The lady's fearless candor gave me heart in a way. I felt no need to soften what I'd come to say. She needed to comprehend the danger she faced.

"Madame, please believe that concern for the safety of one of your own children has brought me here. Your daughter Lianelle lives in mortal danger."

"Lianelle? At school? What danger?" Her guards fell away instantly, to reveal a mother's dismay.

"Reliable evidence has convinced me that the Conte Ruggiere has allied himself with a conspiracy of sorcerers who threaten to renew the Blood Wars. However impossible this alliance seems, you have already witnessed a measure of its gravity. Its merest suggestion has persuaded King Philippe, who staunchly refuses to believe his friend a betrayer, to send these soldiers to detain and question him. I believe your husband delved into this conspiracy in pursuit of knowledge and became enamored of immense and unholy magic."

I ordered my phrases particularly, and observed her expression as I spoke. Curiously, it was not the mention of conspiracy, war, danger, betrayal, or even the king that transformed her yet again. It was instead the words *unholy magic* that caused her eyes to darken and her lips to compress hard enough to stifle an oath.

I held that recognition close, to use when the time seemed right. "Your dilemma, lady, is as difficult as the king's."

"What dilemma? What choice am I given?" Her zahkri could be no better honed than her scorn.

"Last year, near the time of the assassination attempt on the king, your younger daughter learned a terrible secret. These conspirators, who have left a trail of torture and murder across this kingdom, have every cause to silence her. One student from Seravain already lies dead, as does her family. If Michel de Vernase is innocent, then your daughter lives only at a villain's whim. In order to protect her, we must discover what your husband learned of this plot before he vanished. On the other hand, if the conte works in concert with these people, then only his care for Lianelle keeps her safe—and you, of all people, must judge if that is enough. I have not come here seeking confirmation of your husband's guilt, but evidence that can lead us to the truth. I ask you, in all sincerity, to assist me."

Her lips parted, but, for a moment, no sound emerged.

I gestured to a wrought-iron bench. "Shall we sit?"

She shook her head. "We walk. I cannot take tea and chat about high treason and my child's danger as if they were Pollamai's new musicale. Explain to me what sorcerer could have lured my husband, who has deemed every collared mage either fool or fraud, to endanger his child and conspire against a friend he pledged to die for." She struck out across the terrace, and I hurried after. Only when we left the paving for a well-worn footpath did I notice she wore no shoes.

The contessa's every word rang like steel on bronze. Where was the weakness, the bruise I could pressure to break through her armor, the keystone to remove that the structure of her belief would fall open to me? Families were not impregnable fortresses, but human constructs riddled with grievance and secrets. Perhaps I'd caught a hint of one already—sorcery.

"I have no idea who did the luring," I said. "Perhaps this unholy alliance grew out of some advance on the conte's own part. Best we—"

"You think Michel approached a sorcerer to do what . . . work a spell to give him more than this?" She waved at the glorious prospect. "To give him fairer, cleverer children than these he dotes on, or a younger wife to dance with? Or do you suppose it was the hunger for greatness, the driver of all men, that urged him to make his life forfeit and his family outcast?"

This last sounded like old argument, not prompted by

my presence. Perhaps Michel's ambition was the bruise on this family's body.

The path descended into a red-painted pergola, twined with blooming roses. "I would rather learn than speculate, Contessa, and I needs must learn one step at a time. Let me begin simply. When was the last time you saw your husband?"

She strolled a few steps, riffling the last year's leaves with her toes, her arms folded tightly. "On the thirty-second day of Siece last, Michel received a letter from Li-anclle, a letter he claimed private, though what business could be so private a child's mother could not see? Within the hour he rode out without naming his destination or estimating his return. I've not seen him since."

A bitter, angry parting, I judged, leaving resentments so deep that faith, fear, and anguish had not vanquished them after almost a year. The letter would have been Li-anelle's report that Ophelie had obtained the name Michel sought—*the place where it all began*. Eltevire.

"What does your daughter say of this letter and the circumstances that led to it?"

"She's told me nothing, sonjeur. She does not write. She refuses to come home, as she knows I would not permit her to go back to that place. My daughter is . . . uncompromising." The contessa's odd display of conjoined exasperation and pride struck me as a marvel. My own parents had reacted quite differently to bald defiance.

"So, tell me your theory, lady. Surely in all these months you have put together some chain of events to explain your husband's disappearance."

She peered at me through leafy shadows, curious, as if of all questions in the world, she had not expected that one. "I've given it thought," she said. "But I've no supporting evidence a royal investigator would approve."

"My mind is ever open to change."

She dipped her head. "I know Michel was investigating the attempt on Philippe's life. I saw little of him in those two months. That was nothing extraordinary. We chose to raise our children in the countryside rather than in

Merona. Thus his duties often kept him away. But for all these years, he has written faithfully—to me and to one of the children in turn almost every day. Rarely did he write of business. He was a diplomat, negotiating border agreements, modifications to treaties, property encroachments, agreements on trade, ports, and marriages, all manner of things, much of it private. This case was no different. But the world is filled with interesting topics, especially for a mind like his." And hers, I thought, and those of three talented children.

We emerged from the pergola into a grassy bowl dotted with willows. Old stone walls followed the contours of the hillside, harboring rock roses, yellow flax, and stonecrop. A small lake, afloat with ducks and swans, graced the heart of the meadow. Lady Madeleine paused and inhaled deeply, like a prisoner newly released, then continued on the path of brown earth and wood chips that wound down to the lake. I followed. Silent. Listening.

"From the day he took on this task for Philippe, Michel's letters changed in character," said the lady after we'd hiked twenty or thirty metres. "You would say he became secretive. I would say he was consumed, preoccupied. His mind had engaged with something extraordinary—something that intrigued as well as absorbed. My husband does nothing by halves. Since the evening he rode out—"

"Mama! Don't speak to him!" A young man burst from the end of the pergola and cut straight down the hillside, a blur of gangling limbs, red-brown hair, and a voice not yet certain of its timbre. He slid to a breathless halt three metres from us, rapier in one hand, poniard in the other. "Greville de Grouenn says he's but a sniveling poor relation of the king who spreads lies about Papa to gain royal favor. He's brought a *mage* to spy on us."

The youth, a reflection of his mother's beauty on a frame that promised a warrior's stature, quivered in all the righteous fury of fifteen summers.

"Put away your weapons, Ambrose, and behave as a civilized man. Sonjeur de Duplais is here at your goodfather's behest, inquiring into your father's fate. We shall judge his motives for ourselves, not heed soldiers' gossip."

The lady glanced back to me, her brows raised, and the sunlight probing her eyes to reveal a hint of lavender in their depths. "Are you indeed Philippe's kinsman? You don't resemble him."

"Fifteenth cousin. Scrawny, yes, and poor, as librarians are wont to be, but I snivel only rarely. My beliefs have granted me no favor with my liege." I swiveled crisply and bowed to the flustered youth as his rapier wavered between sheath and ready. "Divine grace, young sir."

"You're the librarian from Seravain," said the lady, some understanding awaked in her mind. Perhaps I'd been correct in my guess that her husband had acted as Philippe's eyes on me these several years. "So you *do* know Lianelle."

"Indeed, my lady. Three years I lived subject to your daughter's intellectual whims and frank assessments."

Amusement glanced across the contessa's sorrows like a beam of sunlight on storm water.

Young Ambrose scowled, fiercer than ever. "Mama, how can you tolerate him? He's persuaded the king that Papa's a *traitor*. All these months we've waited for someone to give a rat's ear that Papa's gone missing, and all we've got for it is house arrest and this liar, worming scraps from you to twist into a hangman's noose. He likely wants Montclaire for himself. I'll see him—"

"Ambrose!" snapped the contessa. "Your insults demean *me*, not Sonjeur de Duplais. Heed my word: Take yourself away from here. Now!"

The lad glared at his mother in disbelief. But he slammed his weapons into enfolding leather and raced up the path. Only then did I notice a young woman standing at the mouth of the pergola, watching this display. At such a distance I could judge naught but an unremarkable stature and a fairer complexion than the contessa or her son. Yet the rare shade of indigo that colored her skirt hinted she was no servant.

"Though I may reprimand my son, I will not apologize for him," said Lady Madeleine, following the direction of my gaze. "He but expresses the frustration we've felt these months. Ambrose was squired to an honorable knight, but gave up his place to companion Anne and me. Yet every morn I must apply a mighty tether of duty and guilt to prevent his setting out to search for his father on his own. For my elder daughter, the ordeal has perhaps been worse. Waiting is the slimmest of stilettos, Sonjeur de Duplais, tormenting with wounds that cannot be seen, save in the blood that flows after."

"Indeed so, my lady." So the watcher at the top of the hill was Damoselle Anne, at seventeen the eldest of Michel de Vernase's children, a young woman who could argue the movement of the planets with her father in three languages at once, according to the admiring Edmond de Roble. "I am not alone in sympathy for these months you have endured. All the more reason to seek the truth, be it good or ill."

When young Ambrose passed by her, the girl remonstrated with him. The brother forcefully removed her hand from his back. No family could be so congenial as Edmond and the taverner described.

"You were speaking of the morning the conte left . . ." In search of something extraordinary. Her words had come right off the paper tucked in my shirt: *Something extraordinary happened when your servant went searching for your enemies. He found them. And then he discovered things . . .* What had Michel discovered about himself, and magic, and the truth of the world? About *unholy* magic?

The contessa's vision melted from her children into a deep and somber reach. "I've received no letter since that day. Not a word. Not a scrap. I have walked this land, touched its living bones, felt the sunlight that clothes it, listened to the music of wind, star, and beast song. But the universe no longer speaks love's name to me. I believe Michel found the answer to his great mystery and it killed him."

She left the path and strode through the mead to the marshy borders of the lake, where her zahkri made short, vicious work of cutting an armful of reeds. As I yet stepped gingerly from one tussock to the next, she was already climbing the terraced slopes again, the muddy hem of her gauze skirts slapping wetly against her bare ankles.

Such certainty. Did it derive from her blood-born magic or from some aspect of her marriage, convincing her of that which caused her mortal grief? I was tempted to believe her. Yet logic and evidence declared Michel de Vernase and the Aspirant to be one and the same. And I did not wish him dead, but rather in my clutches, that I might call him to account for the horrors he had caused.

One thing was clear: Madeleine's conviction explained both her willingness to entertain my questions and her lack of interest in pursuing Lianelle's secrets. Her children's future drove her. Forcing Lianelle to speak would not bring Michel de Vernase back to life, and antagonizing Philippe could make her children's lives infinitely worse. Should treason be proved, Montclaire would surely be granted elsewhere, as Ambrose had guessed. And Philippe, as king, judge, and goodfather, would determine their very freedom, as well as marriage, occupation, and sustenance. Only Lianelle, if she remained subject to the Camarilla, might retain some choice in her fate, assuming she survived the Aspirant's plots. This recalled a jarring note in the lady's explanations.

I scrambled up a rock-walled terrace. "Why would you keep Lianelle from Seravain, lady? She is intelligent and gifted. As the daughter of a blood family, I would expect you to encourage her to develop her talents."

"After the Blood Wars, my family renounced magic," she said, snapping off leaves of thyme and rosemary as if they were an enemy's limbs. "Sorcery and overreaching had driven many of our kinsmen to depravity, and my grandsires and grandmeres declared it would never happen again. They deliberately sapped the power in our blood and vowed our future generations to uphold their binding. Cazars do not train. We do not explore our talents. We do not use spellwork produced by others. Our abilities have dwindled near to extinction—except, as it happens, for Lianelle."

I blinked in astonishment. "Then how in the name of Heaven did Lianelle end up at a collegia magica? A father who disdains magic. A mother who denies it, and whose family forbids even the *use* of it."

She grimaced. "My daughter refuses to be bound by anyone's vows. And you must understand, my husband did not so much despise the possibilities of magic as its current practice and its importance in a world 'awakening to its own true nature,' as he said it. But when Lianelle woke us one morning with light streaming from her fingertips and fifty of Aubine's most beautiful moths captured in the beams, even Michel could not deny her. Nor could I. Her raw talent surpasses any in my family's remembrance. Michel encouraged her desire to go to Seravain and explore it. But if your warnings are true, if the least harm comes to my child at that place"—she raised her arms skyward, and the breeze swirled her skirts as if her weakened blood called out with one last gasp—"by the blades of my ancestors, I will call down such a curse on his name that a thousand millennia will not see his shade at peace."

Her cry of anguish echoed from lake and rock and hillside, and she threw down the green mass of herbs that her fist had crushed into a shapeless, scented glob. Clutching her bundle of reeds to her middle, she stormed straight up the hill.

The girl flew down to meet the distraught contessa. "I heard you cry out. What did he say?"

Lady Madeleine, her lips pressed tight, tried to wave off her concern, but the lady's hand was trembling and her complexion flushed.

"Mama, did he hurt you?"

The contessa shook her head.

"At least come inside where it's cooler." The young woman's voice was quiet without being whispery, and her demeanor seemed plain and unelaborated, much like the rest of her. Her eyes darted only briefly my way, as she took the bundle of reeds under one arm and wrapped the other round her mother's shaking shoulders. "Come along if you must."

I almost missed the quiet invitation, and only after a moment did I realize it was addressed to me. "Damoselle," I said. My quick bow was roundly ignored as the two ascended the path.

Though small and slender, like her mother, Anne de

Vernase lacked her mother's and brother's earthy beauty, as well as their resonant energies. Curling wisps of straw-colored hair escaped a single tight braid. Pale skin freckled from the sun, eyes too large, and mouth too wide for a narrow face, she appeared unripe for seventeen, like a plum fallen too early from the tree. Walking any street or corridor in Sabria, she would never draw a second glance.

When we reached the terrace, the contessa shook off her daughter's supportive arm. Anne tossed the reeds onto the bench. Interested in watching as much as hearing, I held back as the two spoke quietly, the girl in an earnest, persuasive posture, yet, in the end, disappointed. The contessa laid her hand on her daughter's shoulder, then walked into the house.

Anne called to me across the terrace. "Come inside and finish your interrogation, sonjeur. But please, make it brief. My mother is feeling unwell, but refuses to retire until you and your companions have left Montclaire."

I bowed again and followed her through a breezy arcade into an octagonal entry hall. Pale yellow walls rose three stories from the blue slate floor, framing open arches that led deeper into the expansive house. The curved arms of a great staircase embraced a gilt-edged mirror taller than two men. The mirror splashed color and sunlight on the unlikeliest of artworks below—a brass telescope with a barrel twice the length of my arm, and an exquisite planetary of silver-inlaid brass. In an odd, lively contrast, earthenware pots and copper urns of fresh flowers had been tucked into every nook and corner. Dante and Jacard were nowhere in sight.

The daughter hurried off toward the back of the house, while the contessa led me into a reception room. The afternoon breeze shifted filmy draperies. Sitting in a high-backed chair where the air from the courtyard could cool her, the contessa leaned her forehead wearily on her clenched fist. I'd never have judged Lady Madelcine fragile. Yet the sultry heat or perhaps the hour's expense of emotion had left her looking drawn and ill. "What else would you have from us, sonjeur?"

Damoselle Anne returned and took a place behind her

mother's chair, laying a hand protectively on the lady's shoulder. Though the girl's fair skin was marked properly with the Cazar sign, she had violated the law by failing to expose it to me. Her right hand gripped the chair back, her knuckles entirely bloodless.

Lady Madeleine was a striking person in all ways, but, somehow, the girl intrigued me more. "My lady, may I address your daughter?"

The lady's long fingers caressed the paler ones that rested on her shoulder. "I suppose you must."

"Damoselle, as I've told your mother, I am here seeking information about your father's activities. I will not lie to you. We've well-grounded suspicions that he may be involved in terrible crimes. But I am interested only in truth, in facts—those that may explain away evidence that we have, as well as those that may support it."

"I don't know anything that could help you." This scarcely audible response reminded me of Lianelle, who, of course, had known a great deal.

"We all know more than we think, damoselle. Tell me, what interests did you and your father share?"

Her brows knitted, as if trying to fathom to what wicked purpose I could put such information. "Natural science," she said at last, pushing several escaped curls behind her ear. "Languages. Foreign lands. Stories. Books." She offered each topic slowly, as a small bite from a much larger feast—a private feast.

"Mathematics?" I asked, and she dipped her head.

"Medicine?" A negative shake.

"Sorcery?"

"No!" Genuine distaste here.

"Yet your sister studies sorcery. She summons animals. . . ."

"Drafi, our stable lad, can make horses follow him about like puppies. That doesn't make it magic."

"And your father's belief?"

Not so quick to answer this time. Again I felt her running through the implications of anything she might say. "Papa believes we should explore what branches of learning fascinate us."

"But does he believe magic to be trickery, ready to be unmasked by scientific advancement, or a true branch of learning, in the same vein as physics or alchemistry?"

"Papa believes—" A quick, tight breath hinted at deeper feeling. "How can I say what he believes? He's gone away." Not *He's dead*.

"Damoselle, do you understand the concept of blood transference—an immoral, illicit, and dangerous practice used to enhance a mage's power?"

"Yes. I've read histories of the Blood Wars."

"Have you ever discussed this practice with your father?"

"Never. Why would we?" Brittle. Short. Out of breath. But not at all weak. Eliciting a reaction from the girl felt akin to pecking stone with a needle.

Hoping to nudge her off balance, I kept up the pace. "You studied with your father for many years, played verbal and logic games, practiced languages, wrote stories and mathematical proofs, I would guess, exchanged correspondence frequently when he was away."

"Yes. All those things," she said without a hint of boasting. But then, I didn't think revealing her thoughts or feelings was Anne's vice. An extraordinary mind must be hidden inside those solid walls.

"Damoselle Anne, have you received a letter from your father since the day he last departed Montclaire?"

Her complexion lost what color it held. "No." So definite, yet so fast—too fast.

"And you've received no letter that could possibly be from him. For if you received a letter lacking a signature or seal . . ."

"He has not written to me. I would recognize his hand anywhere."

"Certainly you would." I pounced without hesitation. Holding my breath, I pulled out the unsigned note addressed to Edmond de Roble-Margeroux and passed it to the young lady. "Tell me, damoselle, is this your father's hand?"

Her eyes scanned the note rapidly. The text contained

naught to indict or condemn. Naught that should induce her to lie.

> *Here at last is the occasion you have pressed for, a chance to return my several favors. Please deliver the accompanying missive to our king in all immediate haste, for his eye and hand only. I'd recommend you seek extended leave from your captain for this journey, as an extended commission will likely follow. As ever, lad, commit. Do not withhold.*

"WHEN WAS THIS WRITTEN?" SHE said, voice dropped to a whisper, which question told me the answer I needed to know.

"I've no way to ascertain that. Perhaps a year ago. Perhaps a month." Let her reveal what she knew.

"Papa scribed it. To Edm— I suppose you know to whom it was written." She hated slipping.

"Your father was young Edmond de Roble's sponsor in the Guard." One step, then another. For the first time, I felt as if matters were coming to a head.

Anne offered the paper to the contessa, who waved it away, covering her eyes with her hands.

"What does it mean?" The girl's soft question did not sound as if she expected an answer.

"We're not sure," I said. But I did know, of course. It meant Michel de Vernase was alive.

Another question had arisen before this diversion, something about letters, but before I could recapture it, a ruddy-cheeked, comfortable sort of woman in a floury apron joined us. She set down a tray holding decanter and cups, and poured wine for the contessa. Lady Madeleine accepted it gratefully, inhaling the rich fragrance before she drank.

The serving woman straightened up, taking my measure with a disdain worthy of an empress. "I suppose you're 'the priggish aristo investigator,'" she said. "Your mage insists you come to His Grace's library right away."

I suppressed a childish retort. Annoyed, not so much with Dante's insulting address or peremptory instruction, but with losing progress to this interruption, I had come near wasting an opportunity. A trusted servant could know a great deal and might not be so carefully schooled as wife or children. "Lady Madeleine, may I speak to your housekeeper?"

The contessa looked up. "Is that necessary?" Evidently my posture spoke answer enough. "Melusina, please tell Sonjeur de Duplais whatever he wishes to know."

"Mistress Melusina, I've only one question. A small thing. How are mages perceived in the village of Vernase? We faced an unfortunate incident on our travels here, and I'm concerned for my companion's safety. He is quite ill mannered, as you've seen."

Melusina flushed and wiped her hands on her apron. "Well, I don't know. We've not had a mage visiting in Vernase in ever so long. My lady, can you recall when the last might have been? Long before the little one went off to school, I think."

The contessa shifted her gaze to me. Despite a weary sadness that seemed to sap her strength more every moment, she understood very well what I was asking. "We've not entertained a mage at Montclaire since Lianelle was three and that woman came from Seravain to validate her handmark."

A woman . . . "Was it Mage Eliana, perhaps, bright red cheeks, one foreshortened leg?"

"No, she was extremely tall," said Melusina, "almost as tall as His Grace and sturdy as a smith. Our little one was but a mite in her hand. She brought that young adept with her—the pretty girl that was so spindly—and as far as I can recall, everyone in house or village treated them both most respectful."

Gaetana and Michel de Vernase. Father Creator! Ten years past and tenuous, but I'd found a connection.

"I really must go." The contessa made as if to get up, but sagged back into her chair.

"Mama, what's wrong?" Anne dropped to her knees beside her mother's chair, chafing her flaccid hands and patting her scarlet cheeks. "Look at me."

The lady did not respond, and Melusina's speedy provision of damp towels and smelling salts and extra cushions changed nothing.

"Has she been unwell?" I said, feeling entirely out of my experience. "Fevered?"

"Please leave us, sonjeur," said Anne, tight-lipped. "You've clearly pushed my mother beyond all bounds of mercy."

"Do whatever is necessary for your mother's health and comfort, damoselle," I said, bridling at the accusation. "But sometime before this day is out, we must take up this conversation again, whether the contessa is fit to supervise it or not." It shamed me a bit to imagine the lady's illness feigned, yet I could not discount the possibility. Beautiful women of good family were not exempt from conspiracy.

Though the desire to pursue my questions had trumped Dante's summons, the contessa's plight induced me to reverse course. "Melusina, please guide me to the conte's library," I said.

"I should stay—"

"Unfortunately, we are not always free to choose our roles in these matters, mistress. Please show me the way. Then you and your staff may attend the ladies. Later, when I resume my conversation with Damoselle Anne, perhaps you could sit as her mother's surrogate."

The grumbling Melusina led me up the stair and along a winding gallery into a library worthy of any collegia. Two walls of book-laden shelves so high as to need stepladders were only the beginning. More shelves held models of temples, bridges, towers. Another wall of shelves held stacked boxes of papers, labeled POETRY, ANNE'S STORIES,

Mama's Wildflower Sketches, and the like. More papers, books, and maps lay heaped on two long tables, or spread on one of three desks that crowded the room. Even the ceiling was in use, with a great star chart fixed to it at one end, and the largest map of the world I'd ever seen fixed to the other.

How could I not compare such a place to the library at Manor Duplais? We owned ten books of Sabrian genealogy bound in red leather, a general history of the kingdom, and a chart detailing the Savin family line back twenty generations—far enough to expose our flimsy connection to the reigning monarch. My blood yet stained that chart, as my father had pressed me against it after he pulled his knife, as if to make sure I would recognize my shame before he gutted me.

As always, my hand massaged my belly. A good thing my father had not studied anatomical charts like those propped on Michel's easel stuck off in a corner.

"Here he is, Master," said Jacard, popping up from behind one of the desks.

Dante had already risen. Though his eyes remained shadowed by his hood, I felt their heat, as always.

"What is it?" I shook off my maudlin history and glanced over my shoulder to make sure Melusina had gone. "I could ill afford interruption."

"Over here," said Dante. "Can you use your senses, student, or must I hold your hand as usual?"

A dozen or more wooden storage boxes seemed to have vomited their contents across the floor. Mostly letters, it appeared. Drawings, scribbles, a litter of broken jewelry, buckles, and pen knives. Opening myself to the touch of magic, I stepped through the jumbled heaps. I assumed I searched for bound enchantment. In the ordinary way, I could detect magical residue only for an hour or two after its expenditure—Dante's for much longer.

In the end, this was easy. When I touched a cube-shaped tin box that sat amid the conte's relics, a sensation of steel nails scraping glass set my teeth aching. I crouched and flipped its lid open.

My breath near left me entirely. A jumble of cloudy

glass and tarnished brass and steel filled the box. I pulled out the thin tubes first, and then three small rusted knives and the smooth-rimmed glass cups, nested one within the other. Last came the stained brass blocks, one small, one large, with levers cocked, ready to pop out the lancet blades.

"Blessed angels," I breathed. "We have him."

CHAPTER TWENTY-SEVEN

9 CINQ
16 DAYS UNTIL THE ANNIVERSARY

No one in the manse, meaning Damoselle Anne, Melusina, Bernard—the balding steward from the stableyard—the housemaids, the gardener or his daughter, the cook or cook's help, or even Drafi, the Arothi stable hand, admitted to having seen the tin box before. None but Anne had ever heard a whisper of transference, save in the same unsavory context as necromancy or death curses or spirit slaves. None knew what a scarificator might be used for.

When I showed her how the little blades snapped out to nick the skin, Damoselle Anne looked as if she might collapse. I told her that even a man with no talent himself could collect blood to infuse a mage. The needed spells could be affixed to blades and vessels—as they were with these artifacts. But the girl squared her chin and said again, "I've never seen such a horrid thing. I can't say why my father would have one, save that he had an interest in learning." She ventured no guess as to whose blood yet crusted the instruments.

Young Ambrose could not be found anywhere in the house, stables, or gardens. Dante did not object when I dispatched Jacard to query the young officer we'd left at the gate. The mage had observed the afternoon's interrogations in silence.

The contessa, rebounded from her faint, wandered into the kitchen as I finished questioning the cook. "Forgive me, sonjeur," she said, puzzling over my simple question. "Transference? Ask Michel. I've told him I've no head for business. Ani"—she waved at her daughter—"dearest, we have guests. Where is Melusina? Why have we not set out refreshments? You must pay more attention to hospitality, Ani. You're almost eighteen."

The lady began to hum a Fassid love song, closing her eyes and smiling as if lost in dreaming. But her voice soon faltered, tears coursing down her feverish cheeks.

"Mama!" Anne grabbed the contessa as the lady swayed and stumbled. "Melusina, help me!"

Daughter and servant coaxed the lady to her feet. The three of them vanished up the nearby servant's stair.

"I doubt her condition feigned," said Dante from the doorway. "Secrets always break those who believe themselves unbreakable."

That could certainly be true. But Lady Madeleine had impressed me as an open heart, not welcoming to secrets. Perhaps that's why Michel did not confide in his wife. The daughter, though . . . Anne's secrets preyed on her.

Jacard tramped into the kitchen, winded from his run up the hill. "The boy's not ridden out."

"Ah! Then it's time to examine my perimeter," said Dante, planting his staff firmly on the slate floor. "Come, Adept!" He vanished through the kitchen door Jacard had just entered.

"Perimeter?" I said.

"The man moves like a greyhound," said Jacard, sagged against a kitchen cupboard, still puffing. "First thing this morning, he raced around the lawns and gardens, dragging that blasted stick in the dirt to create this 'perimeter.' I'll swear he never bound a spell, spoke a key, touched a particle . . . anything, but the dirt turned black behind him. Next he drew a binding circle on the terrace and did some actual spellcasting with silver nuggets and hair and bits of those blasted roots and powders he had me chasing down, but the particles fit no formula I've ever read. I'll swear he's got me twisted end around trying to figure it all out. At least he's let me do his dog work for once: rifling the kitchen pots, examining the ladies' closets, and dragging out every book and box in that damnable library. Naturally, he himself discovered the only useful bit." He sighed heavily. "I'd best go. He doesn't yell quite so much if I keep running, and I've hopes to graduate from dog work before I die. Someday, you must tell me how to figure out what he's doing."

Would that I knew!

As a bellow from outside set Jacard running, a blur of indigo in the passage drew my eye. I set off after it. "Damoselle!" I caught up to the girl in a small yard, walled by red brick service buildings. "Do not think to run away."

She halted immediately. "I am not running away. I just . . ." She tugged her wayward curls behind her ear again. "Why don't you leave? You have what you want. You've pushed my mother to exhaustion. I've never seen her so . . . overthrown."

"Where is your brother, lady?"

"I don't know." Every strained line of her body said otherwise.

"He is not accused. But matters will look very ill if he runs away. Does he know where your father is?"

"How could he know?" she cried, impatience bursting through her reserve. "How could any of us know? Papa has not written in a year. He's sent no message. I've not heard his voice since the hour—" She near swallowed her tongue.

"Since what hour, damoselle?" I said softly. And when she did not answer, I pushed ever so slightly, recalling my lost question at last. "Did your father speak to you in the hour he left Montclaire?"

"Yes." I could scarce hear her answer. "Just ordinary cautions. He asked me to comfort my mother. That's all." I didn't believe her.

"Lianelle would not wish to worry your mother, but I'd

guess she confides in her elder sister. She wrote you about Ophelie, didn't she? About the bleeding?"

"Yes. Those vile instruments . . ."

She pressed her lips together for a moment, her hands plucking at her skirt. She was so controlled for a young woman, so inward, so blank a page when one considered the knowledge and intelligence contained within. The daughter of a worldly man, she could not be so naive as she seemed. If ever a child could be lured into conspiracy, would it not be one like this?

"Lianelle pretends Papa is hiding from those who hurt her friend," she went on. "But *you* think— Sonjeur, my father could not do that to anyone. Ever."

"He spoke with you about transference at some time. Mentioned it."

The sun dropped below the red tile roof, shadowing the girl's pale face. "He spoke of it when we studied Sabrian history. He refuses to hide the world's horrors from us."

Her words fell cold and dry, as if she had focused her good intellect on being a better liar. I cursed the obscuring shadow. "But he *did* hide horrors. Why would he have the leeching implements here? Why would he not show them to you, if they were merely for education?"

"I don't know." She folded her arms and turned halfway round away from me. Fear had tied the girl in knots. Not fear of me, I deemed; Anne de Vernase feared the truth.

"Damoselle, King Philippe cannot ignore the evidence we've gathered, and for right or wrong, innocent or guilty, he will judge your father's fate. And yours. You *must* speak those things you know—for your own future, for the future of your family. I am skilled only in guessing, but you, an intelligent young scholar, must know there are spells to detect lies. Believe me, you are not good enough to evade them. Tell me what your father said about his journey on the morning he left Montclaire."

As from a septic wound touched by a blade, the words burst forth. "He said that some men present a face of such reason and nobility to the world that the world cannot conceive the cruelty and corruption behind it. He said it was his duty to take down such a person, no matter—no matter how highly placed or how close to our family. No matter consequences. And he said someone at Seravain had given him the means to do so."

Father Creator . . . the last link in the chain. "Who, damoselle? Who was your father planning to take down?"

"He said it was better for us not to know such terrible secrets," she said, all fever drained away, along with hope and self-deception. "Because we would have to live on if his plan went awry."

Better, indeed! His children had to face Philippe's wrath.

"And it all went awry, didn't it?" she said. "My mother believes he's dead. My sister now believes it, too. Our servants, his soldiers . . . even his friend in Merona has stopped writing. So he must be dead."

"What friend?"

She waved her hand in dismissal. "Some woman at court."

Woman? The world paused. "*Who*, damoselle?"

Anne's chin lifted sharply, her guard up again. "I don't recall her name."

I kept my voice even, trying to repair my slip. "So all these months, you've held faith that your father will come home, innocent of any wrongdoing."

"Yes."

"Then, naturally, you've kept all the incoming letters addressed to him."

"Yes, but—"

"I'll see them. Now, if you please."

"But you've no right to see his letters!"

"Ah, damoselle, I do. Your king has given it."

No matter the girl's soft-spoken ways; had she a dagger, it would have flown at that moment. As we returned to her father's upended library, her eyes glinted with angry tears.

Michel de Vernase's unread letters lay in the bottom drawer of the smallest desk in the room. Ten months of letters—letters from diplomats in Aroth, in Syan, one bearing the seal of the Military Governor of Kadr. The conte's correspondence was wide and varied: personal notes about family and friends, minor business of meetings and visits, essays from scholars on a wide variety of topics, none of which interested me at the moment, but might on another day.

When I encountered the letters of importance, I knew. Four of them in a now-familiar hand. Three softened by a year's aging, one crisp as new lettuce. My fingers trembled. My soul rebelled. The day's triumphs fell to ash. But the *agente confide* inside me nodded. *She told you herself. Gave you the clue. "He is an honorable man. Compassionate. Your evidence cannot be credible. I owe him—"*

"You may return to your mother now, damoselle." I charged down the stair. What did Maura owe Michel de Vernase?

One more question for the housekeeper. Melusina busied herself about the terrace, setting a table for three. "A small inquiry before I go, mistress, a matter of curiosity. Damoselle Maura ney Billard, a good friend of the conte, visited Montclaire in the years before he vanished. She is of small stature, like the contessa and her daughter, but somewhat more . . . womanly . . . with smooth, earth-hued skin. Do you remember her?" This was merely a guess, but I scarce noted anymore whether what fell from my lips was truth or lie.

"Oh, aye, certain I do," said the serving woman, each word a coin upon my eyelids. "Such a sweet, refined sort of person. Never comfortable in the country, but 'twas only twice or three times she came, all in that last year. She told me once that the conte had saved her life when she was a girl no older than Ani."

A year ago Anne would have been fifteen or sixteen. The next question popped into my head as if the sky had cracked and revelations come tumbling down like hailstones.

"Melusina, do you think . . . Is it possible Maura ney Billard was the girl who accompanied the woman mage ten years ago?"

The serving woman's thick hands fell still in the midst of spoons and saltcellars. "I'd never thought of it, but, indeed, such shining hair and skin she had, the color of dark honey. Certain and that would explain why she was familiar with the house and family, though she hadn't been back here since she was so very ill that same year. . . ."

And though my mouth tasted of ashes, it was not so very difficult to draw out Melusina's story of how the conte had brought the "pretty, spindly adept" to Montclaire for one night, when she was too ill to remain at Collegia Seravain, some year or so after her initial visit. Michel had whisked her away to relatives the next day, before Melusina could fatten her up with Montclaire's bounty or provide her gammy's remedies for the girl's dulled hair or dry skin or weakness so profound the child could scarce lift her arm.

"Thank you, Melusina." I could scarce speak for heart-sickness. "I believe we are done here. I hope your mistress recovers swiftly. Terrible events, such matters as the king has set me to uncover, touch us all with pain and sorrow."

All of us. Father Creator, forgive us all.

The woman raised her spread hands in helpless resignation. "I'll not say I'm sorry to see you go, but the pain and trouble was here long before you. 'Tis the world's way, not yours. I regret my rudeness this morning."

Numb and weary, I walked away clutching Maura's letters, clinging to a scrap of hope that they might exonerate, not condemn. I stopped under the walnut tree and opened them one by one. They had been encoded with an elementary cipher, not magic, easy to read, even without transcription.

Dear friend: The lady remains resolved to maintain her prerogatives, giving you room to work. Suspicions rise, certainly, but the king will not overrule her. As you predicted. The clues are there to be had should someone clever pick them up. As ever, your debtor.

Dear friend: The money and clothes will be waiting. Gaetana has the lady entirely befuddled, believing she will see the resolution of her desires. The lady is wholly lost in sadness and has no idea of her danger. I hear awful rumors about poor de Santo, but I understand the necessity. Until I know where else to direct my reports, I'll continue to send them to your home.

⤴

Dear friend: Have not heard confirmation of your arrival with the child. QE is restless, and love tempts her to yield, but G soothes her with promises of ghosts. The calls of the dead continue to drown out the pleas of the living. She is not stupid. She knows well she is being set up as scapegoat but is herself too honest to suspect duplicity from those closest to her. I must confess to some guilt at my own small acts. But my faith in you does not and will not waver.

⤴

AND THE MORE RECENT ONE:

Dear friend: My last letter was returned, thus I can only send this to your home. I pray you remain well. The crates arrived at the temple. Food supplies more difficult but arranged. What a surprise it will be when you emerge from hiding. The banners are readied, and the queen persuaded to remain behind. I've wind of a new investigation. I'll tell more as I learn of it.

"LADY," I WHISPERED, "WHAT WERE you thinking to commit such words to paper? Spying on your queen for him? Aiding his plots? Even if he rescued you from bleeding, could you not see he was playing you?"

I found Bernard in the stableyard, told him we would be leaving within the hour, and asked if he had seen the mage.

"He's up to some of his devilry behind the well house," rumbled the steward. "When Sante Ianne returns, he'll banish these daemon mages for good. Mayhap he'll banish you, too, for bringing such a one to this blessed house."

I offered no apology to Bernard's righteous fury, but

walked the direction his trembling finger pointed, past a well house and into a juniper thicket. If the greatest of the Reborn ever returned to Sabria, I would gladly hand over all matters of justice to him.

The prickly juniper trees stretched across a dry slope before the land dropped away steeply toward the backside of the village. Jacard straddled a narrow footpath, maintaining the required ten paces from Dante. For the first time, the adept's face held a trace of fear alongside awe. I halted at his side, no longer surprised to view wonders.

The heel of Dante's ancille rested in a blackened groove in the dry earth. From its white shaft extended a flat film of silver light taller than a man and stretched two metres to either side. The mage shifted the staff along the charred groove, and the film of light shifted with it. When a shift positioned the translucent film across the footpath, a haloed purple shadow hinted at the shape of a person.

"Ah, the lackwit secretary. You've joined us just in time to discover that someone has crossed my little barrier here," said Dante without even a glance over his shoulder. "Were you capable of the simplest disentanglement, Portier—which skill seems to be lacking in all those who study at Seravain—you might discover which of Montclaire's denizens passed here and when."

No magical disentangling was required. "Damnable, stupid boy," I said, cursing idiot children, incautious, duplicitous women, and my own blindness. "He crossed approximately four hours ago, just before the contessa returned to the house."

Bad enough we'd found implements of transference in the house, but the fool lad had heeded his mother's direction and left her. No judge in the world would believe she had not sent him running to his father. And his elder sister, who had remonstrated with him at the top of the hill, knew very well what he planned. The fainting spells. Just enough answers. Stupid of me not to see it coming.

"I can't be sure," said Dante. "I didn't have an opportunity to take an . . . impression of the boy."

"Can you find him?"

"Unfortunately my lack of contact with the lad means I

can't trace him, especially with his four-hour head start on home ground."

"Then our work here is done," I said. "I'll leave word with the guard commander to mount a search for the boy and tighten his watch on the rest of them. We must bring our findings to the king with all haste. Michel de Vernase expressed his intent to take down a 'highly placed' man he deemed corrupt, a man close to his family, a man who presents a face of reason and nobility to the world. His daughter, Anne, can testify to it."

"Remarkable." Gowned and hooded, Dante remained unreadable, the chill timbre of his voice unchanged. "And the magic?"

"He met Gaetana ten years ago, and was fully aware of her interest in transference. Along with the implements you found and my experience at Eltevire, I say we've enough."

"As you will, then. I've no sorrow at putting this idiocy to rest."

Dante hissed, and the silver film vanished. The spent magic showered me as Heaven's light.

CHAPTER TWENTY-EIGHT

11 CINQ
14 DAYS UNTIL THE ANNIVERSARY

I leaned back in the chair, forcing the raw knot that was my gut to relax. "I had to show you first," I said. "There is no hiding them."

Maura laid the letters on her writing table and folded her hands. Her ringed fingers did not quiver. No tears rolled down the silken cheeks that my own fingers ached to touch. No frantic explanations burst forth, no fractured emotions, no demeaning denials or demands for loyalty. Each instance of her serenity served as an incitement to cherish and admire her. And no matter the preachment of reason, my heart yet did so.

She drew her folded hands to her chin. "When the king sent my poor lady to the Spindle, I knew everything had gone wrong. I hoped, naturally. I've lived a year on faith alone—perhaps misplaced, as you assume—though I will not believe that until Michel himself tells me. But I am prepared to answer everything raised by these letters."

Three-quarters of an hour had elapsed since my arrival at Castelle Escalon—much of that waiting until a break in the flow of Maura's supplicants allowed me into her presence to lay out the questions she must prepare to face.

Surely by now the king would know I was returned. Our remaining time could be measured in minutes, not hours.

"You should not have risked coming here. Saint's mercy, Portier, you look so tired, so . . . harrowed. Bless you for your care."

"What blessing do I deserve? All the way from Vernase, I tried to imagine some way to spirit you to safety, some way to discover the entirety of truth. I've no confidence the king will even listen to your explanations. But I swear to you, I will do everything—"

"No oaths, Portier. Once you hear what little I have to offer in the way of explanation, at best you'll think me the world's most pitiful gull. But you must understand: In one moment, I was facing Gaetana's lancet four times in a day, certain I would die soulless before I turned sixteen. In the next moment, this great, strong, handsome man told me not to be afraid anymore, and he carried me off to his home and then to a friend's haven by the sea, where I learned to eat and drink and smile again. Were he to walk in here at this moment and say, *Little girl, kiss your headsman for me*, I would do it gladly. Ten years ago, Michel de Vernase bought my soul and gave it back to me. He just—he never told me what he paid for it."

Easy to understand the price: Michel had kept silent about an incident of transference—a mortal crime in Sabria. My fear was what the world might now pay for his silence. Saints sustain me, I held no blame to Maura. Despair was a disease that blighted reason. Yet I remained an *agente confide*, and thus had to ask, "When did you last receive orders from the conte?"

"Not since the fire on the *Swan*. This fourth letter answered his last. When I received no response, I—" She had begun to doubt, no matter what she said now. I had visited her office in those days, when we both heard the cries of the dead so distinctly in the night. "I waited, hoping for understanding, but none came. So I sent no more reports."

She rose, came round the table, and kissed me on the forehead, suffusing me in her sweetness. Clasping my cold hand in her warm one, she drew me up and into a corner of her chamber. A key on her belt ring opened a narrow door to a servant's passage. "None must see the kindest man in all the world leaving Damoselle Maura's den. Go, dear Portier, and do your duty by our king."

Leaving was not so simple. I kissed her quiet hands and stroked her shining hair, cherishing the weight of her head on my shoulder. "This is not over until I say. Remember that, dearest lady, whatever comes."

I MEANDERED THROUGH THE DARKENING maze, reviewing the long afternoon spent with Philippe, trying to capture what details I might have left out of my report, or where I could have said this or that to be more persuasive, or how, in the Creator's wide universe, I was to move forward. Night was creeping into the world again, and body and mind craved sleep. But it seemed like such a waste of precious hours.

Maura's flimsy explanations had indeed failed to satisfy an angry king. Her implicit trust in Michel's unexplained plan to expose the assassins, including, at the least Mage Gaetana, appeared ingenuous. Her unquestioning compliance with orders she swore were scripted in Michel's hand, and dispatched in letters sealed with his signet—and conveniently burnt once she'd read them—displayed an unbelievable naivete. Philippe had declared her life forfeit.

Oh, he had listened to my arguments, agreed that we had evidence yet to hear, and expressed sympathy with her experience of despair and my own, offered to explain Maura's unshakable devotion. He did not deny that Maura's faith in Michel de Vernase mirrored his own. But he refused to reconsider his judgment, save in the timing of its inevitable conclusion. "She has betrayed her queen, and by her own admission, her actions aided those who tortured a child in the royal crypt and set murderous fire to the *Swan*. Her faith cannot matter. If Michel issued the orders she so blindly obeyed, he will die with her."

The mustachioed Captain de Segur had marched Maura through the crowds of shocked courtiers, her capable hands bound at her back. From the window gallery, I had watched the shallop bear her across the golden thread of the Ley and through the iron water gates to join her queen in the Spindle. The desolate image was scored into my heart.

No wild-eyed feat of arms or magic was going to free her. My only weapon was reason. And so I paced the garden maze, yanking my hair and clawing my arms to drive exhaustion away. *Think, Portier. The Spindle gates are warded by old magic not even its keepers can counter. . . .*

As I rounded a thick wall of gorse and flowering broom, a raven fluttered the branches. Moments later, when hands gripped my shoulders and shoved me into the vine-covered bricks, I recognized the intruder as no bird, but a very tall, very strong, and very angry Ilario, draped in a black cloak.

"You sliming weasel! You scheming toad! How in the name of mercy could you persuade him to leave Geni in that place when she is *innocent*?" He wrenched me up from where I'd fallen and shoved me backward again, this time into a tangle of thorns. "I should wring your scrawny neck, but that would be too kind. By all the Saints Awaiting, I'll see your bowels cut out and burnt do you not go right back and tell Philippe you have no *plan* that requires my sister to stay there another moment. Prisoning will *kill* her."

Without regard to ripped skin or ruined garments, accompanied by a continuum of invective I had not imagined he knew, the chevalier hauled me up from wherever he'd last sent me and shoved me down again, tumbling me head over heels, tangling me in creeping vines, tree limbs, and thorny branches, rendering me incapable of protecting myself, much less providing any sensible answer.

"The *king's* idea," I babbled, "his counselors . . . subjects rabid for justice . . ." *Lord, I understand your anger . . . . It was the only way.*

He batted my hands away whenever I fought to prevent the next uncomfortable segment of my journey through the maze. "To think I had begun to believe you a Saint Reborn. Do you know the Two Invariant Signs?" Another shove. "Refusal to die without meaningful purpose. Inerrant perception of righteousness." And another. "Twice you survived what would have killed any other—on the *Swan*, at Eltevire—and I've never known a man whose honor and compassion grew so much from his bones. But, of course, I *am* a fool."

When my head, still tender from my battering in Eltevire, encountered a much too solid tree trunk, livid lights and unreadable runes swirled behind my eyes. My knees lost all cohesion, and a whimsy stung my thoughts like an angry wasp. Dante . . . everyone would blame Dante for this. When my lifeless body was found, not the finest *agente confide* in Sabria would imagine Ilario de Sylvae had slain me. Me, a Saint Reborn. A most unlikely sensation burbled through my gut, climbing upward until it burst forth, sounding less like wild hilarity than a croaking screech.

The powerful hands gripped yet again and dragged me upright, but only shook me rather than sending me flying. "Blazes, Portier. Are you dead?"

My hands clutched my splitting head. Hilarity faded. "The queen's only held till Edmond's return," I rasped, once he'd let me slump to an earth that wobbled unnervingly.

My stomach heaved bile, and a fit of coughing threatened to finish what Ilario's hand had begun. But he forced a dribble from his silver flask down my throat. Valerian could set a legion puking.

"Try again," he snapped, out of sympathy once the fit was eased. "Why is my sister yet confined when I hear you've brought letters that exonerate her? Her husband refused to address his decisions, and as the royal ass was about to tear down his own palace with his teeth, I chose to go to the source of the confusion. What have you told him, you pigeon-livered stick?"

"Let me tell you what I learned at Vernase," I said, between hawking attempts to clear the nasty taste from my mouth. "Ten years ago, Michel de Vernase made a bargain with Gaetana to stop leeching a young girl. We don't know the terms, or whether that was when he first became intrigued by the power of transference. . . ."

By the time I arrived at Maura's letters, Ilario had settled on the ground beside me. Every time I paused in my recitation, he revisited his litany of swearing.

"Even the leeching tools did not seal his belief about Michel," I said, Philippe's stubbornness maddening me yet again. "He demands more evidence. Yet his heart also demands he free your sister, lord. You know it does. The root of his rage is this dissonance between duty to Sabria and his love and fear for his wife. He believes he must produce the true criminal before he sets her free. If he cannot relieve the suspicions of his counselors and reassure his subjects that this woman is worthy of his love and theirs, whether or not she can bear him an heir, then his reign is cracked—perhaps the very breach these purveyors of chaos desire. Jousting for position will replace scholarly concords. Demesne wars and assassinations will replace exploration for new trade routes. News of Gaetana's execution has already spread like plague. Without confirmation that she was truly rogue, fear and defensive maneuvering will grow between blood and nonblood families. And in whatever case, he must daemonstrate his commitment to justice without prejudice of rank. So he leaves his wife imprisoned. He orders Michel's arrest. And he waits fourteen days for Edmond de Roble to bring him Michel's evidence, praying it will solve the mystery, exonerating both of those he loves."

"And if it does not?"

Such was the likely outcome. "He'll not leave her there an hour more than necessary. Think, lord—if he proclaims Queen Eugenie's innocence today, he must reveal the letters, one of the few cards in his hand that Michel cannot suspect he has."

Ilario scraped his fingers through his hair. "She'll die in the Spindle, Portier. They allow only one family member to visit her, and Antonia has precedence, naturally. Antonia is good-hearted, but she talks of nothing but the way the world should be ordered, and she's never understood Geni. As a child, my sister brought nothing but delight to everyone around her. Now she believes she is Death's handmaiden. If she hears that Maura has betrayed her . . . another friend dead . . ."

"Maura lives until the matter of Michel is decided," I

said. "Philippe recognizes that he needs her testimony, no matter whether Michel or someone else is guilty."

"Sweet angels, Maura a traitor." Ilario's shudder rattled the dark. "She's always treated me equably, never whispered behind my back, never gained advantage at my expense, and I can tell you that is rare enough in this court. But to deliver those vile banners to the *Swan. . . .*"

"She had them made months ago and stored them in the temple, as one of Michel's letters ordered her to do. The phosphorus was certainly added in that time, no doubt along with some clue that would link them to Ophelie, and ultimately, through Maura, to your sister. On the morning of the launch, Maura merely had them collected and delivered to the barge."

"What a daemon-blasted confusion." Ilario sighed. "I'd likely serve as dupe for anyone who rescued *me* from soul death."

"As would I," I said, glancing at him sidewise. "Though I might ask my own brave rescuer yet two more favors."

A stillness enfolded Ilario like his black cloak. Had he even realized how thin his mask had become in the last hour? "And what would those be?"

"You must convince Philippe to proceed with your Grand Exposition—and to expose himself to the crowd by his attendance. Prince Desmond's deathday has been somehow significant to the conspirators. Perhaps merely to lay suspicion at the queen's feet. But Michel has purposely set Edmond's return for that day. If we can lure the villain into some move while the queen is yet imprisoned, we've put a public face on her claim of innocence, while at the same time granting ourselves an opportunity to catch the real criminals as they act. If the villains don't play, we've lost nothing."

"And the second favor?"

"Once we've set the exposition arrangements in motion, Lady Antonia needs must fall ill or be otherwise incapable of visiting the queen, so that you can get me inside the Spindle."

Ilario puffed and spluttered. "Saints Awaiting, Portier,

I didn't hurt you all that awfully! If Philippe doesn't chew my bones to rags, my foster mother surely will."

ILARIO, AS IN EVERY TASK I had set him and so many I hadn't, proved faithful. On the morning after Maura's arrest, Philippe issued a proclamation that Ilario de Sylvae's Grand Exposition of Natural Sciences and Magical Phenomena Honoring Prince Desmond's Deathday had his blessing to go forward.

> *. . . for indeed the despicable, cowardly assault on the Swan blighted our offering of the Destinne's brave launch to speed our beloved son's Veil journey. We invite the Camarilla Magica to join in this festival, for wholesome displays of the fantastical arts shown alongside the glories of natural philosophy, must surely dispel the stench left by the rogue mage complicit in that attack, the canker now excised from Sabria's healthy body.*

THIRTEEN DAYS REMAINED UNTIL EDMOND would return with Michel's answer. Thirteen days until Michel de Vernase would prove friend or foe. Thirteen days to plan how I was to get Maura out of the Spindle and away from Merona.

On the first of the thirteen, Ilario and I spent the entire day with the palace steward, detailing our requirements for the Great Hall and the Rotunda, where we would place the exhibits, and the Portrait Gallery, where we would put refreshment tables. Maura's imprint lay on every message, every name, every idea we had sketched in my journal on that one delightful morning before I'd gone to Seravain and learned I dared not trust her.

On the second day, I sent confirmation messages to the

Collegiae Physica, Biologica, and Alchemistra, to the Academie Musica, and to the various artists and makers of lenses and instruments Maura or I had contacted previously. Lord Ilario's personal invitation to the Camarilla was delivered to Prefect Angloria, along with a gilt-edged copy of Philippe's proclamation.

On the third, I fielded at least one hundred fifty queries from interested participants at my newly installed desk in a minor bulge of the Rotunda. A more difficult task was to counter the various rumors each messenger reported: that the event was designed to mock and humiliate magical practitioners, or that it was naught but a venue for devious mages to upend the king's righteous cleansing of Camarilla interference, or the one spreading like plague from some cult prophet that the Exposition would mark the return of a Saint Reborn.

Late on that third afternoon, a dispatch arrived from the Guard Royale captain at Vernase.

> Thanks to the close watch on Damoselle Anne de Vernase you mandated before your departure, Ambrose de Vernase has been found. While in the village on household business, the young lady attempted to supply her brother with money, clothing, and maps of northern Sabria. The youth and the damoselle have been returned to Montclaire and the watch on the family doubled.

I FORWARDED THE NOTE TO Philippe straightaway. Unfortunately *northern Sabria* was much too large an area to hint as to Michel's whereabouts. Philippe immediately summoned Lady Madeleine and her children to Merona.

Who could not grieve for the young people caught up in this wretched business: Lianelle and Ophelie, Anne and Ambrose, the missing Adept Fedrigo? And Edmond de Roble's fate yet filled me with unreasoning dread. No matter that Gaetana was dead, we would not be done with the evils the Aspirant had wrought until he was in our hands.

On the fourth day—nine remaining until the Exposition—Ilario worked with two painters, a printmaker, and three sewing women to create banners and posters to be hung or distributed throughout the merchant fairs, guildhalls, temples, and academic halls, inviting the distinguished citizens of the royal city to visit the scientific and magical displays. I dispatched personal invitations to the most important scholars and nobles in Merona to attend the climactic events of the festival, and confirmed that the Lestarte brothers were ready to provide a grand fireworks display from a chain of barges to entertain those people we were unable to accommodate at the Exposition itself. In late afternoon, I set out for the east wing to visit the queen's remaining mages.

"WHAT SORT OF EXHIBITION? I am no acrobat or trained dog to perform tricks for ladies, Acolyte Duplais." Mage Orviene's broad face had wrinkled the moment I broached the subject of the Exposition. And once I had described the aligned displays of science and magic, and introduced the idea of his participation, his wrinkles had deepened to ravines. "Dante, were you aware they wanted us to *perform* at this festival?"

Dante's back expressed naught of his thoughts on the matter of Ilario's Exposition. Since Mage Orviene and I had arrived for this consultation, his only comments had been addressed to Jacard, who was scraping some foul mess from the floor inside the circumoccule. The mound of yellow and green muck smelled as if it could be a dead dog dissolving in quicklime. As the adept applied a blade, a pail, and himself to the unpleasant task, Dante observed the sun-drenched landscape outside his windows as if we weren't present.

"I've asked Prefect Angloria to sponsor ten fixed displays to parallel the ten fixed displays of the mundane sciences," I said, smoothing the journal in my lap, as if the prefect herself were tucked away inside it. I needed all the authority I could muster. "Those displays will be open to all guests throughout the morning and early afternoon. But Lucan de Calabria and Aya de Gerson, the Royal Astronomers, will be presenting an optical daemonstration for the late-afternoon program in front of Merona's most influential gathering since His Majesty's coronation. It is only fitting that we provide magical daemonstrations of equal stature, something memorable, that our art might return to the position of prominence it has lacked for so many years. Who better than Castelle Escalon's resident mages to provide them?"

Orviene's small, neat hands kneaded each other in his lap. "But Dante and I have no idea if we hold a position in the royal household any longer, thanks to the cursed Gaetana—may daemons plague her Veil journey! Naturally I had noted irregularities, certain dark tendencies in her work, but I don't believe I shall ever recover from the shock of learning her true depravity. And now Maura ney Billard is arrested, as well. So dreadful, that lovely young woman involved with perversion and murder. Naturally, I've never attached the least suspicion to Her Majesty. Truly, Portier, how could we possibly participate in entertainments, even scholarly ones, with our dear mistress so cruelly detained?"

"No one recognizes that grievous situation more than Lord Ilario, sir mage," I said. "He is confident our good lady will be free in days, if not hours, and feels that elevating her mages to parity with the king's academicians will daemonstrate her wisdom and insight before a noble audience. And what wish could she herself hold higher than that her dead son be honored with her own mages' finest works?"

Orviene blew a resigned sigh and sat back on the couch. "Well, that makes sense, doesn't it? We ought to honor the poor boy. Yes, certainly. I'm sure we can devise something worthy, don't you think, Dante?"

"I work alone," snapped Dante.

Orviene's complexion reddened, and his mouth twitched unhappily. Dante, as a master mage, outranked Orviene. Dante's choice would prevail.

"Daemon spawn!" Jacard's knife must have caught on

something and flipped out of his slimed hand. I glanced up just in time to see the flying blade plop into the gooey middle of the mess. Face curdled like sour milk, the adept stretched out to retrieve it. But his knee slipped, causing his foot to bump the pail, which dumped its contents back onto the floor. A new wave of the vile stench rushed across the room.

Orviene gagged. I clapped my hand across my nose and mouth. Dante erupted.

Across the room before an eye could see him, the mage kicked Jacard sprawling into the muck. "Bumbling toadeater! Get out of my sight!"

The mage's heavy boot gave the adept no time to get to his feet. Jacard, retching, scrambled straight through the mess, clawed at the door, and stumbled into the passage. Face purpled with fury, Dante spun and extended his staff, already belching fire. As Orviene and I gaped, flame consumed the stinking mess, until only charred streaks on the floor and a choking cloud of green smoke remained.

Dante strode to the windows and shoved the casements open so violently, I thought the iron frames might bend. Hands, shoulders, every part of him trembling, he heaved deep breaths of the evening air. Gods, what was wrong with him?

Orviene leapt to his feet and backed toward the door, keeping his chin up and face cold in disapproval. But his eyes were tinged with fear. Likely my own were as well. As when I'd interrupted his work with Gaetana's book, as when he'd struck the stable lad in Vernase, Dante's eruptive violence was no mere choleric temper, no playacting, no considered display to keep Orviene off balance and Jacard at a distance. It could not stem solely from his anger with me or in any other way from his time in the Bastionne, as the incident with the book had preceded his stay with the Camarilla inquisitors. No, this was something else again. *All sorcery requires certain expenditures*, he'd said once. Was this the price of his brilliance? I hated to consider such a destructive cost, not when I needed him so sorely.

Orviene waved a limp hand in my direction. "Acolyte

Duplais, I shall pursue my own daemonstration for the Exposition. Visit my chambers tomorrow, and I'll discuss requirements."

Dante did not turn from the window as the door swung shut behind Orviene. His eyes seemed fixed on the deepening sky, indigo and purple smeared with gold. I urgently needed a private word with him, but could not decide where to begin. And so I waited, wishing I could glimpse his face.

"Why are you still here?" Arms clamped tightly across his chest, staff tucked in the crook of one elbow, he spat the question through a clenched jaw.

I edged closer to him, skirting the swathes of charred mahogany. "I need to know if you'll do this. Before we traveled to Eltevire, you told Ilario you'd some exhibit in mind, something that would 'shock the twittering birds in this palace.'"

"You're to attend this display?"

"Yes, certainly." The question surprised me. I couldn't imagine he'd care. "I can see to your requirements— materials, lamps, draperies, parti—objects to be used. Whatever you wish to be provided."

"I'll bring what I need. Be sure to stand where I can see you. Now, if that's all . . ."

Angels preserve. Unfortunately, I'd only begun, and no stomach-addling demands to stand in his sight when he worked magic could interfere with all the things I needed to say.

"Dante," I said, fingering my journal pages, "I know you wish to be quit of our partnership, but we cannot call our work done quite yet. . . ." His simmering hostility urging me to brevity, I sketched out my growing conviction that the Aspirant would strike one more time on the anniversary of Desmond's death.

"I will place guest registers at every entry and require each man and woman who attends to sign the lists, so that their names can be invoked in prayers for the dead prince. If you were to create one of your perimeters about the hall, Rotunda, and Portrait Gallery, crossing every exit, you could then use the signatures to match these imprints of those who come and go, could you not? We would know who leaves when. Who might be there under a false name. Other things that their . . . keirna . . . could tell us."

"A name scribbled on a page hardly provides enough to pattern a person's keirna clearly."

"I understand that." As ever with Dante, I assumed that the spellwork he had daemonstrated at Montclaire was only a part of what was possible. "But it would allow us to control the scene. Gaetana could have created any number of weapons for Michel before she died, but she'll not be here to wield them. Michel de Vernase knows we'll be watching for a mule. Perhaps he'll decide to try something himself."

Dante's head angled slightly in my direction, so perhaps I'd drawn his interest.

Without looking up, I pursued one additional avenue. "On the night we went into the deadhouse to see Ophelie, you enspelled a brass ring to foil the lock on the main door. I found the ring in a pocket the other day and wondered what capabilities it has. I'll have guards posted about the Rotunda, and Philippe will have his bodyguards. But if we were to corner an assassin, it could be helpful if I could lock or unlock doors at will."

"The spell breaks locks. It cannot make a lock function properly. Simple logic will tell you the difference in the two problems."

Indeed, it was much easier to kill a man than to put an injured man to rights. But I had learned what I needed. I steeled myself. "So, Master, will you honor your oath and build the perimeter?"

So fast I could not see it, he grabbed my doublet and drew me toward him, until our noses were but a finger's breadth apart. His green eyes smoldered, reflecting the glints of the dying sunlight. "Do not test me, student."

I refused to flinch. Somewhere behind those eyes was the man who had tended my burnt hand and who had stretched his magic to its limits to prevent the ruins of Eltevire from falling on my head.

"The Royal Astronomers and the other exhibitors will arrive at dawn on the morning of the Exposition. I'll be in the Rotunda two hours before. Will that give you sufficient time?"

He shoved me away. "Close enough. Perhaps you'll learn something."

I caught myself on the arm of his couch. Tugging my garments around straight, I clasped my hands behind my back, as if I weren't shaking.

"From the day we began this, I've learned from you, Dante," I said to his back. "You have cracked the foundation of my life, and I should hate you for it. But you've rebuilt that foundation with a perspective so much larger and more wondrous—a view of nature and magic that I've not yet begun to explore. I do sincerely regret our estrangement. My letter to the Camarilla was foolish and dangerous and lazy, and I failed to consider the risks—the considerable risks—to you. I regret that more than you can imagine, and I hope . . . Whatever is going on with you, I hope you will recognize and beware its toll." I didn't think an appeal to friendship would move him. Likely I had only imagined we had progressed so far as that.

He did not move. So I retreated. But as I laid my hand on the door latch, his voice rose from a frigid darkness. "I'll serve our agreement on the day of the festival, because it serves my purposes to do so. But at middle-night after it, our confederacy will be ended for once and all. Now get out, and do not bring your mewling face here again."

All these days, even while pronouncing Dante's enmity irreversible and totting up reasons for it, I'd held some buried hope that I was wrong. Kajetan had always called me tenderhearted. Soft. But the chill of that dark room settled deep this time. Filled with regret and apprehension, I left him to his brooding.

At supper two days before the Exposition, Lady Antonia de Foucal fell ill with an attack of spleen and was taken to her room. As she was unable to make her evening visit to her foster daughter, the Warder of the Spindle Prison accepted her written request that the prisoner's next nearest kin, Chevalier Ilario de Sylvae, visit in her stead. The chevalier was most distressed at the doleful venue, shrouding himself completely in black and clutching his famous crocodile charm, though crocodiles had never been sighted in the river Ley.

IT TOOK NO MORE THAN one passage of the three iron water gates bound with hoary spells, one long walk up the steep, twisting central stair, one finger touch of sweating walls, one inhalation of the unnatural gloom, to believe Ilario's contention that his fragile sister must surely die if kept in Spindle Prison too long. I certainly would.

"Prisoner, stand forward," shouted the warder, when we halted our climb before a thick oak door with a barred window.

The bronze key cranked in the lock, spitting a magical residue that tasted like metal shavings. The door swung open soundlessly. A pale figure sat up on a narrow bed, drawing the thick blanket around herself. She pushed bare feet into slippers and made to stand up.

"Dearest Geni," I said, rushing past the warder to bury the lady's face in my embrace before she could stand up and the keen-eyed officer notice the disparity in our heights or the puzzled expression on her face. "Beloved sister."

"Here now," said the officer, "every prisoner, no matter rank, is to stand before the warder."

"Honor binds a Sabrian chevalier to kneel before his queen," I said, releasing the stiff Eugenie, "especially when he pledged himself her own true knight on Grennoch Rock so long ago." I remained kneeling by the bed, head bowed, praying sleep, surprise, and despondency would not prevent Eugenie noting the words Ilario had given me.

"Warder," she said softly, "forgive my brother. He is impulsive and"—she ruffled my hair, pressing downward so firmly as to keep me kneeling—"known to be a bit foolish from time to time. I humbly request permission to sit privately with my visitor."

"Granted," said the warder, gruffly, hanging his lamp outside the door. "The usual time, though. No extension for prattling fools."

"Divine grace, Warder," she said. "And my thanks for the gift of light."

She remained standing until the door swung shut, and the lock clanked. Her hand remained firmly on my head. "Please tell me you've brought good news, brother. It is so good to see you. Refreshing. Though I dearly love Antonia, she says so little of interest. . . ."

Her words died away as nailed boots rang, descending, on the stair. Then she tweaked my hood aside and turned my chin so the weak lamplight shining through the barred square in the door illuminated my face.

"Duplais!" She snatched her hand away and stepped back. "Who sent you? Why are you here?"

"Forgive my impertinence, Majesty," I said, remaining in my genuflection. "Your noble brother contrived to get me here, sending his dearest love and encouragement. At the last, I near had to truss him to a tree to prevent his upending our arrangement and coming himself."

"Our mother consented to this?"

"No, my lady. She is indisposed and knows naught of it. Nor will she ever know, unless you choose to tell her. The chevalier is prepared to reap the consequence of her anger."

"What could persuade him to such a tempest as that?" Her hand flew to her mouth, and she sank to the bed. "Mother of angels, has the verdict come? Am I—?"

"No, no, Your Grace! I bring no resolution to your situation. Of that I can say only that many keep faith on your behalf."

I would not give her vapid assurances. I had done so for Maura, convinced that truth must win out. But I had learned that lesson.

"What news I bring tonight will be hard for you to hear," I said, rising, "but Lord Ilario insists that your devotion to your friends and your passion for justice will compel you to act. And I have no one else. . . ."

As succinctly as I could, I told her Maura's story, both

what solid evidence had reported, and Maura's own testimony. I spoke without sentiment. Without interpretation. The burden of judgment had to rest with Eugenie, for the risks she took would be considerable, in circumstances when her own position would yet be vulnerable.

Ilario's estimates of Eugenie's reaction were entirely borne out. "The only other prisoner in the Spindle is two turns up from me," she said, pausing in her tenth traversal of her cell. "Never in all the woes of this world could I have guessed it to be Maura . . . clever, kind Maura. And never this side of Heaven will I believe she has purposely betrayed a soul to murder. I understand the law, and the need for the king to serve it, else I would be banging my head on these cell walls. But the souls one touches in this life are more important than law. Let Philippe condemn those foul, wretched vipers who so torment young girls. No one will die for *my* sake. Not if I can prevent it."

Nailed boots again rang on the stair. Ascending.

She dropped to the edge of the bed beside me. "Quickly, tell me your plan."

Into her pale, slender hand, I dropped the brass ring Dante had enspelled to break locks. "This is chancy, at best. . . ."

CHAPTER TWENTY-NINE

25 CINQ
THE ANNIVERSARY

"Sonjeur Portier, we need more paper for the Portrait Gallery guest registries," said the breathless young squire as he hurried along beside me, his request almost drowned out by new cheers from the Rotunda. "Could we not just skip a few names?"

"Extra pages are stacked on the table by the service entry," I said, dipping my head to Lord Baldwin's wife and five stair-stepped children, as I sped the length of the Great Hall for the hundredth time since well before dawn. "Skip no one. Shall a small inconvenience cheat our dead prince of his honors?"

"No, certainly not, sonjeur." The squire's voice faded as I left him behind like a faltering horse in a race.

One hour remained until the closing program—the two Royal Astronomers, Mage Orviene, and Dante. Some two hours later the honored guests would flood into the Portrait Gallery for wine and supper and discussion of the varied events of the Grand Exposition, while fireworks lit up the river to end it all. But Edmond de Roble had not yet arrived, nor had any other message or *evidence* from Michel de Vernase. Bless the saints, I had been busy enough to prevent excessive thinking. If Philippe did not find reason to release his wife tonight, then my plan to free Maura was made infinitely riskier. If Philippe did not find reason to release his wife before exacting the penalty for Michel de Vernase's crimes, then Maura was dead.

The day had gone smoothly since I had followed Dante on his circuit of the Exposition venue before dawn, inhaling the vibrant energies of his magic as he embedded a wide gray stripe in the floor at every entrance. Now that thousands of visitors had crossed his boundary, I could only imagine what the shimmering film of enchantment would look like if the mage were to plant his staff in one of the main doorways—uncountable haloed forms jammed one upon the other. Dante expressed no doubt that he could distinguish one from another, though he advised me to require full family names and birthplaces on the registers that he might have more information to distinguish them.

"Heurot!" I called, relieved to see my ever-reliable valet who had been called into service as a footman. "Go round to every entry and remind the door warders that once the tower bell tolls third hour, none but those with court credentials or signed invitations may be admitted to the Rotunda. The morning guests will be escorted out through the Great Hall."

"Aye, lord sonjeur." He'd not gone two steps before he paused and grinned over his shoulder. "Is this day not the world's marvel, sonjeur? Every hour I've thought I'm outside time called to Heaven. The magics are wonders, but these things folk say are not magics have more the look of it than what the mages do! Scholar Rulf conjures sparks with his ball of sulfur and his hand, and that other fellow claims his pump sucks the air right out of his jars! My mind will scarce believe he can silence a bell's ring, the clearest of the god's music. And what I wouldn't give to be allowed to look into the opticum. I heard one gentleman say there were monsters in the water no bigger than a hair from his head!"

"Indeed." I could not but smile at his delight. Though

the intentions of the day had little to do with simple exposition, it pleased me to think minds might be opened to nature's marvels, including sorcery, through my efforts. "Now go on about my mission, lad. If I can manage it later, I'll get you a glance at the monsters."

We raced off in opposite directions. The mass of people circling Philippe's new pendulum in the Rotunda had grown to thirty deep. The heavy golden bob—filled with lead, so I'd been told—had been first released at exactly noonday, the king himself wielding the taper that burned through its thread leash. Suspended from the peak of the Rotunda's dome by fine steel wire, the orb swung in blinding glory, the plane of its swing constantly shifting ever so slightly about its great circle. Philippe's pendulum engineer had set up paper standards about the circle and inserted a slim stylus protruding downward from the center of the golden ball. No other display elicited such noisy delight as did the pendulum whenever the stylus toppled one of the standards.

"Sonjeur de Duplais, what is this horrid marring of the floor? I was told that you were responsible."

Lady Antonia's imperious finger indicated Dante's gray stripe across one entry to the Rotunda. The dowager queen, a living ikon in a cloth-of-gold mantle, clearly disapproved. Her twenty ladies and gentlemen frowned in unison, as if sullied marble ranked among society's worst depredations.

"Divine grace, my lady," I said, bowing. "This is but a fixture in aid of the evening's program, and no permanent defacement." Which latter declaration could well be a lie for all I knew.

"Indeed?" She fluttered a fan, a requirement as the heat and odor of crowded bodies grew ever more oppressive. "Can you give us a hint of what Eugenie's dread mage has in store for us? Dear Orviene has assured me that his exhibition will be soothing, as I was woefully ill these past two days with such spleen as I thought must leave me blind. Such a banging head, such vicious flashes of fever and chills, and a thirst so fierce that I feared I had contracted sweating sickness. So I must insist that no exhibition be too dreadful or too excessive with noise or lights, else it will surely drive me to Ixtador."

Relieved that Ilario's hand had not been recognized in the lady's attack of "spleen," I expressed all sympathy. "Angel's grace, my lady, you appear well recovered for having suffered so terribly. I wish I could reassure you as to the evening's prospects. But in truth, Master Dante does not confide in anyone, certainly not those he holds in contempt."

She touched her fan to her lips, not at all masking a smile. Gossip of ongoing conflict seemed medicament to many courtiers. " 'Tis rumored you do not get on with the fiend."

"Not by half," I said with a helpless shrug, imagining the pleasure of chaining her to the pendulum. "But I would suffer far more than scorn to serve Her Majesty."

"Prettily said, sonjeur. Ilario reports you've been most helpful with this grand folly."

"His lordship is more than kind."

"Well, we must not delve too deeply into an imbecile's qualities." She tapped a red silk slipper on the marked floor. "Do remove this blight when the night is done. Vinegar and coarse wool should serve."

Lady Antonia swept into the Rotunda past the pendulum, trailing behind her the potent scent of jasmine, a growing band of admirers, and a barbed commentary on "Philippe's forever inconsiderate expenditure on mechanical fripperies." Her voice grated on the spirit very like the sour plucks of the virginal on display just behind me.

"Adept Voucon, should I have additional materials fetched for you?" I said, peering over the magnificently carved instrument case.

The stooped, gray-robed sorcerer, acclaimed for playing the virginal without touching either keyboard or strings, was hunched over a loop of cotton string on the floor, frantically adjusting particles of silver, linen, dust, and bone. "Rid this venue of its disharmonies," he said angrily. "I understood we were to work in a purified space."

"Prefect Angloria herself approved this venue, Adept," I snapped. "There are no disharmonies here." Nor anywhere else, so my studies had told me. Many practitioners blamed certain alignments of stars, moon, season, and location for local conditions—disharmonies—that disrupted spellwork. No evidence had ever been produced to support the idea.

I moved on, unreasonably irritated. Excuses, always. No wonder people were skeptical of the art.

A hunger for news sent me in search of Ilario. Indeed, no one could miss him. Resplendent in emerald satin, metres of white lace, and a vermillion short cloak, he was perched on a stool near the opticum at present, offering incoherent explanations of mathematical complexities and magical wonders at a volume that could wake the kings in the royal crypt. As I watched, he theorized that the pendulum's precession about its great circle resulted from a monstrous lodestone being turned by chained daemons in the netherworld, and that Adept Voucon's difficulties with the virginal were surely caused by the nearby vacuum pump. The pump must have removed the very bits of air Voucon was attempting to enchant to shiver the virginal's strings, he said. The appalled academicians would be months in their attempts to recover from his assault on scientific principles.

Before I could take Ilario aside, a siren squeal from the Great Hall raked a claw along my spine. I rushed back to the mobbed venue. But the cry signaled only another lady exhilarated by the sparks of the *virtu electrik,* produced by Scholar Rulf's spinning ball of sulfur, and transmitted through his hand to hers.

The tower bells struck third hour of the afternoon watch, signaling the end of the general exhibition. Ranks of footmen politely urged the guests toward the Great Hall, shooing them away from the pendulum and scouring them out from behind the encircling colonnades.

The Rotunda, a remnant of a pre-Sabrian temple, was a gloomy space, encircled with alternating colonnades and bays. The central dome, some fifty metres above the floor, sat on a ring of arched windows that splashed daylight on its mosaic adornment. Below that circle of light, the thick walls were pierced with only a few small windows, shaped like four-petaled flowers. As these were mostly tucked behind the east and west colonnades or in the two largest half-domed bays on the north and south, the space required lamplight even in the day. It would serve perfectly for the day's culminating events.

On the dais installed in the southern bay, Lucan de Calabria, a puffy, tart-tongued little astronomer, screeched at four laborers shifting a painted screen onto its mark twenty metres from one of the four-lobed windows. In between the window and the screen, two assistants arranged a table on which Lucan's partner, the lean, elegant Aya de Gerson, had set up an apparatus of prisms and lenses.

"Have you everything you need, gentlemen?" I said, one eye on the servants setting out rows of chairs, the other on the west doors where Philippe would arrive. Attendants plumped the cushions in an ornate chair set in the cordoned-off bay reserved for the royal party.

Despite de Calabria's streaming oaths and insults, he asserted the optical display was in good order. Behind the dais, Mage Orviene knelt on the floor, pawing through a leather box. "Dear me," he said in answer to my query, "I'm not sure I have the exact weight of silver for my new work."

"Perhaps Master Dante could provide it," I said, though I'd not seen Dante since dawn and was not about to risk his wrath for Orviene's benefit.

"No, no, no need for that. Once the astronomers have had their fun, I'll just lay out two enclosures. If the one doesn't suffice, I can use the reserve." He clapped me on the shoulder. "Perhaps we'll have rain here in the Rotunda instead of starshine!"

As caelomancy was his specialty, Orviene had lamented that we'd confined the Exposition indoors. But he'd promised to come up with something enjoyable, as long as he could offer his exhibition before Dante's. "The fellow does some clever work. Especially if he's in one of his testy moods. All fire and lightning, even if there's no substance behind it. Anything that follows will seem dull, no matter if it's restringing the Archer's bow in the vault of Heaven!"

I was astonished that Orviene considered Dante's work

to lack substance. How could any trained practitioner fail to recognize such soul-stirring power? Perhaps the agreeable Orviene, who had never reached master's rank, merely suffered a tot of jealousy. I certainly did.

As merchants, officers, minor officials, and guildsmen flowed out of the room in a noisy, sweaty stream, the glittering nobility and highest-ranking academics flowed in. The favored few occupied the rows of velvet chairs between the dais and the pendulum, while the rest stood round the sides of the cordoned-off pendulum circle and behind it. I stood back to the wall, a quarter way around from the dais, on line with the last row of chairs.

I should have been pleased. What commentary I'd heard on the day's exhibition had been favorable. To direct such a complexity of people and movement, and to forward a joint venture of the Camarilla and the mundane branches of learning was no small accomplishment for a reclusive librarian. Philippe's guards were on alert for every kind of physical attack we could anticipate, and despite his erratic behaviors, I believed Dante would hold to his word and guard against threatening spellwork. Please the god, Maura could be free by morning.

Yet my conviction that this was the day of reckoning only grew. Ophelie and Gruchin and the rest of the Aspirant's victims cried out in my soul, hauntings as vivid as Calvino de Santo's spectre. Where was Edmond de Roble? Where was Michel de Vernase, and what *evidence of his discoveries* might Edmond bring?

As if in answer to my worries, Dante strolled into the Rotunda from the Hall. Staff resting in the crook of his arm, expression composed, he did not deign to notice the guests vacating the space around him as he positioned himself along the wall opposite me.

The west doors swung open and five royal heralds marched forward. The assembly fell quiet. The piercing brilliance of trumpets brought everyone to their feet. Philippe strode into the Rotunda, his First Counselor, Lord Baldwin, just behind, and third . . . Ilario.

Despite all, I smiled. *Well done, cousin.* Few observers would attach any accolade to Ilario for the festival's success. His day's inanities could only reinforce the general opinion of him. But for Philippe to acknowledge him in such fashion honored the Sylvae family, especially Eugenie, whose fondness for her fool of a half brother was well-known. Ilario would be well satisfied.

The king strolled down the center aisle, the guests bowing or dipping a knee as he passed. He touched one or another on the shoulder or offered a word of greeting. He stopped for a moment to speak with his pendulum engineer, who had just started the shimmering bob swinging again. After so many hours, its arc had decayed.

The Camarilla prefects sat near the front. Kajetan, taller than his fellows, caught sight of me and raised a hand in greeting. Though I had spotted his silver hair in the Hall that the morning, I had determinedly avoided him. We had not spoken since my letter accusing Gaetana, which meant he would have questions I was not prepared to answer. Protocol would prevent him sharing anything he'd learned from the inquisitors—whether about Gaetana or Dante. I smiled and shrugged, waving helplessly at the mob separating us.

Philippe's return to the dais took him past the seven prefects. They inclined their heads in guarded respect, and he spoke a cordial word to each. The king took his seat without addressing the assembly. That did not surprise me. He was likely stretched tight as his pendulum wire.

And so we began. The lamps in the Rotunda dimmed, leaving the gray air lit by a single window to the right of the dais. Without fanfare, de Gerson, the eloquent, aristocratic royal astronomer, began his presentation on the nature of light. He'd gotten through no more than a few sentences, when his partner, Lucan, objected vociferously, beginning a mock debate. Lucan assumed the role of Massilion, the classical philosopher who had asserted that white light was the purest of the Pantokrator's creations and poured down like liquid from the sun, as it clearly leaked around corners and fell into holes shielded from the sun's face.

De Gerson pronounced that light moved through the aether in straight lines and that colors hid inside it. To Lucan's raucous disdain, he covered the four-lobed window behind their display, and a hole pierced in the screen focused a thin beam of afternoon sunlight through his faceted crystal. The crowd, caught up in their spirited performance, laughed and clapped as the white beam split into a rainbow.

As the two men bantered, my gaze swept the Rotunda. Archers roamed the gallery that circled above us. Guards flanked every door, and three swordsmen stood discreetly behind Philippe's chair.

Lucan, with sly braggadocio, moved a second optical apparatus into place on the long table, while loudly proclaiming that a rainbow was itself one color of light, created by the prism. De Gerson, clever and patient, refuted Lucan's assertion by sliding a slotted board across the spreading rainbow and opening one slot. As a solitary red beam struck the Rotunda wall, people clapped appreciatively. And when he moved the second prism into place and his beam remained red, rather than splitting into another rainbow, onlookers popped from their seats to join the cheers.

Across the Rotunda, Dante stiffened and slid his staff into one hand. The mage's eyes did not rove. His attention, his stillness, his posture, focused entirely inward as they had on the *Swan*. What did he perceive? The optics exhibition involved no magic. I sensed nothing.

The audience murmured and applauded as Lucan, now convinced, closed one slot and opened the next, replacing the red beam with an orange one . . .

Deciding to join the mage, I slipped rearward past a shallow bay and a section of colonnade.

. . . then yellow . . .

I set out across the Rotunda's center, squeezing between the last row of chairs and the roped stanchions that enclosed the pendulum circle.

. . . then green . . .

I had reached some halfway across the row, when Dante's chin came up sharply and his dark gaze met mine. He pushed through the standing courtiers, who paid him no mind. They were laughing as Lucan's slots opened and closed and the beam shifted to blue and then to violet. The pendulum swung, stirring the air. Fouled air. Where? Where?

A man at my elbow snorted, as if he'd fallen asleep, and a woman laughed brashly. Beneath the clapping and laughter, a girl's voice nearby admonished someone named Cato to sit properly.

I rotated slowly, craning my neck, desperate to *see*.

Darkness swallowed Aya de Gerson's violet beam. Lucan must have shuttered the slot in the window screen at the same time, as the entire Rotunda went black as a tar pit. The fouled air shifted as the pendulum swung again, but my eyes refused to accommodate the darkness, no matter how much I blinked or gouged them. It was as if the world had been devoured by the Norgands' Whale of the Beginnings, and I would have thought the guests had vanished with it, save I could yet hear them laughing, clapping, murmuring. In no wise should the room be so dark. Outdoors the sun was yet westering, and we'd left lamps by the doors.

A clatter and a curse, and I could see again. De Gerson was scratching his head, while Lucan straightened the prism apparatus, tumbled over on the table—both men far from their window screen. And Dante . . .

I spun. Dante had vaulted the silk ropes and was darting past the plane of the pendulum toward the center of the great circle and an object that hadn't been there before the moment's darkness.

In the span of an eye blink, I raced to join him. Purple cloth . . . wrapped . . . two metres in length, it lay near the center of the pendulum circle, parallel to the current plane of the swinging bob. In the soft light of his staff, a kneeling Dante was pulling the purple wrappings away.

"Halt the pendulum," I snapped to the horrified engineer who was waving his hands for us to get out of the circle. "Keep everyone away. And fetch Captain de Segur!"

The astronomers' debate halted. The seated guests turned to see what had drawn the astronomers' attention. The chatter quieted, only to surge again in a wholly different note. Restive. Uncertain. *What is it? Where? Who's that? The mage . . .*

"Let me pass!" Philippe pushed through the stirring assembly, Ilario and First Counselor Baldwin right behind him, Captain de Segur alongside bearing a lamp. As they stepped over the silken ropes, Dante pulled away the last of the wrappings, and Michel de Vernase's message to his king lay exposed.

Edmond. Edmond. Edmond. Forlorn hope demanded to name this ravaged flesh something other—a fiend taken from the gallows, perhaps, or a young man consumed by wasting sickness and now relieved of mortal suffering. Heart and mind knew better.

They had wrapped him naked. The fine strong body predicted by Edmond's handsome face and stalwart grace had been no lie. But what lay before us in Captain de Segur's lamplight was but a bloodless husk. Every squared centimetre—face, torso, limbs, fingers, eyelids, genitalia—had been precisely incised, no single wound mortal nor scarce even painful of itself. But surely the young man must have believed himself aflame . . . for all the days of his dying.

I sank to my knees and opened his curled fingers. Twined about one lacerated hand was a purple ribbon looped through a signet ring. The ring's device of an *R* circled by a twisted vine was unmistakable. Ruggiere. Michel. A sealed paper, bearing Philippe's name, had been pinned to the back of Edmond's left hand. I passed the paper and the ring to Ilario, who stood between me and my cousin.

The Rotunda, the muted, restive crowd, the displays and celebrations, receded. My eyes fixed on Edmond's ravaged face, willing him to give testimony to a single critical question. Bleeding was a senseless form of murder, requiring a meticulous touch. Other torments were just as exquisitely cruel in pain and horror, while easier to manage. So why bleed Edmond, whose hand bore no blood family's mark?

Terrible as was the sight and the knowledge of a young

man's mortal torment, more terrible yet were the conclusions of simple logic, as relentless in their progression as Philippe's pendulum. A first, terrifying theory proposed that the Aspirant had devised some way to leech magic from unmagical blood. However, the practices of transference had been thoroughly explored during the Blood Wars, in days when sorcerers knew far more of spellwork. And Dante had sworn Gaetana—and the current practices of the Camarilla—incapable of such greater magic. Logic left but one alternative. Edmond's blood was not as we assumed. . . .

My gaze shot to Philippe, whose face might be the Pantokrator's first rough shaping of granite at the beginnings of the world, but whose fist, marked with the Savin seal as mine was and half hidden beneath his purple mantle, pressed to his breast as if to prevent his heart's disintegration. And into my mind floated the image of the glorious Lady Susanna, retired to obscurity in the country with Philippe's old commander forty years her senior. And alongside the image echoed the story of two men who had drunk each other's wine and covered each other's sins.

I averted my eyes quickly that no one might follow their course and glean my understanding. No wonder then at Philippe's ambivalence at Michel's letter. His faith had compelled him to send Edmond as Michel required, while his every instinct warned him it was a deadly . . . and very personal . . . trap. The agony in my cousin's posture was not the sorrow of a king for his young soldier.

"Cover him," said Ilario, softly. "Angel's comfort, there's naught to be gained by this unseemly exposure."

But what saint or angel could ever comfort the noble warrior king of golden Sabria? None. Not when his oldest friend had murdered his only son.

CHAPTER THIRTY

25 Cinq
The Anniversary

*P*hilippe de Savin-Journia's worst nightmare, so the Aspirant had named himself at Eltevire. So he had proved. So he would prove again unless we made the correct moves in answer to this mortal taunt.

Philippe accepted the ring and the note with scarce a glance. "We continue with the exhibition."

"My lord, surely not!" said First Counselor Baldwin, who had arrived just as I laid the purple wrap across Edmond's face. "No matter who this is, we must—"

"We must do *nothing*," snarled the king, low enough to keep the exchange at Edmond's side. "I know who is responsible, and his vile act will not sully the honors being offered Prince Desmond. Not again. That is what he wants. Portier, see to this." Philippe stepped out of the lamplight, but did not leave.

"Aye, Your Grace," I said, swallowing hard at the responsibility my cousin had just laid in my lap. *Think, Portier.* First the crowd, their voices already risen in fearful speculation. Philippe wished to keep knowledge of this assault on his person—it could be termed naught else—contained.

"Lord Baldwin, if you would, announce that a young gentleman guest has suffered a spasm of the falling sickness and must be helped out of the venue. Say the ailing guest requests that the event proceed in due honor to the late prince. His Majesty has offered his own physician."

A troubled Baldwin flicked his shrewd gaze from Philippe to me and back again. "Sire?"

"As he says."

Philippe's brittle response gave Baldwin direction enough. As if he were a much younger and slimmer man, the First Counselor sprang over the silk ropes and strode toward the dais, bellowing cheerfully. "Everyone, return to your seats and ease your concerns. All is well, though we've had a lamentable incident. . . ."

"Captain de Segur." At my sharp enunciation, the mustachioed guard captain raised his eyes from Edmond's corpus, where they had been fixed. "On bond of life and honor, you will not speak of what you have seen here until His Majesty himself releases you with his word and hand. You will support Lord Baldwin's report in every aspect. Do you understand that I speak with His Majesty's voice?"

I exposed my marked hand on my shoulder, hoping the mark might intimidate him with the possibility that I might muster some magical reinforcement for my authority.

"Yes, certainly." The captain squinted, as if not quite sure what I was. Neither was I, just then.

"Summon two of your most trusted men to carry this young man to"—I glanced around—"perhaps to Lord Ilario's apartments? Chevalier?"

"Certainly. Such a terrible . . . Sante Ianne, so vile . . . wicked . . ."

"And, Captain, double the protection for His Majesty's person, and double the watch on the outer gates and on the exits from the Great Hall, the Rotunda, and the Portrait Gallery. Search the alleyways, the courtyards, anywhere someone could hide. The one who's delivered this victim must not slip out with the departing guests."

De Segur slammed his fist to his chest and hurried away.

I had little hope that his search would be useful. Michel himself would not have risked carrying a corpse into the palace. If we could discover *how* the body had been brought here, we might have better fortune finding *who* had done it. Sorcery. I'd wager my eyes on it.

Dante examined Edmond's lacerated skin, his feet, his back, his eyes, touching and not touching, in the meticulous way he examined everything. Philippe watched from the shadows.

"Someone's carried him across Dante's perimeter, sire," I said. "With the god's grace, Dante will divine who it was."

"There can be no grace here," murmured the king, barren as the wastes of Eltevire. "What in the cursed realm of Heaven will I tell his mother?"

Edmond's mother. A young warrior's beloved mistress sacrificed to political necessity, married off to an elderly friend to shield mother and child from disgrace, and to save Philippe, the scion of a blood family, the unexpected king, from Camarilla penalties for promiscuity. The story would explain a great many things.

"He's been dead more than a day," said Dante, kneeling up. "There's no rigor. What blood he had left is well settled in his legs—he was standing or, more likely, hanging." Raw wounding encircled Edmond's wrists. "No bound enchantments cling to the corpus. Given more time, I might be able to determine where he was kept."

"Can you learn how he was brought here?" I asked.

"I doubt that." Dante shrugged, rising.

Restive murmurs among the guests had yielded to excited babbling and pointing fingers. I excused myself and hurried to the back of the pendulum circle where people pressed against the silken ropes, craning to catch a glimpse of the fallen man. Surely someone had noticed the bundle carried in.

"Scholar," I said to a young academician. "A word with you . . ." Two sharp-eyed ladies and a gentleman with a shock of red hair pressed close behind the young man. "Did you—or any of the rest of you—happen to notice our ailing gentleman stumble into the circle? We're seeking the rest of his party. But his tongue is a bit thick, as happens with the falling sickness, so we could not understand the names. He's wearing a purple mantle...."

Though everyone behind the stanchions wished to speak, none had anything useful to report. They had been watching the light beams or the pendulum or had looked away just then. Several mentioned the lights going dark, but no one had observed anything odd or anyone looking ill.

When I returned, frustrated, to the pendulum, two guardsmen with a litter had joined Ilario and Philippe. Dante had vanished. "Where's the mage?"

"Says he's gone to 'check the perimeter.'" Ilario knelt at Edmond's side, tucking the purple wrappings about the young man's long limbs.

"Bear the poor gentleman carefully, lest he suffer another spasm," I whispered to the guards. "Keep gawkers away. As you can see, his sickness shames him. Chevalier, will you show them where to lay him?"

The soldiers lifted Edmond's enshrouded form gently and followed Ilario through the parting crowd. Once they had gone, Philippe crooked a finger at the lamp. I held it close as he broke the seal on the letter.

After only a moment he refolded the paper and passed it to me. "You need not fear you've erred in your conclusion, cousin."

What have I learned?

First: To explore the new, one must not fail to look behind and inward.

Second: Setbacks on the field of battle winnow the weak.

Third: All secrets are writ in blood.

Never more in your shadow.

Curiosity begged me to probe Philippe's understanding of this message. But the man had receded to an untouchable distance, as if Discord's Worm, lurking beyond the horizon, had sucked down the roiling ocean. Only the king remained. He pulled a slender scroll from his brocade waistcoat. "Dispatch this to the warder at the Spindle. At middle-night I will come down to the docks to welcome my wife home."

An unseemly rush of relief and excitement engulfed me. Father Creator, by morning, Maura could be free. I needed to notify an accomplice that our game was on. I needed to get to the harbor before the cordon of guards tightened around it to protect Philippe. Yet the Aspirant's accomplice, and all the answers he could provide, might be lurking in the Rotunda.

As I wrestled with the conflicting demands of duty and desire, Philippe strode back down the aisle to the dais, his authority like a gale wind sweeping away his guests' doubts and fears. "We have done for our ailing gentleman what can be done," he announced. "So let us declare this an interlude to savor the wine and delicacies in the Portrait Gallery, then return and proceed with this extraordinary event. I would see what these mages have to offer that can match our astronomers' exceptional presentation." The king bowed to his two astronomers as would his own most gallant chevalier.

The assembly applauded and cheered. Conversation burgeoned as children were released from their seats, and ladies called to friends, and gentlemen expounded on the afternoon's events to any who would listen. Philippe and Baldwin led the way through the wide doors. The glittering guests pooled behind them and flowed like a mighty river into the gallery.

I had never imagined a king's life to be so like a player's, or a spy's, forced to live masked and walk through scenes no matter the state of his health or his heart. As with so many of the grand destinies explored on my boyhood nights, truth was altogether different from the dreaming. I could not run off to play rescuer. Not yet. I had a murderer to catch.

Once I had dispatched a messenger with Philippe's orders to the Spindle, another to the Lestarte brothers that they should delay the fireworks display until middle-night, and left a brass token in a palace alleyway to alert my evening's accomplice, I hurried into the Great Hall. The exhibits had been dismantled. A few, like the virginal, sat atop wheeled carts, waiting to be hauled out.

A sheen of silver flickered beyond the colonnade at the far end of the hall. Even at so great a distance, Dante's magic shimmered in my veins, as unlike the sorry residues of the day's magical displays as this palace was to a bondsman's hovel. I stayed away from him, though, not wanting to associate our activities.

Each of the twelve entrances to the Great Hall remained manned and guarded. I interviewed the registrars and scanned their lists, paying particular attention to persons who had arrived in the last hour. Most names were familiar, though oddly . . .

"No one at all passed the door between the quarter hour and the half hour?" I asked the registrar at the southwest door. The gap only struck me because the registry for the southeast door had shown the same quarter hour with no entries.

The young woman peered at her page full of time notations and signatures. "None. We don't have the servants sign each time they come through. We just tally them on their own list as you told us. But . . . I suppose not."

I returned to the registries I'd already examined. Every entry register exhibited the same quarter-hour gap. The tower bells had struck sixth hour as Edmond was carried away, which meant the Rotunda would have gone dark no less than a half-hour previous—approximately the same time interval, which meant . . . what? That everyone in Castelle Escalon had gone blind for a quarter hour?

Magic, surely, yielding just time enough for someone to carry a body in and leave again. Perhaps Dante's perimeter could tell us whose magic had left us blind.

Unfortunately, Dante had left the Exposition. Indeed, no one had seen the mage since he'd been "working his devilry" in the Portrait Gallery. Damn the man! Where had he gone?

I raced up the stair and around the long route to the east wing, calculating the time I had to get questions answered. The supper interlude would consume at least another hour and a half. Once the king returned to the Rotunda, Orviene would begin his daemonstration. And then Dante would be needed on the dais. And he wanted me in the Rotunda. Saints knew why.

Jacard's chair outside Dante's apartments sat empty. I barged in without knocking. The mage was not at home. I was not tempted to linger. The air in his great chamber squirmed and wriggled as if I were immersed in one of the royal fishponds. He had wanted more time with Edmond's corpus, so I took off for Ilario's apartments.

Michel had surely intended Edmond's murder to daemonstrate his own superior strength and cleverness, as well as a serious vulnerability in Philippe's household. Vulnerability to sorcery, to intrusion, instilling fear, uncertainty, and suspicion in the court, and in Philippe himself. The Conte Ruggiere had proclaimed himself an enemy so bold as to murder the son of Philippe's friends and perhaps . . .

My suspicion of Edmond's parentage would explain Philippe's confidence in his choice of heir. How much better than some random courtier would be a son of his own body, a well-educated, well-trained young noble of intelligence and modesty. Though a bastard could not inherit directly, anyone's name could be scribed on the Heir's Tablet in the royal crypt. Perhaps that was when Michel's rebellion had begun. *Never more in your shadow.* Perhaps the common soldier raised so far above his station, for twenty years the king's closest friend, had expected his own name to be etched in stone.

Captain de Segur's two men stood watch outside Ilario's door. "Sorry, sonjeur," one said, barring me from approaching. "Chevalier de Sylvae commanded none is to enter."

"I am the chevalier's secretary, Savin-Duplais," I said. "Inquire."

Moments later, Ilario was dragging me toward his small sitting room. "Blessed saints, Portier, the lad was so hurt, so . . . damaged."

Edmond was laid out on the divan. Dante was bent over him, scraping at the lacerations.

"There you are!" I said, relieved. "What have you learned?"

The mage corked a glass vial and tossed it into a cloth bag that rattled as if it held more such vials. "I'm trying to understand what was done here. The spells used on him are the same used when they took your blood—which means only that they used the same implements. It is likely his injuries were inflicted by the same who inflicted the first of your leeching marks—this Aspirant. Not surprising. Clearly they planned from the first to kill him. One-and-twenty days since he left here, and he was dying for most of that time. But whyever would they leech a man with no blood family connection?"

"Cruelty, taunting, smirking. Michel's telling us he still has tricks." The words burst out of me without thought. For reasons I had no time to explore, I could not tell Dante what I suspected about Edmond's parentage. "Or perhaps this was sheer vengeance. We found Eltevire. Forced him to destroy it and retreat before he knew how to use it. Transference is only a means to some greater magical end, and Eltevire, in whatever perverse way, represents that end. Michel's letter, setting up this murder, came to Philippe the very night we returned to Merona. And then Philippe set the dogs on Michel and his family. The conte must have been furious, doubly so when he lost Gaetana. I doubt we'll know more than that until we question Michel himself."

Dante lifted his dark brows, then turned back to examine Edmond's fingers. The damnable mage likely knew I was withholding. But the matter was too private—for my cousin, for Lady Susanna, for the queen—and it was only a guess. Ilario stood in the doorway, fondling his crocodile charm, eyes averted.

"So, what did you learn from the perimeter?" I said.

Dante untangled the purple mantle from Edmond's long limbs. "Michel's son is here."

"Ambrose!" The startling news pushed aside speculation. This was bold. Brazen. My doubts about Michel's stellar family were rapidly diminishing.

"The boy entered the Exposition early in the day. He lied about his name, but a pattern on the perimeter shield matched the one at Montclaire. I found no evidence of his leaving."

"What of the contessa or the daughters? Have they even arrived in Merona?"

"None of them crossed the boundary, as far as I could tell. Alas, the boy did not accompany our dead man. Mayhap he was a scout, though. An hour or so after he arrived, a gentleman brought in a 'sickly cousin determined to see the displays.' Evidently the cousin had fainted, and two of the guards helped carry the man in. They deposited him on a bench under the colonnade so he could recover. The impression on the perimeter showed only three men crossing the perimeter together at that time, not four, but then, my enchantment reveals only living persons, not dead ones. Sadly, neither the guards nor your registrar glimpsed the sick man's face. They didn't worry, as the person who brought him was familiar—a householder, too. The fellow made a tick mark by some earlier signature on the servant's list; thus he scribed only the sick man's name on the registry—*Largesse de l'Aspirant*."

"*Gift of the Aspirant*," I said, mouth awash in bitterness. "And, naturally, no one could remember the householder's name or could say which signature on the servant's list he annotated."

"Not a one of them." Dante buckled his bag.

"And so this mysterious householder waited and placed Edmond in the pendulum circle when the Rotunda went black to hide him," I said. "That was done with magic, wasn't it? You sensed it. I was watching you. I'd wager the householder left the palace right then. Every guest register shows a quarter hour gap just at that time."

"Just before the light vanished, I detected a burst of infantile spellwork, scarce stronger than a beginning student's. And you guess rightly. I found a second impression of the mysterious householder, a few hours later than the first—very likely the time of the darkness. He departed."

"Did he work the darkening spell?"

"Perhaps. I'd too little to go on." Dante hefted his bag, retrieved his staff, and slid the hearthside gargoyle that opened the hidden panel in Ilario's wall. "Now, we've twittering birds yet to shock, student. Are you coming?"

"I'd best leave the way I came," I said. "But I'll be there." Considering Dante's erratic behavior, his insistence on my presence could not but leave me uneasy, but I reminded myself that he had saved my eyesight, the use of my hand, and my life twice over. He had earned my trust. Sadly, I was finding it harder and harder to give.

As the panel closed behind Dante, Ilario laid a silk sheet over Edmond. "I'll summon the Verger," he said. "My physician will swear to whatever I tell him. He'll assume he was drunk when he examined the 'ailing guest.'"

"How will my cousin bear this?" I said, softly.

Ilario glanced up sharply, as if to see if I understood fully what I asked. He nodded slightly and expelled a long breath. "Rock-headed as he can be, abrupt, unforgiving, shortsighted, tyrannical when it comes to matters in which he has no interest, Philippe de Savin-Journia was born to carry his office. He'll do what's necessary to see Sabria safe. Not even this will break him."

"Will you meet with him tonight?"

"Yes. He must set Geni free now. If I have to challenge him to a duel, I'll see he does it."

I smiled at his ferocity, seeing both the Ilarios I knew at once, as if the man stood before his own reflection in a distorted mirror. "No challenges, Chevalier. He's already sent orders to the Spindle. He'll meet her at the harbor at middle-night."

"Saints and angels." Ilario's head sagged against the wall. But after no more than a moment, it popped up again. "What of your mysterious plan to aid Maura? Will this help? Set it back? If you'd just tell me what I stuck my neck into . . ."

"Your sister will send word that she requires her full

honors for her return—proper clothes, her ladies. She is vindicated and does not wish to skulk back to the palace like a freed convict. You should support her in her request." I hoped to tell him without *telling* him.

"Certainly, I will support her. Though . . ." No one could twist his face into a mournful knot as could Ilario. "Portier, this is not a night to press Philippe."

"He *must* accede to her requests, lord. Please. Your sister desires it."

After much groaning reluctance, and varied attempts to coerce, threaten, and plead his way into my secrets, Ilario agreed, as he had for the past ten days, to remain ignorant.

"Your sister promised to be sensible, lord. I reminded her there were other ways to help Maura if circumstances did not settle right tonight." In actuality, however, she had recognized, as I did, that her own freedom would likely signal Michel's guilt—and reduce Maura's life to days, if not hours.

Ilario knew these things, too. "If Geni comes to harm from this, I'll come after you, Portier. At which circumstance you'd best remind me that she would have locked us both in a hermitage for not telling her about poor Maura." He was not jesting.

He walked me to the door. "Do you believe Dante about the magic? A spell that could make twenty door wardens fail in their duties and erase every speck of light in the Rotunda seems more than student's work. The mage seems . . . off . . . since you came back from Vernase. He doesn't so much as insult me anymore."

"I'd think you would appreciate that." A glib answer, but I had no other, save that Dante meant what he said about being finished with us. "I make no guesses about Dante just now," I said. "But I'd not . . . He is cooperating with me today, as he did at Montclaire, but he vows our partnership ends tonight. Something's twisted him—the sorcery he's working, anger about his interrogation at the Bastionne—so I'm inclined to believe he means it. I find myself wary of him, and you should be, as well. But then you've been wary of him for a long while."

He waved off my concession. "I've lived at court many years. I don't trust anyone save you, *student*."

I could not but laugh at his perfect mimicry of Dante's inflection. But he sobered quickly, his palm weighing the green silk spall pouch at his waist. "This is getting much too heavy, Portier. Keep yourself safe."

I laid a hand on his shoulder, wishing I could assure him that all would be well. I had come away from the Spindle with the impression that Eugenie de Sylvae resembled her half brother in many ways of importance, certainly in courage, loyalty, and determination. But belief would be impossible until the queen walked on shore into her husband's arms with no alarm raised.

As I started down the corridor and the east wing stair on my way back to the Rotunda, I considered the "darkening" magic. With Gaetana dead, who would Michel charge with delivering his dreadful message to Castelle Escalon? We had assumed all along that other magical practitioners were involved, like Quernay at Eltevire. Assuming such a spell would take training . . . I paused for a moment and closed my eyes to recall the young men and women lined up with Orviene behind the dais, matching faces and names with the household roster of adepts and acolytes I'd jotted in my journal not long after I'd arrived here. Only one face was missing, as it had been for more than a month. . . .

"DANTE!" I CALLED, BREATHLESS AFTER pelting down corridors and stairs to catch him on his way across the Great Hall.

Staff in hand, he paused, his glare a heated poker between my eyes.

I kept my voice low. "You use the impression on your perimeter and the signature on the Registry to develop a pattern, yes—this *keirna* that identifies a person?"

"Yes."

"And magical artifacts can tell us a great deal about the practitioner who enchanted them. Like a signature of another kind. You could use it to explore keirna, as well?"

"Yes."

"Try this." He recognized at once what I deposited in his hand, altering his course abruptly for one of the entrances to the Great Hall. I retreated to an adjacent entry and pretended to review the entire day's guest list, while watching Dante.

Holding what I had just borrowed from Ilario in one hand, he planted his staff on the gray stripe that crossed the threshold. As the guards, the registrar, and scattered guests watched in awe, the silver sheen spread from his staff like a stiff curtain to either side, smudged and layered with shapes of every shade of purple, gray, and blue, as if a crowd stood just beyond it.

Moments stretched. Tame applause echoed from the Rotunda. The gawkers and stragglers remained quiet as if the mystery would ultimately be revealed to them, only to sag in disappointment when Dante lifted his staff and walked away without anything exploding, melting, or catching fire.

Eyes and mind yet dazzled with magical residue, I awaited him behind a cart loaded with tables and crates marked VACUUM JARS and PUMP. The mage dropped Ilario's crocodile charm into my hand. "Cleverly reasoned, student," he said. "It appears Adept Fedrigo has not drowned after all."

CHAPTER THIRTY-ONE

25 CINQ
THE ANNIVERSARY

"Sonjeur de Duplais!" The swordsman in red and gold livery hailed me from across the Great Hall. "We found the young man."

"Adept Fedrigo?" I bit eagerly at the possibility. "Already?" Having just spent half an hour passing along his description, I was astonished.

"No, sonjeur," said the guardsman, reversing course as I fell into brisk step beside him. "The Conte Ruggiere's lad. Scholar found him hiding in his cart. Rousted him, and the boy bolted. Door guard chased him into the west wing, where we caught him squeezing into a closet."

The west wing. The king's residence. The guard's livery should have told me. "A closet?"

"Captain said we should inform you before questioning the boy."

"Exactly right."

After traversing innumerable ever-wider stairs and more elegantly appointed galleries, the guardsman turned from the broad, well-lit corridor, which I recognized as leading to Philippe's study, into a clean, spare servant's passage. Two soldiers flanked an open door. Standing inside the cramped mop closet, his gangling limbs in a knot, his tanned cheeks exhibiting a distinctly scarlet cast, was a fuming Ambrose de Vernase.

"Am I under arrest, librarian?" Much to his disgust, his voice chose to display its erratic timbre, sorely diluting his attempt at scorn.

A gray-bearded soldier passed me a sleek dagger with an ivory inlaid handle. "He carried this."

"What would you suggest we do with a man found sneaking into the king's residence with a weapon, Lord Ambrose?" I said evenly, slapping the weapon on my palm. Inside, I was cursing politics and hotheaded children and greedy, ambitious men who made children their pawns.

"I wasn't sneaking anywhere. I was going back to *my* residence, my father's apartments, where we're being held prisoner by our betrayer kin—"

I clapped my hand across the boy's mouth. "Are you an entire imbecile? Think where you are and speak in a civilized manner."

The ruddy color drained from his complexion. My suspicions that Michel de Vernase's children knew facts of importance ran high, and I *would* have their secrets from them. But I'd no time for coddling a fool just now, and I'd not see a rightfully troubled youth imprisoned for thoughtless words.

As he stewed, I turned to the guards. "Was no watch placed on Conte Ruggiere's family when they arrived here?"

"Two men outside the door, night and day, sonjeur," said my escort. "We've no idea how he got past them."

"But here he is, not a spit from His Majesty's own rooms," snarled the bearded guard. Clearly *he* believed the worst. "The conte's apartments, where his mam and sisters lie, are two corridors over."

Ambrose lifted his chin and glared at us all. He could not possibly comprehend the danger his father had put him in.

"You've stayed here with your father in the past," I said. "You know your way about. Why would you mistake a closet—?"

Of course. I would wager my year's pay that one would find a hidden panel in the back of this closet. Philippe would have given Michel apartments that communicated with the royal suite by way of the palace's hidden ways. Michel might have shown his son the intriguing passages, but more likely the boy had spied his father using them. It was certainly not my place to reveal them to the guards.

"Well, no matter. It's easy to get confused in so large a place," I said. "So you were visiting the Exposition. Have you an interest in scientific advancement? Or is it the magic draws you?"

He didn't even pretend. "I wanted to see *him*. The king. My own *goodfather*. I wanted to ask him how he could believe a man who saved his life ten times and spent most of every year away from home in his service could ever betray him. I wanted him to tell me with his own mouth."

"And did you see anyone you recognized this evening?"

"I wasn't looking for any but him," he spat. Not the least twitch of guilty withholding marred his youthful fury. If raw passion exposed truth, then Ambrose de Vernase knew nothing of the night's events.

"I don't think there's more to do here," I said. "Lord Ambrose must be returned to his mother, whose welfare he should consider ahead of childish whims. Being His Majesty's goodson, wise in the ways of politics and royalty, he surely knows that until he reaches his majority, his mother is held equally responsible for any libelous word or treasonous act on his part."

Ambrose's rose-gold complexion faded to puking yellow. One would think I had slammed a boot into his groin.

"As for escape, such a noble young man's word should suffice. Is that true, Lord Ambrose?"

Eyes narrowed, he gave something of a positive acknowledgment with head and shoulders.

"Good." I held out the boy's dagger. "Then, of course, you will place your hand on your weapon and swear by your mother's safety and your own honor that you will not leave your father's apartments by *any route*—door, window, or *other*—until such time as your king gives you leave. Do you so swear?"

"I do—" Ambrose had already spoken by the time he comprehended the "any route" part. When his eyes shot up to meet mine, I made sure he could read my understanding of his evasion. His mouth clenched in resentment. "I do. But I'll make him answer. Be sure of it."

Sacre angeli! I gripped his shoulders and shook him. "Treason is not a contest, Ambrose. Nor are you a child, whose thoughtless transgressions can be indulged and forgiven. Cool your emotions and heed reason. Your path is grown exceeding narrow this night."

His demeanor did not change, which did not mean he failed to comprehend. I hoped.

"Take him back to his mother. Tell her to put a leash on him."

"Whatever my father's done, he has good reason," said the boy, his dark eyes filling with angry tears. "But you and your mage and . . . and the lord who put you up to it . . . have done worse. You think you can hurt people and no one will guess. I'll see you pay for what you've done."

Though he wrestled and squirmed, the guards marched him away held securely between them.

The young palace aide who'd fetched me shut the closet door. "I may be speaking out of turn, sonjeur. Forgive me, if so, but you seem to have the lad's interest at heart. I don't know that the contessa will talk sense to him. The strain of the conte's disappearance . . . his situation . . . she is not the same woman as visited here in the past."

"How could she be?" I murmured as he left me. Confirming that, indeed, a hidden passage could be accessed from the dark corner of the closet did nothing to soothe my unease.

STARS SHONE INSIDE THE ROTUNDA'S dome. Or rather, silver lights dotted the blackness that filled the great vault, some randomly scattered, some clustered into familiar patterns— the Arch of Heaven, the Bowman, the Three Oxen, the Winter Cup. Some of the "stars" above our craning heads whirled and spun. Orviene adjusted a wooden cylinder and a disk of silver in his spell enclosure, made an entirely unnecessary circling wave of his arm, and a fiery chariot drawn by six giant eagles flew across a silver crescent moon. The compact and powerful charioteer was surely meant to be Sante Ianne the Reborn, though the saint of wisdom was commonly portrayed as returning on the back of one eagle rather than driving six. Perhaps Orviene was a cultist like Ilario, or perhaps the chariot was merely a dramatic image, chosen because the mage couldn't think of anything more interesting.

Was pure illusion the best Orviene could offer? Thanks to Ambrose's misbehavior, I'd arrived at the Rotunda only at the end of Orviene's display, but I was already sorely disappointed.

The chariot circled the vault. The air smelled faintly of rain. My hair and limp shirt collar shifted slightly in a wispy breeze, a poor reality out of proportion to the chariot's size and speed. The children enjoyed Orviene's work best, squealing in delight as he produced pink and yellow lightning and a rain shower that spattered on doublets and bodices, but felt more like swarming gnats than water droplets. The adult onlookers applauded politely as a grand gesture produced a red-orange sunrise entirely lacking in heat.

As the smiling mage bowed to the audience and made the required obeisance to a stone-faced Philippe, footmen turned up the lamps. The true daylight outside the thick walls had faded. But despite the passing hour and whatever drowsiness might have been encouraged by wine and supper and a less than stirring daemonstration, not one soul left the chamber. Guests whispered to their neighbors, and fingers pointed to a shadowed space beside the dais where Dante stood, eyes closed, forehead touching his staff, as if in prayer.

Knowing Dante was more likely to be engaged in spellwork than prayer, I felt my own excitement rise, though reason insisted I should be gnawing bricks by now. Maura was waiting.

I planted my back on one of the columns that supported the vault. Let Dante open his eyes, if he wanted to know where I was.

Orviene left the dais to a scattering of applause. Seemingly oblivious to several scornful comments about "tricks to amuse children," he began chatting amiably with guests seated on the front rows, as he packed his materials into a bag.

"Get you gone, mage!" Dante's voice cracked the restive quiet, as he emerged from the shadows, his staff jabbing at Orviene's paraphernalia. "These folk have serious magic yet to see this night! Take your trinkets with you."

When some of the guests tittered, Orviene—complexion purpled—snatched up his bag and hurried off, abandoning his enclosure strings and metal chips.

The shocked murmurs quieted quickly, as Dante stepped onto the dais. His blue silk robes rippled, and his collar gleamed, the fine gold inlay reminding all that this was a master's collar, not the plain silver of a lesser mage like Orviene. His white staff began to gleam of its own light, brighter by the moment, while the lamplight dulled—flames not snuffed or reduced, but muted in quality as if the air grew thicker.

My skin shivered, itched, half numb, half heated, as do pursed lips when one blows a single low note for much too long.

"We've been asked to show wonders," Dante said, leaning on his staff, his ruined hand hidden inside his flowing sleeve, as always, "and I, a crude man, unaccustomed to what noble lords and ladies and celebrated scholars deem wonderful, have watched and learned this night. The astronomers created slotted shades and built apparatus to daemonstrate what they cannot explain. But any alley brat lucky enough to find a shard of broken glass on a sunny day might do as well."

The onlookers gasped as a rainbow of light shot from the top of his staff, red, orange, yellow, green, blue, violet. And they clapped as the colored rays bent and joined together into a single white beam, like a single stem emerging from a spread of colorful roots.

I did not applaud. My gut constricted, because I heard his heated scorn glaring like a summer sunrise, and even halfway across the room I tasted the bitterness feeding his magic. Could no one else sense it? Why were those nearest him not squirming backward? Had my body not been pressed against a solid surface already, I would have done so.

"But I celebrate these academicians of the natural world as you do. They attempt to learn. They map the heavens and theorize about its structure and movements. They quantify and record and seek answers, and create"— his white beam bent and moved, traversing the upturned faces, pale and dark, young and old, smiling, amazed, puzzled, until it reached my own, near blinding me with the glare—"magnifying spectacles, so that lowly secretaries with weary eyes may read the words they scribe for trivial men. Useful things."

Laughter rippled through the silk- and satin-clad rows and lapped at my shoulders from those behind me. Heat rushed to my cheeks, and my hand came up to shield my eyes, which were not wearing the spectacles at the moment. Was this why he'd wanted me here?

Even as humiliation burned, I could not but contrast the searing heat of the beam with Orviene's simulacrum of sunlight. Every person Dante's light touched must realize the same. After what seemed an age, the beam moved on, and so did the mage's introduction.

"But even a king's astronomers cannot lift you into the heavens, any more than they can take you inside their beams of light. Not yet. And so next, we saw the practitioner deemed collar-worthy by the Camarilla Magica attempt such a journey. But he teased you with air painting, no more real than the inhabitants of this ancient dome."

The white beam and its bright-colored roots vanished. Now the staff, raised high, gave off a broad, spreading glow that illuminated the vault, immersing all of us below in a sea of shadows.

Long before the days of Sabria, a people called the Cinnear had built the Rotunda, choosing the ribbed dome, resting on its ring of glass windows, as a repository of their god stories. Centuries later, a Sabrian king had hired artists to cover the painted scenes of beast gods and legends we did not know. In the arced recesses between the vault's ribs, the artists had laid richly colored mosaics of our own god and the stories of our hero saints.

Though much of the gold background had since flaked away, exposing the faded paintings underneath, and the pendulum suspension cog protruded from the dome's peak like an unsightly wart, the luminous figures of the Pantokrator and his servants still had power to awe. In the daytime, the thin bracelet of glass about the dome's base bathed them in sunlight, revealing the richness of lapis and jade, coral and amber. But touched by Dante's shuddering luminescence, the angels' wings seemed to ripple as in a mighty wind, and the eyes of the saints, dark-outlined as prescribed by the Temple, widened as if they had just taken notice of earthly life. Their backs bent, their raised hands reached down toward us all. . . .

The air boiled, thick as a posset. My wind-whipped hair and collar stung my cheeks. Terror wriggled its way into my craw, though it had no name and no shape that made sense.

I shook my head and blinked, and the saints and angels retreated to the ceiling. Shivering, I forced my eyes from the vault.

"Heaven's gates, so beautiful," murmured a woman just beside me, her sighs merging with a chorus of awe from the rest of the chamber. What did she see? Did no one feel the danger? Gowns, scarves, lace, and hair riffled, disarranged by the wind of angels' wings.

Dante lowered his staff, and every eye shifted his way. "Perhaps you would rather travel to places of your own choosing," he said, and he twirled his staff in his hand, now pointing it at the wooden dais. Spinning in place, he quickly scribed a circle with a rill of blue flame.

As one, the onlookers inhaled, but did not cry out or panic, for the fire did not spread or grow. Inside the circle, Dante crouched down—I could not see what he did—then rose up and settled into his meditative posture, eyes closed, head pressed to the carved hornbeam staff. "Consider regrets," he said, "those unfortunate things you would change. We could travel into that demesne. . . ."

All around me, people closed their eyes. Like sheep.

Like herdbeasts allowing themselves to be led into worse
danger. Oh, I knew regrets, but I would not play. I held my
eyes open.

But darkness bloomed from his circle of fire, blinding
my common eyes. And with night came memory and a
fiery wounding. . . .

*The knife rips down my left arm, and five different
places on my chest and back and side, as if my father
is trying to carve the cursed mark—the interlaced S
and V—into every part of my wretched flesh. Into my
heart.*

*Get up, get up! On your feet, Portier, or die this
moment. Sweet angels defend! Grab the madman's
wrist. Ignore the pummeling; that hand holds no
blade. Hold on. . . .*

*The gut wound, explosive agony moments be-
fore, cools. A blessing, save that my legs are losing
all feeling at the same time. Blood pulses weakly
from my belly and arm. Numb feet stumble side-
ways, dragging the scrawny madman along with
me, his face contorted, bloody.*

*"Master! Help me! Dufreyne . . . Garol . . .
Mother . . . someone!" My calls bring no succor, and
he does not stop his flailing. The earth wavers . . .
light shimmers . . . fades into gray . . . Let go and
he'll strike again . . . and you'll die. Retain your hold
and you'll collapse . . . and die. Choose.*

*Let go, then. Strike at his throat. You've one
chance. . . .*

*Released, the madman staggers backward. My
weakened hand scarce grazes his throat.*

*The floor rushes upward. Breath will not come. A
cold black glove envelopes limbs, belly, back, squeezing the heart . . . inexorably . . . stilling its struggle . . .
then brushes lips and tongue with numbing frost . . .
and, with two black-clad fingers, closes my eyelids.*

No! Please, give back the light! I am not finished.

Father Creator, this is wrong! I am destined...
meant...

Smell is the last of the senses to fade, so it's said,
and the first to return. Thus the aroma of cedar and
juniper, old leaves and dry grass, dampened by
mist, should be a reassuring replacement for the
odor of evacuated bowels and blood-soaked wool.
But I know where I am, and I will not look upon it.
And so I shutter thought and belief and the eyes I
cannot feel.

Sweet angels carry this plea to the One Who Judges.
Was I not born for more than failure? For more than
petty striving? I cannot... will not... accept this.

A soughing wind rattles twigs and grasses—my
only answer. Despair replaces breath. Cold stone re-
places heart. And two lumps of unfeeling wood shove
me upright and set themselves one before the other. I
am terrified to look, lest seeing make it real, lest I spy
the First Gate barred and know I will wander in this
cold, lifeless place for the duration of the world.

Please, I don't belong here! I am Other! Destined!
Hear me....

A hammer falls upon anvil, and I am falling...
falling... seared, crushed, starved, burnt. Bursting
agony in my lungs sparks streaks of acid on skin,
through flesh. My nostrils clog with choking
lavender.

"Onfroi went mad and killed my boy. My child."
Her sobbing whispers blare through skull bones like
trumpet blasts. "I had to stop him."

"Give me the fire iron, Dame Duplais. No one will
blame your son for defending himself. If he lives,
he'll not remember elsewise."

❦

THE HOLOCAUST RETREATED AS SWIFTLY as it had come. My
backside was planted on the Rotunda floor as boots and
slippers, skirts and ruffles, breeches, leggings, and old-
fashioned puffed pantaloons brushed past me. Murmurs

filled my ears—sobs, fear, muted curses. Occasional out-
bursts of anger or wonder: "The man's a devil ... My
grandfather ... cruel ... So cold ... So real. What pleasure is this? ... I smelled his stink ... her scent ... our
garden ... real ... So perfect, I could almost touch it ...
Marvelous ... Daemonic ... Real ... What kind of Souleater's servant is he? I *saw*."

"Are you well, sonjeur?" An elderly man wearing the
sky blue gown of a mathematician held out a hand to me.
"I'm not sure what this cruel mage just showed us, but
you're not the only person it's struck low."

Wrung out as old rags, I let him draw me up and prop
me against the pillar. But I could only shake my head in
answer to his queries, and he soon moved on, as the Rotunda emptied of its unsettled population.

Words could not describe what had just happened. Nor
could I shudder or weep or rejoice or rage, though reason
swore I had justification for all those things. I could not
feel anything save the same conviction that had accompanied every enchantment Dante had worked: What I had
seen was truth. Three truths, to be precise, and when was
Portier de Savin-Duplais anything but precise?

I had not killed my father.

My hysterical mother, she of the too-strong lavender
scent and ever-fractured emotions, had slammed a fire
iron into his neck, attempting to save my life.

And on that same night, I had died.

CHAPTER THIRTY-TWO

25 CINQ
THE ANNIVERSARY

My head felt hollow as a burnt-out log. Come another magical wind, it could surely blow through one ear and emerge from the other.

I had died. I had felt the Veil's chill finality on my cheek, smelled the sere and lifeless grasses of Ixtador. And then I had come back. Not as an infant, like a Saint Reborn, and probably not because I had pleaded with a distant god that I had died too early. Surely Ophelie had pleaded the same. And yet, I had screamed: "I am Other . . . destined . . . meant. . . ."

The arid wash of sanity smothered my creeping shivers. *Idiot. Saints wield true magic.* The pleas had been but a recurrence of childish dreams, my hope to serve some purpose in this world.

Kajetan had summoned a physician, so he'd told me after. The man must have been blessedly skilled to induce my heart to beat again before my last tether to life was severed. For all these years I'd thanked Kajetan for saving my life, but only now did I understand how near a thing it had been. He'd saved my mother's life as well, for to slay a noble husband was, as yet, a crime indefensible, according to Sabrian law. How could I not have remembered any of this?

Could simple knowledge of the truth leave the quality of the world so different? The air of the Rotunda sparked and shivered, as with Scholar Rulf's *virtu electrik*. Footmen's boots struck the marble with a brittle snap. Light, color, and space existed in their own right, no longer subordinate to the physical objects that produced, displayed, or shaped them. I inhaled the emerald of the floor medallions and the petal-shaped voids of the windows. The cool curvature of the column at my back inverted, enfolding me as a mantle. Every perception seemed richer, sharper, more intricate in detail, as if my body, knowing it had once been dead, devoured every sensation of life three times over.

None of this was inherently terrifying. I should relish the taste of the human world. I should rejoice at the weight of murder lifted from my soul. I should grieve for my mother's fractured mind, and marvel at an act of maternal feeling from a person I had deemed incapable of such. So why did chill fingers crawl down my back, and my stomach insist it housed naught but writhing snakes? Why did my hands tremble?

Across the Rotunda a clog of courtiers on their way to the refreshment tables blocked the doorway to the Portrait Gallery. The volume of their conversation was rising by the moment, its tenor angry, tense, and fearful. Men glanced over their shoulders uneasily and spoke too loud; couples clung to each other. Some children clutched parents' necks. But a few little ones dragged along behind, facing backward, glowing as if anticipating more . . . More what?

The tower bells rang tenth hour of the evening watch, giving me fair warning. Two hours remained until the queen would be brought from the Spindle, when I had to be in Riverside to steer the future course of my life.

I walked briskly toward the Portrait Gallery. Something brushed my cheek—a moth?—and I near leapt out of my skin. No one stood within ten metres of me. The chairs were empty, shoved out of their orderly ranks. Soon

I would be left alone with the servants come to sweep and the curious footmen come to haul out the chairs.

"Portier!" The steward's third secretary hailed me as he emerged from the crowded Portrait Gallery doorway.

"Divine grace, Henri. Do you need help with those?" De Sain's long fingers clenched three wine cups. The soft slurp of wine against metal carried across the distance between us.

"No, I'm off to relieve Gufee at the west door registry," he said as I joined him.

Our steps echoed in the increasingly empty Rotunda. "You and Gufee can pass along word that the tallies can stop as soon as the king retires to Riverside. I'll be off writing my report." A flimsy cover for my absence, but enough, I hoped.

"Can't say I'm happy to loll about this place another hour," he said. "Now I understand your fear of that mage. I'll have nightmares till I'm gray-headed." His voice had quieted noticeably at *that mage*.

"What did you actually see, Henri? I couldn't get a good look from the back, and I've heard so many different things."

"Ask someone other." He raised his wine cups. "You'll be sure I've drunk fifty of these already."

"Tell me," I said. "For a while, I was thinking the angels were going to fly right out of the vault. Or that Sante Marko and Santa Claire thought to raise me up to the dome and throw me down again. Can't seem to shed it." Which must explain the tremors in my hands.

Though Henri ducked his head as we strolled through the pooled lamplight and past the silently swinging pendulum, his gaze flicked repeatedly about the gloomy Rotunda, as if he did not wish to see anything, but couldn't resist the looking. "When the mage drew the darkness from his ring of fire, I saw my da, who's been dead since the war in Kadr. Only—"

"Only what?"

"Only he didn't look as he did when I saw him last . . . or ever." The secretary dropped his voice even more. "He was wearing a rugged coat covered with sand. In fact he was climbing a great dune, the sand flowing over him and under him like water. And his face was hollow as if he'd starved and scared as he'd never been in life. Portier, I could near touch him, he seemed so real."

"Surely it was only your imaginings taken shape. Knowing he died in a desert war. Recalling the last time you spoke . . ."

"Angels preserve, he didn't speak! My heart would seize if a voice had come from such a haunting. But I could smell . . . When he was off at the war, Da would chew areca nuts till his tongue was red. To keep him square, you know, relaxed, and ready."

"So you imagined you smelled areca?" My mother was forever in debt to a local spice merchant who imported the odd fruits from the south.

"Take a whiff of my sleeve, Portier. I've not been near an areca nut in seven years." He poked his elbow out.

Feeling a bit foolish, I bent close to the dark blue satin and sniffed. Permeating Henri de Sain's sleeve was a rich aroma something kin to spiced olives. Unmistakably areca.

"It doesn't seem likely," I said, trapping my tremulous hands under my elbows. "Yet powerful sorcery did take place here. It lingers."

"Lots saw phantoms tonight, I hear," said Henri. "Lots felt things . . . movements . . . they couldn't see. Lots won't speak of what they experienced. Myself, I've got to get out of these clothes. The stink makes me think he's going to step out from around the next corner."

The bell rang the quarter hour. My steps slowed. "We'll talk again, Henri. Angels' peace this night."

"Aye, and to you, Portier. And all of us." He sped toward the west doors, juggling wine cups.

I needed to go, to make ready for Maura's escape. Yet magic held me in the Rotunda, drawing me to the center of the night's mystery.

Dante's fire had seared a grooved ring some four metres across into the wide, fitted planks of the dais. I almost laughed. The mage had made himself another circumoccule. And he had spilled—splashed—something inside the circle to stain the pale wood dark. So what had he done?

I stepped across the sooty boundary to examine the stain. But before I could take a second step, my chest tried to fly apart. Unseen fingers probed, tweaked, and pinched as if plucking out my body's every hair one by one. Knees, elbows, and hip joints cracked and splintered, scraped like glass on steel, ground bone on bone.

I backed out hurriedly, and the sensations ceased. Was Dante's spellwork still active inside the circumoccule? This could not be residue; never had I experienced such a complex, physically painful reaction to spent magic. It would not have surprised me to find my bones reattached in some altogether new alignment.

A sweeping lad with a flat face and angled eyes ambled across the dais, pushing his scant litter of sand, soot, crumbled leaves, bits of straw, and broken glass. He touched his forehead politely as he passed me. His path took him straight through Dante's circle and all the way to the edge of the dais until his sweepings cascaded from the edge onto the floor below. Then he reversed course and slogged by again, his broom gathering a new pile of debris, mostly dust.

That he crossed the circle a second time without so much as a start answered the very question I would ask him. He felt nothing. What I had experienced must be residue detected by my trained senses, and not some unfolding enchantment that anyone might experience.

Staring at the circle, I considered whether the effects would be so severe if I breached it with only one hand. As I debated, the sweeping boy passed by again, pushing another pile of debris. Amid the sweepings was an object very like one of the astronomers' prisms. Once the youth had shoved the mess off the end of the dais and started another round, I stepped down and poked a finger into the piled sweepings. What I had thought a valuable prism was but a chunk of broken glass.

However, as I turned away, I noticed a corked vial amid

the detritus, which would not have been so remarkable, save that it was clearly labeled EXPOSITION in Dante's distinctive, left-handed script.

Three short strikes of the tower bell reported another half hour lapsed. Time to move. The earthenware vial, painted dark blue or purple, felt empty. Stuffing it into my doublet, I turned to go.

I'd gone only a few steps when a muffled argument back under the colonnade behind the dais rose to a yell. ". . . find it or I'll conjure a hound that rips flesh from idiot slaveys and set him on you!"

Dante burst out of the dark colonnade, robes flying, hesitating only briefly when he caught sight of me. "Have you naught better to do than idle in this empty cavern, secretary?"

"Alas, I'm assigned to all aspects of the Exposition," I said, tagging after him. "The displays, the program, and the cleaning. Though I've hardly a head for business just now, thanks to you."

His determined course took him onto the dais. I followed, stopping at the circumoccule. He kept going until he reached the back of the platform. "I chose not to clean up my mess immediately after my daemonstration," he said, reaching behind the dais and pulling out his bag, which contained the vials with the scrapings from Edmond's wounds. "I greatly dislike questions from the ignorant."

"But, as always, I am willing to risk your annoyance in the cause of learning." I stared up into the dome, where the mosaics were scarcely visible in the gloom. "What, in the name of Heaven, did you do here tonight, Dante?"

"The birds are atwitter, are they not? I've always considered lenses more fascinating than prisms, especially for those of limited vision."

"Indeed. What I saw . . ."

"We are finished at middle-night. Did you forget?" He stepped up to the dais, dropped a plug of lead into the charred groove, and set the heel of his staff atop it. A sputter of white fire, and the plug softened just enough to settle solidly into the trough like a well-constructed dam.

"There. I'd recommend these planks be burned. You'll see to it?"

"Certainly," I said, stepping into the circumoccule. Naught but heat bothered me this time, a billowing stink of hot lead from the plug, and a waning prickle of fire from the rest of the broken circle. *This* was residue. I could not say what the other had been. "But I need to know—"

"I'll offer you one more thing, student. If you should catch this charm-peddler Fedrigo, ask who taught him blanking spells." From the bag Dante pulled a length of white string, threaded with black silk, and crushed it in my hand. "Now get out of my way. We are quit."

As he strode down the length of the dais, his gaze scanning the platform, I inspected the string. It yielded naught but a magical residue the texture of stonedust. Entirely confused, I crammed it into my pocket.

When Dante stepped off the dais, he paused and poked his staff at the sweepings pile. Then he kicked the large chunk of glass so hard it shattered against a column, spraying shards all over the newly swept floor. He walked away, quickly swallowed by the gloom under the colonnade.

His anger over something missing . . . something dropped, perhaps . . . I pulled out the vial, uncorked it, and sniffed. Cedar, henbane perhaps, and— I upended the vial over my hand, shook it, slammed it into my palm until a single droplet rolled out. Blood.

I stared at the telling bead and again at the dark stain in the center of Dante's ring. So he had worked a *vitet*, a vital spell, an enchantment that incorporated blood as a particle—or in Dante's case, one that incorporated the blood's keirna in the pattern he wove. Vitets were not illicit, as long as the blood was freely given to the practitioner, but they were as complex and unstable as human souls. Theory suggested this particularly affected the one whose blood was used.

A void yawned in my belly. My fingers rubbed my chest, where cross-hatched scars reminded me of pain, blood, and smoke. The Aspirant still had the half litre of blood he had taken from me. *This* blood could not be mine . . . surely . . . else Dante . . .

The tower bell pealed the quarter before eleventh hour, shaking me out of my paralysis. Father Creator! I sped through the Great Hall and snatched up the bundle of clothes I had stashed at my desk early that morning. Shedding my *agente confide*'s responsibilities and my disturbing memories for a task that supported no delay, I charged out into the night.

CHAPTER THIRTY-THREE

25 CINQ
THE ANNIVERSARY

As I traversed the open arcades, courtyards, and broad stairs of the palace and the upper city, the Rotunda's oppressive anxiety faded. No longer did I have the sense that at any moment I would bump into something I couldn't see. Yet my perceptions remained in their altered state—as if all my senses had been given spectacles to remove the world's blurred edges.

Lamplight glinted through the seams of doors and shutters and winked like fireflies. Laughter and music from taverns shimmered on the air like bronze bells. The darkest, quietest alleyways were redolent with scent—yesterday's fish, smoked pork fat, wood shavings, forged iron, an overflowing midden, tansy growing in the seams of old walls—not a hodgepodge "stench of the city," but each scent distinct in itself, pleasant or not as its nature and my appreciation prescribed. My perceptions gave me an extraordinary confidence. By the Souleater's Worm, the villains would not count Maura among their victims.

No one must see me in the next hour, at least not to remember, so I kept to Riverside's back streets, well away from the Market Way that led from the heart of the upper city to the harbor. A golden haze swelled over the rooftops—torches blooming along the wide boulevard to light the way for the king. Rumors would be flying.

A dull thud rattled the shutters along the lane and set the dogs howling. White fire blossomed over the river, a cascade of light as if the stars were melting. *Not yet!* I needed to be at the harbor, as near the main pier as I could get before the turn of middle-night.

No further bursts occurred. The Lestarte brothers must only have been testing their launchers. I slipped into a darkened warehouse that smelled of new cut oak, char, and pitch. Inside, dangling his feet from a cooper's wagon bed, waited Calvino de Santo.

The disgraced guard captain had been more than willing to aid in this night's work. I had warned him his actions would be viewed as conspiracy to treason, but he relished the chance to save another pawn from a fate so like his own.

"So it is tonight," he said, returning the brass token I'd left him in a palace alleyway.

"He sent the release order." I kept a wary eye out the doorway. "No one challenged your leaving?"

"My night's taskmaster believes something I ate gave me heaves. I offered him good proof. The gate guards are so accustomed to my skulking about all night, they never noticed me walk out. I'll walk back in when we're done. I've a thought where to take the lady. I know summat—"

"No! You mustn't tell me." My skin popped out in gooseflesh. "If I'm arrested, I must not be able to reveal her destination. I'd take her myself and damn all, save I must be here to bring de Vernase to trial."

"Skin your worry, sonjeur. Under an hour and I'll pass her to someone reliable. None'll be able to get her destination from me, neither."

We confirmed positions and timing, and I left him. Riverside residents flooded the streets, pointing to the sky over the river. Some brought torches or lanterns to light their way home. Some paraded with pipes and tabors, as if this were the grape harvest festival or a frost fair on midwinter's night.

I pulled a black cloak from my bag and donned one of Ilario's out-of-fashion hats, expensive enough to name me respectable, old enough to bear no connection to Ilario, and wide enough to shield my face from easy view. As I neared the river, I angled through the steep lanes toward the remote slip where Massimo Haile's barge had been moored on the day of the *Swan* fire. No one had used it since that ill-omened day.

The tower bells told the second quarter of eleventh hour, as I scrambled down the muddy bank, tucked in between the old planks and water's edge, and drew the voluminous cloak over my entire self. When the Guard Royale set their protective perimeter around the harbor, I would already be inside it.

The half hour stretched long and anxious in the pitch dark, my every sense twisted to extremity. Cold mud crept into boots and breeches. My mind worried at the earthenware vial and its telltale drop of blood, pawing through evidence—conversations, dates, and times. I longed for light to consult my journal. My conclusion did not change: Dante could not be the Aspirant. Even the thought, dismissed, appalled and terrified me. No matter passing doubts, no matter his erratic behavior, I refused to believe Dante was bent.

When the tower bells rang middle-night, I poked my head from my shroud and gratefully shed every consideration but the present venture. White, gold, vermillion, and emerald fire seared the night sky all up and down the river. No kingdom in the world could produce the intense colors of Sabrian fireworks. Magic, some called it, though I knew our alchemists had found the secret in their minerals. I crept out from my hiding place and straightened my borrowed hat. Another burst of mixed yellow and green provided a springlike bower of light for the shallop emerging from the Spindle's water gate.

Boots squelching, I scuttered along the steep bank toward the central harbor. When the bank began to flatten and voices murmured nearby, I assumed a drunkard's meandering gait.

With a fierce satisfaction, I noted some two hundred

courtiers gathered at the pier. Outside the ring of the Guard Royale, a thousand or more citizens of Merona trilled their pipes, thumped their tabors, and set up howls and cheers at each burst of colored fire.

Wandering up the bank, I waved at no one in particular and fumbled with my breeches, as if I'd relieved myself at the riverside. Unnecessary playacting. The guards faced outward toward the common mob, and the eyes of the courtiers were fixed on the approaching shallop or on the wharfside street above the mudflats where blazing torchlight illuminated the waiting King of Sabria.

The heavy night breeze flapped pennons and shifted cloaks. I forced myself to breathe as the rowers shipped oars and glided the last metres into the pier, tossing lines to those on shore.

Liveried dockhands assisted the flock of ladies, fifteen or twenty of them indistinguishable in dark, hooded cloaks, onto the wide pier. The queen, regal in her pale cloak and gown, glittering with diamonds and rubies, stepped out of the shallop last. Every eye was drawn to her.

A lanky man in emerald satin burst free of the waiting nobles and into the chattering cluster of gentlewomen as they walked up the pier. He embraced each of the brave attendants in turn, swinging her round in exuberance, as his great cloak filled like green wings. Ilario.

Rebecs, shawms, and pipes spun a wild and merry gigue, and the crowd erupted in disbelieving laughter as Ilario danced with the ladies along the pier and muddy bank. When the chevalier bellowed at other men to join in the celebration, a goodly number did so.

Reluctant to involve him in our risk, I had not asked Ilario to create such a distraction, but I blessed it. With all eyes at the center, no one noticed when another fellow— I—in black cloak and gray hat, embraced one of the queen's dark-cloaked ladies and danced her away from the new arrivals and into the crowd of dignitaries.

I'd never felt such an embrace—the softness I had imagined the first time I'd seen her, the desperate thanks, the radiant affection that her great eyes spoke with my name. "Dear, kind Portier."

I swept my voluminous cloak about her. "Switch cloaks with the one in my bag." I whispered. "Quickly, as we dance."

In the press of the crowd, it was unlikely that anyone noted that the gray hat was swept from my head and trampled underfoot, or that when I released the lady from my enveloping embrace, she wore a hooded summer cloak of bright blue. On this night, the brighter color was the better disguise—Eugenie's own suggestion. By the time Ilario released the laughing gentlewomen, and they strung out along the boardwalk laid across the mudflats from pier to wharfside, no one pointed out that there were fewer ladies by one than had been rowed out of the Spindle.

Maura and I ambled up the boardwalk with the rest of the queen's guests. Two sobering, solid lines of the Guard Royale flanked our path, holding back the raucous mob. Maura shook so violently that I feared someone would notice. But I gripped her tight and babbled noisily of kings and queens and the ridiculous Chevalier de Sylvae, and bent down to kiss her once—which was entirely foolish, but seemed to calm her at the least. Her lips were cold as Journian frost.

At last Eugenie, too, stepped onto Sabria's shore. Ilario bent his knee before her. She raised him into a long embrace, but sent him on and walked up the long path from the pier alone. At last, beneath the blazing torches, she knelt gracefully before her king. To the cheers and wonder of the citizens who'd come to the riverside thinking to see only fireworks, Philippe raised her up and bowed before her in turn, greeting her not as a prisoner indulged, but as Sabria's rightful queen.

Only as the royal couple strolled hand in hand down the wharfside toward Market Way did some sharp-eyed observer point out the orange flares spit up from Spindle Prison. Almost lost in the fireworks, the warning of a prisoner's escape caused only murmurs at first. *But the queen's released . . . king's come to fetch her . . . other prisoners? . . . There, look, another flare!*

More serious shouts soon followed. As Maura and I mingled with the protected elite on the wharfside way, guardsmen spread quickly down the shoreline all the way to Massimo Haile's slip.

I blessed my guiding angels that I had not followed my first instinct to get Maura out of the crowd quickly and go back the way I'd come. Unfortunately, the second line of guardsmen constricted about our party of courtiers. Of a sudden, my plan to slip quietly into tiny, dark Fish Lane where Calvino de Santo waited seemed incredibly naive.

The royal couple, oblivious to the rising disturbance, mounted their waiting horses, as did Lady Antonia and Ilario, who waved his feathered hat and blew kisses at every person wearing skirts and some who didn't. Philippe's bodyguards encircled the four and escorted them on a slow progress up the boulevard. The rest of us, including the queen's ladies, were held back by the orders of Captain de Segur, the very captain I'd sworn to obedience beside Edmond's body. Cursing fortune and my discarded hat, I ducked my head.

The captain dispatched searchers into the dockside lanes, then climbed atop a cart to address the restive party. "Honorable ladies and noble gentlemen, one moment please," he bellowed. "We've signs that a prisoner has taken advantage of this happy occasion to escape the Spindle. For your protection, we ask you to remain here. We'll escort you to your conveyances a few at a time. . . ."

"Portier, move away from me," Maura whispered.

I gripped her hand the harder and scoured our surroundings for a way out. My anxiety was not at all soothed by the sight of another boat lamp halfway across the strait between the Spindle and the shore. Once the boat landed, Captain de Segur would know exactly for whom he was looking.

A soldier burst from one of the steep side lanes and ran to the captain for a hurried conference. My heart lurched as the captain's sharp eyes roved our party of anxious nobility and lit on me. "Sonjeur de Duplais! Please join me here."

"Fish Lane," I said softly, ducking my head in the captain's direction. "Ten houses in. As soon as you're free to go." I squeezed her hand and dropped the bag containing her black cloak.

Spirit aching at abandoning Maura, I pushed through the grumbling party. "What is it, Captain? I've duties."

He jumped down from his perch. "Fortunate you're here. We've found the fugitive."

It required every bit of discipline I possessed to refrain from looking over my shoulder. "Indeed?"

"The sorcerer was hiding on a balcony overlooking Market Way, exactly where the king was to pass. We need you to identify him."

"A sorcerer . . . Fedrigo!" I spluttered, relieved and astounded. "But I thought—"

My racing mind shifted tactics. Captain de Segur surely realized that Adept Fedrigo was unlikely to be the prisoner escaped from the Spindle, but he couldn't be certain until the boat landed. And without doubt the noblemen and ladies surrounding us were entirely unused to standing in the damp wind surrounded by soldiers. They were ready to mutiny.

"Well, heavenly legions, that's excellent, a fine job!" I shouted, slapping the captain on the shoulder. "Certainly, I'll come with you. Now the fugitive is found, we can allow His Majesty's friends to be on their way unhindered. Bravo! His Majesty will be delighted."

No more than that was required to stir the prickly aristocrats. They began to clamor as one and push through the ring of guards. Only a few hours had passed since I was issuing orders under the king's authority. De Segur had little choice but to follow my lead. The captain ordered his men to release the guests to proceed home as they would.

As the party dissolved, I gripped Captain de Segur's hand firmly. "Sir, you are a credit to the Guard Royale. As you witnessed but a few hours ago, this murderous Fedrigo's infamy ranks second only to that of de Vernase himself in the king's mind." That was most certainly true.

"Then we'd best make sure this man's the one we're supposed to be hunting, hadn't we, sonjeur?" said the captain, his syllables crisp.

"Certainly," I said, then held my breath for a moment as a bright blue cloak vanished up Fish Lane. *Godspeed, sweet lady.* An iron yoke slipped from my spirit, leaving me with an odd certainty: Maura would be all right.

MY AWARENESS OF ENCHANTMENT GREW stronger the farther into the alley the young soldier led me. With every step, it galled my spirit worse, grinding, gnawing, making me want to retreat.

Never had my sense suggested a rightness or wrongness about spells it detected. It merely signaled that one existed and registered its relative strength. Dante's door wards bit, but that was the *effect* of the spell, and had naught to do with my perception of its existence. In the same way, magical residues presented as more pleasurable or less, but I had never correlated a pleasurable sensation with a worthwhile end or vice versa. But this enchantment clamored evil. Whoever had created it, Fedrigo or other, was someone to be wary of.

The fugitive had been trapped at the blind end of the alley—the back of a ramshackle warehouse, flanked by a tall fence and a deserted house. Face down in the weedy corner, the large man bucked and thrashed, while two soldiers sat on his back, one of them attempting to bind the prisoner's ankles. A young officer held a lantern.

"Captain de Segur sent me to identify the fugitive," I said.

"He ought to have sent more hands to hold the toadeater," said one of the soldiers, a burly man whose knees clamped the prisoner's waist and whose fist snarled the prisoner's hair. His own head looked to have been scraped on the splintered fence. "Or mayhap an iron to crush his skull."

"Hold the light down here," I said, and I crouched where I could see the captive's face.

The prisoner growled at me fiercely, but I could see enough. His dark beard was trimmed closer than last time I'd seen him, and other men could have a neck the same width as their heads, but I would never mistake the nose that looked as if it had been broken ten times.

"I do believe you've earned your king's favor, gentlemen. Please sit him up. And you"—I nodded to the young soldier who'd fetched me—"notify Captain de Segur that this is indeed the man we sought. Remind him that His Majesty wished to be notified the moment we found him." The guide sped away.

"Sitting him up" was a violent business. In the end, the two guardsmen had to bind Fedrigo's thick hands and truss knees, arms, and ankles before they could prop him against the warehouse wall.

"What vileness were you about tonight, Adept?" I said. "Bleeding more children? Or delivering another murdered soldier to your king?" In answer, he hawked bloody spittle in my face.

"We've not got a word out of him," said the young officer, cradling his own left wrist to his chest.

I wrenched open the adept's sleeves and shirt, but found no evidence of transference. "So, unlike Gruchin or Ophelie de Marangel, you are a willing conspirator," I said. "Gaetana's creature. The Aspirant's creature."

He grinned, fresh blood staining his teeth and leaking out the corners of his battered mouth.

"Where is Michel de Vernase? And what's this spellwork hanging about you like a dead man's stink?"

He widened his eyes like an innocent child accused. He was not afraid, though. True, Fedrigo did not know of Dante's perimeter. And we could not use it at trial to link Fedrigo with Edmond's body without revealing Dante's role in the investigation. But we could surely roust the door guards who helped him carry in his "sickly kinsman" wrapped in purple. Why was he not worried?

I snapped my attention to the officer nursing his damaged wrist. "Your messenger implied the prisoner posed a danger to the king. In what way?"

The young greville flushed. "He was lurking on a balcony overlooking Market Way—the place where it gets narrow going round Sweeper's Rock. Looked as if he were going to drop a rock right down on the king's head. Turned out it was only this book."

The officer held the lantern high. A splintered board protruded from the fence as if Fedrigo had been trying to rip an escape route through it. An open book lay over the tip of the board, as if a reader had marked his place. The large, tattered volume—seven or eight centimetres thick, its wide pages limp with the damp—drooped from the narrow slat.

"This was the *weapon* he held on the balcony?"

"Aye. Ready to drop it over the side, till Orin kicked open the door and took him down. He never got a chance. Though it's not exactly a man's weapon, is it, pig snout?" The biggest soldier slammed a boot into Fedrigo's side.

Despite the blow that pumped more blood from his mouth and left him slumped awkwardly, Fedrigo grinned again, sly and wicked. Eager.

I sat on my haunches, at eye level with the book. Perhaps my perception of magic had been stripped and clarified back in the Rotunda, just like my other senses, for, as sure as my name, I knew this book held more death in it than any weapon I'd ever come near.

Thwarted at his game of magical chaos when we destroyed ElteVire and Gaetana, Michel de Vernase had retaliated by eliminating Philippe's heir. But the king had surely not found time to scribe a new name on the tablet in the crypt. His death would ravage Sabria. This time Michel meant to kill.

"Has anyone touched it?" I said. "How did it get in this position?"

The three soldiers looked at one another. "None of us had aught to do with it."

Fedrigo's eyes flicked from me to the book and back again.

"In the fight on the balcony . . . did the book get dropped or juggled?"

Orin, the young greville with the broken wrist, had been puzzling at my questions, but this one triggered something. "It didn't. I thought it was odd. When I came after him, I thought he'd drop it and run, but he curled up around the thing, then kicked me so hard I near took a dive off the balcony myself. By the time the others showed up, the villain had ducked out."

And led them here. Cornered, he had tried to rip through the fence . . . then placed the book.

Carefully I lifted the worn leather cover, so thin a wind would wrinkle it like paper. Recalling the banners on the *Swan*, I shielded my eyes with my free arm, but no spits of fire leapt out. The title page read *Covenants of Civil Properties in the Demesne of Challyat*, which meant nothing to me. Naught seemed hidden between its pages. I lowered the cover gently. The board creaked.

The impact of the book itself wouldn't kill, even with a square hit on someone's head. But memories of the *Swan* would not leave me, nor would Ophelie's family or Gruchin's. "Have you a fondness for fire, Adept?"

Fedrigo shrugged, but the roused hunger on his bruised face answered all. A spark on the Market Way at its narrowest point—the oldest houses in Merona—would rage through Riverside like summer lightning in the maquis, and up the hill into the city proper.

Now his eyes were on the book, Fedrigo could not look away. A man who loved fire. A man unafraid, perhaps because he *intended* to die. Which meant we all would die . . . and Philippe, too. I had just sent him notice that one of his son's murderers sat in this alley. *Saints defend us.*

So, Portier, you can try to move the book to a safer place—like the river—or you can sit here and wait for this little trap to fall and explode or whatever it's designed to do.

"One of you bring water," I said, in focused urgency. "Enough to douse the book and more. Hurry!"

Fedrigo's smug expression told me that would not be enough.

"Greville Orin, get you to the palace and find one of the mages—Dante, if you can find him, or Orviene—and get him to come here. Tell them that Duplais says there's a challenge here that devil's fire will not explain. And hurry. Whatever you do, make sure the king keeps away. He *must not* return to Riverside. Do you understand?"

"Understood. I'll spread the word of more fireworks to come at the river, as well." He set the lantern well away from Fedrigo's feet. "Hagerd, be alert. The prisoner is your charge."

"Good man." Better than me to think of a way to empty Riverside without causing a riot.

I crouched near the book like a useless schoolboy, Fedrigo's sly grin driving me to distraction. Had he some alternative trigger to ignite the book? Surely he'd not have perched it so precariously, if so. I dared not move it, but the torn plank could give way at any moment. The imagining had sweat beading my brow and the burn scars on my hands twinging.

"Did *you* work this nasty spell?" I mumbled, knowing full well Fedrigo would not answer.

But the answer came anyway. The magic that hung about the book was huge, not simple. Even I could sense so much. But Dante had called Fedrigo's magic that darkened the Rotunda *infantile*. Darkening spell . . . *blanking spell* . . .

I pulled out the wadded loop of silk-threaded string Dante had given me and dangled it in the air. "Perhaps the one who taught you to work blanking spells is the same who ensorcelled this vile book. We're going to discover who it is whether you speak or not. Whether you die or not."

Fedrigo's smirk faded. His thick neck reddened and spittle dribbled from his mouth. Perhaps his voice had been muted like Gruchin's.

"Not a twitch," growled Hagerd, pressing his sword tip to Fedrigo's belly.

Gaetana hadn't bound this spell; Michel's vengeance had flared to murder only after Eltevire was destroyed and Gaetana dead. Nor had Fedrigo; if Fedrigo was capable of sophisticated spellwork, why would he have used something *infantile* as he deposited Edmond's body? Certainly an experienced spellworker could bind his spells poorly if he wanted. If he had reason. If he wished to make investigators think him incapable. . . .

I twined the looped string about my fingers. And I recalled an impatient Dante poking his staff into an enclosure loop before it could be picked up—one of two loops laid side by side behind the dais in the Rotunda.

"Souleater's bones," I whispered. "*Orviene* taught you spellwork." The incapable Orviene, who had somehow earned a mage's collar. So kind he was . . . so concerned for his poor missing adept. Orviene had asked me if Ilario might know why Fedrigo had gone to the docks on the day the adept was supposedly knifed, yet, when questioned, he had reported Fedrigo perpetually short of money and in the habit of gambling. Indeed, Orviene had pointed me repeatedly at Gaetana, and I, like a dotard, had followed his accusing finger. Of all men, I should have known to look harder at a fool.

Narrowing his eyes and curling his lip, the adept squirmed, and the swordsman shifted his blade to Fedrigo's throat. The magic grated at my spirit, growing like a canker, like raw poison. Gods, where was the man with water? What if Dante refused to come?

I glared at the damnable book and imagined how Dante would proceed. He would see an overused book, smudged and worn. My enlivened senses could smell the dusty shelves where it had lain, the smoky lamps that had illuminated it, could hear the voices reading it, discussing, arguing over it. *Covenants* meant lawyers and magistrates and registrars and property disputes. Angry people had used this book. Maybe that's why it was so tattered. None were so angry as Fedrigo, a man who burned innocents for pleasure, who would burn himself to keep his master's secrets.

Yet those who had made the book's pages—those who shredded the old linen, soaked and washed and pulped it, spread it in its frame, pressed and dried it—had no clue as to what might be written upon them. Paper could hold poems or stories, accounts or covenants—endless possibilities. And those who brewed the ink, and the binders and printers, for this was a printed book . . . all their labor and invention had gone into a volume destined to hold a cruel and evil spell to murder a king and fire his city. I inhaled deeply of the Riverside stench, of the fishy harbor and the dry wood of the warehouses—every sensation crisp and hard-edged and alive.

Fedrigo, scarlet-faced, growled and rocked his massive body, as I pulled off the link belt I wore over my tunic, clipped the ends together, and laid it gently around the book. He roared, even as Hagerd's rapier bit his fleshy neck.

I grabbed a fistful of dirt and laid it atop the book, evenly so as not to upset its balance, and sat down near the warehouse wall. Closing my eyes, I built the rune in my imagining, encircling the book as it lay on the plank, incorporating everything I'd considered. Dark curling lines for the inked words, ragged white strips for the paper, rectangle for the presses . . . and before I knew it, I was painting the rune with red blotches for anger, and orange, blue, and white arrows for flame, black claws for evil intent. . . .

Fedrigo began to slam his bound feet to the ground. The soldier kicked him, and I wanted to scream at them to stop, for I felt the heat rising. Not in my flesh, but in my bones. In the part of me that understood these things, a part of me I had not visited since I was a child and felt the stirrings of power that made me dream of magic.

I considered *coolness*, *damp*, and *stillness*, and the heaviness of dirt that could smother a fire.

Fedrigo yelled, wordless, guttural, gurgling yells. The swordsman grunted and crashed to the ground, his legs kicked out from under him. But I did not see the plank give way and the book fall, because my eyes were focused inward, where walls and barriers toppled like paper standards struck by the pendulum.

"Sonjeur, the book!" This time the blaze seared my cheeks, and the crackling quickly rose to a thunder like fifty horses galloping together.

Fedrigo's agitation erupted in crows of triumph.

But I sought the power that lived in the pattern I had made, and I joined it with what lived in me, born in my blood. And as if the spout of flame had been sucked into my veins, enchantment roared through me, unruly and awkward, but building, rushing, towering, shivering my foundation, swelling heart and lungs and filling me with torrents of magic. I spread my arms and bellowed in the triumph of a lifetime's longing.

I did not need to open my eyes to know the book was ash or that Fedrigo glared at me with such hatred as would eat a man's heart, for I had built his hate into the keirna of his book, and I had quenched it with the glory of my art.

CHAPTER THIRTY-FOUR

30 CINQ
5 DAYS AFTER THE ANNIVERSARY

*The trial of Michel de Vernase-Ruggiere, Maura de
Billard-Vien, Orviene de Cie, and Fedrigo de Leuve
for murder and high treason began and ended on 30
Cinq in the 877th year of the Sabrian Kingdom in the
city of Merona. Philippe de Savin, King of Sabria,
Duc de Journia, Protector of the Fassid, Overlord of
Kadr, sat in judgment, in company with a Judicial
Scribe and seven Magisterial Advisors, drawn by lot-
tery, as prescribed by Sabrian Law.*

*Of the four accused, only Orviene de Cie and Fed-
rigo de Leuve were in attendance. The Conte Ruggiere
and Damoselle ney Billard remained at large. A mage
of the Camarilla Magica sat as family advocate for de
Cie and de Leuve. The Chevalier de Vien refused to
send a representative to his daughter's trial, stating that
the family maintained no further interest in Damoselle
Maura's person or fate. Representing the Conte Ruggiere's family was Damoselle Anne de Vernase. . . .*

I LEAFED THROUGH THE NEAT pages, meticulously penned
by the judicial scribe and delivered to me for review,
scratching out a word here or there, replacing a sentence,
correcting not the testimony itself, but its articulation.

My cousin had insisted I complete the task immediately following the trial's adjournment to ensure that no questions remained unanswered before he announced his verdict publicly.

Countless activities came to mind as preferable for a soft summer evening after such a long and arduous day. I would have liked to close my eyes and recapture the sweetness of Maura's embrace. I would have liked to write a letter to my mother and tell her I'd be home to visit soon, and express my hope that perhaps she would be feeling well enough to walk in Manor Duplais' lavender beds with me, as I knew she enjoyed that above all activities.

Magic, too, beckoned at this sunset hour, when the world itself donned a mantle of mystery and all things seemed possible. All these days, even when concentrating on this trial, my spirit had existed in a state of exaltation. So much to learn, to explore. Everything I'd read and studied lay before me like mysterious lands and oceans lay before the *Destinne*'s prow. Twice in the days since, I had ridden into the countryside and spent an afternoon creating simple spells, just to confirm this renewal was no cruel imagining. Each success but fed the yearnings that had ever lingered in my innermost heart, a deep and hungry burn like that of raw spirits or swallowed lightning.

But I would work no magic at Castelle Escalon as long as Dante remained there. He would sense it, and I was not ready to tell him. Somehow his terrible spellwork at the Exposition had shattered the walls and barriers he'd claimed stifled my magic, in the same way it had broken through my memory of my own death. I wanted to believe he had given me this unparalleled gift knowingly, as a friend. But until I understood what was happening with him, I would tell him nothing. It grieved me, but I dared not trust him.

So much for the Invariable Signs of sainthood. For those first few moments after magic had scalded my veins, Ilario's beliefs had come upon me in a rush of wonder. I had eluded Death three times, once so close as to smell the grass of Ixtador Beyond the Veil. What if I *was* Other? What if the recurrent dreams of my youth—the battlefields, the flood, the rescue that had gotten me chained to a rock—were the true memory of recurring lives?

I had quickly recovered my sanity. If I were a Saint Reborn, my inerrant perception of righteousness was, if not broken, then entirely confused.

And so I corrected a paragraph, then approved a swan's graceful glide to its landing in the swan garden pond. Another paragraph and I watched the sky change color. After so many sultry days, the breeze ruffling the pond smelled of rain to come. I breathed deep, hoping that the most refreshing of all scents would cleanse my blood as Dante's sorcery had cleansed my head, for it seemed as if the facts and implications of this investigation had taken up residence in my veins and arteries, so that if I were to cut my arm I would bleed evidence. Appropriate, I supposed.

I turned another page. Two-thirds of the testimony was my own. The remainder I had elicited from witnesses, for my cousin had designated me Principal Accuser.

Calvino de Santo had testified to Michel de Vernase's actions in the aftermath of the previous year's assassination attempt. In return, Philippe commuted his former captain's sentence. De Santo could now find work and rebuild his life—outside of Sabria, I hoped, lest someday his king discover his role in Maura's escape. I wondered if Gruchin's spectre would yet haunt him outside the palace walls.

Audric de Neville had testified haltingly of Ophelie de Marangel's death. Philippe had granted royal clemency for the killing stroke Ophelie had begged from the old chevalier.

Chief Magistrate Polleu of Challyat testified that the fire that killed the Marqués de Marangel and his family had been traced to a carpenter's apprentice, whose money box at home contained receipts for *the building of crates to specification,* signed by Maura ney Billard. The apprentice's wife identified Fedrigo as a customer she had spied delivering "white paste in a jar of water" just before Ophelie's home burned. The carpenter's helper himself could not testify, as he had died in a fall less than a week after the Marangel fire. That small fact I recorded in my journal, another death to the Aspirant's account.

Henri de Sain witnessed to the shipments of crates by Maura ney Billard, bringing a solidity to the case that masked some of its more speculative elements.

A palace guard and a registrar identified Fedrigo as the householder who brought an "ill kinsman" into the Exposition, revealed later to be one Edmond de Roble-Margeroux, dead son of the king's great friend, Lord Olivier. Captain de Segur's soldiers witnessed to Fedrigo's attempt to murder Philippe by dropping a fire-spelled book on his head.

Orviene had tried repeatedly to defend himself, babbling like a terrified child of his blindness to Gaetana's and Fedrigo's plotting. He claimed never to have seen the spelled book, and that the enclosure string turned over to the Camarilla had never bound a fire spell and was never his at all.

The Camarilla advocate sat silent through all this. His participation would have made no difference. Orviene and Fedrigo would be bound over to the Camarilla as soon as I verified the transcript. They would be dead by middlenight. The imagining did not grieve me.

Lianelle ney Cazar de Vernase initially refused to testify, until the Principal Accuser took her aside and pointed out that she could sit either in the witness chair or in her father's empty prisoner's box, accused of complicity to treason. The prospect of beheading at dawn the next morning tarnished the luster of defiance.

To give full credit to the girl's courage, however, she agreed only to give yea or nay answers. Though it made my questioning more difficult, I was happy at the solution. I was able to squeeze the story of Ophelie and transference out of her, while avoiding the matter of Eltevire or its disturbing nature. I avoided any testimony that might reveal Ilario's or Dante's roles as king's *agentes*. For Ilario's sake, if no other, our confederacy would remain as secret as I could manage.

Certainly, the most damning of all witnesses was Anne de Vernase, who identified Maura's letters, verified her fa-

ther's signature on the letters that had sent Edmond de
Roble to his death, and reported Michel de Vernase's last
words to her: that it was his duty to "*take down*" persons
he deemed corrupt, "*no matter how highly placed . . . no
matter the consequences.*" Nothing more was required of
her.

Throughout the day the girl had listened to every word
unflinching, never once meeting the eyes of her royal
goodfather or anyone else in the chamber. When I had
done with her questioning, it required three prompts for
her to remove herself from the chair. She could not seem
to take her eyes from the bloody lancets and scarificator
we had found in her father's library.

It surprised me that Lady Madeleine would have sent
her daughter alone into such an ordeal. Bad enough the
girl had been forced to witness to her father's infamy. At
the end when Philippe gave Anne an opportunity to speak
in Michel's defense, the girl had shaken her head and remained silent.

Philippe's own demeanor, grim and settled more than
angry, had not wavered throughout. He did not present
Michel's last letter in evidence, but told his advisors that it
laid out frustrated ambition as motive for Michel's crimes.
I did not believe that was all, but it was enough for the
Magisterial Advisors that Philippe was convinced of Michel's guilt. The burden of judgment was the king's alone.

And so we arrived at the verdict.

*Michel de Vernase to be declared Outlaw, Abductor,
Murderer, and Traitor, stripped of Title and Demesne, neither to be housed nor succored in any wise
under penalty of Treason. Upon his arrest to be taken
to Spindle Prison, there to be stripped, flogged, and
executed by beheading, his body burned and ashes
scattered in an unknown location, according to the
law of Sabria.*

*Maura de Billard-Vien to be declared Outlaw and
Conspirator in Treason and Murder, neither to be
housed nor succored in any wise under penalty of
Conspiracy. Upon her arrest to be taken to Spindle*

Prison, there to be executed by beheading, according to the law of Sabria.

Fedrigo de Leuve and Orviene de Cie to be declared Murderers and Traitors, to be remanded to the Camarilla Magica for the crime of Blood Transference. If the penalty adjudged by the Camarilla is in any wise lesser than the following, then to be returned to Crown custody, taken to Spindle Prison, there to be stripped, flogged, and executed by hanging, their bodies burned and ashes scattered in an unknown location, according to the law of Sabria.

AND IT WAS DONE.

Without hesitation, I signed the document in the space reserved for the Principal Accuser, capped my ink, and wiped my pen, and again wondered if I had done right.

My life held too little of faith to understand how Maura could have done what Michel told her without questioning, yet my conviction of her innocence remained unshakable. I had risked my life and carved out a piece of my honor to save her. Never again could I call myself an honest man, else I must give myself up as guilty of conspiracy as outlined in the verdict. And I would do it all again.

It was not love that made me believe. Though it might have grown to that, we scarce knew each other. We had spent perhaps six full hours in each other's company—both of us bound in secrets. Since that last cold kiss, my dreams of her were already altered. Her soft, self-contained beauty had become that of an indelible artwork, not a living, breathing woman. I wished her safe and happy, but the ache of not knowing where she was—and maybe never knowing—had quickly become manageable. Someday I might discover that I had been duped. Until then, I would rejoice in her freedom and believe.

Having tied up the documents and gathered my materials, I returned to the palace, waiting in an anteroom as the transcript was signed by Philippe and the Magisterial Advisors, sealed by Philippe's ring, and installed in the judicial archives. An attendant was dispatched to summon the family representatives to hear the verdict read. By morning, heralds would be spreading news of it throughout the kingdom.

Shortly after the arrival of the Camarilla advocate, two masked inquisitors, and four adepts, Anne de Vernase arrived. I rose when she entered the waiting room, bowed, and exposed my hand. She returned neither the greeting nor the gesture, but rather faced the judiciary chamber door with hands knotted in front of her. Great gods, what cruel mother sends a seventeen-year-old child alone to hear her father condemned?

The girl's flighty curls were already escaping the tight braid she'd worn for the trial. She appeared altogether small and pinched, as well she might. No matter what secrets she yet held, I felt sorry for her.

"Damoselle," I said quietly, when the attendant stepped out, "though I understand your distraction, I would advise you to maintain protocol while you are here."

Her brow wrinkled, and she flicked a glance at me as if my meaning might be written on my face. I waved the marked back of my hand at her. "It is the law. I don't mind one way or another, but others might. Especially today."

With a shaking breath, she set her lips tight, returned her gaze to the door, and exposed her hand on her shoulder. She was trembling.

"Perhaps we should send for your mother." Out of all the verbiage I had directed at her that day, it surprised me that this suggestion broke her composure, evoking a spearing glance of hatred and contempt.

The door to the judicial chamber burst open, and the masked inquisitors came out, followed by the two sorcerers, shackled and shrouded in dark wool sewn with iron rings. An attendant held open the outer door.

"Damoselle de Vernase," said one of the Magisterial Advisors, poking his head from the inner chamber, "enter."

But the girl stood paralyzed, her face devoid of color, her eyes like copper medallions fixed in horror on the bullish Fedrigo—unrecognizable in his shapeless hood and gown. Holy angels, her father was reportedly a big man, like the adept.

"Creator forgive you, *Fedrigo*," I said, stepping close to the hooded giant. "No other can."

He growled and rattled his chains. The adepts shoved him forward.

The second, smaller prisoner stepped out of line, stumbling in his shackles. "Good, kind Duplais," Orviene babbled, "tell them I'm no good at magic! My father bribed the examiner at Seravain. I swear to every god and saint, I know nothing of spelled books . . . nothing of leeching . . . I didn't see their evils, their depravity. Please, do you know what's done to you in the Bastionne? Help me. Tell them. . . ."

The masked inquisitors wrenched him into line and shoved him through the door. I felt ill.

"Damoselle, present yourself." The summoning advisor waved at the attendant holding the door. "Mardullo, have the boy brought right away. This'll not take long."

Anne swallowed hard and followed the impatient advisor into the judiciary chamber.

For a quarter hour, I sat with throbbing head in my hands, trying to remember why I had ever taken on this investigation. Just as an advisor opened the door of the judiciary chamber, two members of the Guard Royale escorted young Ambrose into the waiting room. "Good," said the advisor. "Bring him in. And you are required, as well, Sonjcur de Duplais."

In the front of the square, somber room, Philippe, his seven advisors, and his judicial scribe sat at the same long, polished table they had occupied the entire day, the empty witness's chair facing them on the right, the four empty prisoners' chairs facing them on their left. The few rows of chairs reserved for observers remained empty, save for one on the first row where Anne de Vernase sat alone.

The guards installed Ambrose beside her. The youth, casting hostile glances about the room, gripped the arm of his sister's chair and bent his head her way. "So he did it, did he? Judged him guilty? Isn't it a relief we've a kindly guardian to care for us?" At least the lad did not bellow as

he had on the night of the Exposition. Standing just behind them, I was likely the only person in the room who
heard.

"Quiet your tongue," said the girl, intensely still, eyes
fixed on her folded hands. "You must *think*, now. For your
family. For your life."

Lord Baldwin motioned me to the witness chair. He
served as examiner this time. "Sonjeur de Duplais, please
recount your knowledge of the traitor Michel de Vernase's
son."

As the boy sneered and rolled his eyes, I gave an accurate rendition of what I had seen at Montclaire and at Castelle Escalon. I did not report his insolence word for word,
but no one in the room could fail to imagine what *insult*
and *exuberant expressions of anger and resentment* meant.
This judgment was quick:

*"Ambrose de Vernase to be declared a Danger to the
Crown and a Risk of collusion with a known Traitor, to be
held in Spindle Prison until the Traitor Michel de Vernase
is apprehended or until the King of Sabria determines he is
no longer a Danger and a Risk, according to the Law of
Sabria."*

The judicial scribe passed me the document to review
and sign. I wished I could argue that the judgment was
harsh or unfair. But no sovereign with a mind would leave
Ambrose free to carry tales to his father, to join him, or
to be used as a pawn in Michel's cause by anyone else.
House arrest would have been more generous, but at fifteen, Ambrose was clever and well trained. He had already eluded soft guardianship. And once word got out as
to his father's crimes, Ambrose might not be safe outside
the Spindle.

"I won't!" said the boy, reaching for his sister. All traces
of youthful defiance fled. "Ani, tell them. I don't know
anything!"

Michel de Vernase's children, faces pale and rigid with
shock, were forced apart, one to be returned to her mother,
the other remanded into custody of soldiers who bound his
hands and would row him through three iron water gates
into a dank and lonely prison. If the conte himself had

been in that room, I would have snatched a guard's dagger and shoved it through the blackguard's heart. No matter their secrets and conspiracy, Michel had made these two and put them here. *He* was responsible.

I assumed this was the end of the day's ordeal. But as Philippe thanked and dismissed his advisors and scribe, he commanded me to stay behind.

The cold sweat that popped out under my layered garments had naught to do with the stuffy judicial chamber. Surely my cousin would have kept his advisors behind if he planned to enter another charge to the day's tally. I stood beside the witness box I had so recently left.

Philippe rose, removed his purple robe, and dropped his heavy pectoral chain and diadem onto the table amid the papers, ink bottles, bloody implements, and damning letters. He mopped his damp forehead, stretched his back and shoulders, then moved to the end of the long table where a decanter held enough wine to fill one cup. He lifted the vessel in query. "You've expended more words today than the rest of us together."

"Thank you, sire, but no. I've not the vigor to lift a cup just now."

He refilled his own and sat in one of the advisors' chairs, beckoning me to take a seat across the table from him. Instead of drinking, he set the cup on the table, fingering its stem and the embossed tree on its bowl. "My wife seems well recovered from her ordeal."

"I am gratified to hear that, lord." That he began with this did naught for my simmering nerves.

"She set Maura free, you know. Pretended a fainting fit. While the warder escorted one of her ladies to fetch smelling salts from the boat, she used a spelled ring to unlock Maura's cell. And what guards could keep count of a bevy of queen's ladies dressed in identical black, hooded cloaks on a night when fireworks lit the sky? It is much easier to manipulate your warder when you are the reinstated queen with full honors, rather than a prisoner awaiting release."

Exactly so. I smiled inside, even as my neck shrank with the imagined slide of cold steel.

"I understand why she did it. I forced her to find a place to take her stand. Putting her in the Spindle . . . one of her nature, so fragile in heart. No necessity—none—has pained me so. Payment must be made for such an insult, and this is mine. Indeed, when it comes to it, I am grateful to pay. But *damned* be this rift that must now persist"—his fist slammed the table so hard, the advisors' empty cups rattled and his own near toppled—"*damned* be these corrupted mages and the villain who used them, and *damned* be this office that must shape our privacy. The whispers about her will never be silenced."

Astonished at such a personal confessional, I trod carefully. "Your lady queen may be fragile of heart, lord, but she is a woman of extraordinary strength and conviction. I did not understand that before observing her close to. Perhaps, with your generous reception and public engagement, others will see those qualities, as well."

My cousin's finger dabbed at droplets of wine jarred out of the cup by his outburst. Then he dropped Dante's spelled ring on the table beside his cup. As it spun and settled, he raised his eyes, every bit a king's finest instrument, to meet mine. My body demanded to crawl under the table.

"It is well you told me from the beginning that you were a *failed* sorcerer, Portier, else I'd have to think you conspired with my wife to free the young lady. I apologize for that."

I wondered if vomiting would be excessively dramatic at this point. Philippe made no sign that he noticed how near it I was.

"You've done me great service, cousin, no matter that I detest the truth you've uncovered. It was a difficult task I set you. But your conduct has been exemplary, and you've shown extraordinary intelligence and insight, as Michel himself told me a lifetime ago that you could. I wish you to take a permanent position in my household and continue to sort out such complicated matters. Only a fool would believe the Aspirant has abandoned his ambitions just because we know his name and have lopped off his magical arms."

He sipped his wine.

"You may name the office as you like—aide, special counselor, royal investigator. *Agente confide* is no longer applicable, as my greatest enemy knows you work for me. But I will make clear to all that my earlier public assessments of your character, intellect, and motives were but a screen. Or"—he toyed with Dante's ring, then shoved it in my direction—"less comfortable, but perhaps more useful, we could leave such unjust assessments as they are and install you in some minor post, allowing you to remain . . . underestimated."

I was entirely wrung out, and if he intended that as punishment, it was a clever one. "Sire, you are most generous, and I am so very honored, but . . ."

For my life, I could not have explained why I did not grasp a royal appointment with both hands and crow to the powers of Heaven that now I would have leisure, means, and opportunity to find my way in the world. The art I had just reclaimed could not be practiced in the mouldering halls of Seravain, and I had no desire to live in a forest hovel as Dante had.

"In no wise can I make such a decision tonight."

"I understand," he said. "I've had few days so difficult as this. Take a little time." He tapped a fingernail idly on the table. "Have you heard that my wife plans to retain this other mage—your Dante?"

"No, lord." This news stung like a slap from an icy hand. Dante and I were finished here. The household acolytes and adepts had been advised by the Camarilla to return to Seravain.

"I don't like him."

"He did you good service, lord. Without him we'd never have unraveled the deception of the arrow, Gaetana's interests, or the meaning of the spyglass or Eltevire."

"But tell me, cousin, what he did five nights ago—tell me it was cleaner, healthier than the spyglass magic."

And, of course, I could not. Philippe would not reveal what he'd seen. Perhaps he wasn't ready, as I was not.

He rose and extended his hand. "We did right today, Portier. No decision in this life is perfect. Would I could

see ways to make such complexities more just, more nuanced. But that will take someone more subtle than either
of us."

I kissed his ring. "Aye, my lord. We'll leave that for the
future. And we'd best catch the villain first."

Likely he noticed I spoke only of Michel. And that I
was not such a fool as to take Dante's ring.

~

UNABLE TO CONSIDER SLEEP, I decided to roust Ilario and tell
him of the trial. "My lord's off meddling," said his surly
valet, John Deune, who answered the chevalier's door.
"Summat to do with the traitor's wife, no matter such is no
proper concern of a gentleman."

The ever-awkward Deune took as much ridicule as his
master, and with far less grace. I wondered that Ilario kept
him on. I surmised no danger that the testy, dull-witted
valet would decipher his master's secrets or develop ties
with more clever courtiers who might.

I trundled off in search of the Lady Madeleine, curious
as to Ilario's "meddling." A footman told me the Chevalier
de Sylvae had headed off swearing and cursing, "as was
wholly unlike himself," after visiting the Conte Ruggiere's
private courtyard. "'Twas surely the strange goings out
there," he said, embarrassed. He could describe what he
meant only as *unlikely* compared to his experience of
noble ladies.

Following the young man's direction, I threaded a
snarl of west wing passages into the dark corner of a
walled garden. The scent of jasmine hung heavy on the
summer night, and clicking beetles and trilling night-
birds were accompanied by the rhythmic scrape of steel
on dirt and stone. Someone was digging . . . and humming. I drew aside a cascading vine.

A woman dressed in soiled white gauze sat inside a ring
of fifty lit candles, plunging a spade into the dirt. Mounds
of freshly turned earth pocked what had once been a
square of grass and curving rose beds. The rosebushes
themselves were broken and straggling, petals littering the

ravaged yard. Cascades of flowering vines lay in great heaps, ripped from the enclosing walls.

"Mama, please come inside." Lianelle de Vernase crouched outside the ring of candles. "Ani's back. We need to tell you about Ambrose."

"But I cannot, my darling!" The woman leapt up and whirled around, her gown knocking several candles to the grass so that Lianelle had to stomp on the little flames before they set the lady or the garden alight. "So much yet to be done. I must bury every blossom before I go in, else how will they grow? Neither father nor son will come home till all the flowers are buried and risen anew."

Madeleine de Cazar's cheeks, arms, and flushed cheeks were smeared with dirt, and spittle ran down her chin. Her hair, unbound and tangled, flew wild in the night breeze. Her eyes flared excessively bright in the candlelight . . . and bore not the least scrap of reason.

No wonder Anne and Ambrose de Vernase harbored such spearing hatred. And no wonder at Ilario's distress . . . ever the chevalier at a woman's trouble. I refused to believe my questions had done this to Lady Madeleine, nor that Ilario would imagine it so.

Father Creator! Fear a viper's fang in my craw, I bolted for the east wing.

Dante's door stood open. Beyond it lay a horror to chill the soul. The mage's staff belched a scarlet whirlwind that had trapped Ilario at its heart. The young lord hung in the red mist above the circumoccule, a blur of pale skin, flailing limbs, and ragged lace and satin, spinning like a child's top.

"Was it the priggish librarian who allowed you to imagine you have a mind, peacock? Perhaps I must send you through the glass and leave you a splotch on the paving to convince the earnest little insect that I mean what I say."

As I held speechless in the doorway, the red blur raced toward the windows, the garish reflection doubling the dread spectacle. But before a disastrous collision, the scarlet light vanished in an explosive brilliance, and Ilario plummeted to a heap at Dante's feet.

"Th'art a devil, mage. A dastard." Speech slurred, the chevalier pulled himself to his knees. "Don't need a fine education t'see it. You must heal the— Oof."

The heel of Dante's staff slammed Ilario's belly hard enough to shove him backward. "*Must*, cloudwit?"

"Stop this," I said.

"Must heal . . . contessa . . ." Another blow and Ilario gasped and doubled over. His hand twitched toward his sword, but he merely clenched his fist and shook it feebly . . . impotently . . . at the mage. Merciful god, he was not going to break his mask.

"*Must*, fool?" Another vicious blow.

Ilario groaned. "You. Ensorceled. Lady."

The mage raised the staff again.

"Dante!"

The mage's head jerked up, and his cold green eyes met mine. With a snarl, he slammed the staff down on Ilario's shoulder. Ilario bellowed in agony.

I charged. "Stop this, you misbegotten Souleater! Are you mad?"

Ilario bellowed, as the carved hornbeam landed yet again, this time on his upper arm. The bones cracked and ground. A quick blow to his side silenced his cry, just as I skidded to my knees and threw myself over him.

"Get this whining, lying dancepole out of my apartments." Dante raised his staff again, but it did not fall.

Shielding the chevalier's head, I slid my arm under his shoulder on the side opposite his injuries. "What's happened to you, mage?" I said. "Since when is Ilario the enemy?"

"He burst in here, threatening murder and issuing orders. I'll not have it, no matter who he is."

"Did Madeleine de Cazar threaten you?"

"Creeping aristos who dabble with secrets and sorcery break themselves." Much as he had opined at Montclaire.

But the lady's sudden collapse violated every expectation . . . and Dante had made a point of touching her. And of all men, I knew that he could influence the minds of others. God's hand, he *had* done it.

I helped Ilario to his feet. Expecting the cursed hornbeam to land on my own back, I guided him into the passage. Though no hand touched it, the door slammed behind us.

Ilario cradled his left arm and gritted his teeth as I half carried him away. The moment we arrived at his apartments, I dispatched a gaping John Deune to fetch the chevalier's physician. "What were you thinking?" I said as soon as I had him on his couch, pillows supporting his arm. His complexion was the color of alabaster.

"Devil drove the woman mad," he spat through clenched teeth. "Jacard saw him work the magic. Couldn't leave it go without a word."

"But you knew you wouldn't draw a sword on him, either."

"Never thought he'd—" He tried to shrug, a disastrous move.

When he had finished puking up his last meal and lay wasted and trembling on his couch, he summoned a wobbling grin. "Could've. Could've taken him. Easy. Some of us have to live on could'ves."

The physician came and went, leaving Ilario trussed in plaster and linen. I shooed away John Deune with a promise to see the chevalier imbibed the prescribed poppy extract.

Despite a posture rigid with pain, Ilario made it clear he would do no such thing. "Can't," he said. "Might blab something I oughtn't."

The consequences of his chosen life seemed worse by the moment. "Can I fetch anything to help you sleep?"

"Stay till I'm snoring," he mumbled. "Might be tempted to throw myself off the balcony if I heave again."

For the next hour, I recounted the events of the trial and its aftermath. "I'd a mind to drop in on Dante after speaking to you," I said when I'd gotten through most of it. "Thought to inquire if it was my blood he used that night."

"Dante's gone rogue, Portier. He's more dangerous than the Aspirant or Gaetana or Orviene or any of them. Geni says not to bother my head, that she has 'an under-

standing' with him. But Madeleine's been in that courtyard seven days. Refuses to go inside. Refuses to change
her garments. Sleeps where she drops. They try to coax her
out of the sun, but it's all they can do to get her to eat or
drink. Curdled my blood. And my good sense, obviously."

"I've been unconscionably blind," I said. "He has such
a unique and marvelous vision of the natural world. I've
never met a man whose passion burned so singular . . . and
so bright. After Eltevire, I was certain we'd come to the
beginnings of true friendship. But he was so angry when
he found out I'd written that letter to the Camarilla. . . ."

"You're more a mush-headed idiot than my sister. Risk-
ing your lives for Maura against all evidence. Neither of
you willing to condemn this villain mage. At least Geni
doesn't claim to *like* him." He shifted uncomfortably, and
I stuffed a silk cushion under his rapidly bruising left side.
"You did not cause this, Portier. The Camarilla might
have scared Dante a bit. Any sane man would get over it.
And she's no friend of mine, but Michel de Vernase's wife
is no weak-minded ninny. No *strain* or *questioning* broke
her."

"I know it," I said. The admission wrenched my spirit.
To imagine I'd allowed such talent as Dante's to plunge
into an abyss of wickedness pained me more deeply than I
could speak. But the escalating violence, breaking a woman's mind, coldly and deliberately brutalizing a man who
posed no threat to him . . . Such acts daemonstrated a
ruthless intent far beyond playacting—beyond healthy
anger. Beyond humanity. Not even I could excuse him any
longer.

"Indeed, I've been the world's greatest fool," I said,
wishing I dared down his neglected poppy extract and
sleep for a year. "So tell me reasons. Why harm the contessa if he thinks to join Michel's depleted band? Naught in
her answers hinted at complicity in anything criminal."

Ilario raised his brows in disbelief. "You really must
learn more of the wicked world, Portier. What does one do
to announce one's arrival in a new milieu? You daemonstrate your power to the elite in a small, but very important
way. Force them to take note of you. If the one whose at-

tention you crave is a villain, then you daemonstrate your power in villainous ways. If the elite decide you are a valuable addition to their circle, they invite you inside."

This is exactly what I had set Dante to do, only we had purged the palace of its villains. But perhaps that was not the circle he aspired to. "That cannot explain this particular villainy," I said, feeling the sealed testimony of the day begin to rip open. "This will not endear him to Michel. If *Michel* wanted her silenced, he could have done it any day this past year."

Ilario drained his cup of wine and passed it to me to refill. "Ah, you see, Dante's act will only gain attention if Michel is a part of the circle he wishes to join. Its nature just tells us that Michel is not the *sole* part of it."

My conclusion followed immediately. "And not the most powerful part."

"He's made a bid to join them, Portier."

I returned to my apartments profoundly troubled. I could not disagree with either Ilario's premises or his conclusions, so clear and obvious when I looked back at the days since Eltevire. Why had I held such fierce certainty in Dante's character? I must be the world's purest idiot. Recalling the mage's pitiless face as he splintered Ilario's bones shook my very soul. What could drive a man to such a reversal of character?

Loyalty and causes, no matter how noble, meant nothing to Dante. His mutilated hand testified of pain as wretchedly familiar. For a man of his talents and will, I doubted any physical danger could coerce. And certainly no personal ties could be used to force him to some behavior unwillingly. Family was anathema, and he recognized no friends. Which left desire.

What Dante loved and desired was magic. He had been willing to sacrifice his physical well-being to delve deeper into sorcery. Had something he'd seen or heard in the Bastionne convinced him he would learn more on this divergent course? Certainly scruple would not restrain him in its learning or its use. What Sabria had seen on the night of the Exposition had likely been but the first hints of his delving.

Father Creator. I had brought him here. I was responsible for whatever he wrought.

But so was one decision made, at least. I sat down and penned an answer to my cousin.

My gracious lord:

You have honored me as kinsman and servant, in no wise more than by today's most generous offer. Your trust humbles and gratifies me. Forgive me, sire, but I cannot accept the position. My search for honorable service necessitates a different path. In concern for my fellow agentes confide, I would ask that no tale of this investigation—and no defense of me—be released beyond what is already public. My deeds and prayers ever seek your welfare and that of our beloved Sabria.

Your kinsman,
Portier de Savin-Duplais

ON THE TENTH DAY AFTER his queen's release from Spindle Prison, Philippe de Savin-Journia returned to his Presence Chamber to conduct his public business and welcome a troupe of traveling players who would present a masque in celebration of his birthday. To the surprise of his courtiers and the pleasure of the king—and all gossips—Queen Eugenie graced the audience with her presence. Her pale rose gown trailed behind her like shredded clouds as she made her obeisance.

I had never seen such a genuine smile on my cousin's face as when he raised her up. Open, illuminating, transforming, that smile explained a great deal about Philippe's soldiers' and subjects' affection for him.

The king led Eugenie to her chair across the dais and one step lower than his own. She whispered in his ear. He kissed her hand. The chamber rang with cheers and joyous applause.

I stood in the mass of courtiers along one side of the Presence Chamber observing this happy evidence of reconciliation. Gossips would note that Queen Eugenie's household had taken on a new shape this day. Certainly Lady Antonia was there, as always, her browless eyes scrutinizing the assembly. Ilario stood close, as well, in a rakish, feathered hat and his most outlandish doublet of yellow brocade, skirted to his knees and rife with silver beadwork that rivaled Eugenie's gown in elaboration. Bands of beaded silk strapped his shoulder and arm, broken in a riding accident, so rumor had it. The colorful crowd of acolytes and adepts was reduced to a pale, subdued Jacard and the queen's new First Counselor, the gaunt, dark-browed mage at her right hand. Gaetana's and Orviene's place was now Dante's alone.

Retaining him made sense. Naught had happened to change Eugenie's desire to feel her mother's hand and ensure the happiness of her dead children. The dread I had carried since the Exposition, reinforced at the sight of Madeleine de Cazar's madness, settled deeper in my belly.

"It is our delight that our queen joins us today in the business of the realm," said the king, now returned to his chair in front of the great planetary. "Before we welcome these visiting players, she wishes to announce an appointment. My lady . . ."

"It is my pleasure to name the new administrator for my household," said a beaming Eugenie, ignoring the chill that spread like hoarfrost from her First Counselor's grim countenance. Strong and determined, her voice carried all the way to the back of the Presence Chamber. "Someone to bring order to my frivolous life and see to the comfort of my dear ladies and valued counselors. A gentleman of quiet demeanor and superior skills—and excellent family connections."

Suppressing a sigh as I noted the hard twitch of Philippe's brow, and a shudder as Dante's gaze speared me with green fire, I made my way forward to kneel at my gracious lady's feet.

EPILOGUE

MIDSUMMER

The Midsummer Fete was quiet this year. All celebrations pale after the Grand Exposition, one short year ago, and the public notice of Michel de Vernase's trial and conviction. The traitor is not yet found; nor, thank all benevolent angels, is Maura.

My work in the queen's household is satisfying, and I am fading into bureaucratic anonymity—as I intend. But I am free of business for the evening and so wander into the Great Hall and Rotunda for my nightly visit, a habit I took up on the night I finally admitted Dante had turned. It is here I've found confirming evidence of my fears.

Until Ilario's Grand Exposition, and excepting the occasional coronation or royal wedding, the Rotunda and Great Hall had stood quiet and empty for more than three centuries. No longer.

Sitting on a bench placed for viewing the great pendulum, I watch wisps of light dance over my head. The glimmers are not sunbeams, for the sun failed more than an hour since. Nor are they some reflection of the passage lamps kept lit for the pendulum engineer and guards making rounds. Those lamps are few and hooded so that their weak, steady light falls on the floor.

No, these floating threads of blue, purple, and green can be seen everywhere in the Great Hall and Rotunda, though chiefly in the dome, occasionally illuminating a saintly hand or angel wing or dark-rimmed eye. Staring will not capture them, as they manifest themselves just as the eye gives in and blinks.

The whispers are just as elusive. I'm not sure anyone else has heard them, though every palace conversation since Prince Desmond's deathday speaks of palace hauntings. No one comes here alone anymore except for me, and even a companion's breathing would drown them out. But after so many nights, I know they are getting louder. I dread the day I'll be able to distinguish words.

What disturbs me more is the smell: cedar and juniper, dry grass and old leaves, touched with moisture and laced with a faint tinge of rot. I cannot find a source for it save in my memories of Eltevire and dying.

Dante has caused this.

One evening as I sat here, sensing these changes, watching the lights dance in the vault and spread into the Great Hall, I recalled something he had said just after the Exposition: "I've always considered lenses more fascinating than prisms."

And so I considered lenses. Which led me to think of spyglasses. And of spectres and of perimeters that might identify those who crossed. But magical perimeters could also serve as an enclosure for spellwork—a great circumoccule—a boundary. And if magic rose from every aspect of nature and not solely from the blood of a practitioner, then how much power could be derived from the keirna of seven hundred onlookers opening themselves to magic in a temple that had witnessed a thousand years of the human and divine?

Thus I began to think of the Rotunda as a great lens, and all of us who'd sat here on that night as peering through to see . . . what? Splinters fractured from the world we knew, as the rainbow colors of the Royal Astronomers were fractured from white light? Or had we been given a view into another place altogether?

These ruminations but affirm my decision to remain at Castelle Escalon and discover the truth. To keep watch on the one who made this happen. In the queen's service I can stand close by her mage. And if Dante and his allies are lulled into believing my uncomfortable service to the king finished, all the better. No matter that my inerrant perception of righteousness is flawed, I see now what I am. I believe I am destined ... meant ... to stand against those who seek chaos. Against him.

Reaching into my boot, I pull out a heavy disk of silver and flip it high overhead. The coin catches the light of the lamp as it spins, twirling, glinting, displaying its two faces. For the span of a few heartbeats it hangs in the air, then drifts slowly to the floor.

Saints watch and guard us all.

ABOUT THE AUTHOR

Carol Berg is a former software engineer with degrees in mathematics from Rice University and computer science from the University of Colorado. Since her 2000 debut, her epic fantasy novels have won multiple Colorado Book Awards, the Geffen Award, the Prism Award, and the Mythopoeic Fantasy Award for Adult Literature. Carol lives in the foothills of the Colorado Rockies with her Exceptional Spouse, and on the Web at www.carolberg.com.